Alexa's Gold

Donan Berg

DOTDON Books
Moline IL

Alexa's Gold

DOTDON Books are published by

DOTDON Personalized Services
514 17th Street
PO Box 1302
Moline IL 61266-1302

Author e-mail: bergdonan@gmail.com
Order copies: psitsdotdon@msn.com

Library of Congress Control Number: 2017939016

ISBN 13: 978-1-941244-15-9 (E-book)
ISBN 10: 1941244157

ISBN 13: 978-1-941244-13-5 (Paper)
ISBN 10: 1941244130

First U.S. Edition: August 2017
10 9 8 7 6 5 4 3 2 1

Donan Berg wins 2016 1st Place Romance Gold Award

Donan Berg's novel, *One Paper Heart*,
topped the Feathered Quill 2016 Romance Awards.
Enjoy a taste of *One Paper Heart* later in this book.

Author Berg also earned the romance
winner's circle seven times in
The Dixie Kane Memorial Writing Contest.

What others say about his novels:

A Body To Bones

"A winning plot . . ." Kirkus Discoveries

The Bones Dance Foxtrot

"Clues eventually fit together in clever and significant ways . . . dramatic tension builds around which woman Jake will pursue." National reviewer.

For family and friends.

We all share life with special people be they grandparents, parents, spouses, brothers, sisters, sons, daughters, godchildren, cousins, nieces, nephews, guardians, or friends.

In meaningful little ways, remember to say thank you to each of them.

If you find my fictional story triggers a warm feeling, a happy heartbeat or a joyful recollection, I dedicate all the blissful moments to you and yours.

Books by

Donan Berg

Novels

A Body To Bones
First Skeleton Series Mystery

The Bones Dance Foxtrot
Second Skeleton Series Mystery

Baby Bones
Third Skeleton Series Mystery

Adolph's Gold

Abbey Burning Love

One Paper Heart

v

Alexa's Gold
Short Stories

Bubbling Conflict and
Other Stories

Amanda

Alexa's Gold

Donan Berg

Chapter One

"**R**ich men don't date exhausted women." Grandma's oft-repeated admonition ebbed into the minutiae of Alexa Hovey's grief. She squeezed the steering wheel of her battered F-150 pickup. The tension that distended the light-blue veins on the backs of her slim hands reverberated to grip her fragile heart.

A squeal from Alexa's two-year-old son, Samuel, shredded her veil of invisible melancholy. After the rural Iowa county gravel road ruts jiggled Samuel's Popsicle, orange melted-ice drips stained his Chicago Cubs bib.

Alexa welcomed her son's distraction. He reigned as her life's never-ending joy. His throne a child seat belted onto a faded-gray fabric bench seat. When Alexa's rust-pocked red pickup crested a pointed hill, he laughed. She swallowed a sharp inhale when her vehicle's front suspension hung in midair, momentarily weightlessness, until the spongy, in-need-of-repair-shocks bounced her and Samuel. Alexa's strained seatbelt stretched without a tear.

"Whee, Samuel," Alexa shouted as her butt thumped her seat a second time. Buoyed by the exuberance of Samuel's giggling, she vowed to protect him without the need for a father figure.

Alexa's peppermint Lifesaver stuck like a barnacle to the roof of her mouth. She lowered the driver's window and, without guilt, spit the half-dissolved disk into the dust-filled afternoon air. She doubted the suspicious neighbors Grandma decried in their long distance conversations would see the disk, or the airborne saliva, fly. *And, if one or two did, so what?*

Samuel's glee a full pivot from his whining and chair-kicking in the office of Grandma's estate attorney, their last stop. The black-haired, angular faced Attorney Brad

Alexa's Gold

Haberkorn had tried to calm Samuel without success. Samuel's tantrum disturbed Alexa less than her mother's telephone shrieks last week that culminated in Mother's threat: "If you don't share, you'll get nothing, not one red inheritance cent."

Alexa bit her tongue when her mother's rage rambled on to Mother's speculation about Grandpa's hidden treasure. Alexa honored her sworn promise to Grandma not to verify Mother's theory one of Grandma's recipes held the clue to buried gold coins.

After two coughs she raised the driver's window to within a half inch of full closure to shut out the road's dust. Alexa harbored no doubt her hoarseness would heal and the sale of Grandma's farm would guarantee Samuel a safe home, fund his college nest egg, and buy her a SUV. She never spoke of her SUV desire, which would be her first new car of her twenty-eight years. Similar to Samuel's bedtime teddy bear, Alexa was adamant in her belief that material possessions brought comfort without reciprocal love.

The glass-encased church bulletin she passed announced the 2010 Easter week services. Alexa's anticipation rose since Mr. Haberkorn said Grandma's farm was two-to-three miles west of the church. Alexa's purse carried Grandma Anderson's last mailed postcard, which she had cherished since its receipt the week before Christmas. With words few and letters scribbled large and wavy, Grandma's mailed expression of her love for Alexa and Samuel infinite. Also in Alexa's purse, a copy of Grandma's will that gave Alexa the farm and all associated assets except for $1.00 individual bequests given to each of twelve relatives. The first named relative was Alexa's mother.

"Honey, don't touch your sticky fingers to your pants." Samuel raised his chubby right hand to his uncombed dark brown hair. Alexa swiveled her head to the deserted road.

3

Samuel's giggle shifted her gaze to him. He patted the crown of his head. Alexa's frown, exaggerated by the muscle tenseness beneath her facial skin, softened when Samuel's grin displayed a lower gum gap where a tardy front-tooth hadn't yet sprouted.

Alexa flipped down her windshield visor. While the action gave relief to her eyelid squint into the setting sun, the visor did nothing to sweeten the spring's smell of decomposing manure spread between withered corn stalks. Sagged wood-slatted snow fences a sad reminder of December's snowy blizzard that had prevented Alexa's four-hour journey from her Chicago apartment to attend Grandma's funeral. Alexa longed to show Samuel his great-grandmother's farm and drive herself into the farmyard of her childhood's greatest memories.

Alexa remembered her yellow-flowered sundress and dashes across Grandma's lawn to chase the buoyant dandelion seed parachute. The tug-of-war between wind and gravity upon the dandelion fluff ball scrolled in slow motion beneath Alexa's raised eyelids. Her fantasy staved off the nebulous fear tremors that her mother would be at the farm with tools to install new locks.

Her glances to Samuel and her desire not to drive past the entrance to Grandma's farm distracted Alexa from the Iowa landscape undulation peppered with bright red barns and picturesque square white houses. Grandma hadn't divulged why she blessed Alexa with the farm and not Alexa's divorced and remarried mother who lived in Ohio. Alexa doubted her opinionated Grandma's dislike of divorce severed a mother/daughter biological bond.

"That's your unpredictable grandmother," Mother had said in a conciliatory tone that evaporated after Alexa refused to sign a legal paper that renounced her will beneficiary status.

Alexa bit her lower lip. To avoid shame she had capitulated. For two years she lied to Grandma that the U.S.

Army had deployed Samuel's father to Afghanistan. Alexa's plan to explain the truth to Grandma in person never materialized. When fate and Grandma's stroke denied Alexa the opportunity, she forced all regret deep into her heart. Alexa lived day-to-day with a manufactured rationalization distilled from unforgettable cowardice that Grandma's health wouldn't have withstood the truth.

"Honey, we're almost there. Look. A green tractor."

Samuel's miniature blue eyes gazed at her and not at the landscape's rolling hills.

Alexa slowed to read a posted RFD number. The name Erickson on the mailbox signaled Alexa was within three farm entrances of Grandma's. She counted aloud, "One." Samuel raised his right hand forefinger. "Two." He added his second right hand finger. "Three." His giggle filled the cab and Alexa's heart with playfulness.

Alexa swiveled her head left. Joyful moisture welled behind her eyes, a throat lump formed, and then she gasped.

The large oak that shaded Alexa's dandelion chases now sawed to a three-foot wide stump.

The two-level front porch roof of Grandma's log-cabin-styled house sagged in multiple places. One broken windowpane allowed a tattered inside lace curtain to flutter. Plywood nailed over a far window. Wood stain blistered. Caulk between logs cracked or missing. And then . . . and then . . . her gaze bumped across three rows of evenly spaced stewed mounds of black dirt, clay clogs, and white clover blossoms next to holes dug in the front lawn. Alexa tallied twelve piles before she quit her count in disgust.

Who else sought Grandpa's buried treasure? His stashed gold. She had to find Grandma's apple cake recipe. Alexa's right hand re-crossed her heart as she mumbled last summer's pledge to Grandma not to reveal the recipe clue Grandma hadn't fully explained.

Alexa coasted to a stop. Her right hand reached into her

5

strapped brown leather purse to remove her cell phone and Brad Haberkorn's business card. He'd promised to recommend a local Realtor. Her budget envisioned three or four weekend trips to rehab, list, and sell.

"Mr. Haberkorn, I'm at the farm. You didn't tell me Grandma lived in . . . ah . . . in a ramshackle house. The likes of which haunt the streets near my Chicago apartment."

"Hang up. I'll speak with you directly."

Alexa, pleased that Samuel hadn't chewed his Popsicle stick, switched her gaze left. She did not understand why someone parked a three-windowed, two-toned tan mobile home under an unlit yard security light and in front of a dense spruce windbreak.

Four knuckles rapping on the dusty window glass next to Samuel startled her. Samuel, restrained by his seat harness, reached his arms to her. She recognized Attorney Haberkorn. "It's okay, Samuel." Alexa's right hand on her driver's door steadied her until her launch landed her dark-blue sneakers on gravel. She stretched her torso erect and, behind her opened door, self-consciously smoothed the billowed sides of her white cotton blouse. The blouse and designer denims purchased last week at her favorite thrift store.

She glued her gaze to Mr. Haberkorn's profile until they met at the F-150's front bumper. The toothy smile she gazed up at resembled his law firm's online bio photograph. He radiated an awkward shyness. She had been pleasantly surprised the thirty-year-old online birthdate was in reality true. His blue blazer, not seen in his office, struck her as nerdy with its white pocket protector flap imprinted with Baker, Haberkorn Law Firm.

Alexa's ingrained big city paranoia caused her to keep a two-arm length separation. "You surprise me, Mr. Haberkorn?"

He arched and relaxed his trimmed dark eyebrows. "Please, you can still call me Brad." She nodded. "Probably not what you expected."

Did he refer to himself or the farm? *Be Cool. Assume house.* He'd intimidated her when behind his office desk, not acted flirty. She'd play it safe. "It's been three years. I have this . . . ." Her purse hung from her left shoulder. She fumbled to retrieve her wallet from inside her purse and unzip a photograph compartment. "Here's what I remember." She showed Brad a snapshot of a smiling woman and a child standing on the lawn in front of a blurry white farmhouse.

"Assume that's you with Mrs. Anderson." He cradled the photo between his right hand thumb and four fair-skinned fingers. His manicured fingernails consistent with right palm flesh devoid of calluses.

"Yes. I was eight, no seven." She stowed the picture and wallet in her purse.

He gazed past her right shoulder. "You could see the beauty even then."

Alexa's cheeks warmed from the inside out. She'd already authorized his fee from Grandma's estate and had expected him to be polite, not a rural Casanova who made her feel he searched deep into her soul. Her trance broken when Samuel cried "Mommy."

"Excuse me." She circled Brad, unlatched Samuel's door handle and swung the door toward her. With her purse tossed onto the bench seat, she unfastened her son's car seat buckle. Samuel's untied bib became her temporary washcloth to wipe his face and hands before she straddled his legs on her right hip. "No," she whispered in response to his wiggles. "You'll fall into a hole if I let you run."

Feet square beneath his shoulders, Brad's once distant dark smoky eyes floated up and lazily descended in his direct gaze at Alexa. He stood patient; his unbuttoned sport coat hung limp. With Samuel on her right hip, she rejoined him a foot from the driver side front fender.

She'd stockpiled vacation days and saved gas money before she telephoned to advise him of the new dates for her twice delayed Iowa trip. A flutter of small brown birds from the windbreak spruces attracted her gaze to the mobile home. The birds landed on, and then darted from, the home's roof as she stared.

"Land tenant Oscar Erickson." Brad began. "He owns the trailer. Son Joe lives in it."

"Was that agreed to by Grandma?" She searched Brad's eyes for a clue.

"Don't recall." Brad folded both arms to his chest. "Likely something oral."

Alexa gazed to the front lawn. "If the son lives here, why didn't he stop this digging?" Brad rotated his waist and tilted his right shoulder toward Samuel. His right hand's feeble attempt to high-five her son failed. "Thought you knew your grandmother moved into in a nursing home last summer. Joe Erickson works highway construction. Doubt he's here very often."

"Then why not put the mobile home at his parents?" She squeezed Samuel tighter.

"Independence I would gather." He shrugged, squared his shoulders, and refolded his arms. "Anyway, the Erickson's are friendly folks. I'm sure they'll accommodate whatever your wishes are. I've collected the cards of three local Realtors for you to interview." Two of Brad's right-hand fingers extracted business cards from his white-shirt pocket.

Her left hand thumb and forefinger clasped the stacked cards. "Thanks." She crammed them into her rear jeans pocket. Alexa cleared her throat, puzzled as her right eye caught Brad's right hand stretch open his front pants pocket.

"Forgot to FedEx you these two keys."

What else has he forgot to tell her?

8

"Think they're both for the house," he continued, "but not sure." He closed his right-hand fingers around a purple key fob. "I've a duplicate set of these and others in my office. I'll gladly relinquish them to you after probate's final distribution."

When his right hand fingertips grazed against her outstretched left palm, her hand trembled, and dropped six inches. Unleashed energy tingled her nerves until it fizzled at her shoulder.

Samuel squirmed against her right side as he reached his right hand for the dangling keys.

Alexa snatched the keys, careful to avoid Brad's second touch. Her left hand forced the fob and its two keys into her front jeans pocket opposite Samuel.

"Your son looks like he could be a handful."

"What can I say?" Her left hand helped solidified her right-hand grip on Samuel. "He's a growing boy." As Brad's gaze lingered to probe her eyes, she tempered her impulse to let Samuel become a relationship bargaining chip and averted her eyes.

"If you have any question, please call me. I'm parked near the machine shed."

Before Alexa lifted her gaze, she listened to the gravel crunch as he briskly strode away. Annoyed at herself for not uttering a courtesy good-bye, she elevated her left hand. The dust cloud of his departing Buick offered no hope he saw her belated wave.

Alexa steadied her son's tiny rubber soles on the pickup's fender. Except for Grandma and Grandpa, Alexa couldn't recall a time when any adult said to her they were glad she visited. The mid-April twilight lengthened the spruce tree shadows and neither mother's car nor any other interrupted their steady farmyard advance.

She grabbed her purse, and with one right foot kick, propelled the pickup's driver door shut with a loud click. Alexa clutched Samuel and scurried thirteen elongated

strides across the paper-strewn side lawn. She bounded up
the four wooden steps to a redwood-stained twenty-by-
thirty-foot rear deck.

Her sneakers left a dusty trail. Grandpa Henri's favorite
three-legged stool straddled the threshold of the
farmhouse's kitchen door.

Rats. Had Brad or Mother beaten her to Grandma's
apple cake recipe? Alexa believed Grandpa Henri, while
his death was suspicious, had neither betrayed Grandma's
recipe clue nor unearthed his golden coin treasure.

"Anyone here?" Alexa shouted. The sound of her voice
died without a response. She repeated her question as she
stepped around the stool and into the kitchen. The sun's last
fading ray streamed through the window above the sink to
highlight her toes. She toggled a wall switch. The ceiling's
1930s light fixture didn't even flicker and Alexa decided
she had neither light nor time to check any basement fuse
box.

In Grandma Emma's post-Thanksgiving telephone
conversation, Grandma said she'd tucked a typed apple
cake recipe into her recipe collection. Alexa grabbed
Grandpa's stool and set Samuel on it. Her upper and lower
oak cabinet and drawer rummage discovered no cookbook.

Alexa hoisted Samuel to her right hip. Her left hand
flung aside the dining chair that propped open the pantry's
six-panel solid wood door. With plans to be quick, she
guessed Grandma locked up her county fair recipes. In
Grandma's five-by-eight-foot walk-in pantry, plank-board
shelves wedged a four-drawer black metal file cabinet into
a far corner.

Alexa's slender left hand fingers yanked the key ring
Brad had given her from her front blue-jeans pocket. She
surmised the smallest key had the best chance to pop the
pushed-in oval lock in the cabinet's upper left corner. Her
left hand thumb and forefinger pressed the key shaft teeth
to engage the lock's inner tumblers. Alexa focused every

10

pound of her one hundred and twenty pounds to rotate the key. Her second effort deepened a key edge imprint into her reddened thumb. Its flesh resembled soft tinted putty.

A loud click behind Alexa propelled her to twirl one hundred and eighty degrees. Samuel's scream stung Alexa's right eardrum. Alexa's left hand grasped the light fixture chain that dangled a foot above her head. She pulled. Nothing happened except a soft click. Samuel's wail pierced their black hole darkness.

"Samuel, Samuel, it's all right. Mommy's here."

Small fingers squeezed her neck. The salty wetness of Samuel's tears dampened her chin. She lowered Samuel to the floor, and he clutched her left leg.

Alexa's right elbow bumped a hard, unknown object. *Ouch.* Keys jingled when the fob and its circular metal ring hit the floor. She crouched to retrieve it and her effort failed. She patted the closed panty door until her right hand grasped its doorknob. Two hard twists failed to turn the reluctant doorknob. She stretched her right-hand fingertips high to search the two-inch molding above the door for a spare key. *Who put a pneumatic door closer on a pantry door?* She dismissed her grumble to worry about how she and Samuel could escape. Her nostrils inhaled the doorjamb's disturbed dust that floated past her face. After her right-hand fingertips discovered no doorknob unlock button, her fingertips confirmed a slot outline for the insertion of a key not within her grasp.

Alexa stretched a pocket's denim to dry her right hand wetted by a swipe of Samuel's face. She dared not dump her purse to find the keys FedExed to her last week by Attorney Haberkorn. Alexa encouraged Samuel not cry as she guided him to her right leg. She clutched her purse to her midsection. Her bent right index finger snagged her Grandma's farm building keys.

Alexa fumbled in the darkness to insert each of Grandma's four keys. She tried teeth up and teeth down.

None fit. *Stupid attorney sent the wrong keys.*

Had Mother sunk her claws in? Mother's telephone threat to deny Alexa her inheritance had ignited a restless apprehension within Alexa and hastened her trip to Grandma's Iowa farm.

"The farm's mine!" Mother's scream ricocheted in a never-ending loop within Alexa's skull. "Grandma Emma wasn't in her right mind to give it all to you. Neither your pretty face nor throwing yourself at that young attorney grandma hired will work, either."

Mother can go to hell. Shrouded in darkness, Alexa cringed as her deep-seated maternal hatred bubbled to the surface. This day it eclipsed her need for Samuel to enjoy extended family stability to compensate for a missing father and dead grandparents. Until Mother's call revived her anguish, Alexa had taken to heart that all humans bore a personal cross. Today she vowed to redouble her effort to ignore Mother's selfishness and reconcile without wrecking her and Samuel's future.

The fear in Samuel's pleas fueled Alexa's helpless frustration. She rapped her right hand's bare knuckles on the wood door. After six rap sequences, Alexa sucked her right hand's two middle knuckles and, without the taste of blood, gulped a deep breath of musty, dry air. Her dread continued to escalate. While she racked her probation-officer-trained brain for a tidbit that offered her hope for escape, her left hand rubbed her foolishly bruised knuckles to soothe the aching joints.

File cabinet contents would save her. Prior visits taught her Grandma kept a vise-grip or locking pliers in its bottom drawer for stubborn Mason jar lids. Either tool would provide her with the leverage necessary to twist and expose the doorknob's interior lock mechanism and allow her to retract its bolt.

Thanks, Grandma.

Alexa's left hand separated Samuel from her leg. She

dropped to her knees to fish around and past Samuel's sneakers for the dropped key ring. Her dry throat exploded with an itchy, raspy cough. She apologized to Samuel. The panty's confined space augmented her search effort. With the fob in hand, she stood.

Two key attempts proved as unsuccessful as her first try had minutes earlier. With the second key anchored in the key slot, she forsook her key effort to brace her hands on the cabinet's top left and right corners.

"Don't move, Samuel." Alexa's blue sneaker toe kicked the lowest drawer. Pain in her right big toe persuaded Alexa to pivot and bang her right heel against the drawer. When she crouched and yanked each drawer, none budged.

Alexa cursed the blackness and smelled the sour, sweaty odor of oncoming fear—her fear. She'd never considered that irrational fear would ever freeze her brain. Her parked pickup outside had a flashlight in the glove box. Neither could she retrieve it nor could her two-year-old Samuel transform into a sheet of paper, slip under the door, and toddle to her pickup.

That's it. She reached into her left front jeans pocket for her flip-phone. Gone. Then she remembered. She'd plugged it into her pickup's cigarette lighter to charge. This very moment it drained her vehicle battery as she lamented her bad luck. Alexa dispelled all worries for Samuel's immediate safety with the belief they would discover a way out of the pantry before dehydration. Her right hand wiped a forehead beaded with moisture, this time hers.

Alexa patted the air to locate a shelf's edge for balance. She leaned back and twice slammed her uplifted right sneaker sole square against the pantry door. The hinges jiggled. Neither the lock nor the hinge pins dislodged. She coughed twice into the crook of her right arm and listened. Silence. Tingles beneath her jeans denim crept up her left calf. Her extended left hand verified it wasn't Samuel. Alexa shook her raised left leg. Unsure of the results, she angled her left heel to her right knee and swatted at her sensation's creator. *Damn bug.* The faded skin prickles and Alexa's grab of Samuel's small right hand calmed her.

The rumble of tire treads and crunched gravel seeped into the pantry.

"Help!" Alexa bellowed. "In here." Her expelled breath unnerved her when it bounced off the door into her face. Alexa clamped her right hand to her mouth. Her eagerness to hug Samuel one last time, rather than the budding anxiety of not knowing who entered the farmyard, swelled her brain until logic overpowered emotion.

She positioned her useless keys to protrude outward from between her curled right hand fingers. She didn't need two fingers pressed to her wrist to count her blood-vein throbs to realize her heart thumped against her chest's rib cage.

Alexa pressed her left ear against the crack between the pantry door and its doorjamb. Metal hinges, other than those in proximity to her, creaked. Faced with a choice between another shout and silence, she chose the latter. She choked what could be her last breath at the bottom of her throat. Her right hand assured her that her body shielded Samuel.

Footsteps in an ambient hush slithered through the pantry door perimeter cracks. Alexa flinched when the footsteps abruptly stopped.

She speculated the rhythmic clicks had indicated heeled boots. Alexa exhaled softly when a banged kitchen screen door seemed to confirm the person exited. She castigated herself for a lack of courage. To compensate she squared her five-foot-seven frame, raised her fists, and alternated head-high blows to the wooden door that imprisoned her and Samuel.

Her ears detected renewed hinge squeaks, but no footfalls.

"Come out whoever you are," a loud voice demanded.

14

"I'll call the sheriff."

Alexa's brain cells registered no inkling of who called out. The male huskiness deeper than her remembrance of the last Iowa man encountered, i.e., Brad Haberkorn.

"Mommy, I'm scared."

"Ssshh, Samuel. Mommy has to think." *Calling the sheriff could be a good thing.*

"Come out now or I'll smash the door."

"Can't," Alexa shouted. It wasn't until her word flew from her lips that Alexa realized its ambiguity. She edged herself rearward and squeezed Samuel against the file cabinet she'd tried to break into. The clang of metal against metal alerted Alexa to shield her eyes. She sighed in relief when her left forearm, laid across her eyes, blocked two wood splinters. She peeked after a second thud. Light streamed into the pantry. The wedged head of a sledgehammer encased by the door panel her ear had pressed against. The door's knob dangled.

An electric lantern's beam glinted off aviator sunglasses perched atop the stranger's cropped sandy-brown hair. When he faced the hole Alexa peered through, each hazel eye a spot of color amid his bronzed facial complexion. His perfectly centered nose accented its flatness.

Alexa discounted the stuffy pantry heat as the genesis of her warmed cheeks and renewed forehead moisture. As she stepped into the kitchen, his eyes penetrated hers to reach her soul and devour her essence. This never happened in Chicago where city street pedestrians bustled or party-goers bumped bodies beneath a bar's mounted strobe lights with neither men nor women slowed by exchanged glances.

"Pleased to meet you," Alexa said. She didn't know if Iowa etiquette required she offer her hand. That she carried her son hampered her left arm extension. Plus, she needed her free right hand, studded with key points, to strike out, if necessary.

15

He squared his stance. "You ain't robbing this place, so who are you?"

Her curiosity aroused, Alexa asked without inflection, "How'd you gather that?"

"Deduction. Pickup with Illinois plates too far from the Iowa border and thieves rarely tie a stroller to the tailgate."

Alexa realized she didn't have to gain this guy's everlasting confidence. If she and Samuel could drive away, they'd be safe. Grandma's recipe caused her to hesitate.

The stranger tapped his Red Wing boot's right front toe twice on the floor.

"My grandmother owns this place." Alexa's breath hitched. Did she give away too much information? She grasped for salvation. "We're waiting for her attorney. He's late."

"Great lady. She lets me park my mobile home here."

He sounded sincere. Alexa wouldn't ask him if he dug the front yard holes or pocketed Grandma's recipe. She thanked him for her freedom and, with Samuel on her hip, edged past him and out of the kitchen. She risked his presence safeguarded Grandma's home.

"Mommy, me hungry."

"All right, Tiger. I'll wash you at the Lakeview Inn and we'll find a restaurant."

In her rearview mirror, yard-light-generated shadows gobbled up Grandma's farmhouse and Alexa's girlish childhood memories. Shouldn't she expect Jeffrey the Monkey and Grandma's nighttime friendly ghost, who thrilled Alexa years ago, protect Grandma's recipe until daybreak?

* * *

Undampened by the morning dew sprinkled on Grandma's front lawn, the county road added a dusty dragon's tail to the fast approaching blue sedan. Alexa's left-handed grip

on a hoe tightened when the sedan fishtailed and veered
toward Grandma's driveway.

A gasp twitched in her throat. She kicked aside the half-
filled black plastic bag and dashed to Samuel, who crashed
his Hot Wheels racer into pebbles at the gravel driveway's
edge. Samuel squirmed to free himself from her two-
handed grip. Alexa retreated three steps and willed the
flight reflex out of her calves. Samuel's blue and white T-
shirt absorbed the moisture in her palms.

A sedan engulfed by settling dust appeared to be Brad's
Buick, but a twenty-something skinny blonde emerged. A
digital camera dangled from the intruder's wrist.

"Close your mouth, Tiger. You can't eat dust."

As the woman wobbled forward on clunky elevated
clogs, Alexa's critical eye discerned a pronounced chin
cleft, red lipstick too bold, and clumpy mascara. Alexa
quelled her gut reaction to run to her hoe before the
passenger door opened.

"Good morning." The woman's voice shrill. Her
slender fingers, tipped in fire-engine-red nail polish, parted
a black portfolio she had slipped from under her right arm.
She handed Alexa a white and red striped Realtor business
card with embossed black type that read: "Red Roof Realty,
Jon Grundy."

"You're not Mr. Grundy."

"Daughter. He messed up his appointments. Apologies.
Didn't know if I was to be here this morning at eight-thirty
or nine o'clock." She squinched her eyes. "Whatever. My
name's Susan."

Alexa refused to speculate how this Susan, in a blue
knee-length white-belted dress with a white frilly collar,
could induce overall-clad grizzled males to buy farms.
What did an aspiring fashionista know about acreages or
land values or farmhouse remodeling? Samuel weighed
heavy on Alexa's right arm. She hoisted him higher on her
right hip. "He could've rescheduled."

"People tell me that all the time." Her unencumbered left hand reached toward Samuel's chin. Alexa spotted Ms. Gundy's gesture and frowned. Ms. Gundy fisted her extended fingers. "Show me around. I'll snap the pictures needed for your listing."

Alexa pressed her lips and swallowed. She hadn't committed the listing to Mr. Grundy. One of the three Realtors she'd telephoned from Brad's cards declined to offer a market analysis; the third scheduled to arrive later between one and two p.m. To save the gas needed for a return trip to Rosie's Cafe, Alexa had purchased ice, canned cola, and two vended sandwiches to fill her orange cooler. It stayed cool in the shade beneath Grandma's rear porch and ready for her and Samuel's lunch.

Overwhelmed by the huge radiant grin on Susan's face, Alexa mumbled, "Guess you can look around, but I still haven't made a final decision on who to list with."

Susan's smile faded. "You lead."

Alexa began with the barn's ground level. Boarded milk-house windows blocked the sun from its dingy walls and dirt-streaked floor. Through an interior doorway, stray sunbeams flitted across rusted stanchions. Alexa denied Samuel the opportunity to crawl on the concrete floor.

She let Susan climb the two-by-four boards nailed to the wall as an improvised wooden ladder and peer into the barn's loft. Susan reported twine-tied straw bales piled within a foot of the barn's peaked roof congested the hayloft. Alexa didn't object to the sweet smell when showered by a broken alfalfa bale stacked with the straw. Alexa had no idea why Susan snapped a picture of the ladder. The two exterior photos made sense. Metal cages affixed to the cavernous machine shed's ceiling skipped Alexa's attention until commented on by Susan.

Alexa gazed at the farmhouse and volunteered, "Haven't completed my inside tour." While smashed pantry door images filled her brain, she defensively added,

"Probably needs work."

"County records indicate it was built circa 1912. Buyers today seek these houses."

"They do?" Alexa shifted Samuel to her left hip. She tugged on a braided rope tied to a backyard oak's horizontal limb. Seemed strong and secure. If she could find a decent used tire, maybe Samuel could swing like she did when she visited as a little girl.

Alexa, with no trust in the front porch's safety, interrupted Susan's stare at the mobile home to suggest they enter the kitchen via the rear door.

"Pretty musty," Susan exclaimed as she skirted the kitchen table.

The wooden table legs creaked when Samuel grabbed the table edge with both hands, bent his knees, and swung.

"Stop it, Samuel." She picked him up by his armpits. "Let's wash your hands." Alexa questioned if he could since she hadn't tried the sink's faucet.

Susan's camera flash startled Samuel.

Alexa relented when Samuel wiggled and lowered him to the kitchen floor. She wiped his hands on her jeans and guarded the pantry entrance. Susan clomped into the parlor. Moments later, Susan's footfalls ascended the stairs. The upstairs floorboards directly above Alexa's head creaked. She gazed at the ceiling, happy to find no visible plaster cracks.

She turned the knob next to the cast-iron sink's goose-necked faucet. Nothing. An unsuccessful retry both deflated Alexa's sliver of hope that a repair would be doable and inflated her fear of a humongous plumbing bill. Alexa chose not to open any cabinets for Susan, which she guessed, by the stained and oiled grain, were all oak.

Ms. Gundy's wide grin surprised Alexa when Susan clomped into the kitchen. "Lovely old house." She rolled a marble across the kitchen floor's black-and-white linoleum. "Ouch."

19

"You hurt yourself?"

"No. The marble's speed increase tells me this house has shifted. Suspect you got a foundation problem. An engineer, or a friend I know, can tell you how bad."

"There's no water either."

"Well's probably shut off to prevent frozen pipes. No big deal."

Samuel toddled to the marble and kicked it. With shaky steps, he chased the rolling marble.

"Samuel, that's not yours."

He plopped onto his butt and his right hand grasped the green marble.

"Honey, give it back, please." Alexa feared he'd choke if he dared try to suck it.

Samuel shook his head no.

Susan's shrill voice interrupted. "Let him keep it. I buy a new bag every year."

Alexa squatted and forced Samuel's right-hand fingers apart. Without a verbal condemnation, she pocketed the marble before she wedged a chair between the kitchen door and its jamb. She poked her head outside to determine if a last minute wind shift blew yesterday's pungent manure smell in a direction the screen door didn't let filter into the kitchen. Stones pinged against metal.

Alexa gathered up Samuel and stepped onto the porch. Yard dust swirled to announce a second visitor. A tall, sun-tanned hunk of the "Survivor" television show mold leaped from his Ford F-250. Alexa didn't need the aviator sunglasses atop his head to recognize him. Alexa smiled within herself at her word "hunk." The slangy descriptive term never seemed to be polite, but it fit the man who, less than twenty-four hours earlier, had rescued her and Samuel.

"Hey," Susan called out. The voice from behind startled Alexa.

The hunk's right heel skidded in the gravel. His left foot propelled his abrupt turn. He stared. An uncomfortable queasiness enveloped Alexa until Susan called out a second time. "Joe. Expected your call."

Susan's portfolio scattered dust as she plopped it on a porch rail. Her clogs clumped on each porch step as she hustled to meet the man she hailed as "Joe." Either her hip sway or her shoes mesmerized Samuel.

"Didn't expect you'd be here until late Saturday," Susan said.

"Lightning forced work shutdown thirty miles west. It's headed this way."

Alexa believed him. A freshened northwest wind cooled her cheeks. Clouds started to build on the western horizon. The largest sported a dark gray bottom that trailed black wisps like frayed open-weave lace. Alexa lowered her gaze from the heavens as she neared Susan.

Samuel tugged at her right earlobe. "Mommy, I gotta tinkle." He'd worn big boy diapers for the last month. While Alexa suspected the padding to be thick enough to absorb an accident, she feared he'd not surmount his last potty-training hurdle if she ignored him.

A coy smile teased Joe's lips.

Susan interjected, "House doesn't have running water."

"Well, little man, did mommy teach you about trees?" Joe's sheepish grin widened. Alexa forced her lips apart but her cheek muscles feigned a smile. She gazed toward the spruces. She'd not let Joe drag Samuel there.

"Bring him this way," Joe interrupted. "Trailer's got a bathroom. Follow me."

"I've got to run." Susan swiveled her gaze from Joe's butt to Alexa's face. "Give my office a call tomorrow after lunch, or, if I knew where you're staying, I could try to reach you."

"Lakeview Inn."

"Of course." Alexa watched Susan sashay toward her Buick. "See you later, Joe," Susan called out before she veered to the porch to retrieve her portfolio and camera.

Alexa's eyes bopped from room corner to ceiling inside Joe's mobile home impressed by its cleanliness and neatness. Perhaps Brad spoke truth that Joe didn't stay very often. As she tended to Samuel in the bathroom, her right thigh chilled when against the outside wall. The dull thuds beyond the sixteen-inch louvered jalousie window dotted with raindrops reminded Alexa of a cousin's quip that storm sheltering in a mobile home was akin to living inside a snare drum.

Upon her bathroom exit with Samuel in tow, she heard a male voice, not Joe's, from a forward room. Alexa saw no male when she passed the galley kitchen to arrive at the living room. Joe stretched his legs from armrest-to-armrest across the cushions of his brown-plaid couch. His naked shoulders closest to Alexa; his stocking-covered feet at the far end.

"Radio says it will be a terrific storm," Joe said. His green T-shirt lay crumpled beneath his shoulders. He tilted a sweated clear beer bottle to his lips. The strange male voice, interrupted by waves of over-the-air static, touted used cars.

Alexa glared at the bottle. "I do thank you. We'll be going now."

"You're welcome to stay. I'm not expecting anyone." He rose, strutted across the floor past her, and set his bottle inside his apartment-sized refrigerator. "Didn't mean to drink in front of the little man. Kinda forgot. Not used to daytime company."

"We don't wish to impose." She gripped Samuel's hand and opened Joe's storm door.

A wind gust stretched the aluminum door's safety chain taut, fluttered interior living room curtains, rustled Venetian blinds, and flickered the kitchen's fluorescent ceiling light.

Joe leaped forward. "Let me corral that door."

His breath moist and warm on the left side of her neck

22

as he reached past her waist for the handle. An eerie wave of self-consciousness coursed her body. Her tenseness triggered by proximity to his naked chest, his bicep bulge, and his callused fingers. Nerves within her spine smarted in a rhythmic zigzag. She couldn't force herself to gaze into his face.

Samuel crab-walked to and jumped onto Joe's sofa.

While Joe's left hand clutched the door handle Alexa had released, he sucked in his abs to squirt past her onto the wooden stoop's square landing. He rotated toward her. "Can now see what spooked the superintendent. There's a wall cloud."

"Is that bad?" She regained her composure. *Stupid question.*

"Spawns tornados. Mrs. Anderson let me join her in the basement year ago last spring when a tornado leveled four buildings just north of here in Fernton."

"We can do that." After the four words tumbled from her lips, Alexa inhaled deep. For the past three years, she'd shied away from men her office friends introduced her to, and, even then, her intuition often crashed and burned. Sure, this Joe smashed her and Samuel's pantry escape route, but then he had no expectation they were isolated at the farm. With an inaudible exhale, Alexa succumbed to the realization that Grandma trusted the Erickson's, or otherwise the mobile home wouldn't be there. She waved at Samuel.

"Go ahead, I'll bring the little man, lock this door, and meet you on the back porch."

Past the mobile home's corner, a forceful wind gust retarded Alexa's steps. Wind-slanted rain pelted her chin. Her right forearm protected her forehead and eyes. Humidity sucked a lightning flash from the underbelly of a cloud. Before Alexa mouthed "a thousand four," thunder rumbled less than a mile behind Grandma's barn.

Alexa exchanged raised forearms to protect her eyes

23

Donan Berg

against the sheets of unrelenting rain. Her short twenty-
yard run from the mobile home to the porch mustered her
last reserve of strength and speed. Rain soaked her clothes,
especially her cotton blouse. Her motel room's full suitcase
of dry clothes useless.

Samuel's joyful squeals caused her to glance rearward
past her right shoulder. Samuel's left hand fingers,
unprotected by Joe's collapsed umbrella, stretched to catch
raindrops. On the wooden porch deck, a lowered Samuel
danced and stomped his shoes in a shallow warped-plank
puddle. His high-pitched giggle punctuated a thunder echo.
When Alexa shook her head at him, he clapped. With
dexterity and speed, Joe's outstretched hand prevented
Samuel's porch step tumble into a six-foot diameter lawn
puddle.

Alexa rushed to direct her son's energy toward the
kitchen door.

When she passed Joe, he said, "He must be a handful?"

"Everyone says that." She retrieved her lunch cooler.
"I've two sandwiches we can share."

"I'll be right back." Joe hesitated until Alexa re-
established a grasp of Samuel's right hand. Joe then
splashed to his mobile home as he tilted two umbrella ribs
into a shifting wind. Samuel dropped two blocks and
clapped when Joe straddled the kitchen door threshold and
twirled his umbrella. Joe displayed a plastic sack tied to
each wrist.

"Bread, summer sausage, trail mix, pop," Joe said.
"What more do we need?"

Alexa trembled. A draft shivered her torso where her
wet blouse clung to her skin. "Sounds like a feast."

While Joe didn't mention beer, he'd slipped on a green
T-shirt with the word "Guinness" brazened in white across
his chest. Alexa "moon-walked" to a kitchen counter.

"And, drum roll." Joe set the food bag on the table
while his left hand hid one bag behind his back. His right

24

hand rustled plastic. "Wha-la. Brought this shirt. Yours appears awful wet."

Alexa allowed the shirt's long sleeves to drape toward the floor as she accepted the shirt Joe offered. She didn't want to say anything to highlight her inner anxiety. Women who jog or sunbath on Chicago's Oak Beach exposed more skin than her rain-induced clinginess. Joe hoisted Samuel onto a kitchen chair.

"Thanks." Alexa sidled to the parlor. "I'll be right back."

When she returned clad in Joe's shirt, its sleeves folded to her elbows, Samuel sat on her cooler, a summer sausage slice protruding from his lips. She assumed Joe, not Samuel, repositioned the cooler against the kitchen's lower cabinets. Rain splatters wet the western window. Alexa lifted her son to extract two ham sandwiches and two colas. She offered one of each to Joe. As she bit into hers, lightning flashed and thunder boomed three seconds later. Joe lifted an am-fm radio from his plastic bag. The DJ's deep bass voice interrupted a country western song to announce a National Weather Service tornado warning for Lake County. He urged county residents to shelter in place.

Joe grabbed Samuel. "Suggest we find the basement."

Alexa banged cabinet doors until she located matches and two large two-inch white candles. *Thank you, Grandma.* At the bottom of the basement stairs, Alexa brushed a cobweb from her hair and her right forefinger flicked a silverfish thoracic shell. A chrome-legged old Formica dining room table and three rickety chairs occupied the pillared room's center. Without electricity, the sun's disappearance intensified the storm's dark scary elements. Diffused light projected through four basement windows, each eight, twelve-inch glass-blocks, faded.

Samuel clutched Alexa's left leg. She used her wet blouse to wipe each a chair and then slap at a spider that sprinted across the tabletop. When posed to light the second candle, Joe suggested she wait in case the storm lasted.

Alexa suppressed her prior frightful captivity memories of being rope-bound and gagged in a boarded-up, abandoned, utility deprived Southside Chicago house basement.

Booming thunder blanched Samuel's face. A lightning bolt flashed outside a west window. A second flash at a window across the room didn't entice Alexa to investigate.

"Haven't heard the train yet," Joe quipped. His facial features shadowed.

"What?"

"You know, a tornado speeds in with the roar of an approaching train."

Alexa didn't want to think about tornado devastation. Her cell phone rang. With clipped phrases she agreed to delay the afternoon Realtor appointment.

Joe tested two chairs and slid one to Alexa. Candlelight flickers created masks on Samuel's and Joe's faces. Grandma, alone on a prairie farm in the midst of a harsh Midwest winter, probably appreciated she had a strong young man nearby. On second thought, Alexa was positive Grandma did. Why Grandma hadn't mentioned him in their telephone conversations puzzled her.

Still, no male, however kind or persistent, would chisel a chink in the wall she built to protect her heart. Infrequent Internet dates augmented by best friend double-dates allowed Alexa to hone her emotional defensive skills and relationship avoidance techniques.

The deepening black velvet fingers of darkness horrified her. She could neither abandon Samuel nor the lifeline Joe represented. "Have you lived on the farm long?"

"Close to four years. Your grandmother treated me terrific from day one."

"Mommy, me hungry." Samuel scrambled onto his mother's lap.

Alexa unwrapped her sandwich, tore off a two-inch piece, and placed it in Samuel's right hand. "What do you say?"

Samuel lips cracked wide. "Thank you."

Chair leg scraps against the concrete floor alerted Alexa of Joe's interest. His forward lean permitted luminous light streaks to cross his cheeks.

"Grandma never mentioned your mobile home."

"Don't know why. I praised her sesame seed cake to everyone."

Blunted floorboard creaks above them crept to the room's center. Alexa and Joe's gaze converged at the basement stairs. Joe blew out the candle. Alexa tightened her grip on Samuel.

A doorknob's metal clinks pierced the unlit stillness. A voice called out, "Anyone here?"

Alexa's abdominal muscles tensed; anxiety rivulets disrupted her nascent comfort with Joe's presence. Fate or luck served her by his selection of the chair between her and the stairs.

"In the basement," Joe shouted.

Alexa swallowed hard. Bravado without weapons better served by a wait for the intruder's possible disinterest in an abandoned farmhouse.

Joe stood, fists clenched. "Identify yourself or get out." The depth of his tone radiated strength or camouflaged his anxiety. "You're trespassing."

The expansive beam of a high-powered flashlight preceded black oxfords and khaki trousers as they descended tread after tread. Alexa's squint strained to piece together the man's features.

"Alexa, are you all right?"

"Of course she is," Joe replied. "Who are you?"

"Brad, Brad Haberkorn." He lowered the beam.

Alexa chided herself for her failure to recognize the pants and the voice. "Why you here?"

"Received a telephone call from Red Top Realty that Susan Grundy left you at the farm. Called the Lakeview Inn. They said you hadn't returned."

He shined his flashlight into Joe's face. "Didn't expect to find you down here."

Alexa stood and walked three paces to be within an arm's length of Joe and Brad. Both men physically similar, broad shoulders, torsos tapered to the waist, Joe two inches taller than Brad. Their movements born of either athletic competition or physical labor.

Alexa fought off the urge for further comparison. She predicted her elliptical-trainer-lubricated joints equaled their flexibility despite her smaller frame. As much as either or both physically impressed her, there'd be no chink in her armor.

"As you see, Samuel and I are okay. Not the Hilton, but safe."

"Thank God. Spotter radioed in tornado funnel touchdown near Cook's Corner."

"That's east of here," Joe said. "Should mean it passed us by."

"Blue skies in the rearview." Brad gazed at Alexa. "Lydia Skelton make it?"

Alexa appreciated the simple question. "Ms. Skelton telephoned. I promised I'd wait."

"Good. Call me when you decide upon a Realtor."

Silence engulfed the basement until Joe scrapped his chair leg on the concrete.

Without a lip visual, Alexa heard Brad say, "Guess I'll go then." His light-outlined frame ascended the stairs. Faint overhead floor creaks faded.

Joe relit the candle. "Didn't realize this place for sale."

"I'm not a farmer. Don't believe I'd survive in isolation."

Joe passed his right palm through the candle flame. A second time he counted the seconds before he flinched.

28

"It's not the depression you read about."

"Grandma enjoyed spending hours and days baking. The gene wasn't inherited."

"Bet if you use your Grandmother's recipes, you'd surprise yourself."

Alexa didn't respond. She attributed a gunned engine outside to Brad's departure.

"He didn't have to drive out here." Alexa noted Joe's first hint of jealousy.

She refused to allow Joe to draw her into a full-scale macho battle, but courtesy deserved respect. "Think it nice Brad exhibited concern."

"Aw, nothing special. We folks always give our best to strangers."

Alexa fought not to expose a preference for either man. "Didn't mean to exclude you."

"Didn't take it that way." He wiped his hands on his jean-clad thighs. "Let me check outside. If the storm's truly passed, no use for us to hide in this basement."

Alexa counted to twenty. The floor creaks stopped and, against her better judgment, she let Samuel crawl up the basement stairs ahead of her. The door to the rear porch stood ajar.

Whether Thor or angry nature gods, no higher spirit threatened destruction. Tree twigs and leaves lay scattered on the gravel. Her stroll to the front lawn while Joe entertained Samuel greeted Alexa with an unexpected discovery. The winds blew away half the litter. Tidbits of shredded paper sheets fluttered in the branches of a ten-foot oak on the lawn's eastern perimeter.

Interrupted by a metallic gray Nissan Altima, Alexa's thoughts galloped from trash to Samuel's whereabouts. Quick strides found her son tucked safe in Joe's arms.

"You got a visitor. I'll entertain the little man inside my trailer."

Samuel giggled atop Joe's shoulders. Alexa unleashed

her tongue to warn, "No beer."

"Of course not." Joe's exasperated eyes mirrored her father's when, as a little girl, Alexa repeated the same question four to five times. Alexa wished to retract her words. Since that wasn't possible, she shrugged.

Joe twirled Samuel. "Little man can have ice cream, okay?"

Alexa's cheeks warmed. "Fine." The words "not too much" sank into her throat unspoken.

A plump woman in her fifties approached Alexa from the direction opposite Joe's departure. Her garish flat-heeled silver pumps subdued by her dark blue-jacketed skirt suit.

"Terrible storm, wasn't it?" Alexa nodded. "I'm Lydia Skelton. Skelton Realty." She offered her right hand.

"Alexa, Alexa Hovey." They shook hands. "You see much damage?"

"Scattered branches. Nothing substantial. My father helped the Andersons buy this place."

"Didn't know that."

"Trust me if you want to know what's going on in Lake County. Your grandmother was a terrific lady. No one baked better. Could never persuade her to share those secret recipes."

Alexa didn't interrupt. She'd been trained as a probation officer that nods and silence often encouraged the speaker to get to the heart of the matter quicker.

"Don't know why your grandmother allowed this trailer without rent payments. Musta been because she had a soft spot for Oscar Erickson. He helped your grandfather, bless his soul, bale hay. Trouble is the land's been crop-farmed for years without rotation, which might depress the farm's value. And, this fine house." Ms. Skelton sighed. "Terrible your grandmother wasted her last days in that nursing home."

Alexa's right sneaker toe scraped a dandelion head off

its stem.

"Don't worry. I'll get you top dollar. You can take that to the bank."

Alexa lifted her gaze when the words stopped. Alexa's jumbled thoughts capped by the wish Grandma hadn't died. Samuel deserved an adult male role model. Although she didn't relish competition with Susan Grundy, her son's positive reaction to Joe emboldened her.

Alexa suggested to Ms. Skelton they tour the barn, the machine shed, and the house in that order. On their trek to the barn, the warmth of Grandma's old Christmas sweater battled the cold front's chill. Alexa's step froze when Ms. Skelton's honey-coated self-promotion switched to "Bet you treasure your grandmother's recipes. Be a great estate sale draw."

Alexa rotated her torso left before she stuck her right hand, first two fingers crossed, into her front jeans pocket. "Grandma never shared." Alexa's assertion half true. True if one meant neighbors. Not so if Alexa included.

"Well, if you find them, don't destroy any. Our county ladies club would love to produce a cookbook to finally outsell the Clover County women's edition."

Alexa uncrossed her right-hand fingers and pointed her forefinger to the barn. Their perfunctory barn and machine shed tours provided no smiles for either.

"Let's have a look at the house, shall we?" The self-assertive lilt that had grated Alexa's nerves returned. She forgot the urge to say "see ya" as she quickened her pace to stay astride Ms. Skelton. "Don't suppose there's central air conditioning."

Alexa shook her head. "Haven't found electricity or running water."

"No problem. Trust me. Like I said, I'm known to find high-price buyers. One can always repair or update utilities. Now old world craftsmanship . . . ." Her gaze flitted to the kitchen door. "That's something modern tradesmen have never learned, if you know what I mean?"

Ms. Skelton's exaggerated wink struck Alexa as phony. *Choose naive or pompous. What a Realtor choice.* Maybe she should forget top dollar, run a newspaper ad, and accept the first offer before the next tornado swirled Grandma's barn and house roofs across cornfields. Any money she pocketed would be greater than what she might have imagined.

"I told your mother the prospects for a quick sale at normal prices would be hard."

"What?" Alexa stared at the woman. "You spoke with my mother?"

"Brad Haberkorn let it slip that your mother may be the eventual farm owner."

Alexa's right-foot sneaker kicked an empty cola can. It clattered to the driveway's edge. Mother's threat had blossomed into action. No doubt her stepfather egged mother on. Alexa never doubted Mother's full-time job with medical benefits jetted his three-week courtship into an altar-ending affair. Alexa had no proof of her stepfather's poverty but her Mother's wedding ring accompanied by a pawnshop receipt didn't indicate independent wealth. His wholesale business conducted at flea market tables didn't list him in *Who's Who* or generate gold-embossed dinner invitations from Donald Trump.

"Mr. Haberkorn didn't tell me. Grandma wrote my name in her will."

"Listen, honey, I'll be on your side. Treat me right with the listing and you'll be okay."

"This is all rather confusing. You still want to look around?"

"Of course." Ms. Skelton's gaze at the mobile home hardened. "That still Joe Erickson's trailer?" Alexa nodded. "Woman to woman, I'd be careful of that guy. He's flashed his eyes at several young ladies, my daughter-in-law included. She had her heart broken after she . . . well . . .

you know what I mean."

Alexa didn't, but neither did she wish to encourage further conversation. Joe acted a gentleman to her and Samuel. Grandma had warned her how rural gossip stung and hurt innocents. She'd keep her guard raised, confident of her strength to ferret out evil motives.

After twenty minutes inside the house, Ms. Skelton announced she'd seen all she cared to see. Although she snapped no pictures, the Realtor's ooh's and aah's at the farmhouse's Old World carpentry struck Alexa as authentic.

Alexa waved as Ms. Skelton's Altima drove out the farmyard. When certain Ms. Skelton wouldn't return, Alexa knocked on Joe's door.

"C'mon in."

Joe, on his hands and knees with Samuel on his back, played the horse. "Lone Ranger, can Trigger rest now?"

Alexa laughed at the living room scene. Priceless joy radiated from Samuel's eyes.

"Mommy, me stay." His right-hand toddler fingers stroked a miniature Colt .45 replica.

"Not today. We've a room at the motel."

Joe slowed his rise to allow Samuel to slide off. He then picked up her son and plopped him on the sofa. His socks eliminated carpet friction to speed up his pivot to face her. "You decide?"

"Not yet," Alexa replied.

"Then you're coming back?"

"'Fraid so. I thought selling would be easy. From what little I know about real estate, a buyer's first impression overwhelms later discovered value. Very important Grandma's house doesn't scare away potential farm buyers."

Alexa couldn't express her alternative thought: Maybe living with Samuel far from city crime would benefit them both. Her final decision had to calculate the net of

Grandma's farm rent to supplement a rural Iowa job not yet attained.

Joe's derriere dented his sofa cushion. Samuel, on Joe's right knee, pointed Joe's fake pistol at the ceiling.

"Samuel, please give that gun to Joe. Mommy doesn't want you playing with any gun."

Joe wrestled it from Samuel's fingers. "It's only a cigarette lighter without fluid."

Alexa blew out a sigh. "Samuel shouldn't get the idea he can play with guns."

Joe's right forefinger pressed a release. The gun-like butt separated from the cylinder and barrel. A flint and blackened wick appeared. Three flicks by Joe's forefinger failed to produce a flame. He clicked the disjointed pieces together and stuffed the lighter beneath a sofa cushion.

"Thanks. Don't know why I blab on like this."

"It's the storm. Strangers bond when disaster looms."

She bit her lower lip. "Guess so. I'll make sure you get your shirt back."

"No hurry. Sister gave it to me at Christmas. Never liked its long sleeves." Joe laughed.

Alexa couldn't help but take pleasure in his laugh, an honest laugh. Unpretentious. That Samuel sat on Joe's right knee without his normal squirms another positive sign.

"C'mon, Tiger." She stretched her arms to Samuel. When he didn't move, she slid her soles closer, and placed her hands under her son's arms. With a twist, Samuel rested on her left hip.

Joe didn't twitch or flinch. "Will you call me the next time?"

"Sure." Her voice strong, unequivocal.

Alexa lingered until the mobile home's door latch clicked before she put Grandma's house in her sights. She'd never considered her nostalgia and Grandpa's gold tied her future to Iowa.

Joe impressed her as exceedingly nice, level headed,

concerned, and not pushy. Lydia Skelton's comment about his breaking female hearts a soft cerebral echo.

Alexa chided herself not to drop her vigilance nor relive past agonies. She'd disengage herself from all Iowans who inflicted harm. And her mother if what was said proved true.

Golden sunrays ascended behind the barn's roof. Alexa soaked in Mother Nature's majestic rejuvenation. She clutched Samuel and abandoned her fanciful poetic dream.

Into Samuel's right ear she whispered, "You like Joe don't you?"

Chapter Two

Alexa thanked God for her cell phone ring, a welcome break from best friend Belinda Marchiori's marathon questioning about Alexa's Iowa trip. While she drummed her fingers for a secretary's connect, she gazed out a window seven stories above Chicago's LaSalle Street. On any other day, the hovering gray clouds stripped joy from Alexa's enthusiasm. Her thoughts flipped between money for a new life and the crush of past reality.

"Yes, Brad. No, I've not decided." She laid the cell on her desk and activated its speaker.

"You need to."

Alexa pondered if Brad was on her side. "Why? Because my mother will if I don't?"

"Where does that come from?"

"Don't ask." She twisted her desk phone cord around her right hand index finger.

"I apologize if I didn't tell you your mother sent me a

letter, but you shouldn't worry. The will says you inherit the farm as your grandma's sole beneficiary. That's what's important."

"What about the crops planted? That mobile home?"

"Oscar Erickson has a contract for this year's planting that the court will honor no matter who owns the land. Don't know if there's a contingency on the mobile home."

"What about next year?" Line static forced Alexa to lift the handset to her left ear.

"Why worry? Aren't you going to sell?"

The contrarian in Alexa tested him. "What if I don't sell?"

"Now I'm confused. When your grandmother met with me to create the will, she said you grew up a big city girl and wouldn't ever change. She expressed a strong desire not to let any farm proceeds fall under the control of your mother's husband."

"Guess headstrong Grandma considered him a womanizer." Alexa pressed her lips together. "I shouldn't be so cruel."

"Won't categorize your grandmother. She really loved you. No one else remembered to call her on her birthday. She remarked once last year she would've planted dandelions if you'd been there to chase them across the lawn. Memories twinkled in her eyes, uplifted her spirits."

Tears welled behind Alexa's eyes. Grandma never let Alexa halt their phone conversations without her promise to call again. She never realized Grandma valued beyond measure her infrequent trips. "Why do I feel your reminiscences hide something?"

"They don't." His voice dropped. "You've got to trust me."

"What about the recipe?" Alexa remembered Grandma's county fair ribbon drawer and Lydia Skelton's cookbook contest. While Grandma guarded her recipes with a sentry's vigilance, her devise of the apple cake recipe baffled Alexa.

"Your grandmother insisted on its inclusion. Yet, she wouldn't explain its significance except to say it honored her late husband and a favorite saying."

"That's quirky, even for Grandma."

"Did she have a favorite saying? A bible verse?"

"Grandma often said 'In God We Trust, All Others Cash'."

The line's intensified static drowned out Brad's reply, if any.

Alexa waited a minute. "Brad, you still there?"

"Yeah."

"I'll talk quick. Losing battery. If anyone asks, I'm still deciding upon a Realtor. Between us, I need a foundation and exterior repair estimate on Grandma's house."

The line went dead. Alexa opened her desk drawer and crammed her cell into her purse.

From the next desk Belinda asked, "You okay?"

"Sorta."

"Tonight might be a good night we share a drink after work."

"Can't. Gotta pick up Samuel from day care."

"No excuse. You pick up Samuel. Drop him off at my mother's near Lincoln Park Zoo and we'll start at Merkle's."

Alexa double-parked her F-150, lifted Samuel from his car seat, and ran up the stairs into Belinda's mother's house. She scribbled her cell phone number on a Chinese takeout menu for Mrs. Marchiori and promised Samuel his mommy would be early.

Belinda followed her to the pickup, not yet ticketed.

The bar crowd at Merkle's numbered less than twenty. Proof the Cubs weren't playing at Wriggly Field, two blocks away. Alexa slid into the inside banquette seat that stretched along the sidewall beneath TVs and wall-hung memorabilia. Merkle's hamburger basket special with the cheese-sprinkled fries made her decision easy. Belinda ordered two glasses of pinot noir.

"I tried not to eavesdrop, but is your mother messing up your life again?"

Alexa bowed her head. She could open her heart to Belinda; her confident and best friend since the City of Chicago employed them as probation officers. Their job was to counsel homeless and abused teenage girls, not to be troubled themselves.

"Guess so. To what extent I don't know. It all revolves around Grandma's farm."

Belinda sipped her wine and held the rim to her lips long enough to permit a patron to walk past en route to the restrooms. "So, what about other relatives?"

"I'm an only child and my one uncle died four years ago." Alexa shifted table condiments to allow the server to place her basket in front of her. "Grandma surprised me. There's a large mobile home parked opposite her house."

"Frisky Grandma?" Belinda's spirited eyes dominated by a sly smile.

"Son of the land tenant. Nice guy. Real hunk, if you're interested."

"Now you're talking." Belinda drained her wine glass. "When you going to invite me?"

Alexa bit into a fry and swallowed. "Hadn't planned to."

"What?" Astonishment flashed in Belinda's eyes.

Alexa gulped a pinot noir mouthful. She prayed Belinda faked her hurt.

"You'll hide a delicious hunk from my deserving eyes?" The furrow of Belinda's brow deepened. Alexa mortified her tease crept past merriment to the point redemption required.

"He's said to be a Casanova. Spreads legs like Thanksgiving turkeys, enjoys the stuffing, and then tosses away the bones."

38

Belinda tapped her fork. "You know that for a fact?" Alexa clamped her lips tight before she blurted "Heavens no. Second . . . third-hand gossip." Alexa dismissed her catty guilt; she hadn't nicked their friendship.

"Field trip; field trip." Belinda's taps repeated. "I'll borrow my cousin's camper." Her taps escalated into a rhythmic chorus.

* * *

Alexa, from the passenger's seat, directed Belinda's SUV into Grandma's farm. Both had cashed in a personal day to escape Chicago with the Thursday rush hour exodus. The digital dash clock read: 9:50 p.m. No yard light shone. Belinda's mother tended Samuel until Monday.

En route, Alexa had telephoned Brad to leave a message that after two weeks she still hadn't decided whether Susan or Lydia deserved the listing. While at a gas station, Alexa missed his voice message that the judge had issued a temporary injunction against Alexa, or anyone acting on her behalf, from selling the farm without court approval.

"Looks cool," Belinda said.

"Morning light may change your mind."

While feral creatures near Grandma's house howled, chirped, and buzzed, Alexa helped Belinda lock the unhitched camper's stabilizers into the gravel. After Alexa crawled in, Belinda's nasal breathing, not the tight inside quarters, delayed Alexa's sleep.

"Belinda." Alexa raised her voice a notch. "Belinda, turn over."

"What? Where's that hunk you mentioned?"

"Go back to sleep."

Alexa lay awake. Her earlier scan showed Joe's pickup absent. Perhaps she'd see him Saturday. While Joe accepted Samuel, how many questions would Joe require answers to? She only trusted Belinda to know her true story. Alexa flattened her left ear against the pillow and drifted into a starless void.

Belinda shouted, "Wake up. Morning. Time to party?"

Alexa groaned. Belinda's annoying quirky belief a day should begin when the sun crossed the eastern horizon even survived tedious mountain-less drives. Alexa's encrusted eyelids peeked to confirm sunrays streaked the sky.

Alexa pushed her green sleeping bag to her waist. She gawked at a fully-dressed, makeup-applied Belinda. "If your hunk shows, I'm ready."

"I can see. Let me find my jeans, and we can explore Grandma's house."

Alexa's key unlocked the kitchen door. Nothing appeared disturbed from the day of the storm and its tornado warning. She followed Belinda's exploration.

Alexa's right hand encircled a WD40 can. She sprayed the basement water shut-off valve until the lubricant streamed along the valve stem. The circular valve resisted. She sprayed a second time. Her right hand's left-rotation pressure prevailed. She hustled upstairs. No water spewed from the kitchen sink spout to reward her efforts.

"Could be the well," Belinda said. "My folks had one in the suburbs."

Together they found the well next to the barn. Alexa's set of keys solved the first stumbling block when one unlocked the pump padlock. Alexa carried no keys to overcome the farm's no electricity hurdle. The REA office she called promised a lineman visit Monday.

When Susan from Red Top Realty telephoned to inquire about the listing, Alexa parlayed Susan's eagerness to extract Susan's promise to retrieve a key from Brad's office and be present when the electrical guy showed.

"What about the mobile home?" Belinda asked.

Alexa's right forefinger pointed. "Separate line. See that pole."

"Lucky my cousin's trailer has a chemical toilet." Belinda laughed. "Wouldn't want my butt to itch from poison ivy."

A Buick inched into the farmyard.

"Your hunk?"

"Attorney handling Grandma's estate." Alexa waited for Brad to exit his vehicle before she walked towards him. Belinda dawdled.

"You get my voice mail?" Alexa shook her head. "Your mother filed a claim to invalidate your grandmother's will and invoke Iowa's intestate law."

"What in the blazes does that mean? I've heard possession is nine tenths of the law and I'm here and Mother isn't." She tried to speak in a calm professional tone while she floated in a new ocean of chaos. "I paid you what you said I owed. Now you say I've wasted my money."

"It's not that simple. I can't prevent your mother filing a court paper."

Belinda strode within speaking distance. She stopped with her hands clasped at her waist. "You saying Alexa loses this farm even if her grandmother's will said she should have it?"

"Not exactly."

"Lawyers." Contempt glazed Belinda's utterance. "Slimy bastards no matter where you live."

"Hold off, Belinda." Dishonor or shame streaked Brad's eyes. "Do I need a new lawyer?"

"Can't answer that," Brad replied. He averted Belinda's stare. "At your grandmother's will appointment she said what's in the copy you received. I asked about a bequest to your mother, but Mrs. Anderson said to leave out all mention of her."

"Unless you can one hundred percent tell me this is my farm, you better go."

Brad's shoulders slumped as he backtracked to his Buick.

Alexa stared at him without speaking. Belinda's hand

gripped her right shoulder.

With the Buick out of sight, Belinda broke the silence.
"Real shame." She stepped forward and winked. "If he
weren't a lawyer, he qualifies for my hunk category."

"You're suffering a strong case of hunk mania."

"If one gets to pick an ailment, that's all I'll say."

Alexa shrugged and enlisted Belinda's help to carry
cleaning supplies from the SUV trunk into the house. She
realized neither she nor Belinda had eaten breakfast and
without electricity they had no working stove or
refrigerator. "Ready for breakfast at Rosie's?" Alexa asked.

"Anywhere."

Alexa prompted Belinda to select a booth far from the
four locals seated along the counter. Alexa doubled
Belinda's breakfast special order. Two gentlemen wearing
bib overalls passed. The second's right hip thumped the
backrest behind Alexa and his hurried "sorry" told Alexa
the men landed at the corner booth behind her.

"They'll have a difficult time selling the Anderson
place." His gravel voice low and distinct.

A tentative, halting voice responded. "Why? Land's
tillable."

"Have you forgot? It's cursed."

Alexa forced herself not to turn around. The trying-to-
take-it-all-in Belinda waved to the server who balanced two
breakfast plates. Alexa slid her water glass aside and shook
her head when the server asked if there would be "anything
else?" Alexa had no guarantee the man spoke of her
Grandma's farm; she desired to hear more. Grandma often
said the number of Andersons, most unrelated, filled more
church pews than any other family name. Alexa touched
her right hand forefinger to her lips to signal Belinda not to
speak.

The gravel-voiced one continued. "Recall when Mrs.
Anderson tried to sell two, three years ago. The buyer who
outbid Oscar Erickson died in a car wreck our sheriff

couldn't explain."

"Coincidence, pure coincidence. That's all it was."

"What then about those bones? The body of Mrs. Anderson's husband never found."

Alexa swallowed hard.

"Two witnesses vouched he drowned fishing in Minnesota."

"Yeah, and six months later . . . after the coroner's inquest, both owned new cars."

Alexa gasped. Behind her, denim rubbed Naugahyde. She twisted to the noise and caught one man peer above his wire-rimmed glasses to stare at her. He pushed his eyeglasses upward, shrugged, and then, without a word, rotated to his buddy. The server brought the men breakfast plates and their conversation ceased.

Alexa's mind wandered to her attendance at Grandpa's memorial service and the hushed church vestibule conversations. She had agreed it plausible the Mississippi River current forever carried his body away. The county sheriff said that even happened in Iowa rivers. When Alexa visited six months later, Grandma exhibited fewer depression symptoms.

Belinda pointed toward the restroom door. Alexa fished three singles from her purse for a tip and dillydallied alongside Belinda's SUV.

"Too bad I didn't bring my cast-off-devils kit," Belinda said. She stopped at her SUV's driver door to chuckle.

"Quit it. Gossip, that's all." Alexa's fingers unlatched the passenger door, and she slid in to latch her seatbelt first. "Those guys need to learn life is not a conspiracy."

Belinda inserted her ignition key. "Just in case I'll tuck my silver cross under my pillow."

Alexa gulped. "You got one of those?"

"Yeah." Belinda cocked her head toward Alexa. "Uncle gave me one at confirmation."

When Belinda's SUV entered the farmyard, Alexa's

scan found no Joe. She dismissed her interest and left the kitchen door ajar.

A bottle of concentrated Pine-Sol, packed for interior cleaning, challenged Alexa's creativity. She forgot it needed dilution. Belinda suggested a stream search and boiled water. Alexa shook her head. Grandma hadn't invested in a portable propane stove.

Disappointment tugged at Alexa as she pawed through rags and groaned when dust swirled from kitchen cabinet shelves. After a cough, Belinda led Alexa to the backyard, but not before she grabbed a black plastic bag to finish her exterior trash collection.

A half-filled bag at her feet, Alexa's right hand tugged on the braided rope that hung from the backyard oak's lowest limb. Ever louder putt-putts alerted Alexa to an approaching tractor. Mud-caked John Deere wheels crunched to a stop in front of Belinda's SUV.

"Good afternoon." A lanky man with tan-weathered skin and brilliant eyes that reminded her of Joe leaned forward. His quilted brown vest touched the tractor's steering wheel.

Uncertain if she should flee or stay, Alexa breathed easier when Belinda rounded the house's west corner. "Hello," Alexa replied.

The man rocked rearward, swung his left leg, and jumped off his tractor. "Name's Oscar Erickson." His five long strides closed the distance between them. "Bet you're Mrs. Anderson's granddaughter." He stood six-foot.

"Yes." Alexa shook his hand, almost winced from his grip. "Alexa's my name."

"Your grandmother was a fine lady. People in these parts would do anything for her."

Even cover up a murder? She gulped. Be sociable, Alexa admonished herself. "Nice for you to say. I loved her very much. You know Grandma long?"

"Thirty, almost forty years. Both this farm and mine

down the road surveyed in the federal government's land grant homestead program." He winked. "I don't go back that far, but farming's been in my blood all my life. My kin's buried next to your grandparents in the Christian Church cemetery on the road to Lakeview."

Alexa didn't have the courage to broach the subject of one or two graves.

"Anything you need, just ask." His right hand rubbed his chiseled jaw line.

"Where's the nearest stream?"

"A mile over yonder." He pointed in the barn's direction. "Why?"

"Well pump not powered yet. Hard to clean without water."

"Easy fix. Joe's got water in the mobile home. I'll unlock. Fill as many buckets as you need. Don't look puzzled. We trenched a special electrical line and a water line when first moving the mobile home here. Made it easy to calculate the charges."

"Oh."

He reached into his right overalls pocket. "Okay, got'em." His right hand grasped a ring of keys. "Rain earlier this week kept Old Betsy out of the east forty. Must uproot the quack before the corn reaches knee high." He tipped his straw hat. "Push the lock when you're done."

Alexa watched Oscar's long strides arrive at Joe's mobile home and then return him to his tractor. She waved as he drove his tractor to a rutted path that skirted the barn.

With two buckets filled, Alexa and Belinda began their scrub upstairs. As to who would scour the claw-footed bathroom tub, Alexa lost the coin flip. Without further visitors, Alexa raced to duplicate Belinda's energy. At five p.m., an exhausted Alexa suggested they wash up in the mobile home and drive to Rosie's for dinner.

Dusk encircled them as they returned to the farm. Light spilled from the mobile home window Alexa knew to be its

45

living room. They had left no mobile home light on.

As they stood in the farmyard, Belinda asked, "Your hunk home?"

"Doubt it. No truck." Alexa stepped left to avoid a puddle. "Probably a timer for security."

"Or to keep the ghosts away."

"Quit it already." Alexa entered and exited Belinda's camper with her flashlight. She set the flashlight on the back porch rail to telephone Samuel and say good night. She promised him mommy would be home Sunday.

With a flashlight beam for guidance, Alexa strode toward the machine shed. Belinda tagged along and asked if the machine shed might be a garage. Alexa shrugged and jumped when Belinda's hand poked her in the small of her back.

"Why stop?" Belinda's voice quizzical.

Alexa crouched. "If this shed isn't being used, squirrels didn't make these." She pointed a light beam at two sets of soft tire tracks. Wet mud traces, in the lower recesses, intrigued Alexa. *Water should have evaporated.*

"Maybe that hunk of yours parks here?" Belinda's left cheek near Alexa's right ear.

"Saw his truck. It doesn't have a set of duals like what's here."

Belinda jumped the light beam. "Didn't you say there's a land tenant?"

"You saw him earlier. Tractor tires have different ribs. Like those at the edge of the grass."

"Anything missing?"

Alexa rose. "How should I know? Let's take a look."

"Whoa, Nancy Drew. I agreed to clean, breathe fresh country air, and let my fiancé chill for a long weekend. I ain't no detective."

Alexa strode to the machine shed door. "Stay put then."

"Ain't gonna stay out in the open by myself." Belinda helped Alexa push the overhead track shed door twice their height to the right until it crashed against its stopper.

Alexa walked two paces into the machine shed's interior. Nothing in her light beam struck her as suspicious. Corrugated steel panels fastened to trusses formed the roof. Similar steel panels screwed into a vertical wooden framework created walls supported by square eight-inch posts sunk into the earth. A concrete slab floor extended from the front door three-fourths of the wall length with packed dirt beyond. Alexa couldn't tell if someone disturbed the leveled soil. While jagged cracks radiated in spider web fashion, no saw cuts showed patches repaired the original concrete.

"Seen enough?" Belinda asked.

"Yeah. Guess so." Alexa was happy to depart a shed where echoes swirled.

"Good. Giant spiders may drop on our heads any minute from those wire cages hoisted to the ceiling. Those cobwebs darker and thicker than cotton candy."

"Critters drop only in alien movies."

Belinda held the flashlight in her right hand, pushed with left as Alexa mustered every ounce of arm and leg strength she possessed to jerk the machine-shed door closed.

"You got more than one chair for your back porch?"

"Two-seat swing in basement we can carry up or we can use kitchen chairs. Why?"

"I packed a Citronella candle and pinot noir. This can be vacation, right?"

Alexa laughed. "Wine's good." She'd banned alcohol from her apartment when first pregnant and thereafter to set a good example for Samuel. She missed him dearly.

Belinda, on the porch, clinked a glass to hers. "Here's to the new Baroness of Iowa."

"I'll take it, but medieval history says it's an inherited title."

"Who in the office, or the six million souls in Chicago,

will know?"

Alexa chuckled and shook her head. "Or care." Glass in hand, she sipped and strolled between two candles spaced on the porch railing. At a distance, two, then three fireflies flashed their tails of light. *A marvel of nature.*

"This could be a great place," Belinda said.

"I'm not a farmer."

"Who cares? Your grandmother never rode a tractor, and she gained an income."

"I guess." Alexa gazed into the spruce trees. Here she wouldn't have to deal with big city gangs. Her superficial glee clashed with the stillness and boredom, its cousin. "What about our commitment as probation officers to help and protect all the teenagers named in our case files?"

"There are others."

"Yeah. Jaded ones. Lifers like Tanya who care more about their paycheck than those we're supposed to steer to productive and happy lives."

"We'll always have types like her. Bigger question is how you want to live life."

Alexa glanced at Belinda without a word. She'd heard Belinda pose that question in the hospital when Alexa lay punched and brutalized by a girl's boyfriend's gang. A girl she'd tried to help stake out a clean life, free from smoking pot and snorting drugs.

"You have a refill left?" Alexa extended her right hand with its empty glass.

Belinda poured, tipped the bottle up, and then emptied it into her own glass. She shifted in her chair. "You haven't answered my question."

"Don't know. Nothing's easy. Thought I'd be blessed by having money from the farm's sale. But now it's no slam-dunk."

"Your mother again?"

Alexa didn't like horror movies, nor wish to discuss Mother. "You heard what I heard earlier. Mother's selfishness is not a surprise. Let's drop her. Then there's Samuel."

Belinda put up her right hand, palm out. "Hold on. Samuel's a kid."

"Well, maybe now, but my job tells me he will need a father figure."

"Didn't see a ring on the lawyer in the off-the-rack sport coat. What if he springs a trap to jettison your mother and rides to your farm rescue?"

Alexa repressed her tingling memory of Brad's touch. Her secret reaction might not last forever but it would today. The shield of Belinda's sarcastic and cynical lawyer putdowns also protected Alexa. *Can't trust them.* He wrote Grandma's will, knew her wishes, and he's not telling Mother to take a hike. Probably cashing in. "He's not my type."

"But if you're horny?"

"Quit it." Alexa's spongy legs bounced her torso like her pickup brakes.

Belinda jumped to her feet and pressured Alexa's shoulders. "You okay?"

"Must be the wine." Her left palm pressed the porch rail to steady her. "I'm okay."

"Thought your body swooned as a golden knight galloped through your fantasy."

"It's the wine." Alexa handed Belinda an empty glass. "Nothing more."

"If you say so. I'll die if we don't feast our eyes on your farm hunk tomorrow."

* * *

By noon Saturday, Alexa had lugged the last of four filled black trash bags to the home's southern wall. She wiped her brow. Munched granola bars substituted for eggs and bacon. Belinda had moaned longer about sweat ruining her makeup than no proper breakfast.

A near-empty bottle of Pine-Sol rested on the kitchen table. With diluted Pine-Sol in buckets, Alexa attacked the kitchen and Belinda the first floor parlor. Both saved the Liquid Gold for the oak woodwork and kitchen cabinets. After an afternoon of scrubbing and trips to Joe's mobile home for fresh water, a tired Alexa reached for her cell phone on the kitchen counter. The displayed time a quarter past five.

Alexa called out, "Enough for today, Belinda."

"One more rinse swipe and you'll have the spiffiest parlor west of Chicago. Ready for My Lady to courtesy and wiggle her fan at bachelor suitors a Sunday calling."

"What's that?" Alexa gazed at her hands. Their rash-like redness and finger-joint stiffness endurable. "What's that about lady bachelors?"

"Checking if you had your ears on."

Alexa peeked around the corner into the parlor. Grandma had praised cleanliness as being next to godliness. "Will tell Richard you scrub great. He'll think you're domesticated."

"Don't pour it on."

"Right." Alexa gazed across the parlor's faded red carpet and through the yellowed lace curtain she promised herself to replace. She spied a familiar pickup enter the farmyard and rushed to the rear porch.

In a contrast to its prior gravel-spitting arrival, the F-250 coasted to a stop. Joe jumped from the driver's seat with a brown paper bag squeezed under his right arm. Across the hood, he called out, "Heard you were here. Stopped at the Kum & Go for a few items."

Belinda, who still wore her yellow rubber gloves, sided up to her.

"Wow!" Joe exclaimed. "There's two of you. We'll have a party."

"After supper. I'm committed to driving Belinda to Rosie's." Alexa realized that a later party with Joe wouldn't happen if he validated her suspicions about his beer drinking. *Alexa, you hypocrite. What about last night's wine?*

"Nonsense. I've bought four steaks and coleslaw. My grill will blaze in nothing flat." He smiled and hoisted his paper bag. "How does your friend vote?"

Alexa's head swiveled from Joe to Belinda. Alexa's right hand forefinger curled to touch her thumb. She hoped Belinda read her signal.

Belinda hesitated. Her hand brushed aside a forehead curl. "I'll vote grill."

Joe beamed. "Your place or mine?" He laughed.

"If the grill's outside your mobile home," Alexa replied, "we'll visit you." She darted to Grandma's kitchen to collect her cell phone and then realized that the bathroom to freshen up in was in Joe's trailer.

Belinda stood in the kitchen door. "Did I do all right? He looked at me kinda funny."

"You did fine. Work perspiration and mascara highlighted your raccoon eyes."

Belinda bowed to catch her face reflection in the door glass and shook her head. "Rats." She turned. "He's hunky, twinkling eyes. Bet he likes you."

"Let's go or he'll think we've changed our minds. I'll grab the potato chip bag. Neighbors shouldn't call empty-handed." The lilt in Alexa's voice filled the kitchen.

She watched Joe set up the grill as Belinda ducked into Joe's bathroom first.

Joe flung a lit match onto the charcoal. The rising heat flaked jelled fat burnt onto the grate. Joe streaked his wire brush from side to side to knock the flakes into the ashes. He propped three webbed lawn chairs, two green and one pink, against his trailer's skirt. On a four-legged card table next to the grill, Joe centered a Coke six-pack, three plastic glasses, and an ice-cube tray.

Joe smiled and bowed. "Welcome to Joe's Fine Dining.

Seat yourself."

While his actions were helter-skelter, Alexa noted a stiffness in Joe's smile. The expression akin to an actor's opening night or the initial interview with one of her case clients. She couldn't duplicate Belinda's laugh.

"What we waiting for?" Belinda whispered. She arranged the chairs in a single line with alternate colors before she plopped into the one farthest from the grill. "This is great, Joe."

Alexa left Belinda to fend for herself as she hustled to Joe's bathroom. When she returned she splashed two ice cubes with Coke. Water droplets on the chilled can wet her fingers. When she raised a second can, Belinda waved her off.

Alexa popped a can at Joe's request and handed it to him. He took a swig and ducked inside the trailer. In less than two minutes, Joe swept past a seated Alexa. Bloody beefsteaks forced white butcher paper to his right palm. Alexa guessed each weighed twelve ounces, more than twice her weekly diet. Flames flared when the first steak hit the grill.

"Eight minutes to a side okay?" Joe asked.

"Don't know time," Alexa replied. "Well done, no blood, works for me."

Joe gazed at Belinda. He waved a wooden-handled elongated fork. "Well, pretty lady." Belinda blushed. Her the lip skin with the small dark brown mole stretched by her smile.

"Medium well. You know, a little pink in the middle."

Alexa, on her own initiative, retrieved plates and utensils from Joe's kitchen. She handed a plate to Belinda and kept two in her hands. Joe scooped Belinda's steak off the grill and gazed at Alexa. She'd taken a bottle of A-1 and the coleslaw from Joe's refrigerator. If not for the stored beer, Alexa rated the electricity to the refrigerator's condenser a colossal energy waste.

"You fine ladies have everything you need?"

Alexa echoed Belinda's yes without the added head bob. Joe sat between them; his shoulders slumped. Between bites he smiled at Alexa a time or two. With each bite, the silence between the three lengthened. Once, with his cheeks bulging with coleslaw, Joe reminded her of a squirrel munching acorns beneath an oak tree. The laugh corralled in her throat required every ounce of her willpower not to erupt into a liquid belch that sprayed bits of steak.

"Too bad I don't have marshmallows," Joe said as he collected the plates and silverware. "All I can offer is beer."

"That's okay," Alexa assured him. "Coke is plenty."

Belinda rose to her feet. "I'd like to thank you, Joe, for your hospitality."

"You're welcome."

"If it's all right, I need to visit your bathroom before I call it a night. Boss lady worked me hard today."

Alexa hadn't signaled Belinda to leave. The sun, radiant in streaks of red and orange between pancake clouds, touched the horizon. Two minutes after Belinda disappeared around the corner of Joe's mobile home, Alexa heard Belinda's always hard-closing camper door slam shut. She assumed Belinda desired privacy to telephone Richard. Alexa had apologized earlier for her unintentional interruption of one lovey-dovey conversation. Great for Belinda.

"Want a beer, or mind if I have one?"

Alexa waved, her right palm exposed. "Go ahead. Not for me, thank you."

Joe returned with two bottles, one uncapped. The second he laid on the ice tray's chilled water. "So how is the little man? You said you had to telephone him earlier."

"Samuel's fine." Despite Joe's masculine lure, she stayed rooted between the armrests of her chair. "He talked about your playing horsy with him most of the trip home."

"And . . . ." Joe stood and repositioned his chair to face

53

her rather than be alongside.

"And, what?" Her stomach completed a half gainer.

"What did Samuel's mother say?" His eyes lingered on the tip of her nose.

Her clasped hands dropped into her lap. "I said you were nice."

"Nice? Only nice?" The subdued flash in his eyes wasn't a twinkle. "Were you upset about the beer?" His lips twitched.

Her chair became unsteady as she squirmed forward. She shifted her weight rearwards. "Forget what I said. No . . . no I wasn't."

"You must understand. I don't join the fellows at bars. Come home every chance I get. Like tonight. We've extra overtime tomorrow. I'll drive back early. My limit's two. Tonight and always."

"I can appreciate that." If it wasn't true, a paunch would've replaced his muscled abs and branded him a liar. "You don't have to justify yourself."

His right hand reached toward hers and then, before a touch, he dropped it to his thigh. "It's not justification. You should know the real me." He gazed for a second at a sun half hidden by the horizon. "You big city women fall for men, like Brad, with college degrees. Since you first came, he's made more trips to this farm then in all my years."

"Education's nice, but honesty's nicer."

"Guess you like that 'nice' word. I enlisted in the Navy before I understood the importance of a piece of paper. Earned my GED when winters meant construction layoffs."

"That's great."

"Is 'great' higher or lower than 'nice'?" His eyes twinkled. "Don't answer that. I was trying to tease, but it sounded mean."

"You're not mean. If you were mean, Samuel wouldn't have acted like he did."

Joe's hand reached forward a second time and this time

54

it rested on hers.

After a minute Alexa jerked her left hand, not vicious, but forceful enough to free it. "Sorry." Her voice softer than it need be. "Think I should first know you better."

"I'm not trying to seduce you. Saw in my bathroom wastebasket one of those feminine plastic things so I know the timing's not right."

Alexa clasped her cheeks. Her hands absorbed the furnace blast. She hadn't given the applicator discard a second thought. Neither could she let on his comment revived recurrent, uncontrolled nightmares. Thirty captive hours elapsed before the first assault. The gangbanger-boyfriend of her client Nina shouted the morning after her abduction "I don't do sluts on the rag." Alexa's SWAT team rescuers arrived on day twenty-two.

Words escaped from between her palms to ask Joe to bring her a beer. After he departed, she reached into her pocket for multiple tissues to soak up and wipe away her tears.

"You sure," he asked. "I should've kept my mouth shut." He handed her an uncapped bottle. "Should've learned not to be so blunt."

"Don't change. Women adore honesty. We think it's nice." She chuckled. And when Joe laughed, she marooned a mouthful of beer in her mouth to let the shivers cool her cheeks. She pressed the chilled bottle to her cheeks. "I have a question."

"Shoot."

"Are you and your father the only ones who use the machine shed?"

"I don't, except in the winter. Dad always drives back and forth. Why?"

"Saw large tread ruts. Wondered who made them."

"Show me." Joe's right hand snatched his second bottle from the ice tray.

Alexa left her beer on the card table and led Joe to the

machine-shed door where, in the failing daylight, she crouched. "Here."

Joe, next to Alexa, bent forward, his weight on his right knee. "Tandem wheels. Handful of county pickups have duals." He shifted to be on all fours. "This nick." His right forefinger pointed to a quarter-inch of raised mud. "This might identify the exact vehicle."

"Anything ever been stolen from the farm?"

"Nothing here to steal, except perhaps the farmhouse's copper plumbing."

Alexa stood. Joe's explanation caused her to reexamine why she thought her discovery important. Her precious Samuel and her life embraced worries greater than tread impressions.

Joe brushed his knees to dislodge dirt particles from his jeans. "Could be lovers needed a place to park." He smiled. "And, I'm not planting any suggestion."

A strange rustle captured Alexa's attention.

Joe also tweaked his head. "Could be a raccoon disturbing the old lumber pile."

She could've accepted that explanation until Belinda stepped around the machine shed's corner with a flashlight in one hand and a cell phone in the other.

"You sleepwalking?" Alexa asked.

"Couldn't sleep." Stray light beams highlighted muddy shoes. "Decided to explore."

Alexa didn't buy her explanation but wouldn't say anything with Joe present.

"Did you know there's an old car behind the barn?" Belinda asked.

"Sure," Joe said. "Mrs. Anderson said her husband junked it. I looked at it once. Block pistons frozen tight. Had to have cracked an oil gasket."

Alexa squeezed Belinda's elbow to shine her flashlight on the tire tracks. "Joe says these are common tandem wheels."

Alexa's Gold

"Okay then. I'll be heading to the camper. Good night." Belinda strolled away.

Alexa wondered what else Belinda found or searched for. Belinda had explained at work she walked for exercise but to stumble around strange property in the dark was suspicious.

"I'll add my door light to the yard light," Joe suggested. "We can enjoy the breeze."

"For a few minutes."

Joe handed her the unconsumed beer. Alexa's hands welcomed the task. Two sips seemed to please him. True to his word, he finished his second beer and reached for the last Coke.

Alexa asked Joe what he knew about Grandpa's sudden death.

"Was in the Navy when it happened. Mrs. Anderson kept to herself about it."

When the breeze died, gnats swarmed from the grass. Alexa asked Joe to use his bathroom before she said good night. She pocketed the discarded tampon applicator. Outside the mobile home, she didn't resist Joe's hug. The same light she'd seen the night before in Joe's home shone into the farmyard. The hug and the light brightened her pathway to Belinda's camper.

Soft snores proved to Alexa that Belinda lay snuggled in her sleeping bag. Alexa stretched out on top of hers, her eyes focused on the ceiling. Her careless discard of the applicator careened Joe's comment into repressed memories. She feared recycled nightmares. Her therapist's diagnosis confirmed they'd never completely vanish. She filled her brain with thoughts of Samuel's Popsicle to forestall the often-unbearable terror.

With her mental guards on high alert, Alexa refused to disagree with the proposition that sex didn't equal love. Her grandparents had been so alike. Both inbred with strong farm values and a deep love for each other and the land.

Not so with Mother's seething animosity bred to the point of non-communication.

If in love opposites attract, she and Joe fit that mold.

She prized his honesty, even if she suffered embarrassment. Yet, it wasn't coarser than the sexual slurs and gutter epithets her case subjects hurled at her. And, she'd parroted the sleaze-ball language so often the girls she interviewed realized Alexa possessed courage stronger than the wearing of a do-gooder badge.

Alexa tried to sort through her jumbled thoughts. That Samuel took to Joe shined as a positive. But how she could maximize Samuel's happiness perplexed her.

She could live in a rehabbed farmhouse, rent the land, and languish until Joe's summer weekend work return or his winter layoff days. Her inner voice said she wasn't Grandma. Alexa agreed. Even with Grandma's recipes, she doubted her skill to win a blue ribbon. Her probation job challenges, despite the risks, energized her and, every so often, she'd rescue an at-risk teen.

No final decision loomed when she heard a vehicle leave the farmyard. Alexa assumed she'd fallen asleep and that Joe's early morning work departure awoke her. Belinda snored. Daybreak didn't intrude. Alexa patted her pillow to her ears and closed her eyes.

She awoke to the silence of Belinda's empty sleeping bag. Upon her exit from the camper, Belinda shouted at her. "Joe left you a note."

"Huh?" *There was no unanswered question.*

Belinda leaned across the porch rail. "Taped to his door. You gotta tell me what it says."

A white envelope taped to the mobile home's door bore Alexa's handwritten name. She tore its flap. Scrawled inside was a note. "I've left my door unlocked. Please lock when leaving. When you come back, there'll be a spare key in the glove box of the old car behind the barn."

"What he'd say?" Belinda asked. Her breath impatient

and gentle on Alexa's neck.

"Home's open. And where he'll hide a key."

"Great guy. I should be so lucky."

"I'm sure he saw that rock on your finger." Alexa tore up the note.

"Oh. Guess he's honorable for not trying to . . . you know. Do you think his manhood's as tanned as his face?"

"How the . . . the blazes should I know? Go take a shower. Make it cold."

If Alexa sounded upset, deep down she wasn't. A nosey Belinda was the willing price she paid for a great friend, even if Alexa exasperated by her brashness. Alexa pounded on the bathroom door to hurry Belinda's shower.

Belinda repeated Alexa's impulsiveness by repeated raps on the same door and shouting, "Alexa, did you hear? You got company. Better be decent."

Alexa slipped into flip-flops, zipped her denim's fly, and finished tucking in her long-sleeved T-shirt. She hadn't expected visitors and her bra lay in the camper. She folded her nightshirt under an arm and saw a familiar Buick when she rounded Joe's mobile home.

"Sorry to bother you." Brad's eyeballs rotated every which way, except at her. She didn't wish to jiggle. "The judge Saturday granted your mother an injunction hearing."

"What's that mean?" Her gaze encompassed his ever-present blue blazer.

"It's preliminary to deciding the validity of your grandmother's will."

"Do I need to be there?"

"That's why I drove out hoping to catch you."

Irritation crept into her voice. "You could've telephoned." She folded her arms, and that pushed her breasts up. She let her arms fall to her sides. Brad's unsteady gaze focused above her chin. His neck veins bulged and his skin's paleness ebbed. *He can't be mad; she's the one who deserves to be upset.*

"True. But in case you had any question I wanted to answer personally."

"Why?" She choked off asking if Mother bribed him to have her give up the farm.

"Please understand that I'm on your side."

He read her mind?

"As a court officer I have legal limitations that conflict with advising will beneficiaries."

He'd said enough. She wanted him to leave and leave fast. "Okay. You've told me. What date? When?"

"Judge didn't say."

Then why didn't he leave? She stared at his crotch. Street girls had told her the tactic provided them the distraction needed for a dash to safety.

He shifted his weight from foot to foot.

Alexa's design changed from ire to devilish amusement.

Brad shuffled his feet. "I must call you with the exact day."

Alexa didn't understand his double-talk. He said he didn't want to use the telephone and now he does. Had he'd driven out to instill vague worry or to torment? *Lawyers! Ugh!*

Brad's right-hand fingers wiped his brow. His lips parted. No words. He yanked a white handkerchief from his rear pocket to wipe his brow a second time. "You and Joe getting along well, I presume, for him to let you use his trailer."

"He's been great." Why she didn't use her word "nice" a mystery.

"Must be going. Sunday church luncheon." Brad's 180-degree-turn dislodged a dozen pebbles before his Buick proceeded east.

Alexa ambled to the rear porch.

"If I let my mommy's babies jiggle like that—"

"Quit it. You didn't let me shower first." Alexa laughed

as she folded her arms across her chest.

Belinda's initial snort developed into a full belly laugh.

"God perhaps intended one purpose for female milk glands." Alexa paused. "Forgot Eve ate the forbidden fruit and twisted Adam's perception."

Belinda, in her merriment, grabbed the porch rail to prevent her forward topple.

"Quit it. I've uttered enough blasphemy for this Sunday. Let's tidy up and stop at Rosie's."

"What about the tire tracks? Someone may return?"

"We'll take a cell phone picture and lay a board across." Alexa didn't believe her plan foolproof, far from it. She hadn't quizzed Belinda about her possible Saturday night walk discoveries. She doubted Belinda had tripped on Grandma's apple cake recipe.

Alexa herself puzzled why she had encountered no recipe in the pantry or any cabinet. She'd pried open the pantry cabinet and destroyed its lock. Farm records, no recipes.

Chapter Three

For two weeks Alexa hadn't heard a peep from Brad. Her heart slithered fast toward panic the day an oversized envelope marked "Official Business" stood propped against her apartment door. Her heartbeat slowed when she read the sweepstakes entry contents.

Samuel, ever since his return from Grandma's farm, nagged her to play horsy. She did a time or two, but her spine ached to support his increased weight.

"I'm a big boy." Samuel joyously proclaimed the first

day he wore tidy whities.

"Yes, you are." Alexa returned his beaming grin and led him to her pickup. She dropped him at daycare en route to the downtown Chicago Lake Street ramp near her office.

"Do mommy's babies crave the country life?" Mirth populated Belinda's tease as she approached Alexa and Tanya in the probation services lunchroom.

"Quit it."

Belinda spun a chair to join her two co-workers. "What? You tease the sport-coat attorney and run? Bet his eyeballs still bob as we speak." Alexa shook her head. Belinda redirected her salvo. "Hey, Tanya, you ever dream of being a farmer?"

Tanya's raised sandwich never dropped beneath her chin. "Nope."

"See, Alexa, if you find a hunk at a farm and you own the farm, latch on. It's destiny."

Alexa frowned. "Quit it."

"Be a sport. If I hadn't promised my charms. Could be yours. Saw the hunk's eyes sparkle."

"He ain't my hunk," Alexa snapped. "You suffer from radiation off that rock you wear. Puts you in an otherworld universe. You envision Prince Charming in every man you see."

Tanya cocked her head. "My husband said something similar in his sleep one night. Thought he muttered sweet nothings because I laid beside him."

"In your dreams," Belinda replied.

Question marks dotted Tanya's gaze. "No! His dreams."

Alexa shook her head. Her two officemates orbited personal fantasy worlds. Alexa to herself admitted there were days she craved to see Joe again. He'd been nice, more than courteous.

When her cell phone rang after lunch, she accepted Brad's information and promised she'd be available in three weeks, on a Friday, in Iowa's Lake County courtroom. After she hung up, she wrote a short note addressed to Joe in care of Oscar Erickson to inform him of her plans. For a sign of trust, she added a postscript with her cell phone number.

Alexa steeled herself to telephone Mother. Each fended off serious questions with vague clichés and protestations of "being fine." Within the one minute connection neither mentioned the court hearing. Alexa sighed, heartened Mother hadn't changed her number.

Alexa's days dragged. Her only smile when office gossip circulated that Belinda had, in melodramatic fashion, dramatized for colleagues the farm cleaning burden Alexa imposed. Belinda's best charwoman exaggeration was how she, with a can of Brasso, had to shine the pull ring and each chain bead to the overhead tank that flushed the upstairs old-fashioned toilet.

She circled and re-circled the court date on her home and office calendars. Irritations rose. Susan reneged on her promise to meet the REA lineman required a revisit and an extra fifty dollar charge. Farm electricity encouraged Alexa's mind to jump to flowing tap water and functioning toilets.

Joe seemed to be the only Iowa resident she could trust; yet, directory assistance informed her he didn't exist. Gossip impeded her call to Oscar. She missed Joe's voice and could only listen to her cell message he'd be at the farm Friday evening. She *69ed the number. A recorded message filled her ear that she'd dialed a pay phone that didn't accept incoming calls.

The Thursday evening before the 11 a.m. Friday court hearing, she confirmed Belinda's promise of her camper and their next day's four a.m. departure. She dropped Samuel at Tanya's.

Alexa, in a gray pants suit she wore for Chicago court appearances, strode through the early a.m. orange glow to hop into Belinda's double-parked SUV and buckle her passenger seatbelt. Belinda forced a smile. "You will do fine. Did your attorney prep you on what to say?"

"No. And, if truth be fatal, I didn't ask."

"You can't be defeatist."

"I've pondered long and hard. Samuel, my blessing, came from my hurting. I can't expect another blessing without cost."

"Sure you can. Your grandmother loved you. Didn't you spend precious dollars on long distance when she had no one to talk to?"

"Yeah." Alexa sucked on a peppermint, her third since her alarm rang at three a.m.

"Consider that your hardship and she rewarded you in her will. Bet her spirit has a hand in getting you and Joe together. I never met her, but from what you tell me, your grandmother was, and is, a wise soul."

Alexa swallowed her last mint as Belinda maneuvered into two street parking stalls in front of the Lake County courthouse. Its reddish brick, layered gothic style, commanded an entire city block. Alexa's pulse didn't quicken until she stepped onto the second floor landing.

"Alexa, how nice to see you." Mother's voice dripped with charm. Her right shoulder touched a gentleman's tailored pinstriped black suit. "I'd like you to meet Mr. Axelrod. He's my attorney. Came all the way from Des Moines. He's so kind."

Not distracted by his tight lips or steely eyes, Alexa also ignored Mr. Axelrod's offered right hand. "Mother, you didn't tell me you planned to be here."

"I'm so sorry if I caused you distress. My mother left so many details undone. Who'd have known your grandma's mind had deteriorated so after your grandfather's passing."

"What?" A knot rose in Alexa's throat. "There's only the farm, no animals."

"But that land tenant has been late with his accounting

64

every year and your grandmother let it slide." Mr. Axelrod
nodded. "Who's to know how much was swindled. Mr.
Axelrod says the rent paid lagged average Iowa yields for
high-grade black loam."

No Mother. Not another scheme. After Mother's second
husband divorced her, Dad told Alexa of Mother's close
call to escape prison for under-the-table payoffs from store
suppliers. Mother defended the trips and exquisite jewelry
as all gifts. While Alexa gave Mother the benefit of the
doubt, she also believed her Chicago policeman Dad. His
detail of how payoff schemes exploited legal loopholes fit
Mother's situation.

When the outside chimes struck eleven, Brad
materialized between two wooden doors to announce the
judge would be ready in five minutes. Belinda whispered
she'd wait in the corridor. Alexa followed Brad into an
empty courtroom. Mother and her attorney trooped behind.

Brad pointed Alexa to a front row seat. Mother sat
across the aisle. The two attorneys assumed seated
positions at counsel tables inside the railing. A bailiff asked
all to rise. A black-robed judge entered and requested all to
be seated.

Alexa leaned forward to hear every word. The judge
asked Mother's attorney to explain his basis for a farm-sale
injunction prior to the court's determination of the will's
validity.

Mr. Axelrod's voice boomed. He asserted Mrs.
Anderson was an impressionable woman who had been
manipulated by her land tenant, one of three will witnesses.
Mother smiled.

Alexa assumed the attorney meant Oscar Erickson.

Mr. Axelrod handed the clerk two blue folders. "My
expert's evaluation details that the land tenant I speak of
swindled no less than $15,000 from Mrs. Anderson each
year."

Brad buttoned his blue blazer as he stood to address the

judge. He challenged the proffered swindle evidence as extremely dubious. While he admitted two subpar payment years existed, he handed the judge certified copies of area weather summaries to show those crop years experienced excessive rain-induced flooding.

"Your honor, Mrs. Anderson never rented her entire acreage for she followed her husband's practice to rotate sections in and out of the federal soil bank program. Therefore, I tender counsel and the court these redacted federal government income statements received late yesterday.

"And . . ." Brad paused to stretch his frame to its greatest height. "Even if the court disqualifies Mr. Oscar Erickson as a will witness, two other valid signatures remain to comply with Iowa's Testamentary law, which the court knows requires but two will signators."

Alexa, ready to clap, rubbed her hands together in glee. She didn't read law, but Mother's slumped shoulders and downcast expression encouraged Alexa to think positive.

The judge thanked all present and stated he'd rule within two weeks. Alexa rushed past Mother's glare. Her corridor elaboration to Belinda added a special emphasis on how Brad stood tall, put force behind his words, and that, from her vantage point, the judge appeared impressed.

Mother left without a good-bye.

Brad entered the corridor and motioned Alexa he wished to talk. "I'll contact you when I hear from the judge." He bent close to Alexa's left ear. "Looks good for you. I can't say more."

After Brad exited, Belinda inquired, "He ask you for a date?"

"Heavens no." Alexa didn't understand Brad's behavior. He acted standoffish and then whispered words she should prepare for a celebration.

What had she misunderstood? The judge said nothing about the validity of Alexa's farm inheritance. If Oscar

Erickson was the culprit, why wasn't he in court?

Alexa's stomach growled. She grabbed Belinda's forearm. "Let's have lunch at Rosie's."

Belinda ripped into four pieces the official-looking document she yanked from beneath her driver-side windshield wiper.

"You get a ticket?"

"Nah. Warning. I'll toss the pieces at Rosie's. Don't want these hicks to catch me littering."

Alexa gazed around Rosie's parking lot until she spotted a trash container for Belinda. She walked toward it and pivoted when she heard a whistle behind her. The male adolescent with acme blemishes hadn't whistled at her, but at a Jaguar XKE exiting the parking lot. The Polk County Iowa plate said: "LAW1." If that was Mother's lawyer, Alexa dreaded going inside.

She pushed Belinda to enter the restaurant first. There sat Mother, alone in the corner booth Alexa and Mother had occupied weeks before. Mother's wave showed she had seen them.

"Hello, Mother. You know Belinda don't you?"

"Heard you speak of her. Care to sit down? I haven't ordered."

Alexa couldn't refuse, no matter how adversarial or distasteful. She hoped Belinda's presence minimized Mother's cuss words. They slid in opposite Mother. The server promised drinks when she wrote up their burger orders.

"Don't know why you're fighting me, Alexa. My lawyer says all went well."

Alexa laid her forearms on the booth's tabletop. "Ain't fighting anyone."

"Yes you are. We all know Grandma wasn't in her right mind when she signed that will. She may have liked you, but she wouldn't screw me or other relatives no matter how distant."

"Grandma sent me a postcard last December. Her words weren't jumbled. Her steady hand wrote the same way she always did."

Defiance surfaced in Mother's eyes. "And, I suppose you will use that as evidence."

"Nobody's asked. I'll always cherish that postcard."

The server delivered two colas and one iced tea and returned to leave three burger baskets.

Alexa's mother clamped a burger with her thumbs and fingers. She lowered it from her chin. "You know." She fixed her eyes on Alexa. "We could make a deal that would be a win/win for both of us. If you fight me, you'll lose and end up with nothing. But we don't have to fight."

The humorless bite in Mother's tone cramped Alexa's stomach. She arched her back with no intent to trust Mother or ask for the tiniest deal element. Mother never offered charity.

"Your frown is so unbecoming, daughter. With our agreement I tear up the paper my lawyer filed so you inherit the farm and then you agree to sell it to me for $50,000."

"Don't think that's wise, or even possible."

Mother persisted. "Why not?"

Before Alexa could formulate her reply, Belinda tapped her shoulder and pointed toward the entrance door. Joe gazed their way and smiled when Alexa enthusiastically pumped her left forearm. He strode to the booth.

"Sorry to interrupt. I'll just say hi and be gone."

Alexa's voice sprinted out her words. "How come you're in town? We didn't expect you at the farm until later or maybe in the morning."

Mother frowned.

Alexa didn't press her questions. To be civil, she said, "I'd like to introduce my Mother, Ruth. You know Belinda." Belinda smiled. "This is Joe Erickson, Mother. He lived at the farm with Grandma. That is, he parked his

68

mobile home there."

"Pleased to meet you." Mother's tone so icy it approached consuming icicles.

"Your mother was a gracious lady. I never knew a woman with such spunk."

"If you say so," Mother replied.

"Think it was two summers ago she sat on her porch all upset. She'd chased Daisy, my Dad's dog, away from a flower bed she's planted and locked herself out of the house." Unaware if Joe would continue, angst invaded Alexa's psyche. She squirmed in her seat.

Mother's gloom lifted. "Goes to show Grandma's mind lost ability to remember things."

Alexa foresaw mother's tact. She'd twist anything Joe said. Best if she changed the subject. "So tell us, Joe, why you're not working."

His left hand rubbed skin beneath his eye. "Paving machine gear broke. Company can't get repair part flown in until tomorrow night. Foreman told everyone except two mechanics to skedaddle. I can't joint concrete not poured."

"Will we see you at the farm?"

"That's where I'm headed. Nice meeting you all. Enjoy your lunch." He flicked his upright right thumb into the air. Only Belinda waved in response.

After Alexa received her doggie bag, she imparted to Mother one last piece of information. "Realtor pointed out farmhouse foundation unstable. That'll have to be addressed."

"And I suppose this Joe treats you well. He knows about your son?"

"His name is Samuel, mother, not son or little boy. It irritates me you never refer to him by his name. He's your grandson. Don't forget that."

"This son of yours brings shame on our entire family." Mother raised her eyebrows at Belinda. "I won't say more, not in public with others present."

69

"Just because I didn't go to Planned Parenthood doesn't make me a bad person. I might not know who Samuel's father is and I'll not chase tens of candidates with the stick of DNA testing."

"You made me lie to my friends. I felt so degraded."

"What! Telling them I went wild with a soldier on furlough from Iraq who shipped out for a second tour only to return home on a flight to Delaware with six other flag-draped coffins."

"Your family didn't need to know the whole truth. Shame enough you weren't married."

"And divorce wipes the slate clean?"

Daggers flashed in Mother's eyes. "How dare you?"

Belinda interjected, "Thank you both for lunch." Her left thigh nudged Alexa. "We'd better be leaving. There's a line at the door."

Alexa slid out. She faced her mother. "I'll tell Samuel his grandmother loves him."

"Don't be snide. If you can drain all that pent up venom out of your system, remember what I said about the will. Fighting won't do either of us any good. Think hard. Call me at the Lakeview Motel. I'll be checking out very early tomorrow. I have a long drive."

Belinda said good-bye. Alexa, on her way out, paid the full tab and tipped the server. Not until she placed her right hand on Belinda's car door did Alexa tense her abdominal muscles to forestall the nausea that threatened to climb her esophagus. Mother's public facial contortions had constricted every vein in Alexa's body.

"When your mother's spleen gushes, it gets to you, doesn't it?"

"She's been like that since Samuel's birth. First she disowned him, which might be better." Alexa bit her lip. As to Mother, she couldn't be generous. She climbed into Belinda's SUV.

Belinda slowed so as not to hit a left-turning vehicle.

70

"You don't have to answer, but was there a reason after the attack you didn't get an abortion?"

"I prayed. The chaplain said I'd been a strong person after my father was shot in the line of duty on a Chicago street. Mother wailed from the funeral procession until her psyche cracked. She pounced on the next bar Casanova, divorced him after a quickie marriage, and now lives in Ohio married a third time. I don't want to be Mother."

"Understand, but raising a son?"

"Let's stop at the Kum & Go. We can't rely on Joe grilling steaks."

Belinda circled the gasoline pumps to park at the end of the building. "Before we go inside, why did you chose to raise your son, sorry, Samuel."

"Samuel's the love of my life. I've read where many great men overcame wretched childhoods and dysfunctional families. My son has, and will continue to have, a loving home. Chicago policemen, who either worked with or knew my Dad, have offered me both moral and financial support. If I need a babysitter, my refrigerator has a list of fifteen."

"I've seen that list, impressive. But won't you lose that moving to Iowa?"

"Haven't planned to move. Selling the farm is my goal."

"Then your mother's idea isn't so farfetched?"

"Except Grandma didn't trust Mother. At least, that's the strong hints I gathered."

Combined, their food shopping lasted ten minutes and Alexa counted a further fifteen before she and Belinda drove into the farmyard. "We need to check if there's electricity."

"You do that. I'll unhitch my borrowed camper."

Alexa's sneakers kicked up a dust trail before she bounded up the rear porch steps. She toggled the kitchen wall switch. The ceiling light fixture failed to glow. She

71

hopped up on a kitchen chair to learn it had a bulb not encrusted with black residue.

Alexa felt a tap on her right calf. "You check the fuse box?" Joe asked.

"Why?"

"The yard security light has been on every night since, I don't know, two weeks ago. Never used to be. Suspected you had the electricity turned on. I'll find the box in the basement."

In the dim basement light, Joe finagled with what he called an old-fashioned fuse saying Alexa dodged a major headache in that extra fuses were stockpiled on top of the metal fuse box.

"Let's give it another whirl. See if I guessed right."

Alexa flipped the kitchen switch. The ceiling light flickered and stayed on. "Thanks, Joe. You're nice to have you around."

His grin stretched his cheeks. "Nice enough to say yes to a drive-in movie tonight. Historical epic about Australia."

"A drive-in? Didn't they all unplug their projectors by the late '90s?"

"Not the Flamingo. They show movies Friday, Saturday, and Sunday nights."

"Don't know. Belinda will feel abandoned. She's spent all day at my side and she drove here with the camper and all." Joe lowered his gaze. "Maybe a rain check?"

"What's Belinda like?" Joe's question phrased like he wouldn't be pacified with evasion.

Alexa rotated the kitchen sink faucet and deep orange-tinted water spewed forth into its left-side basin. The well worked and Alexa basked in the glory that electricity nudged civilization's amenities from slumber.

Joe upped his vocal volume. "Shopping maybe? Listening to musical groups live?"

"Oh, sorry." Alexa let the water run. "Shopping, more

shopping, and musical concerts."

"Good." Joe's left shoulder brushed hers. "Tonight's the first community outdoor concert. Heard town chatter earlier today about a traveling band. Name I've never heard of. The shops don't close until ten or eleven."

"Should I presume you want me to ask her?"

"Seems more reasonable. Say it's all my idea. I'll shoulder any the blame."

Alexa left Joe in the kitchen. Not until halfway across the farmyard did she see Belinda come forth from around the corner of Joe's mobile home.

"What's up? Had to use the bathroom."

Alexa's right sneaker toe kicked a pebble. "Would you be hurt if I left you alone for a couple hours tonight? Joe asked if I'd go with him to a drive-in movie. I'll say no."

The pout competed with the glint in her eyes. "And you'll be forever bitter I caused you to be an Old Maid."

Alexa hugged Belinda. "Thanks. Joe says Lakeview stores are open late tonight and there's live music on the street. We could drop you off."

"No thanks. Camper's unhitched. I'll drive. That way if I get bored because they don't have the proper Popsicle flavor or I can't kidnap an unsuspecting farm boy—"

"Don't even kid about that."

"Sorry." She raised her right forefinger. "I have one condition."

Alexa inhaled. She reeled in her enthusiasm, already halfway to cloud nine.

"I get to use Joe's bathroom first."

Alexa, in her blue jeans and sweatshirt work outfit, passed up Grandma's tub, not yet scrubbed, to wait her shower turn in Joe's trailer. Her court pants suit hung in Grandma's closet. Her mental image of Ellie Mae Clamplett convinced her not to cover her hair with a bandana. City peers would approve of her designer jeans with their manufacturer-created knee rips and red sequined blouse. She didn't know about Iowans. She sighed. After all, it was a drive-in. Who'd know what she wore if she didn't visit the concession stand?

"Wow!" Alexa exclaimed. "You'll knock the guys over." Belinda pirouetted in her mid-thigh black mini skirt. The capped-sleeve powder blue blouse with its to-the-neck collar didn't detract from the charms hidden by its stretched fabric.

"Got sandals, but I'll wait until town. See you later."

Through the frosted bathroom window, Alexa heard Belinda's SUV wheels spin. Alexa frowned into the mirror as her hairbrush battled tangled curls. Her belt buckle prong almost slid into an unused hole. Either her work stress or the worry about Samuel accounted for her lost weight. Her mind's inner told her to forget the world's cares for fun, fun, fun.

Joe acted the perfect gentleman in helping her climb into his F-250.

"How'd you get cleaned up so fast?" she asked to break the elongated silence.

"Used your grandmother's bathroom. Had to drag myself outa that claw-footed tub." A sly smile touched his lips. "If you visit more often, I can get real used to it."

She skipped her cleaning question. "But . . . but the water, it was orange. Filled with iron."

"After ten seconds, it ran clear. No problem."

The countryside twilight feathered Alexa's senses unlike lamppost light circles on grimy city streets. Grandma's trash-free yard and Joe's mowing had helped to restore Alexa's childhood memories. Samuel could help plant petunias for curb appeal. If Joe's dad agreed to a rent advance, Alexa could hire caulkers and a contractor. But that wasn't her date scheme.

"Beautiful, isn't it?"

"What?" Alexa asked.

"The country. You can roll your window down."

Alexa's Gold

Alexa braced for the manure smell, but it wasn't there. The fresh aroma of green cornstalks and soybean plants swirled into the cab. She swallowed her peppermint. The roll that served as her crutch to fend off nervousness now an empty wrapper. "You love it here, don't you?"

"In a word, yes. It's all I've known. I've been in Des Moines for the I-35 reconstruction. While it's what I do, it's not at all enjoyable." Joe's eyes focused straight ahead.

"Why didn't you become a farmer?" Alexa didn't want to interview, but the question flowed to her lips.

"Takes money . . . unless you inherit." Joe's eyes rotated toward her without head movement. "Tough to get a loan." His throat seemed to tighten. "Only farmers like my dad with family land and equipment financed years ago can prosper. And it's a roller coaster. To use the bigger tractors, you need to rent more and more acres. It's a vicious cycle."

"I've met you father. He doesn't have a new tractor with a cab and air conditioning."

"That's Old Betsy. Cultivator's on it year-round. Dad's like a man reliving his boyhood."

Her right hand reached for the panic handle. "I don't like to relive memories."

"Sorry. Last turn. See the screen ahead."

Alexa tilted her chin up. Above the trees loomed the exposed screen support structure of what had to be the last 1950-era movie drive-in. Joe inched along the curved entrance road. Cars packed with teenagers honked. At who, she didn't know. A flock of pink plastic flamingos surrounded the ticket shack where a bald man poked his head out to stare deep into each vehicle.

"We've got to park in the last row. Operator thinks big trucks block views."

"You come here—" Alexa wanted to say "often." She deferred. Joe's eyes waited, focused on hers. "Here for the popcorn, too?"

"I'll be back."

Alexa smiled as Joe knocked on her passenger window. She unlatched her door, and he handed her a large buttered popcorn bucket. Joe rounded the hood to deposit two Cokes in the front seat's center console before he settled himself.

"Thank you." Alexa squirmed closer to him until blocked by the console. "You have to help with this." She extended her bucket. He took three kernels. "More . . . please." He smiled.

When the feature presentation title appeared, Alexa realized there'd been no cartoon. The desolate Australian outback filled the screen. Her body tensed with a man's on-screen murder.

"You okay," Joe whispered.

Alexa welcomed his concern. "Fine. I closed my eyes."

Dramatic music swallowed by the clops of horses. Joe slid his right hand behind her left shoulder, along her seat's top contour. She relaxed. When she opened her eyes, the screen didn't matter. Joe's eyes twinkled in the dim light, brighter than any heavenly star. It felt like ages since she'd been out with a male who didn't wear diapers.

"You've added a goal to my life," Joe said.

"What's that?"

"Well, never really had a mission. Guess that's a Navy word for a life plan. There's work. Family gatherings. Rarely anything else."

"And, now?"

"Your Grandma said I needed to find, and I'll use her words, a nice woman."

Alexa laughed. Her emotional release elevated her to the feel-good zone. "You said?"

"I'd nod and quickly change the subject."

Alexa didn't consciously rest her head on his hand. He cupped it against her skull. "Bet Grandma didn't let you get away with that?"

"You're right. She said she had a granddaughter I should meet."

She artfully throttled her pulse surge. "You're kidding?"

"No. She said it more than once."

Grandma's mawkish advice filled Alexa's ears. After Samuel's birth, she deflected Grandma's marriage inquiries with a lie her fiancé attended college. While she hadn't meant to lie to Grandma, her judgment lapse spiraled and augmented her guilt. Her Mother's restaurant offer rekindled the notion Mother may have spun a wilder story to the point where Grandma understood Alexa lied. If so, Grandma didn't let on. Tears welled in Alexa's eyes.

"You okay. Preview didn't indicate this movie to be sappy. *The Three Stooges* would've been a better choice."

"Not the movie." *That was honest.* "Thinking of Grandma."

"She was kind, a beautiful lovely person." Joe sounded wistful. "There's a lot of her in you."

Alexa's cheeks warmed. "Thank you."

Joe's left hand picked up a napkin.

She let him dabbed at a tear high on her cheekbone, the first of many. "You can't be enjoying this movie with me falling apart this way."

"We can rent the DVD if we miss something. We have so little time together. I want to spend all my time in your company. Would it be all right if I kissed you?"

No date had ever asked her before. She nodded, twisted her shoulders, and leaned toward Joe so their heads split the console width. His lips brushed hers. Her popcorn bucket hit the floor.

"Forget it," Joe whispered.

Her tentative kiss responded to his. She wouldn't lose control. Her eyes closed. Their noses bumped. She peeked and flickers of florescence from the movie screen streaked Joe's face. He jerked his head from her.

"Did I do something?" Her heart pounded against her ribs.

"Nothing you shouldn't do again. Find I sometimes need to breathe."

Alexa laughed.

"You have a great laugh. Or, should I say 'nice'."

"Quit it." Alexa regretted her jump to dismiss his tease.

"I'm sorry." Joe pressed his lips together and his eyelids drooped.

"Don't be." Alexa rushed to repair her impulsiveness. "You've proven I rely on 'nice' too often. It's in my genes. Give me time and you'll see I can change."

"I'd like that, especially the spend time part."

He leaned sideways, twisted, and kissed her softly. Their lip contact a gossamer tingle. She cradled his left hand in hers. When the lovers kissed on screen, he squeezed her left shoulder. Alexa lost empathy with the actors well before a chorus of engine revs announced the movie's end.

Homestead lights dotted the rural Lake County landscape. The security light at Grandma's farm bathed Belinda's camper and SUV in yellow light. Alexa owed her friend another big favor. At first she wondered why Joe's F-250 barely crawled into the farmyard. Then, she remembered the gravel crunch that forewarned her of all visitors.

Joe's mobile home sat as a bulwark of darkness. Alexa reasoned he switched off the front room light that always shone or else its bulb had burnt out.

Joe didn't need to whisper inside his F-250, but he did. "Do you think Belinda's asleep?"

"If she shopped until she dropped."

"You can sleep in the mobile home. There's an extra bedroom."

Alexa's endorphins marched within her veins in a state of readiness while her conscience urged caution. At this precise moment she liked Joe enough to take it slow. He'd shown respect for her as a person and she didn't believe he'd offered anything other than a roof to sleep under.

"If that's too close," Joe continued, "I'll sleep on the sofa."

"No, no, it's not that." She repressed the painful memories of a man's sweaty scent. "With Belinda here, I mustn't."

"Knock on my door if she's locked you out."

In the light of a quarter moon shadowed by clouds, Joe and Alexa embraced.

Alexa dropped her arms. "Thank you for a wonderful evening."

"Maybe next time I'll not interrupt and you can open your eyes to the movie."

Alexa clasped her right hand to her mouth to stifle a laugh. Except for Samuel's occasional antics, her laugh hadn't been spontaneous in a month of Sundays. "I might say something about that." She stretched her chin higher for one last kiss.

She got in one last word as he strode away. "By the way, I carry a member card for DVDs. Good night." Alexa's ten fingers fumbled with the camper door handle. She entered on tiptoes.

Belinda's voice pierced the darkness. "You're home early."

"Short movie. No cartoon."

"You didn't look upset outside or like you needed a rescue."

Alexa found it difficult to fill her voice with indignation. "You spied on us?"

"What are best friends for? Cuts the number of day-after questions."

"We'll talk in the morning. I'm tired."

"Lip-lock?"

"Quit it. Next time I'll do a Columbo on you. Your sweet honey allure and exposed calves had to have males flitting up and down your shopping aisles."

79

Belinda's chortle ricocheted off the low ceiling. "One maybe." Alexa heard the rustle of a sleeping bag not her own. "That's all I'll say. Sleep tight."

Alexa was positive Belinda faced the wall before her last comment and didn't see her darkness-disguised toothy smile. Glorious ringlets of light skittered beneath Alexa's eyelids as she lay supine on her sleeping bag. If you loved someone, were you supposed to see their face in your dreams or not? She couldn't remember. Images of Joe's twinkling eyes delighted her no matter which way she jostled her head.

Years ago Grandma had prodded Alexa to put wedding cake under her pillow. Alexa lamented she needed Grandma's recipe. Pleasant, yes, nice, very nice, memories of her evening with Joe at the movies escorted her to dreamland.

Belinda's repetitious snore woke her.

Alexa's nose against the camper's window seal detected smoke. Her tongue's faint taste confirmed. Quick rubs of her right hand fingers failed to chase the blurriness from her eyes. No streaky dawn rays clashed with the yard light's yellow glow. Where had she tossed her jeans?

She whispered Belinda's name.

Out of the interior darkness a weak voice responded, "Not now. I'm tired."

Alexa scrambled to unlatch the camper's door. Its curtain fluttered. Alexa's throat swallowed the stinging wisps of smoke swirled by the breeze. Her right hand thumb and forefinger press quelled the eyelid blinks that resembled the wings of a hovering hummingbird. Alexa's left hand recoiled from the chilled, dewy metal of the sloped camper front.

A flash of flame, brighter than the steak grease flare from Joe's grill, blinded her.

She hurled herself onto all fours in the dusty gravel, a reflex action from an office boot camp weekend meant to heighten instincts and teach survival skills. She grimaced and flicked from her skin a sharp rock partially imbedded into her left palm. Her pain succumbed to fear.

Alexa shouted Belinda's name.

A second flame flashed. Alexa's ears filled with the irregular pops neither microwave popcorn nor vinyl siding fighting a polar vortex. Stingers of devilish heat, reminiscent of an opened oven door, struck her upturned face.

Who had fireworks?

"Joe, Joe," she screamed. Her lungs ached without air. *Couldn't no one hear her?*

Chapter Four

"**A**lexa, what's happening?"

Pain oozed into Alexa's wrist from her left palm. It distracted her thoughts. She rotated her eyes to squint into the camper's shadows. Wasn't that Belinda? But where was she? Alexa's voice quaked, "You got your cell phone?" She crawled in full retreat, past the hitch, toward the camper's unlatched door. It banged the camper's sidewall.

Belinda emerged in a black sports bra and red biker pants. "What did you say? Did the Martians attack? You lose an earring?"

"No jokes. Call nine-one-one." Pushed to her feet by her right hand, Alexa yelled, "Now."

"They're asking what the emergency is."

"Fire." Alexa screamed, "It's a fire."

"They're asking where?

Alexa calmed her voice. "Grandma Anderson's place.

81

Two farms from Oscar Erickson."

"They want to know the RFT number?"

"That's RFD and I don't know. Tell them to find the glow out their window." Alexa didn't desire to be sarcastic. This wasn't Chicago. Didn't everyone say they knew Grandma Anderson?

"The lady said she'd pulled the volunteer fire siren. Said to stay calm."

Alexa slid her feet into flip-flops. "You see Joe?"

Belinda reached into the camper for a blue T-shirt. "No."

"Ouch." Alexa's right toe smarted where Belinda stepped on it. "Hand me some towels."

"They'll burn."

"I'll run into Grandma's house." She patted the outside of her jeans pocket to confirm she had her keys. "I can soak them in water."

"It's too dangerous to go into Joe's trailer."

Alexa ran to the camper's rear. Across the farmyard, grayish smoke poured from the mobile home's unlit living room window. Flames flashed behind the kitchen's window. Joe had to sleep at the far end of the hall. She could stay outside, pound on his window.

Belinda tapped her right shoulder. Alexa turned to grab two towels from Belinda's extended left hand and dash to soak them. Water dripped from the towels as Alexa jumped off the rear porch. She ran to where Belinda stood, shielded by Joe's F-250.

Arriving vehicle tires skidded, unimpeded by the farmyard's loose gravel. A Buick driver flung wide his driver's door. Brad shouted, "Heard siren. Fire pumper coming."

Alexa evaded his outstretched arms and ran to Joe's mobile home.

She circled wide of its front door, opposite side of the living room window. With one towel pressed to her face, she edged forward. *Please God, please.*

Darkness resided inside the mobile home except where yellowish flames pulsed. She pounded her fist against the last window. "Joe, Joe," She inhaled heated air. "Fire. Fire."

A pop and flame flash her only response.

Sweat rivulets streamed down her face. Her skin tightened. She pledged to fight off the blast of an opened oven door until Fate slid her onto a wire rack. She hit her right hand knuckles on heated glass until they hurt. With her left hand wrapped in a wet towel, she swung until fatigued.

Sirens blared closer and closer. Strong arms about her waist dragged her rearward.

She laid prone on a gurney. A uniformed Black man leaned forward, his hands pinned her.

"No, no," she screamed. "Please don't hurt me again. I didn't give Nina to the cops."

"Young lady, you don't have to worry about the police," the man's modulated voice said.

"Sir, let me speak to my friend." Belinda's right arm cleared the gentleman aside. "Alexa, you're safe. It's not 2007. Breathe deep. You did everything you could. Oscar Erickson wants to talk with you, but I told him to wait. Breathe deep. Breathe deep."

Belinda's blurry image faded into darkness.

Chapter Five

Alexa hung on to the oak tree rope with both hands. Her feet planted as a shoulder-sway fulcrum. Her senses frozen in a childhood fantasy, free of last night's bitter taste of swirling embers. She rocked in opposition to the budding branches above her. Each swing designed to scour the smoky odor from her singed hair.

Her purse, its strap slung over her right shoulder, bumped her hip. It contained Grandma's cherished postcard. She envisioned "Jeffrey the Monkey" sat on the oak's tree branch just out of her reach. Grandma pretended Jeffrey cured measles, chickenpox, flu, and winter colds.

Grandma had promised she could hug Jeffrey forever. He would be always be the same, even if you grew up. If you moved away, Jeffrey would wait for your return. And, he could hug back. You only had to believe. Alexa believed, then and now.

Grandma said she prayed that even if she wasn't there, Jeffrey would be. If his tree felled or burned, he'd twirl to a nearby oak.

Alexa clutched the rope to her chest. She wanted to climb it to sit next to Jeffrey. No injury prevented her from trying. While deep breaths pained her, the fire hadn't scarred her skin. Her hair's singed ends would, in time, be no more.

Alexa called out, "Don't move, Jeffrey."

Wooden planks behind her squeaked. Alexa's gaze twisted to the rear porch.

"Who's there?" Belinda asked.

Alexa relaxed her grip on the rope. She whispered to the sky, "Stay, Jeffrey." Jeffrey clapped. Alexa felt safe.

"Alexa, it's past three and you haven't eaten all day."

"In a few. Promise." Alexa returned her gaze to Jeffrey. She couldn't tell Belinda. Dark memories had nurtured and spewed too many demons from the recesses of Alexa's brain. Mention Jeffrey the Monkey and Belinda would truly think her crazy.

Belinda's breath on Alexa's nape announced Belinda's closeness before her arm comforted Alexa's shoulders.

Alexa's fingertips touched the rope and, with a sigh, she let go.

"If not something to eat, maybe a relaxing bath upstairs."

"No." Alexa screamed. She jerked free of Belinda's embrace. "I don't want to see Joe."

"It's okay," Belinda said. "Let's talk. Follow me."

Alexa did. She sat on a kitchen chair on Grandma's rear porch. Her gaze never left its wooden boards. When Belinda placed a cool glass in her hand, she sipped, careful to keep her vision below the porch rail. Alexa nibbled once and couldn't eat the tuna sandwich Belinda offered. Pain in her throat blocked food swallows. Her stated and unstated questions of "why me?" went unanswered.

She heard the sound of gravel crunching. She hoped against hope that if she didn't look up Joe would swagger toward her.

The shadow of a human enveloped her. "How's your breathing, Alexa?" The bristles of a neophyte mustache highlighted the gentleman's face. With his white dress shirt's top button undone and his paisley tie knot stretched, both matched his loosely draped charcoal suit coat.

"It hurts." She coughed.

"You can expect that for at least a week. I treated you last night at the hospital. By your actions I deduced that the hospital environment caused you more harm than being an outpatient. It's no problem. Don't like to see my patients strapped to a bed. Kicks and screams upset others and does you no good."

"Don't remember being like that."

"No matter. What I like is that you're up and walking. Your friend must be a great help."

"Belinda's the best." Alexa's gaze focused on the stethoscope that protruded from the doctor's right suit coat pocket.

"You're strong like your grandmother. She was eighty-

85

four when she left for a better world and, unlike other seniors I tend to who require a regimen of pills, she didn't. I need to check your lungs and heart. It's a precaution. Just breathe deep when I ask."

Alexa followed the doctor's instruction as he pressed his stethoscope at seven locations on her chest and back.

"All's progressing well. I'll leave my card in case your regular physician needs further information. It's been a pleasure to meet you."

Alexa nodded. Her gaze only followed the departing doctor until he left the porch.

"You did great," Belinda said. "If you'd eat . . . that would be even greater."

"I meant what I said about you. You can tease, but you're still the greatest."

"Must be the medicine talking."

"What? Remember no medicine."

"Gotcha." Belinda laughed.

Alexa's throat gagged on her exploding laugh. "If today's, what, Sunday, what time are we leaving for Chicago?"

"We're not. Called the dictator and explained there'd been accident and that you were in the hospital. Fibbed a little and said I didn't know the hour the doctor planned your release." Belinda smiled. "Asked for week of medical-emergency sick leave not deducted from our banked hours."

"He agreed?"

"Not until I had him speak with Brad, what's his last name, yeah, Haberkorn."

"Brad was at the hospital?"

Belinda set the tuna sandwich plate on a swing cushion. "All night."

"Dreamed he tried to pull me from the flames."

"A dream? No way. That happened. You were like a WWII kamikaze pilot attacking that mobile home.

Shouldn't have given you those towels."

"Was he hurt?"

"A little, I think. But, like you, he fought off the EMTs."

"You exaggerate." Alexa's right fingertips brushed her forehead, no hair strands touched.

"No way. I may get high probation officer marks, but no one reaches the true soul of our client girls like you do, especially these last two years. Mother Theresa would be proud."

"I'm no saint. Don't even go to church regular."

"Don't go there. Religion isn't on my to-do list. I'm talking humanity. That's more important than churches, choirs, and robed gray-haired guys shouting from raised pulpits."

Alexa lifted her gaze. "So where do we sleep tonight?"

"We got the camper. Or, you can lay on your Grandma's bed upstairs. The wash machine in the basement doesn't seem to work so we must wait a day to buy sheets."

"Camper's fine. I'll rinse out underwear in the sink." Alexa closed her eyes. She didn't know if it was exhaustion or what. After an undetermined silence she heard whispers.

"I don't know if we should wake her."

Alexa opened her eyes. "Gotcha, Belinda."

Brad stared at her.

"Where's Belinda?"

"I'm right here."

"I didn't hear gravel." Alexa perceived the bafflement that consumed Brad's face.

"He gotcha, Alexa," Belinda said. "He didn't know if the farmyard was a crime scene or not so he parked on the road. Crossed the front lawn to the back porch."

"What crime scene?"

Brad leaned forward. "The fire. Chief suspects arson."

Alexa's head throbbed. Her eyelids fluttered. "I didn't

set no fire."

"Of course not. No one suspects you set the mobile home fire that killed Joe Erickson."

"Omigawd." Alexa's shoulders collapsed, and she listed right.

Belinda hugged Alexa. "She didn't know. Should've told you."

Brad's left hand covered his mouth. "I'm so sorry."

Alexa's skin rippled with shivers; tears cascaded down her cheeks.

Brad muttered, "Alexa, I'm so sorry."

"Brad." Belinda patted Alexa's left shoulder. "I think you should leave. Call me."

"Don't have your number."

"Oh. Come back tomorrow. Alexa should be calmer by the afternoon."

Through teardrops and out-of-focus-vision, Alexa watched Brad step off the porch. She hankered for Joe's shout he'd bought steaks. She didn't care if beer filled his refrigerator. He'd been honest. A quality she admired. He'd not been an Internet charlatan who'd say anything to add her to his trophy list. Joe had been real. His kisses tender. His intentions honest, and she admired that.

Samuel had reacted to Joe's goodness. Alexa grateful Samuel recognized the present and little else. It spared Samuel a lifetime of lament as to the life Joe would've given him.

Alexa sighed. Grandma's world offered her and Samuel neither short-term peace nor long-term solitude. A revived Jeffrey the Monkey created for her but a temporary diversion. Her roller coaster life returned her to the reality Samuel required a father figure. She'd toilet trained him without quenching his question of "show me how to do it, mommy." He'd need a strong model to become a self-realized, well-adapted adult man.

On the rear porch, Alexa rested her aching muscles, if

not her tortured mind. When the sun lowered itself to the horizon, she beseeched Belinda to sit next to her.

"You're my friend. I can hide from others, but not you. Tell me why Joe hasn't visited. He has to know about the fire. I remember his face in the mobile home window when I pounded."

"You need to be a strong person. Joe died in the fire."

Alexa lost control of her sobs. Her chair tilted sideways, but she didn't tumble.

"He's with his creator. A better place," Belinda whispered. "You did all you could. The firemen did. The ambulance crew exhausted themselves to save him. He'd been in the smoke too long. My regret is I didn't respond quicker to your cry."

"What you're saying confirms what my heart has dreaded all day."

"You can survive this."

"I know we've been trained to say that to the relatives of street victims. I've mumbled it numerous times. The SWAT team leader who ended my captivity said those exact words when he lifted me off that bloodstained mattress in the third abandoned house. I want to believe."

"You have believed. And, you're a survivor. Always remember you're a hero. If you weren't, you wouldn't have rushed to save Joe."

"But I didn't save him." Alexa wiped a tear from her right cheek.

"You tried. That's what's important."

"Maybe if I'd agreed to his request to sleep in the trailer."

"You have to believe it wouldn't have made a difference for Joe. Things happen. You acted in accord with your belief of what's right. That's important. Right now only God above knows what caused the fire. We have to respect that."

When the sun's rays sank below the horizon, Alexa

understood the world hadn't stopped its rotation. Be it ever so close, she couldn't gaze at Joe's mobile home. She acceded to Belinda's urgings to rest in the camper.

Mother Nature's strong breeze replaced the lingering burnt smell in Alexa's nostrils with the fresh aroma of field-spread manure. Alexa's memory revisited her bouncing pickup ride with Samuel. Her scattered thoughts circled her 2007 attack. She'd been strong then and last night was definitely no worse.

Tires crunched gravel. Alexa lifted her head. Brad?

Two strong raps rattled the camper door.

"Miss Hovey? Sheriff Edwards. I'd like a word with you, please."

Alexa tucked her knees and swung her legs out of her sleeping bag. "Just a moment."

Belinda stood with a khaki-uniformed, clean-shaven man, aged forty to forty-five. When Alexa paused in front of his lean and muscular frame, he had to be six-foot.

Belinda suggested they move to the rear porch. "There's a yellow bulb there that won't attract moths and flies."

"Good idea," the Sheriff replied.

Belinda nudged Alexa forward with soft jabs to the small of her back.

The Sheriff climbed the porch steps first. "I'll stand." He removed a small notebook.

Alexa flopped rearwards onto the chair cushion still flattened by her extended afternoon sit. Belinda positioned herself nearby on the porch swing.

To Alexa's relief, the Sheriff slowed his rapid fire background questions when she said she served the City of Chicago as a probation officer.

"Where were you when the fire broke out?"

"In the camper with Belinda." She gazed Belinda's way to see her friend's nod.

He swatted something unseen. "When was the last time

Gold

Alexa's Gold

you saw Joe Erickson?"

"Yesterday evening. We'd gone to a drive-in movie." Alexa filled the silence. "Came back here between ten and eleven. In case you're interested, the movie was about Australia. Think that was also its title."

"How did the fire appear?"

"Don't understand."

"Smoky, large flames, small flames, things like that." From below his brass nameplate, the Sheriff extracted a pack of cigarettes from his breast pocket. Returned it without opening.

"First smelled smoke, then at the corner of the camper. A large flame flash."

"Hear any explosion?"

"Several small pops. Don't know why."

"See any fire outside the trailer?"

"No."

"Where in the trailer did you see flames?"

"Front part, say living room. Faint light streaked hazy black shadows when I peered in a back window. Flames leaped to lick the ceiling. Saw an outlined figure move. I pounded on the glass pane that reflected flames. White eyes inside stared out at me, large white eyes I'll never forget."

"You recognize who it was?"

Alexa thought she heard a low moan. "It could've been her." Belinda gazed at her feet.

"Joe," Alexa murmured. "Sure it was Joe."

Belinda rose to stand next to Alexa. Her grasp stopped Alexa's shoulders from trembling.

"There was a grill. Know when it used?"

"Night before. That's right. Friday. Belinda, you tell him."

The Sheriff shifted his gaze upward.

"That's right, Sheriff. He called it a party. Joe had steaks. He doused the coals."

"I'll contact if I need more. Trust you'll feel better."

91

"Thank you."

After the Sheriff stepped off the porch, he gazed at Joe's trailer for two minutes. A cloud of puffy white smoke trailed his head when he strode away. Indistinct radio voices crackled and died. The sound of a high-powered engine faded into the night.

Chapter Six

Alexa tossed and turned. She'd won a game of rock-scissors-paper with Belinda. She let Belinda sleep in Grandma's bedroom while she chose the upstairs bedroom she'd slept in as a child.

When a child, the twin bed hadn't allowed her barefoot toes to drape its edge. The clinical white sheets Belinda purchased Monday separated the mattress from Grandma's multi-flowered handmade quilt. Alexa, careful not to glance too far left, fixed her mind on Jeffrey the Monkey who sat on the window's outside ledge.

Jeffrey, you should ride with me to Chicago. You can't shake your head no forever. Samuel will love you and grow in the joy you bring. Every child needs joy. That's why I refused to abort Samuel when his life stirred within me. No adult should have the power to deny joy to a child.

"Alexa, you up," Belinda shouted from the bedroom door's other side.

"Yes."

The bedroom door opened. Belinda modeled the navy-blue prairie-style empire dress she'd purchased. Its hue close enough to black to be appropriate for Joe's scheduled 2 p.m. funeral. Alexa planned to pair her gray pants suit with a new deep purple blouse she purchased on Belinda's shopping trip. "I'll meet you in the kitchen."

Alexa pushed aside the bread and sliced beef Belinda centered on the kitchen table to slurp plain yogurt. A door knock interrupted her noon lunch. "Come in."

Alexa rotated her torso and momentarily gasped at the suited man's resemblance to Joe.

"Thank you," Oscar Erickson replied. Belinda invited him to join them.

Oscar cleared his throat and pulled out a chair. "Alexa, I apologize if I waited too long."

She raised her right palm. "Don't."

"It's been so hard. Joseph was next in line to farm my land. Leah and I lost a son in childbirth after Joseph and neither of our two older daughters has any desire to run a farm. They're like you. Both ran off to the big city."

Alexa didn't believe she'd abandoned a way-of-life. Her family, especially her Dad, chose Chicago for his life and his livelihood. In Mr. Erickson's time of grief she couldn't challenge him or quibble with his choice of words. "Joe . . . Joseph was very kind. You should be proud."

"We are. And proud of you for your attempt to save him." His gaze drifted as his voice weakened. "We know no other woman . . ." Oscar's right fist smacked his chest. "We can't say 'thank you' too often. Always remember that Leah and I are here for you, always."

Alexa couldn't forestall her stream of tears. She wiped her cheeks with a napkin. "I'm sorry."

Oscar skidded his chair away from the table. "After the funeral there'll be a reception in the church hall, then later a private family get together at the farm. Leah and I'd be honored if you and your friend stopped by. I don't believe you've meet Leah. She and your grandmother traded recipes a time or two. My wife's made an apple cake recipe in Joseph's memory." His eyes moistened. "He'd eat the whole pan if nobody looked."

Alexa didn't see his tears, although she witnessed Oscar's white handkerchief dampen. "We'll do that."

* * *

In the throng of mourners that surrounded the Erickson family Christian Church Cemetery plot, Alexa stood stoic as she grasped Belinda's left hand. Silent and rigid sentinel oaks and spruces funneled prayers to the heavens. Stretched canvas strips suspended Joseph's metallic bronze casket six inches above his excavated grave. The funeral service minister bowed his head and then lifted his gaze to the blue sky dotted with cottony clouds.

"Lord, we ask not why but glorify you in your wisdom. Although human life is brief, Joseph shared the grace you bestowed upon him with others. Grant unto him eternal rest."

Alexa nudged Belinda. They stepped noiseless across the grass. Behind them arose infrequent wails and the rhythmic clicks of a gear that lowered a heavy weight. Alexa halted at Belinda's SUV.

"He touched you, didn't he?" Belinda asked.

Alexa's answer escaped before she realized it. "Yes."

"That's a good sign."

"What?" Alexa tried hard to follow Belinda's logic. She failed.

"I'm no certified romance counselor, but for the last three years you've sashayed through the dating motions and avoided any hint of commitment."

"That's not true." Alexa fought the constriction of her cheeks, the press of her lips.

Their silence and smiles acknowledged three women who passed within earshot.

"Sure it is. I twisted your arm to sign up for online dating. And, what happened? You go on dates. Never a second with the same guy. The odds aren't that terrible."

"You saying I'm to blame."

"Only you can answer that. I've never been through the wringer, so to speak, as you. If I you, I'd probably be in a straightjacket screaming and collecting on-the-job disability until the day I die in restraints with bed sores."

"Don't think so." Alexa's right foot flattened three white clover blossoms. "It really doesn't matter. Would've gone out with Joe again."

"Saw you reflect the sparkle of his eyes. That's why I'm afraid for you."

"Afraid of what?" Apprehension stirred Alexa's interest.

"That you'll convince yourself why should I try again? That you'll hide in your 2007 shell."

"Hello," Brad said. His voice soft and near.

Alexa trembled. How much had Brad heard? After a moment of reflection, she sighed. She shouldn't delay his task to help her with Grandma's will. Their initial-day infatuation shelved. As Grandma expected, she'd be able to move on with her life.

"Hello," Belinda said.

"Sad day. This community has too many."

Alexa bowed her head as if her soul mustered a silent assent. The inquisitive community drained her energy. The preacher's eulogy left her heart strings broken.

Belinda gazed at Brad. "You going to the farm?"

"Custom says only family and closest friends. Although I've known Joe, I'm not family and my community clients have been, what shall I say, sometimes at odds with Oscar Erickson."

"Oh," Belinda replied.

"You both have a nice day. And, Alexa, please think about what you wish to do when the judge issues a decision."

While Brad's eyes expected a verbal answer, Alexa bobbed her head without conviction. He didn't protest and ambled toward a second cluster of mourners.

Belinda chided Alexa, "You weren't very polite."

"He's a lawyer."

Belinda shrugged and said nary a word on their trip to the Oscar Erickson homestead. A young gentleman directed them to a grassy parking spot.

When the farmhouse door swung in, a petite, wiry woman, her cheeks drawn, appeared. Her left hand clutched a black prayer book. "Welcome, come in."

"Who is it, Leah," asked an unseen baritone voice.

"Emma Anderson's granddaughter."

The unseen speaker commanded, "Have her come in."

"Joe was so kind," Alexa said. "I'd like to introduce Belinda. She's my best friend." The interior house layout appeared to be an exact duplicate of Grandma's.

Leah pointed for Alexa and Belinda to step left. "It's an honor to have you in our house. Weren't the reverend's words wonderful?"

Alexa nodded. A dozen, perhaps fifteen, persons filled the parlor and the kitchen. Joe's framed picture, draped in black, hung in the parlor. Alexa assumed it had been a high school graduation picture, but then remembered Joe's GED certificate remark. She concluded further thought unimportant. No picture could duplicate his sparkling eyes alive in her memory.

"I'll find a drink and hang out on the back porch," Belinda said.

Alexa picked a glass of lemonade from a tray. She sipped. After a moment, Oscar Erickson approached.

"I'm so pleased you came." Alexa recognized his voice as that of the unseen.

"From what I know, neighbors help each other."

"You would've loved Joe."

Alexa's neck muscles wrung her throat like a dishtowel.

"I know your grandmother appreciated his help," Oscar continued. "I'm sure you're aware she wrote a letter that, upon her death, gave Joe forty northwest corner acres."

An inkling of unexpressed doubt nibbled her numbness. "Wasn't told."

"She did. The letter exists, filed away in my papers. You want to see it?"

"If you say the paper exists that's enough for me."

"It would've been a start for Joseph. Given him a taste of the land that would all one day be his. You have to understand Joseph would've never asked your grandmother for compensation."

"Grandma was a generous person."

"How right you are. Please enjoy yourself. I need to say thanks to others."

Alexa milled amongst the guests, but felt no real connection to any of them. Belinda at the last moment appeared at Alexa's shoulder to rescue her from one inquisitive woman who claimed to be Joe's aunt. They excused themselves, each with a mumbled thank you.

Belinda shifted her SUV into gear. "I hate funerals, even when I know the family."

"Sorry you had to endure this. What could I do considering the father's personal invitation?" Belinda nodded. "Oscar said Grandma wrote a letter giving Joe forty acres upon her death."

"Is that legal?" Belinda slowed to turn into the Anderson farmyard.

"How do I know? Grandma's bank account never overflowed. It may have been her way to repay Joe for his kindness and also keep him nearby."

"Forty acres times three thousand dollars per acre."

"How'd you get that number?"

"Open ears on the porch." Belinda clicked her key fob to unlatch her SUV doors.

"Then Grandma lavished on Joe land worth one hundred twenty thousand."

"She could've hired a visiting service cheaper."

"If I have to deal with it, I will."

"Might be other things, so to speak, that'll crawl out of the woodwork?"

Alexa's vision focused on the parked Buick. "Maybe we should ask Brad to leave?"

Belinda unbelted herself. "Why?"

"I'm exhausted."

Brad, without his blazer, stood motionless alongside his Buick. Alexa detected no smile.

On their circuit to Brad, Belinda whispered to Alexa, "This fellow must really dig you for him to always show up where you are."

Alexa paused her footsteps as she activated her cell phone to reveal no messages. "Don't know. I've had my cell phone off since the funeral's opening hymn."

"That could explain it." Belinda threw a conniving glance. "Maybe? I'll be quiet now."

"The judge made a ruling." He turned to Belinda. "I need to talk privately with Alexa."

Belinda frowned and resumed her walk toward the rear porch.

"Should I be concerned?" Alexa asked.

"In a way yes, in a way no."

"C'mon. Lawyer talk. Tell me the truth. Use words with meaning."

"Judge received a document that says your grandmother gave forty acres to Joseph Erickson before she died. That impacts your grandmother's will giving you everything."

"Oscar Erickson today told me about that. How can that affect anything? Joe's dead."

"Fire chief believes there's evidence that your mother set the mobile home fire." His stoic expression never fluctuated. "If that's true, then the judge might believe your mother acted on your behalf to deny Joe Erickson his portion and keep everything in your family."

Her jaw tightened. "That's preposterous."

What about Mother's offer at Rosie's? Brad's

speculation muddied everything. Mother's offer required Alexa to inherit. Was Brad cruel to imply Grandma's will convicted Mother of arson? How could she explain anything without indicting Mother? If Mother rebelled against any neighbor getting one acre of Grandma's farm, what would she do if she discovered Oscar Erickson, through his deceased son Joe, gained forty acres?

Brad cut short her musings. "The letter doesn't qualify as a devise of property since there aren't two qualifying signatures. While any judge, in a heartbeat, would toss the letter giving Joe forty acres, this result doesn't negate the incentive it gives your mother."

"Well, she wouldn't kill anyone."

He shrugged. "What the fire chief believes is a different story."

Alexa repressed her anger that Brad didn't support Mother. "You should leave now."

"I'm only here to protect your best interests."

"Sometimes I wonder," Alexa mumbled. Unable to face him, she gazed off into Grandma's backyard. She sensed Belinda was posed to run to her rescue. "You do what you must. I've got to return to Chicago to protect my livelihood."

"The Sheriff may want to ask you questions."

"I've already answered the Sheriff's questions. If there's anything you need, you have my cell phone number. I'm not hiding. I have a son that needs me."

Brad hung his head. A second later he uttered, "Okay."

Alexa stepped aside and watched Brad's Buick turn right when it reached the county road.

"Why'd you act all uppity to send him away?" Belinda asked.

"Why not? He wasn't nice or helpful."

"He might be the only person here in Iowa you can count on."

"Doubt that. He's a lawyer. The more convoluted the

more he can justify upping his fee."

Chapter Seven

For two weeks Alexa tried to bury her anxiety with office casework. When idle, thoughts of Joe's fiery mobile home exhausted her. The white eyes. Flames leaping chin to forehead. Hot metal. Towel-wrapped fist pounds. Wild fear. Intact window glass. No escape. The image of a burned out mobile home shell she gathered in a quick rearward glance from the passenger seat of Belinda's SUV forever scarred her memory.

Since Samuel's birth she'd resigned herself to the fact Chicago men never respected her. Too often the men acted as if springing for the dinner check guaranteed they'd bounce on her sagging bedroom mattress. Joe hadn't. At the movie he'd asked her if he could kiss her. Odds had to be that other eligible men with similar dispositions existed. Alexa doubted her chances to meet one.

She gazed out the office window onto a busy North LaSalle Street.

"You planning a trip back to Iowa?" Belinda asked.

"Not really. Samuel and I will drive out early Saturday, return late Sunday."

"Wish I could come with you."

"That's okay. I need to ask Oscar Erickson in person for an advance to begin repair on Grandma's house foundation. Also, get an update from Susan on the listing."

"You can't do both by telephone?"

"It's important I sort through Grandma's keepsakes and recipes. Can't ask strangers."

Chapter Eight

Alexa smiled at Samuel. His tongue licked before his mouth sucked a Popsicle. Had she softened too much? Her pickup bounced along the county road, an hour from Rosie's Cafe.

Grandma's free-of-litter yard pleased her. After she unbuckled Samuel from his car seat, Alexa marshalled her courage to walk towards Joe's mobile home. Samuel toddled onto the grass in pursuit of a white moth.

Visual images swirled in her head. The most vivid a drive-in movie scene of a bombed Australian city where the hero searched the wreckage to rescue the heroine. And before her the burnt shell of Joe's mobile home, its roof collapsed. No crane magnet strong enough to uncover Joe clinging to life beneath the metal scrap awaiting salvage.

The vehicle-crunched farmyard gravel behind her announced a visitor. She cocked her head to see Brad's Buick. It stopped and his strides detoured right to tweak Samuel's chin.

Samuel scampered to hug Alexa's right leg. She pursed her lips. Brad's extended his right arm didn't encourage Samuel to give up his clutching grasp.

Brad stood two arm lengths in front of her. If he had something to say why didn't he say it?

He cleared his throat. "Received your message about the foundation. Suggest you hold off. The judge hasn't yet signed the order approving your inheritance."

Alexa squeezed Samuel's shoulder. Words a street-wise teen would shout behind a jabbing finger flooded her mind. Even if one of her clients couldn't hear her, it wouldn't be her. How could she say mumbo-jumbo? "Is this more legal gobbledygook?"

"Just a cautious judge." Brad's right hand stroked his

khaki trousers.

"Why? Didn't Grandma's expressing herself before witnesses who swore truth tell the judge what she wanted?" She fixed her gaze on his eyes as his wandered left and right. "Grandma depended on you to do it right."

Her sharp emphasis of "on you" accused him of failed stewardship, negligent, if not deliberate.

He bowed his head. "I did everything by the book, followed the law."

"Really?" Her right hand removed a Lifesaver roll from her pocket and, without using her left hand, popped one into her mouth. Samuel's wide eyes followed every supple twist of her fingers. Without sealing the roll, she stuffed it into her front jeans pocket.

"If you don't believe me, there's not much more for me to say." His left foot stepped rearward. He ignored Samuel's left hand swung in his direction.

Alexa grabbed Samuel's left wrist, pulled his arm to his side, and released her grip. With her right hand fingers curled in a fist, she knuckled her right brow to hide her trembling lower lip. The chill of abandonment galvanized her spine.

Three rearward steps and Brad pivoted toward his Buick.

Alexa crunched her Lifesaver as Brad's Buick departed. Samuel's struggles and wiggles to reach her jeans pocket required her to hoist him onto her left hip.

"C'mon, Tiger. We'll grab your blocks so you can play while Mommy works."

Alexa skipped Grandma's larger bedroom to begin with her childhood room. Last month had shown the kitchen cabinets to be empty except for mis-matched glasses, a blue-patterned dish set, and silverware. The bulky parlor furniture resisted her efforts to expose every corner. Neither did she desire to attack the basement's cobwebs nor the insects that thrived in damp dark spaces.

Samuel stacked Legos in the upstairs hallway. She glanced at him from the room's doorway. His smile eased her fears. Two blankets and a winter quilt filled the small-dresser drawers. Girlhood clothes no longer there. Bedroom walls she remembered as pink now a pale drab green.

"Kaboom," Samuel shouted. His right hand slammed a wood block into a Lego tower.

She leaned against the bedroom doorjamb. "What was that?"

"Superman."

"Honey, Superman leaps tall buildings. He doesn't knock them down."

Samuel's grin exposed his missing tooth. "Me hungry." Alexa hustled to act upon Samuel's clue he'd be fussy if not fed.

Alexa paused inside the entrance to Rosie's Cafe. A bearded, stocky gentleman in shirt and tie with a horseshoe ring of brown hair parted two men at the counter. He picked up his order without a word of greeting. Alexa thought she recognized him as Brad's law partner.

The server, after a welcome hello, directed her to sit anywhere. Alexa, after lunch, permitted Samuel to grab an offered sucker at the register, but not to remove the plastic wrapping. She pocketed her change and the sucker and buckled Samuel in before their return to the farm.

Alexa plopped Samuel in the second floor hallway next to his blocks. "You can have this sucker later." She added his plastic shovel so he could scoop.

In Grandma's bedroom Alexa separated closet clothes into one pile for donation and a second for discard. After the closet she opened the top drawer of Grandma's dresser. Its golden oak matched the headboard that sported appliques popular in the 1930s.

"Samuel, you okay?"

The renewed sound of tumbling blocks assured her he hadn't gone exploring.

When her eyes spied a costume jewelry ring she'd
adored, Alexa slipped her forefinger into it and wiped it
across her tie-dyed T-shirt. The ruby red glass sparkled.
She left the jewelry drawer contents in place. Three cleared
large drawers grew the discard pile. The last rested on the
bed.

Alexa tilted it. A yellowed envelope lay cradled in the
space between the drawer's slide supports and the dresser's
bottom. The greeting card envelope crackled to Alexa's
touch. She sat cross-legged on the bed. Dried glue streaked
the unsealed flap. She unfolded the once creamy paper
inside to find its left corner decorated by a single red rose.

Alexa read Grandma's handwriting:

"September, 2007.

"Dearest Alexa,

"I know you're going through difficult times. May
God's hand lead you to the joy I've seen you experience so
many times here at the farm."

Alexa allowed fat tears to trickle from her eye ducts to
her jawbone.

"Childbirth can be difficult. You'll forget the pain when
your baby boy or girl lays a warm cheek on your bosom.
And then, without a doubt, when those baby eyes twinkle."

"Mommy. Sucker." Samuel's hands struggled to grip
the bed's quilt. Alexa stretched her right hand to tug on her
son's belt at the seat of his pants. He scrambled to sit in her
lap.

"In a minute. Mommy's reading Grandma's letter never
sent."

Her left hand held out the letter. Its envelope fell to the
bed. She read more:

"After all these years your laugh lifts me in rapture.
When you're not here, the memory warms my heart and
soul.

"I know you may think it's presumptuous of me, but
you need to think long and hard about who will be the

father to your child. All children need a father.

"You might remember Joe Erickson. He helps me a lot. There's a new young lawyer in town. Brad Haberkorn, nice strong family. I heard he lived in Chicago."

"Mommy. Don't cry."

"It's happiness, honey. One day you'll understand happy tears."

She flipped the paper for Grandma's last words:

"I look forward to your next telephone call. Lucy and Fran from the county club are coming in an hour. I need to bake my special muffins.

"May God Bless. Grandma."

"Honey, let's take a walk. Your sucker's in the pickup."

Alexa grasped Samuel's left hand as his right slid along the handrail. Both of his legs wobbled on each tread. Alexa lugged him from the kitchen door to the front lawn where Samuel tried to run, slipped, fell, and pushed himself up.

Her cell phone rang.

"I'll be with you in a minute, Sheriff."

She opened her pickup door, handed Samuel the sucker, and led him from the gravel to a yellow dandelion bloom growing in the grass.

"I'm sorry. Had to keep my son safe." Alexa listened. "I don't believe it."

"Fire Marshall confirmed the arsonist wedged a matchbook into a living room electrical box and re-attached the plate. Heat from bared wires ignited the matches. You saw the result."

"But Joe should've been able to get out."

"Well, his mobile home was an older model. Fire chief speculates the flimsy wall insulation with no flame retardant properties dispersed toxic fumes worse than flames."

"There's got to be more." Alexa's glance satisfied her Samuel hadn't choked.

"There is, but the investigation's ongoing. Did you see

your mother the night of the fire?"

"Last saw her in Rosie's at lunchtime."

"Did she think you might've been sleeping in the mobile home?"

Alexa swallowed hard. "Heavens no. Belinda and I had a camper. That's preposterous."

"Witnesses tell me you and your mother had harsh words at the cafe and Joe was there."

Alexa switched her cell from her right to her left ear. "No real argument. We were both tense after the attorneys appeared in court that morning."

"Witness said he overheard payoff talk, fifty thousand dollars."

"I accepted no payoff."

"Never said you did. But was there mention of fifty thousand?"

"Mother may have said a dollar amount. It had nothing whatsoever to do with Joe Erickson."

"Let's go back. Last time you and your mother met was Friday lunch at Rosie's?"

"That's correct."

After the Sheriff's good-bye, Alexa pressed her cell's end button.

Samuel's hands sported yellow dandelion bits stuck between his fingers. His sucker lay speckled with dirt on the grass. Alexa's left hand rubbed her neck's nape. She couldn't comprehend what to do next except telephone the foundation repair company and postpone their start. She could ill afford to lose the hundred-dollar deposit by an outright cancel.

After sliding her arms under Samuel's armpits from the rear, she hauled him to the kitchen sink. Samuel giggled when Alexa played washcloth peek-a-boo before she scrubbed his face and hands. While escorting him to the rear porch, she envisioned Samuel as the sole man in her life. He'd eat healthy, keep up his grades, and became the family's second college degree holder.

He climbed onto a swing seat, swung to and fro, and kicked his feet into the air.

Her cell rang. When she answered, whoever it was hung up. Two minutes later another ring. This time Alexa said hello to Susan of Grundy Real Estate.

"Contractor called. Said you postponed repair. Is that right?"

Alexa sat next to Samuel and pushed him and the swing with her legs. "Yes."

"You think that wise?"

"Grandma's attorney says the judge has delayed decision. Don't want to waste my money."

"You think your mother will own the farm?"

Chagrinned at the prospect, Alexa admitted, "Possibly."

"She called me the last afternoon she was in town."

Alexa gulped.

Susan continued, "I told her that if I tried to help her, it conflicted with you."

"And."

"She said she had to talk with Mr. Erickson at the farm. Assumed she meant Joe."

Alexa's jerk-action response jumped through her cell. "You didn't ask?"

"Well, little after five I drove to the Lakeview Inn, but the desk clerk said she wasn't answering her room phone. Assumed she'd gone for supper."

"Sounds logical."

"Not completely. You see, I've a cousin who works there. She said your mother's bed hadn't been slept in that Friday night. Management didn't care because your mother paid in advance. You still there?"

"Yeah." Alexa tried hard to remember if she'd seen her mother after lunch at Rosie's. No. She'd told the Sheriff the truth. "You tell anybody this?"

"Told the Sheriff. Didn't see any big deal. Your mother

probably good and bored sitting in a motel room and left early for home."

"You're right." While not convinced herself, Alexa had to give Mother the benefit of doubt.

Alexa promised Susan two things before she ended Susan's call. First, tell Susan when the foundation contractor would start work and, second, consider Susan's other referral.

Despite her verbal fights and disagreements with Mother, Alexa wouldn't believe Mother had the guts to kill, either murder or self-defense. If a foe had struck Joe with a blunt instrument, poured or sprinkled gasoline, and thrown a match, Alexa could join Mother's rages to this scenario. No way was Mother crafty with matchbooks and electrical outlets to set a fire that destroyed incriminating DNA in its smoke and flames.

"Stay here, Samuel."

Alexa jogged to her pickup to pull a pair of leather gloves from under the passenger seat. She'd test fate and let Samuel swing. If he kept swinging, he earned her promised sucker. She then dashed off to and along the rutted trail that paralleled the machine shed. When she reached the old car, she pressed her right palm to its hood. Her lungs ached. *Why was she doing this?*

Without time to waste, she donned both gloves and tried to open the passenger door. She failed. The driver door creaked with her second pull and swung out. She leaned in, unlatched the glove compartment, and shuffled the paper sheets for a key. None. With her thinking stymied and worried about Samuel, she clicked the glove box door closed and pushed the driver door to disguise her intrusion. To not stress her lungs, she jogged to the porch.

Alexa tried to mentally recreate the events of that fateful Friday. She and Belinda had returned to the farm. Belinda drove into town. She rode with Joe to the drive-in. That provided someone with two hours, maybe more, to enter Joe's trailer with the spare key, jerry-rig the matches, abscond, and allow the plan to work. Alexa sighed. If Susan spoke true, Mother's actions made her a suspect. The lack of a discernible motive created a stumbling block for Alexa.

She needed to engage her mind in non-corrosive thoughts. With this goal, she sat next to Samuel, engaged him in a peek-a-boo game, and then wrapped her arms around his growing body. She relished his warmth and the flood of hospital bassinet memories.

"Daddy."

Alexa froze.

Samuel pointed.

The wet nose of a floppy-eared cocker spaniel peeked around the porch corner.

"Daddy."

"That's doggy, Samuel. Stay still."

Alexa had never seen this or any dog on the farm. The putt-putt sound of Old Betsy crept into the farmyard. Oscar Erickson swung his right leg high and left and jumped off his tractor.

"C'mon Daisy. Time to go home." He snapped a lease onto the dog's collar, tied it to the tractor hitch, and climbed the porch steps.

"Sorry about that. She liked to visit Joe. Don't know what spooked her. Leah opened the kitchen door and off Daisy ran. Expected I'd find her here."

"That's okay. Can you answer me a question?"

"Shoot."

"Did you take the spare key to Joe's mobile home?"

"Why you asking? Sheriff asked me same question."

"Before I had utilities, Joe let Belinda and I use the mobile home bathroom. He left me a note about the key in case we came when he wasn't home."

"You still got the note?"

"Tossed it in the trash. Anyway, how you doing?"

"Been hard. Working helps. I wished they'd give me permission to haul that mobile home away. It sitting there under that tarp haunts me every time I drive over to cultivate."

"Is there a grass cutter in the shed or barn?"

"Don't know. Joe borrowed my tractor mower. But don't you worry none. I'll make sure your grass gets cut regular."

"I can pay you."

"No way. Wife's been asking if you've found your grandmother's recipes. If you find that apple cake recipe that'll make Leah happy . . . and me, too." He laughed.

"Not yet. But if I find it, you'll sure get a copy."

Alexa waved good-bye. When Oscar sat in his tractor seat, he carried Daisy under his right arm. The dog's haunches bobbed as the tractor disappeared around the corner.

Alexa punched in Brad's telephone number and he agreed to meet her in his office.

* * *

Alexa, never impressed by the Baker, Haberkorn Law Firm shabbiness and its side street location, lingered with Samuel near a window while a visibly pregnant receptionist said she'd tell Mr. Haberkorn Alexa waited. The desk nameplate stated: Margaret Skelton.

While the firm's Internet website accurately depicted Brad, not so the firm's office. Telescopic photography camouflaged its crumbling brick exterior and the warped front door. Rich-fabric drapes, gilded art nouveau, and high-end furniture probably rented for reception's one day photographic shoot like a fancy restaurant that covers grade-C plywood table tops with 800-count embroidered cloth.

Alexa followed the receptionist into the first door to their left and guessed that any seat at the room-centered eight-chaired table would be okay. She chose a corner to allow Samuel additional room to roll on the floor and stack his wood and plastic blocks.

"Mr. Haberkorn will be with you momentarily."

Alexa rubbed her bare forearms to counteract the room's chill. Beneath Brad's moist forehead, she noticed he fiddled with his Windsor knot and collar like he'd fastened a noose, not a blue tie. She didn't wait for him to select a seat.

"My apology if I acted rude at the farm earlier today."

"Not necessary." He pulled a chair from the table and straddled it. "Well-meaning persons act different in stressful situations and you have to be under tons."

While she hadn't mentioned her visit's real reason to verify the link between Brad, Mother, and Lydia Skelton, polite ambiguous words to drive the conversation in that direction eluded her. She held off being blunt to save this tactic as her last-ditch recourse.

"Can't understand all this delay with Grandma's will. The delay knots my stomach."

"Hate to say it, but it's a rare client who believes the court acts with any reasonable speed. The judge knows the land won't disappear, so why hurry. He doesn't have to decide on who owns an ice cream cone before it melts."

Alexa laughed. "I'm sorry. My mind asked itself if the judge had ever been outside the courtroom long enough to realize the world plugs in a freezer."

"You got me." His forced smile exposed straight, white teeth. "I must be quicker with a better analogy."

This isn't going well. "Is your receptionist related to Realtor Lydia Skelton?"

"Daughter-in-law. Why?"

"If I were in Chicago, I wouldn't. But here I'm discovering there's family connections that exist on several levels."

"Know what you mean. I lived in Chicago while

111

attending night law school."

"You did? Where?" She glanced at Samuel; his last block finished his tower.

"Beverly."

"That's a long commute to the loop."

"Concerned about inner city violence. Didn't want to be there after dark."

"Many don't." His rationale commonplace, but any Chicago discussion represented a digression from her goal. "You must see Lydia Skelton often."

"Not really. You interested in knowing more about her?"

Brad neither leaned forward nor spoke in hushed tones. Alexa's stomach fluttered. She dared not insinuate Brad and her were birds of a feather. Two inhales steadied her voice to project an objective tone that didn't grasp for personal dirt. "She's likely upset I chose Grundy Realty."

"No doubt, but Lydia's a professional."

"Can't dispute her claim she's represented most county farmers selling. However, I got the impression she doesn't give weight to how buyers think, especially when repairs necessary."

"If you're having Realtor second thoughts, don't. The entire Realtor community with its split commission structure will promote your sale. They understand only one can get a listing. But if they believe you're hard to please, demonstrated by Realtor switches, then word will spread and, while you'll eventually sell, their zeal to negotiate the highest price will be missing."

"No, no. I'm happy with Susan." Alexa cleared her throat. "I understand my mother before the last court hearing talked to you about Realtors."

Brad's shoulders straightened. "Who told you that?"

"Lydia Skelton at our first meeting."

"While your mother may have called, I explained I had a conflict of interest. You were the named beneficiary. It's unprofessional for me to tell Lydia or anyone else your mother called, and I didn't." His undertone screamed don't challenge me.

Alexa then realized how Lydia may have heard of Mother's call to Brad. Loose receptionist lips. Identical way Susan learned of Mother's unmade motel bed.

The receptionist opened the conference room door.

"Excuse me," Brad said.

Alexa pushed her chair from the table and held out her hands for Samuel to sit on her lap. She cuddled the most important male in her life. She'd lifted the gates to permit her date with Joe. With the fire, only guilt remained. Grandma's letter strong evidence she had donned a matchmaker hat. Yet, for an unknown reason, hadn't informed Alexa. Had fate intervened? A voice in the recesses of her mind implored her that Samuel's male role model didn't foreclose the same man from being her life's partner.

"I'm sorry," Brad said from the doorway. "I didn't plan an interruption. So it won't happen again, let's find a restaurant. It's suppertime."

Alexa knew the word "restaurant" meant Rosie's. She didn't want to spark diner gossip.

"Since you hesitate, I won't suggest Rosie's. Let me drive us to Cherry Hill. Luigi's has the best meatballs not squeezed into shape by a Swedish top chef."

Alexa teetered on the brink of hungry. Maybe Brad would drop a hint of what evidence the sheriff has that implicates Mother?

"I'll pack up Samuel's blocks."

"Leave your pickup here. I'll lock my office and meet you out front."

Alexa transferred Samuel's car seat to the rear seat of Brad's spacious Buick. She belted Samuel in before she clicked her front seat passenger harness. The dark-blue leather behind her didn't squeak when she stretched her

shoulders against it. When they passed the drive-in movie screen, she gazed into opposite cornfields.

shoulders against it. When they passed the drive-in movie screen, she gazed into opposite cornfields.

Thirty minutes flew with Brad's commentary of who lived at this or that farm. After Alexa counted three hillside orchards, a Cherry Hill welcome sign announced a town of three hundred. The Snake River S-curve required a quarter-mile bridge to funnel visitors to Main Street. Luigi's occupied the first floor of a squat two-story red brick building. Its vibrant yellow, red, and orange colors lifted one's eyes to the blue-sky ceiling ringed with painted green leaves. One tree branch dotted with little red circles. Alexa assumed they were cherries.

Unlike Rosie's, they had to wait while the hostess seated four couples. When asked booth or table, Alexa requested a booth and a booster chair.

"Pisano, welcome back," said a heavyset man in a soiled white apron and a chef's hat.

Brad smiled. "Luigi, meet Alexa and Samuel."

"Welcome, welcome."

Chapter Nine

Luigi's smile and his festive restaurant atmosphere played over and over in Alexa's memory at work Monday. She propped her forehead with folded arms that protected her nose from the rough break room table.

"Wake up, princess," Belinda teased.

"Please don't kiss me," Alexa murmured.

Like a two-ton crane with a three-ton load, Alexa raised her head.

Belinda sat across from her. "Would not plant a wet

one. First, didn't wish to disturb your dreamland flight. Second, ain't that kind of girl." Belinda chortled. Her infectious laugh AWOL. "You make inroads with that Iowa lawyer?"

"Farm's in limbo."

"What about spreading a blanket between the cornstalks? Picture yourself bathed in moonlight. His soft hands tingle your skin."

"Not in the cards. Had a nice dinner." Alexa forced herself not to take her eyes off Belinda. "Couldn't pry a pearl of useful information from his clamshell mouth."

"Think hard, you might've missed something important?"

Alexa refused to try. Her cough to clear her throat failed. While history told her she traveled less conflicted on a road without Mother, she needed someone to listen. Belinda would be the best. "The sheriff lists Mother as the prime suspect in the fire that killed Joe."

"Even with all the nasty accusations you make about your mother. I doubt she'd murder anyone. If you'd ask me, the sheriff only suspects her because she's an outsider."

A relieved Alexa opened her compact and brushed powder across her shiny forehead.

"You talk to your mother since we saw her in the restaurant?"

"Yeah, telephoned her last night." Belinda's hand motion urged Alexa to continue. "She said she got bored staring at four walls."

Belinda rose, frowned, and then plopped into her chair. "Doesn't she have a gas receipt or something date stamped to alibi her time and whereabouts?"

Alexa shook her head. "Paid cash. She recalled one receipt tossed at an Interstate rest area."

"Bummer." Belinda arched her right brow. "What about her husband?"

Alexa tamped her resentment long enough to admit to herself she hadn't even considered him as trustworthy. "Wasn't home."

"Double bummer. More important, you had dinner with Brad the corn guy. He had to be making goo-goo eyes at you, inching his hand past the knife tip to caress your little pinkie."

Alexa laughed. "All the twinkling eyes came from Luigi."

"Who's Luigi? Another hunk, another dreamboat?"

"Owner of the restaurant we ate at and perfect model for those Italian cartoon chefs. Doubt he'll ditch his lovely wife. She manned the cash register."

"Rats. A little jealousy triangle works wonders. Triggers the target to act before he loses the best woman to enter his life. Nudges the reluctant to the altar."

"Belinda!" Alexa had shelved her secret wish to have a full life with the man she loved.

"Don't be so put off. You got that little voice saying: 'I wish he kissed me again.' And those other flashes. Protest all you want; I ain't buying."

Alexa shook her head. "You're hopeless. Brad's not interested in me; it's mutual. He graduated John Marshall Law School and made it clear his first-hand experience with Chicago females turned him off. They expressed ideals that the only joy in life existed in the shoe department on Macy's first floor. The prissy lace-curtain Irish lassies who grew up and lived in Beverly, where he rented an apartment, cast love-struck eyes only at lads with red hair."

"Winds can change. What have I been trying to hammer into your head for the last year?"

Alexa sipped her cold coffee. "That I'm important. I deserve happiness, and happiness is greater than buying a size-four party dress with size-seven silver shoes."

"Bingo." Belinda's eyes danced. "Give that lady who's

116

about to change her life a prize."

"Store that thought in the lost and found." Alexa rose. "We're got to jump into the case-handling trenches. Drink up."

"My cousin granted me free use of his camper until Memorial Day." Belinda tossed her paper cup into a trash container. "A week from Friday, Samuel and I will go daddy hunting in Iowa. You're welcome to tag along, carry the quiver."

Alexa shook her head. Cupid carried one arrow; he didn't require help. Perhaps before then Brad would call with positive court news. Or, the Sheriff will call a press conference to announce they captured Joe's killer and cleared Mother's name.

Chapter Ten

Belinda's SUV tires droned on, interrupted by the concrete-joint bumps of Interstates 88 and 80. Alexa planned to repay Belinda when Midas returned her pickup with its new front shocks, a serious, but necessary, dent in Alexa's finances.

Old Betsy idled in Grandma's farmyard when Alexa arrived unannounced. She expected the unseen Oscar to be nearby. From the machine shed's west corner, Oscar called out, "Hello, ladies." He lifted his right hand from his overalls front zipper. "Made the last cultivating run today. Found an interesting old coffee can. Suspect a raccoon nosed it into the field."

Belinda straightened her blue baseball cap. "What was in the can?"

"Don't know. Sheriff just left with it. Surprised you didn't see him."

"Saw swirling dust. That's all," Alexa said.

"Yeah, it's been dry for a week." Oscar turned his gaze from Joe's burnt mobile home and its flapping tarp end. "Leah's been beating on me about your Grandma's recipes."

"Haven't found them."

"You keep looking. I'll have to lug a gas can if I don't get Old Betsy home."

Alexa carried Samuel into the kitchen to complete their end-of-trip washing ritual. Through the window she watched Belinda lower the camper stabilizers and unhitch the SUV. They had two hours before lunch. Her agenda, if not Belinda's, ranked basement cleanup first.

Belinda plopped into a kitchen chair. "Do we start in the attic?"

"Later. If we latch the screen door, Samuel can play safe in the kitchen. I'll fill his canteen."

Alexa reached for two pails stockpiled with sponges, spray bottles, and cloths. Incandescent lights tamed the scary basement in a way that candles hadn't. A wet cloth on a square-bottomed broom swatted away years of cobwebs. "This pen in the corner has rabbit droppings."

Belinda frowned. "Last pet I'd ever have. I'll get a dustpan."

Alexa, proud of herself, announced after ninety minutes their task completed. "Last one upstairs is a . . . whatever." She dashed to the basement stairs.

Belinda didn't bite. "I'm too tired."

"You sit with Samuel. I'll check the attic. Plan our attack."

Belinda lifted her pail, two cloths, and the broom. Alexa toted the remaining supplies up the stairs and dumped her armful in the kitchen sink. She grabbed the handrail to mount the stairs to the second-floor bedrooms and then, next to the bathroom door, the attic stairs.

Sweat beads dotted her forehead. Heated air dried her throat. Without a temperature gauge, Alexa guessed the attic was twenty degrees hotter than the seventy-five degrees outside. Three, corded, evenly spaced incandescent bulbs dangled.

Wooden and cardboard boxes tipped on their sides with contents spilt onto floor planks outnumbered flap-sealed cardboard boxes. Alexa righted a dressmaker's form. Its wire skirt topped by a hardy cotton-linen female mannequin. The helter-skelter mess puzzled Alexa. Grandma had prized tidiness, unless dementia ruled, or the last attic visitor wasn't Grandma.

This won't be too bad. She tiptoed through the boxes. Old clothes she'd donate; the heirloom cradle she'd keep. Duplicate farm records required burning. Books and papers she'd trash.

She changed her mind when she crouched to a letter stack tied with a terribly faded red ribbon. The brittle envelopes addressed to Emma Sjodgren, Grandma's maiden name. Maybe Grandpa, maybe not? She rose to lay the four-inch bundle next to the stairs.

Alexa's right foot stepped on a twelve-inch-wide plank that squeaked. Three nails once secured the plank. Alexa counted two empty holes and one square nail, a quarter-inch raised. She couldn't squeeze her right hand fingertips far enough into the crack to secure a hold. The hammer or slotted screwdriver in a kitchen drawer offered her a solution.

Alexa clomped the two levels of stairs to enter the kitchen.

"Mommy. Me hungry." Samuel's hands grabbed for her right leg, missed.

"In a minute, honey. Mommy needs to find a hammer."

"A what?" Belinda asked. Her white socks with feet inside rested on a second chair. "If childcare's this easy, I'll

119

look for a second job."

"It isn't, believe me." Alexa, hammer and screwdriver in hand, skipped every other tread in her backtrack to the attic. The claw hammer, atop a book wedged for leverage, required Alexa to grunt twice to remove the nail. With the screwdriver, augmented by the hammer's claw, she pried the half-inch-thick plank's end six inches higher than adjacent planks. Alexa discerned a second red ribbon, this one brilliant and tied around an eight-by-ten-inch loose-leaf binder.

Alexa removed three additional nails before she jammed the hammerhead sideways under the plank. Her left hand grasped the raised plank end and her right hand pulled the binder free.

Alexa clutched the binder to her breast and left her tools on the planks. She rejoined Belinda and Samuel in the kitchen.

Belinda gazed at Alexa. "Whatcha got?"

"Hidden binder. My guess is it might be Grandma's recipes."

Alexa felt a tug on her right jeans leg.

"Mommy. Me hungry."

Samuel's needs curbed Alexa's excitement. "If you put Samuel in his car seat, I'll join you for our trip to Rosie's."

Belinda slipped her feet into her sneakers. "Don't take forever."

Alexa left the ribbon tied as she re-climbed the stairs to stash the binder in Grandma's bedroom dresser before she rode with Belinda and Samuel to Rosie's for lunch.

After they ordered, Brad Haberkorn entered. He strode to their booth.

"If you're at the farm, I'd like to drive out about four."

"Sure," Alexa replied. "Good news?"

"Could be. See you at four." He responded to his called out name and left the diner.

"Mysterious." Belinda winked. "Must be serious. Can't

talk in front of a youngster."

"Quit it."

Samuel dropped his spoon. It hit his booster chair and then the floor. Alexa gave him hers before she picked up Samuel's spoon.

"No, honey. It's dirty. Finish your mac and cheese."

Alexa spied an across-the-room feminine finger point in her direction. *Probably nothing. Don't be paranoid.* The lady whispered to another.

When it came time to pay, Alexa stood in Rosie's cash register line behind two shoulder-to-shoulder women, one of whom was the finger-pointer.

"Lucy saw Brad and the woman in blue jeans with her kid at Luigi's. Now Brad's here."

"Coincidence?" the second lady asked. "She have a ring?"

"Could. One doesn't go as far as Luigi's except to keep it hush-hush."

A door slam behind Alexa turned the second lady's gaze toward her. The lady hurriedly tapped the pointing lady on her right elbow. The pointing lady glanced rearward before she snapped her head forward. On their way out neither steadied their gaze on Alexa.

Samuel, holding Belinda's hand, toddled to Alexa at the exit door. Outside in the parking lot, Belinda asked, "What was that all about?"

"Gossip. Old lady gossip." Alexa lifted Samuel to her right hip.

"About you?"

"Yeah."

Belinda pressed her key fob to unlock the SUV. "And?"

"Brad." With Samuel pinned by the crook of her right arm, Alexa rubbed her hands fiercely. "They should sew a quilt or volunteer at church, not waste time gossiping."

"What'd they say?"

"We went all the way to Luigi's because we've got the

hots for each other." Alexa ambled past the SUV's hood and opened the rear passenger door to buckle Samuel in. She hopped into the front passenger seat.

Belinda curled her fingers around the steering wheel. "C'mon, they didn't say that."

"Not those exact words." Alexa brushed hair from her eyes. "So what if they used different words? Same innuendo."

"Water off a duck's tail, I'd say. We need to inspect that binder you found."

Their trip's silence interrupted only by Samuel's sucker requests. Alexa caved in after she set him on a kitchen chair. With Samuel calmed, she retrieved the attic binder and untied the red ribbon at the kitchen table. Alexa gathered five loose pages that tumbled across the table.

"Don't touch, Samuel." His retreated left hand inched forward. "Samuel, no."

Alexa refrained from slapping or spanking Samuel. She believed corporal punishment didn't teach, only served as a catalyst for future violent behavior. Alexa didn't forgive her attackers until one year after Samuel's birth. From Nina's boyfriend to the lowest Latin gang recruit, she never told even one. A rival gang knifed Nina's boyfriend six months later at a Taste of Chicago lakefront festival. Alexa had shielded a police sergeant's daughter from public humiliation in *The Chicago Tribune* to learn two abdomen puncture wounds proved fatal.

"These recipes sound great," Belinda exclaimed.

"Agree, but can we really render our own lard for pie crusts? My stove doesn't list rendering between on, bake, and broil. The sugar calories in this cake enough to reach the moon."

Alexa flipped pages. She skimmed a chocolate muffin recipe and a New Orleans mile-high cake variation. Its sensual cake frosting sent her mind on a jazz riff. Dozens of recipe pages were brittle, the majority handwritten. They and the dozen typed pages scribbled with margin notes highlighted Grandma's trial and error. Unnumbered pages and torn pages made it obvious Alexa lacked a complete binder. Belinda muttered her reliance on the index page numbers useless.

Alexa, generally unimpressed by cookbooks, couldn't speak when Grandma's handwriting reminded her of December's postcard. The recipes listed ingredients; Grandma baked in the love.

"So, what do we do now?" Belinda asked.

A kitchen door knock unsettled Alexa.

She scrambled to re-assemble the recipes. With Belinda's help, and without regard to original placement, Alexa slid piled pages under the binder's stiff exterior cover. Vigorous door raps rattled nearby cabinet fronts.

"Just a minute," Alexa called out. She tucked Grandma's recipes into a cabinet drawer.

With his right fist raised, Brad's stern expression greeted Alexa after she opened the door with a doorknob twist. "It's not near four."

"This is too important. I need to talk face-to-face. We can do it on the porch."

"Belinda should hear."

"Prefer it be between us. Protects confidentiality."

"Belinda's my friend. Either say it to the both of us, or leave."

Brad entered the kitchen, said hello to Belinda, and took a kitchen table seat that faced them both. Alexa sensed his tight smile forced when he gazed at Samuel.

"Judge has entered an order under seal."

"What's that mean?" Alexa asked.

"Means it's for parties only. Public doesn't see."

"Why he'd do that?" Belinda asked. Her quizzical face had to have matched hers.

"Sometimes one never knows," Brad replied. "The judge hinted at concern there might not be two valid signatures on your grandmother's will."

"What?" Alexa jumped from her chair. "That can't be. First the delay, now this." Her backside faced the two adults as she bent forward to take a fork away from Samuel.

"If you'd look at me, Alexa, I'll explain." She straightened and pivoted. "Remember there were three signatures on your grandmother's will. I wasn't worried when your mother challenged Oscar Erickson because there were still two. The judge says new information warrants a hearing."

"Lawyer mumbo-jumbo. Speak plain English."

"Margaret Skelton of my office signed as one witness. Now, she says the signature doesn't appear to be hers."

"Crazy." Alexa's lips trembled. A twinge of being played zigzagged through her chest. "Didn't your eyeballs see her sign?"

"Watched your grandmother sign. Not the two office staff." Brad tucked his chin to his chest. "This has never happened before."

"Well, why can't you tell the judge you saw Grandma sign?"

Brad bit his lip. "I can, but, because I'm the attorney, it carries no legal weight. I can't be the attorney who drafts the will and a verifying witness."

"Another stupid law?" Belinda asked.

"Right," Brad replied. His gaze at her no longer than his spoken word.

Alexa's right hand crushed her left hand fingers. "Why would your receptionist lie?"

"Don't know." His eyes plead for mercy. "Really don't."

"You threaten to fire her to tell the truth?" Belinda asked.

"I'd get sued for wrongful termination. Legal staff learn self-preservation early."

Alexa's Gold

As Alexa paced the kitchen perimeter, her right hand fingertips tapped the laminated countertop. Twitches escalated to knot her stomach while she waited for her internal anger to subside. She stared at Brad. His blue blazer and nerdy pocket protector embodied bad news today and, she expected, again tomorrow.

"This must have to do with Mother." Her gaze switched from Samuel to Brad. "Mother will do anything to inherit the farm."

"I can't answer that," Brad said.

"So, what do I do?"

"Suggest you wait. Being a bull in a china shop won't help."

Alexa shrugged. Her stare out the kitchen window didn't change her disposition. "Still think its Mother's voodoo. Couldn't be anyone else. Her attorney know about the judge's order?" Brad nodded. "Then, that's it. Because I wouldn't accept her money, she's determined I lose the farm. Why else would she hire that big city Des Moines lawyer?"

"She's a point," Belinda said.

Belinda's support pleased Alexa.

"Maybe," Brad muttered, "but there's another complication."

"What?" Alexa asked. She lifted Samuel, slumped into the nearest table chair, and then placed him on her left knee. She'd always felt composed when hugging Samuel, even with his two fingers stuck into a drooling mouth.

"Rumor has it there's gold buried on the farm."

"Gold!" Belinda exclaimed. She jumped to her feet. "Wow."

"You said rumor, right?" Alexa asked.

"Said rumor. It's recycled; popped up when your grandmother tried to sell the farm."

"Then . . . if there's nothing else, you should leave. I've got to put Samuel down for his nap." Alexa arose and shifted Samuel to her right hip.

"But this gold." Belinda swiveled her eyes to Brad. "What about the gold?"

Alexa shook her head at Belinda before she gazed at Brad. "Grandma never said a single word about buried treasure. Her only treasure was family and the recipes she kept secret from all who either loved or knew her."

"You find the recipes?" Brad asked.

"No," Alexa lied. She pursed her lips before she covered her lips with her left hand.

Belinda's eyes darted between the three of them. Her voice stilled.

The kitchen door clicked close after Brad departed. Neither woman uttered a word until the blended sounds of an engine and crunched gravel ebbed.

"Why'd you lie about finding the recipes?" Belinda asked.

Alexa shrugged. "Don't know. Everyone asks about them. We've not yet read every one."

"You think there's a clue in them about this gold treasure?"

"Doubt it. The only gold mentioned in Grandma's recipes are the golden raisins she dumps into her muffins. Let me get Samuel tucked in."

"You should rest yourself."

"Good idea." Alexa's left hand grabbed the stair rail. She dismissed her fleeting thought to have Samuel walk the stairs. His drooping eyelids suggested he'd fall asleep faster if carried. She laid him on the bed coverlet in her old room as he continued to suck two fingers. She heard the kitchen door squeak. Belinda likely headed for a walk or a nap in her camper. "Sleep tight, Samuel." She kissed his forehead.

Alexa laid her head on the pillow in Grandma's room. Alexa's stomach twitches flared and died. Changes in position didn't quell the repetition. It would've been better if Grandma had sold the farm and deposited the money.

She turned onto her right side. Fluffed her pillow.

Brad's visit reminded her of the noon-hour gossip crows at Rosie's. No matter. The initial physical twinge of his fingers erased by the bad news he spewed. What had Grandma seen in him? There had to be competent lawyers in Lakeview. When she returned to the kitchen, she'd check the phone book.

Alexa wasn't lured to Iowa by the rationale close friends and neighbors represented the best societal mode. Mother bribed Brad's receptionist? When? How did Joe's fire figure in? Mother had left town without sleeping that last night in her paid motel room. Alexa figured Brad's firing his receptionist would torpedo his community standing. With the receptionist pregnant and maternity leave upcoming, Brad smart to anticipate she'd never return after her baby's birth.

Yet, Alexa resumed full-time work after Samuel's birth. Thus, Brad had no guarantee.

Alexa flopped to her left side. How could she nap with vital questions unanswered? She cast her feet off the bed. She tiptoed across the hall to confirm Samuel slept.

Undisturbed in Grandma's room, she extracted from a dresser drawer the tidy bundle of Grandma's saved letters tied in red ribbon. Guilt twinges flooded Alexa as she stretched the ribbon's knot before she sank into Grandma's cushioned chair. She reached to spread the window curtains and espied Belinda enter her camper.

Single digit postage stamps authenticated their age. All but one came from Grandpa. The odd letter lacked a return address. Opening it first, Alexa read Brandon Erickson's plea asking Grandma to reconsider her rejection of his affections. No words other than the name and that his family would soon buy land nearby gave Alexa any present day clue as to the writer's identity.

Alexa sighed. She searched the remaining eight letters for another from Brandon. No luck. If he'd written other letters, Grandma hadn't saved them. Had Joe known or been related to this Brandon. A sword of ignorance pricked Alexa's mind.

Fate either tricked or abandoned her. Faded ink thwarted her postmark date letter sort.

She opened one from Grandpa. The sweet words didn't correlate with his remembered gruff voice. But then, he was courting, not stomping into the kitchen clad in patched overalls, stained by dirt, farm animals, and his own sweat.

Alexa couldn't believe the words she read. Her Grandpa wrote he worked for Al Capone. He explained he wasn't proud of it, but his speakeasy bartender job in the Wisconsin woods paid twice as much as other depression-era jobs. Grandpa cautioned Grandma not to reply.

Alexa unfolded the crackly page of a third letter written six months later. Grandpa promised he'd soon visit Grandma. He couldn't articulate many details other than that a gang member had ripped off Al Capone. Two bags of heisted bank gold coins stolen. The gang thief found shot. Capone fumed the gold not recovered in the dead man's possession.

Alexa spread the remaining letters across Grandma's bed. She searched for a second gold reference. None. The excitement of Grandpa's mystery gold supplanted the active fragments of her anger Brad had aroused. Deep breaths slowed her rapid pulse.

She raced outside to tell Belinda. Alexa urged her bewildered friend to join her in Grandma's bedroom where the letters remained scattered across the bed.

After Alexa closed the bedroom door so as not to disturb Samuel, she waited with bated breath for Belinda to read Grandpa's two letters that referenced Al Capone and the murdered gang member. Alexa shifted from one foot to the other to still her strong desire to interrupt.

Belinda's eyes widened. Her hands trembled. "Sooo the rumors are more than rumors."

"If the gold's stolen, we can't keep it."

Belinda cocked her head. "Could be a reward."

"More likely we'll mimic the mustachioed Geraldo Rivera who ballyhooed a national television audience to break into Capone's suspected hiding place to discover only sand and an old bottle and no treasure."

"You gonna call Geraldo and tell him he should've run a metal detector across your grandparents' farm?"

"Heck no."

"You going to rent a metal detector?"

Alexa summoned all the courage she could. "Maybe."

"Way to go girl."

"Not right now. Doesn't the person who owns the land keep whatever is found?"

"Guess that's so. You going to ask Brad if that's right?"

Alexa crossed her arms tight. "Never."

"He's your attorney. And he mentioned the gold to us earlier today."

"Yeah, and he said it wasn't a confidential conversation. He might be an attorney, but it's related to Grandma's will. Plus, he hasn't been too adept at getting the court to approve my farm ownership."

"You going to wait until the judge gives you title or whatever?"

"See little choice."

"We could be Sherlock and Watson."

Alexa laughed. "You want to be the smart one?"

"You bet. Call me Dr. Watson."

Alexa reinserted brittle letters into their faded envelopes.

"Wait a minute," Belinda said. "You didn't let me read all those."

"Not much there. Mushy romantic stuff."

"A lost art now that cell phones and the Internet dominate our lives." Belinda's right hand reached for a letter. "What about a clue to the gold's location?"

Donan Berg

"Don't think so. Grandpa didn't steal the coins. He merely tended bar for Capone in Wisconsin, not Iowa, and Grandpa says he heard it all secondhand."

"If your grandfather was smart, doubt he'd write about hobnobbing with the thief. But he had to if the gang all drank at the same speakeasy. Lots of ways he could've known where Capone's gold hid. Don't believe he innocently tripped over it."

"Your brain's working overtime. Slow down or you'll have steam whistling out your ears."

"But, if we found the gold." Belinda's hands clasped in prayer-mode. "Heavens the limit."

"My intuition says there's no gold." Alexa retied the red ribbon. "We need to think this through. I'm thirsty."

Alexa placed the bundle into Grandma's lower dresser drawer. Belinda led them to the kitchen where both filled a large glass with iced tea.

Belinda sipped. "Your grandmother left you an exciting puzzle."

"We're probably fantasizing more than what's real."

"If your grandfather didn't have the gold in his possession, how'd he buy this farm?"

"Inherited it." Alexa leaned against the kitchen counter. "Great-great-granddad staked a claim to it in the 1862 land rush created by the Homestead Act."

"You sure?"

"That's what I remember Grandma saying."

Belinda refilled her glass halfway. "You need to contact Brad."

Alexa stiffened her resolve against Belinda's repeated pressure. "Don't think so."

"Don't be headstrong. This isn't about your feelings. Ask Brad if he'll check the county land records if you don't have an abstract?"

"No abstract I know of. You think it'll help?"

Samuel, his hair tousled, toddled into the kitchen.

130

"Mommy, my pants wet."

Alexa realized Samuel's predicament could have but one cause. With her arms under his armpits, she scooped up Samuel and carried him toward the bathroom. "Belinda, forget the gold until our next trip."

Chapter Eleven

Samuel squirmed on Alexa's right hip the entire distance between her pickup and their eighteenth-floor apartment. She snapped at him once, then felt guilty. Her probation office boss, not her son, had given her twice as many files as her colleagues. His justification she was the most competent struck her as both lame and earned.

The minute she and Samuel entered her apartment, Samuel tried and failed to grab the box of KFC chicken she'd purchased. She pulled out his chair with it booster. He grinned and scrambled onto it. When her son smiled, her world rejoiced. Her right hand stretched forward to press Samuel's hands together. She recited a memorized prayer to bless them and their food. Two plates, two glasses of milk, and ten chicken pieces with coleslaw completed their dinner.

Before she'd eaten the extra chicken wing, her cell phone's programmed ring tone announced Brad's call. She answered his question that her return to Iowa remained indefinite. When she asked about the farm's abstract, he asked her to hold while he retrieved it from the office safe.

"How did Grandpa Anderson come to own the farm?" Alexa asked.

"Inherited it from his father. Land ownership chain

begins with a land grant."

If Brad was in his office, what other ears heard her questions? Alexa tamped her paranoia to focus on being discreet. "Did Grandpa inherit two hundred sixty acres?"

"No. Homestead Act grants were one hundred sixty acres. Hold on." Alexa heard the rustle of paper. *Thank God no voices.* "The year isn't clear, but in the Nineteen Thirties one hundred acres were purchased."

"Don't worry about dates. Who purchased the extra acres?"

"Henri Anderson."

Alexa released a pent up breath. "That's Grandpa. You've answered my question."

"Which was what?"

"Why Grandma owned two hundred sixty acres."

"Is that important?"

Alexa knew its importance to her; however, she wasn't ready to clue Brad in. "Belinda and I had a dispute whether pioneers got one hundred sixty or two hundred sixty acres. With what you tell me, I lost and owe Belinda a drink."

"Sorry. When are you coming back to Lakeview?"

Alexa's glance confirmed Samuel ripped chicken she'd given him. "Don't know."

"Well, next week I have a legal seminar sponsored by John Marshall Law School. I'll be in Chicago and maybe you'd be free to let me buy you that drink you must buy Belinda?"

"What day?"

"Wednesday."

"From experience I know I won't be able to get Samuel's babysitter for that day." Samuel's eyes widen at Alexa's mention of his name.

"Bring him along."

"I won't bring him to a bar."

"We don't have to go to a bar. We can stroll in Grant Park. Find a hot dog vendor. I haven't had a Chicago hot dog in I don't know how long. It'll be fun. I bet Samuel will enjoy it. From here I can visualize the mustard streaks across his cheeks."

Alexa laughed. "Can you call me the night before you come?"

"You'll—" Brad's strong voice interrupted. "You'll do it then?"

"I guess, but—"

"No buts; I'll call next week Tuesday."

With Brad's promise, Alexa closed her phone. She wasn't positive she'd done the right thing. If Samuel benefitted, that would be a plus. With a wet washcloth she cleaned Samuel's face and hands and let him toddle into the living room where she kept his toys. His right fist battered the keys on a toy to emit barnyard animal noises. Samuel giggled at the oinks and moos.

Loud crashing sounds, punctuated by accusatory shouts, filtered through her apartment wall. She readied a call to nine-one-one, but the commotion stopped. Made Alexa think a household male not always an asset.

Alexa speed-dialed Belinda and listened.

"How am I to get a pay grade increase if that stupid supervisor of ours gives me nothing but simple cases any chimp with a clipboard can handle?"

"Calm down, Belinda. You want to take two of my cases? We won't mention it until they're complete and you sign off."

"Too risky. We'll both get fired for insubordination. I was just venting."

Alexa sat cross-legged on her sofa. "Brad called. Grandpa inherited his first one hundred sixty acres and then purchased one hundred acres."

"You think with the stolen money?"

"It was the Depression. Where else would he get money? Wealthy folks didn't tend bar."

"You tell Brad about your Granddad and Capone?"

133

"No. And I don't think he suspects why I wanted abstract info. He said he's coming to Chicago next week and offered to take Samuel and me to Grant Park."

"Cool. You accepted, right?"

Alexa hesitated. "Sorta."

"Don't you see what's happening?" Alexa, her nerves still taut after a tense work day, commanded herself not to let Belinda goad her. "He's hot after your charms."

"Doubt it. He's being nice so I don't sue him for messing up Grandma's will."

"For a probation officer trained to detect lies and hidden agendas, you're naive in your own life. Why should he worry about you suing him? He's got malpractice insurance. He need not keep showing up at the farm when you're there. Now he shows up in Chicago. Did you ask him when he made reservations?"

"No."

"Those ladies in Rosie's more on the mark than you've given them credit for."

Alexa bypassed Belinda's matchmaking to picture herself in twenty years. One image lacked appeal. It'd be a cold day in Hell, MI, before she spent her best years baking on a farm in Iowa.

"You finish your Grandma's recipes yet?"

"Not yet. They're still in my suitcase."

Alexa switched the conversation to the drink she owed Belinda. Samuel had abandoned his toys and mimicked Alexa's crossed legs as he sat four feet in front of the television to watch animals and people fall and create funny faces. When dad tossed his son a ball, Alexa appreciated the act's love, not the batted ball hitting the father's crotch.

After Belinda piled on with additional criticisms of their mutual boss, Alexa begged off and offered to renew their discussion the next day at lunch.

Alexa, to save Samuel's eyes, doubled his distance

from the TV screen and hugged him as they sat on the sofa.
"Sucker, Mommy?"
"Not tonight. Next week."

Chapter Twelve

As a defensive move, Alexa dressed Samuel in a yellow
shirt the color of mustard. While his jeans matched hers,
her patent-leather shoes ranked higher on the stylish pop
culture scale than Samuel's sneakers. Her black shoe color
in sharp contrast to a tucked white blouse she accented with
a necklace of bluish stones and wooden beads.

The night before she'd changed the plan for meeting
Brad. They'd tour Millennium Park after a rendezvous at
the park's Monroe Street underground garage exit.

Conditioned to spy a pair of khaki pants and blue
blazer, Alexa almost missed him in his beige cargo shorts
and short-sleeved polo shirt emblazoned with palm leaves.
She should've known he'd wear black socks with sandals.

"You guys ready for a hot dog."

Alexa smelled Chicago's distinct hot dog aroma,
accented by a slightly pungent onion.

"Will three Chicago dogs be enough?" He displayed
tubular, foil-wrapped packages that warmed the adjacent
air. "Fries and three waters are in my bag."

"Samuel's ready. Let's follow the Chase Promenade
and find a bench or a low wall."

"Come on, Samuel." Brad grabbed Samuel's right hand.
"Your pretty mother can take your other hand."

Alexa's cheeks warmed. She hoped it wasn't too
noticeable as she let the flattery go unacknowledged and

grasped Samuel's left hand. Daffodils and tulips bloomed along the path. Sweet grass scents filled her nostrils. Within four minutes, a free bench appeared in front of them. Brad released Samuel's hand to lengthen his strides and claim the bench as theirs.

When Samuel and Alexa caught up, he plopped the toddler in the bench's middle before he waved a French fry under Samuel's nose. Samuel bit off half and then, mixed with spittle, spit the fry into the air to initiate gravity's descending arc onto the sidewalk.

"Samuel, no. Stop that." Alexa scooped up the mushy fry with a napkin.

Samuel stood on the bench and, without a French fry, spit a second time.

"Do your lips hurt, honey? Was it too hot?" Her fingertip wet with Samuel's salvia failed to discover a blister bubble. A visual inspection disclosed no extra redness.

Brad licked a fry. "Salty, not hot." He wiped a third fry with a napkin.

Samuel bit it twice and swallowed.

The hot dog foil warmed Alexa's right hand as her errant mustard package squeeze yellowed her finger. When sucked the mustard taste overpowered her taste buds. She tore an unadorned hot dog into bite-sized pieces for Samuel. "Sit down, honey." While they ate, all seated, the conversational topics didn't stray from the safety of park amenities, the weather, and the street hubbub in the nation's windy city.

While Samuel didn't ignore Alexa, especially when she held his hot dog, his attention gravitated toward Brad's playful French fry zoom-zoom into the hanger of Samuel's mouth and Brad's help with tilting Samuel's water bottle. All contributed to Samuel's focus on Brad.

Picnic debris collected, Brad asked Alexa, "When's your next visit to the farm?"

"End of next week. Margaret still at work?"

"Today, yes; next week, no. She starts maternity leave on the advice of her physician."

"Does she continue to claim she didn't sign as a witness to Grandma's will?"

Brad hooked his thumbs in his front pockets. "Unfortunately, yes."

"What does she gain by lying?"

"Can't answer that. Supposedly, it's her mother, Lydia, that's behind it."

Alexa stared at the hand-in-hand teenage couple strolling within earshot. She brushed an imaginary bug off Samuel's shoulder to disguise her unease with strangers tuning in. When she excised her anxiety, she gazed at Brad. "That's confusing."

"I'd agree, but the theory expressed in hush-hush terms says Lydia Skelton's still upset she lost a commission when your grandmother didn't sell to Oscar Erickson two years ago."

Alexa shook her head. "That's hard to believe. Realtors must lose sales."

"The farm sale would've meant a huge commission, even split. Thereafter her firm dismissed employees until one part-timer ran the office." Brad's gaze bounced off his shoes. "Two different townspeople claim they saw your mother and Lydia in conversation."

"Doesn't surprise me. Mother will manipulate anyone to gain ownership of Grandma's farm." Alexa stared into Brad's eyes. "When will the judge tell the world I own the farm?"

Brad's unblinking eyes revealed little to Alexa. "Expect any day. Though, can't promise."

Alexa broke off her stare before her self-consciousness gene burst. Loud shouts broke the silence. Energetic pre-teens raced toward the street intersection a half block distant.

Not encouraged by the teens, but by a strutting seagull,
Samuel toddled off to attempt a tail feather touch. Brad
bolted after him. When the two males rejoined Alexa, the
conversation retraced everyday mundane topics. After two
hours, Alexa thanked Brad a second time for the food and
announced she'd have to get Samuel home to bed. Brad
replied he understood and offered to escort her into the
underground garage. She rebuffed him. He turned away as
she carried Samuel to the concrete stairs for their descent to
her pickup.

* * *

Samuel's eyes were at half-staff when Alexa laid him on
his bed. Tired herself, she flipped her shoes. They landed
near her entry door and Alexa detoured left to unload the
dishwasher. She retrieved her cell phone from her purse,
released her jeans' waist button, and stretched out on the
soft contours of her living room sofa, content not to watch
mindless TV. She tried to wipe her mind clear of all
questions, all worry, and all fear, past and present.

When darkness crept in the window, her pensive state
interrupted when her breath hitched. She owed Belinda a
call. Without recall of when she had powered off her cell
phone, she rose to one elbow and brought it to life. The
lighted display showed Mother's seven p.m. voice message
awaited. Alexa listened. Mother, in tears, claimed an Iowa
sheriff had issued a person-of-interest warrant to question
her regarding Joe Erickson's mobile home fire. She pleaded
for Alexa's help.

Living room objects blurred on Alexa. She couldn't
focus on clear outlines of a nineteen-inch television on a
metal stand nor three sixteen-by-twenty-inch pictures with
rocks, waves, and a shoreline. Quiet, subtle shivers slowed
her call to Belinda.

"Your mother going to drive back?" Belinda asked.

"Don't know." Alexa desired to pull away from the

possibility. "Haven't returned her call."

"You ask Brad about it?"

She should've called Mother first. "Didn't get Mother's message until afterwards."

"So, how'd it go? You and the hunk."

"Not too exciting. Samuel had the best time. He ran and tumbled all over that outdoor theatre lawn. Laughed when Brad tickled him."

"He tickle you too?"

"Belinda!" With her exclamation, the phone slipped from her right hand to lay on her stomach. She raised it to her right ear. "Don't let your imagination run wild; wasn't that kind of evening. More like a genteel church social."

"You two make plans to go out again?"

"Not exactly. Said I'm going to the farm two weekends from now. He didn't promise the judge would end my farm title wait by then. And there's my need to scope out Lydia Skelton."

"Why? She's not your Realtor."

"Hmmm. Her name keeps popping up."

"Maybe she's just pushy. Wants to mettle in everybody's business."

"Could be. Mother's trying to reach me. She has to be frantic. See you at work tomorrow."

Alexa's phone showed a new voice mail. She ignored it and overcame her dread to speed-dial Mother. Alexa refused to ponder how Mother would extricate herself this time. Not because Mother had to have everything her way, that helped, but because Mother's entitlement perception focused on material things.

"I'm sorry, Mother. Samuel and I went to the park and then Belinda called."

"That Iowa sheriff threatened me." Her voice volume dipped to be no stronger than wilted flower petals. "He says if I don't answer questions in his office, he'll have me arrested."

139

"You ask your attorney?"

"Don't have an attorney. He wanted too much money. Said that the will with two valid witness signatures didn't give me much chance against you. He praised Grandma's lawyer."

Strands of confusion wrapped themselves inside Alexa's skull, conflicted her brain. Brad had said Margaret Skelton denied her signature on the will. Alexa didn't infer that from Mother's comments. Yet, Mother could be mixed-up.

"You speak with Lydia Skelton when you were in Iowa?"

"She sought me out. Twice asked if I knew the whereabouts of Grandma's recipes. Crazy cockamamie thing about a contest between county ladies. You?"

"I said I found no recipe box." Alexa crossed her left-hand middle finger across her index finger. As stated, she spoke truth. She should've felt guilty, but didn't. "Oscar Erickson asked me about an apple cake recipe. What about you?"

"Not Mr. Erickson, but apple cake, that's the exact recipe Lydia mentioned when she tracked me down the second time. You think they know something we don't?"

The question surprised Alexa. Rare was the occasion Mother sought her advice. Today's question maybe more factual information than advice.

"Small town secrets. Like the gold rumors." Alexa wished to erase her words; shove them in a folder labeled not spoken. She wasn't embarrassed, nor had the words solicited rebuke.

They ignited a spark in Mother's voice. "What gold? Where?"

"Unconfirmed rumors that your father stole, found, or hijacked gold Al Capone snatched in a bank robbery during prohibition."

"My father violated neither law nor the Ten

140

Commandments, not even in a dream. He was a god-fearing man."

"Then that's it. We should forget it." Alexa waited, concerned the line had gone dead, but her phone's connection bar blinked life.

"You bringing up your grandfather reminds me that a person's good name is all we have. You driving to Iowa soon?"

"Weekend after next."

Alexa listened with no deep interest in Mother's proposal she drive to Chicago and ride with Alexa to Lakeview. Mother countered Alexa's two quibbling objections of traffic and inconvenience. Alexa ended their conversation resigned to the fact it would be a family journey to Grandma's farm.

Chapter Thirteen

Belinda's SUV rescued Alexa from having her mother squished in the middle of her pickup's front seat. Ensconced in the back seat with Samuel, Alexa believed he enjoyed their ride the best of all. An animated Samuel giggled at her contorted faces, grins, and tickles.

Two hours of hypnotic rolling-vehicle motion and Belinda's sounds-of-the-seashore CD tired Samuel. His eyelids drooped and Alexa savored the cherry Lifesaver she sucked.

Mother, her head slightly turned rearward, asked, "Is the little bastard sleeping?"

While she flexed her fingers open and closed, Alexa seethed, ready to choke Mother at her next insult. Alexa forced her stare into the rearview mirror to alert Belinda to her smoldering inferno. Alexa bit her lip, cursed Mother under her breath, and forced an exterior calm.

The photographs of Mother at twenty showed her to be stunning, at thirty to be gorgeous, and at forty to be provocative. At fifty Mother exhibited crow's feet, tiny chin sags, and gray in her eyebrows and hair. Wild schemes that Alexa despised corrupted Mother's personality in her sixties to the extent ex-husbands ridiculed Mother by stories of her well-traveled broomstick as testimony to her special hagdom.

Belinda's smile in the rearview mirror cautioned Alexa to be cool and remember her promise to be a saint, if only for a weekend. Alexa didn't doubt her physical strength. Mother's amped up guilt trips threatened Alexa's psychic fortitude to beget mental tremors and nightmares.

Between gritted teeth, Alexa shot back, "Your grandson's fine mother."

Belinda's smile widened. Alexa imagined the "harrumph" look on Mother's face.

Samuel, awakened from his nap, again delighted Alexa with his giggles.

SUV brakes rocked Alexa forward, her right palm slammed the headrest of Mother's seat. "Sorry," Belinda exclaimed. "Looks like we're last to the farm's party."

Alexa strained to see the commotion beyond Belinda's windshield. In her Grandma's farmyard were two sheriff cars, a long-bed tow truck, and a small crane mounted on a truck bed.

"An officer's directing me to drive straight ahead to the barn," Belinda said.

Alexa leaned sideways for a window view. The Sheriff, facing Joe's mobile home, waved his hands upward. A workman wrapped long belts, anchored to a winch cable hook, around the mobile home shell. Since keeping Samuel safe easier in the SUV, Alexa stayed put. Mother slid out of the front passenger seat and skirted a sheriff car to stand next to Oscar Erickson.

"They'll never lift that mobile home chassis onto one truck," Alexa said.

"It's sawed in half," Belinda replied.

Samuel struggled against his car seat harness. "In a minute, honey." Alexa released Samuel and held him on her lap. "See. There's a second tow truck."

The three watched until two flatbed trucks hauled the entire mobile home from Grandma's. With Samuel on her hip, and Belinda trailing, Alexa strode to Oscar.

"Does this mean the investigation's finished?" she asked Oscar.

"For me. Sheriff will impound the front where the fire started. I said scrap everything else. At least it will not stand as a grief monument. Cemetery does that well enough."

Sheriff Edwards exited his cruiser to join the assembled onlookers.

"Mrs. Hovey." Alexa's and Mother's eyes gazed on the Sheriff. "I'd like a word, perhaps in the kitchen." He gazed at Oscar. "Can we keep the tarp? Crime lab desires to return and rake through the debris under the home."

Oscar nodded. "Long as you need. See ya all later."

Alexa recognized Old Betsy's putt-putt. Samuel imitated her wave.

Belinda and Mother proceeded to the kitchen via the rear porch. When Alexa and Samuel arrived, the Sheriff sat with Belinda and Mother at the kitchen table.

"Do I need a lawyer?" Mother asked.

"I can't answer that." The Sheriff removed a small notepad from his uniform's breast pocket. "I only have a couple questions."

He gazed into everyone's faces, lingering longer at Mother's. Alexa massaged her left temple; the spot where her tension headache pain settled. *Sheriff could ask two*

questions on the phone, not issue a warrant. What made
Mother so important?

"A farm coffee can discovery exhibits a curiosity.
Anybody here throw one away?"

After all shook their heads no, he jotted a note on his
pad.

Belinda broke the silence. "I'll play twenty questions.
Anything in the can?"

"Matches imprinted with Lakeview Motel advertising,
candle stub, and a wooden match."

Belinda assumed command. "Those could belong to
anyone, including a town visitor."

"You're right," Sheriff replied. "If anyone of you
misplaced or threw away the can, then my inquiry could be
closed. Since you all deny, it's in the unexplained
category."

"Sheriff, you said you wanted to speak with me,"
Mother interjected.

"Sure did. What time did you leave the Lakeview Motel
the night Joe Erickson died?"

All eyes became fixated on Mother.

"Four, maybe five in the afternoon. Definitely before
suppertime."

"You have any receipts for gas, a meal, or perhaps
another motel for that night."

"Can't say I do." Alexa had expected Mother's sweet,
charming voice. Instead, Mother surprised her with a
matter-of-fact tone that ricocheted as more believable.

"Well, you check and keep in touch."

Nervous energy evaporated from Alexa's pores. Her
headache and queasy stomach steadied.

"If you'll excuse me?" The Sheriff stood and executed
a small bow to grab his wide-brimmed hat from the kitchen
table. "Need to check if the tow trucks made it."

The rear porch screen banged without being slammed.
Brad's right hand caught it before it struck a second time.

Alexa returned her gaze to Brad after a glance at Mother. He stood half in and half out the kitchen door.

"You bring news?" Alexa's voice wistful.

"Not really. Judge had an emergency hospitalization."

"He going to live?" Mother asked in her sweet voice.

"Expect so. Appendectomy's usually aren't fatal."

Mother stood, extracted a glass from a cabinet, filled it with water, and asked if any bed upstairs had sheets. Alexa replied all did and guided Mother to unpack in the third bedroom. She cracked the window in her old bedroom to freshen the air with a cross-breeze.

For her descent, Alexa grabbed the stairs handrail. She gazed at Brad. "Iced tea, perhaps?"

"That'd be great."

Belinda pointed to the empty chair vacated by Alexa's mother. He sat.

Alexa served the iced tea with a question to Brad. "Why's the Sheriff messing with an old used coffee can?"

"It's not the can so much as what was in it."

From the corner of her eye, Alexa caught Samuel's wave at Brad. Brad didn't respond, a glass to his lips. Samuel twisted in his chair to climb down. Alexa lifted him. "Don't say anything." She flipped on the TV, adjusted its rabbit ears, and left Samuel in the parlor.

Belinda spoke with Alexa next to her. "We heard what the Sheriff says is in the can."

Brad's right hand set his glass on the table. "Gossip is there's a matchbook like found burnt in Joe's trailer." Befuddlement ringed Belinda's eyes.

Alexa shared Belinda's puzzlement. She hadn't seen half-burned paper survive the fire. She poured herself a glass of iced water and squared her gaze at Brad. "So? Bet there's thousands."

"Fingerprints." He displayed his left hand, palm out. "Theory is arsonist carried two matchbooks in case he or she messed one up. When one not used, tossed it into the can once the gas or diesel fuel had been sprinkled around the mobile home. But you're right. Triple-A tells motorists to put a candle and matches in a can in case they get stalled in winter."

Belinda coughed. Alexa plopped into a chair.

"You all right?" Alexa rotated her head toward her friend.

"Probably nothing. Maybe I'm allergic to June bugs. Never been in the wilds this often in years. Think I'll take your mother's example and lay down or crash with Samuel." Alexa understood Belinda wasn't comfortable being the odd number. "Call me for the next meal."

"Let's walk." Alexa rose. "Inspect what those haulers left."

She didn't wait for Brad's agreement, expected it. Halfway across the farmyard, he, with a half-full glass in his left hand, caught up. A staked tarp denied Alexa a view of Joe's mobile home site. The spruce branches hid whatever debris they caught.

"I shouldn't ask." Alexa decided to anyway. "You eager for Margaret to return?"

"In a way. Stan's secretary complains every day."

"Maybe that's not so bad?" Alexa hadn't meant to challenge. While these "Green Acres" not her lifestyle, most residents friendly, hateful glares few. The bright side included no money spent to redo her wardrobe for weekend visits.

"You might change your mind if exposed to what's what. Margaret couldn't keep a case file straight for two weeks when she learned of her pregnancy."

His words baffled Alexa. "Joy can do that."

"Can tell you first hand it wasn't joy. Her quick trip to Vegas caught the office shorthanded. Then the café whispers that Carl, her older husband, although legally divorced, had had a vasectomy after his first wife gave birth to their second child."

146

Alexa halted her stroll to the old car. "Complicated, huh?"

"Margaret always desired to keep her baby. I walked in on a heated discussion between Margaret and Lydia, her mother. The clipped comments harsh and also telling. Lydia took Margaret's decision personal. The most vivid when Lydia asked Margaret how she could sit in church Sunday while the congregation ladies, behind self-righteous smiles, blessed themselves for waiting until marriage."

Alexa empathized with the obvious agony Margaret experienced. "Many in this world can be so spiteful without ever having walked in another's person's shoes."

"I guess." He gazed at Grandma's house. "Can't thank you enough for the picnic in Chicago. No one will ever build a huge, stainless steel bean in an Iowa cornfield."

"Shoeless Joe Jackson played big league baseball in Chicago and he shepherded his eight teammates out of an Iowa cornfield."

"Only in the movies. Only in the movies."

"A lot happens in the movies that never occurs in real life." She really believed that. Endless movies had distracted her while she marked time for Samuel's birth.

Brad left Alexa's side for the tarp's far side. He raised his right hand. A shiny medal dangled from a sooty chain. "St. Christopher medal."

Alexa, careful not to step on the tarp, approached him for a closer look. "Mother hangs one of those from her car's rearview mirror."

"Likely has no significance. There's millions."

Brad bent forward and continued to survey the ground. Alexa didn't want to hear of further connection between Mother and Joe's fire. "Tell me, when you were growing up, what's the worst thing you did?"

Brad let the medal swing. "Don't know."

"C'mon. I've heard farm boys are the most mischievous."

147

"Didn't live on a farm; lived in town. My father owned a car repair garage."

"Close enough." Alexa shoved both hands into her front jeans pockets. "So, you gonna tell me or do I have to do an Internet search."

"Ha! Good luck with that." Brad's tone not the least bit angered or annoyed.

"Bet you carved lover's names on trees or into a wood bench?"

He stepped to where his footprints had been. "You'll never know."

Alexa followed. "I can keep a secret."

"Cross your heart and hope to die?"

Lifted from her pocket, her right hand crossed her heart. "And hope to die."

Brad laughed. "Well, guess it won't hurt none after all these years."

"Anybody get hurt?"

"Almost."

"Sorry." Her word barely loud enough to crack the whisper ranks.

"Don't be. I said almost."

Alexa's curiosity raced. Even if Brad's tale wasn't earth shattering or worthy of the Guinness Book of Records, it would be theirs, not monumental, but shared. She gazed into his face to coax it out of him.

"I was in sixth grade. Halloween always tested us for new pranks. The prior year we'd tipped Samuel Jorgensen's outhouse. Took four of us."

"Not original." Alexa's right-hand fingers scratched her neck. "Chicago kids tip sheds."

"Occupied? Mr. Jorgensen ranted for an entire week. Pounded his fist at the cafe and vowed to teach the hooligans a lesson. He named every boy in town. My friend Kenny heard his challenge: we'd never tip his outhouse again."

148

"Bet you did."

Mirth circled his response. "Yeah. And he was in it."

"You're kidding?"

Brad shook his head. "Next year there wasn't a moon. We waited until after ten o'clock. We figured he'd hide in the shadows alongside his house. Two of us watched for an hour and didn't see him. His dog barked inside his house. When the dog stopped, we figured he'd given up."

Alexa didn't need to guess. She encouraged an animated Brad. "But you were wrong?"

"First Kenny crept to the outhouse. Four of us followed. Kenny whispered, 'One, two, three.' We all pushed as hard as we could. A big yell filled the yard before the outhouse crashed."

"Did you watch it fall?"

"Not on your life. I ran." Brad gazed toward the spruces. "The yell wasn't one of us."

"And . . . ." A twinge weaved its way through Alexa's mind. What if he turned the tables and asked her the same question?

"We later guessed the reason we didn't see Mr. Jorgensen was because he sat inside the outhouse. Guessed he didn't hear us to step out and scare us off."

"You do it the next year?"

"No. We heard he wrapped the outhouse in bare wire connected to a battery. Should ask you the same question."

Her head's little voice piped up. "See, be careful what you ask?" *Shut up.* Alexa glanced skyward and counted to ten. "I'll have to think and get back to you."

Brad smiled. "I'll make sure you do."

To fill their elongated silence, she asked, "You know anyone with tandem wheels?"

"Three or four. Why?"

"That's what Joe said. Showed him the wheel marks near the machine shed I thought strange. Pretty common, he said. Want to see?"

Donan Berg

"Wouldn't concern me unless stuff was being stolen."

Alexa wasn't about to mention theft. She sought diversion. "Would Lydia Skelton be one?" She realized her inquiry was a stab in the dark.

"Her eldest son has such a pickup."

"That Margaret's husband?"

"That's him. Doubt his truck. He and Joe never got along. Fights in local bars."

Alexa felt taken in. Joe said he stayed out of bars. "You sure?"

"Reliable sources. After his divorce, Carl Skelton pretty much lived in the Wapsi Bar. Joe waited outside one night, demanded an apology for the untruths Carl spread about Joe gypping one of his friends in a snowmobile sale. It all sounded adolescent."

With Brad's explanation, Joe's honesty score rose. For the world's reality, it mattered little. For Alexa's confidence in judging men, it meant the world, a validation.

Alexa grew mentally tired of tracing the tarp indentations and wondering what truth lay underneath. "Depressing to just stand here. I'm heading to the porch." She didn't gaze at the void she left until she sat on the porch swing.

Brad caught up with her. He leaned his right thigh against the porch railing.

After several creaky swings, Alexa asked, "You have family in Lakeview?"

"Two uncles, half a dozen nieces and nephews."

Alexa wondered if Mother scoured the attic for recipes. Saw the plank she'd pried loose. "What about parents?"

Brad stiffened. "Deceased."

Alexa sensed by his facial-muscle tightness her question unchained an anvil in his chest. She hurried to change the subject. "If you graduated law school in Chicago, why not stay there?"

"Thought about it. Dismissed the idea. Grades not high

150

enough for the big firms and, without family or political connections, I'd drown without a wellspring of clients."

She hesitated several seconds. His answer offered her nothing for a positive follow-up.

"Please don't get mad. I never found Chicago girls, sorry, women likeable. Too demanding is the polite way I can describe it."

"We're not all that way." She had to attempt a sisterhood defense even if there existed quantifiable truth in his judgment.

"Hopefully I didn't say all. Didn't mean all, only the ones whose path crossed mine."

Alexa refused to test Fate and ask the sixty-four-dollar personal question. She harbored reservations about him, humongous reservations. If he'd done the job Grandma hired him for, she wouldn't be sitting on the porch with him, her bank account withdrawn to its last two hundred dollars, and her next paycheck earmarked to pay her apartment rent.

The kitchen door opened.

"Your mother asked about our next meal," Belinda said.

"There's spaghetti, bread, and meat sauce in the bag I brought."

"That'll work." Belinda went inside.

"Guess I should go," Brad said. "Perhaps . . . . When we spoke of movies—"

The crunch of gravel and sliding tires interrupted. Two sheriff cars entered the farmyard. A third blocked the farmyard entrance. Sheriff Edwards and a uniformed woman officer strode to and ascended the porch steps. "Is Mrs. Hovey here?" the Sheriff asked.

Alexa stood. "Y-e-s." Brad shuffled sideways. His left hand cupped her right elbow.

"If you'll stay here, Caroline will go inside the house and request she step outside. We've a warrant for her arrest."

"No. NO," Alexa shouted. Brad's grip restrained her.

Mother edged onto the porch, nonstop tears streamed her cheeks. Caroline marched behind her. Sheriff Edwards advised Mother she was under arrest for arson and attempted murder. He handed his cuffs to Caroline who clamped them onto Mother's wrists, arms behind her back.

A frantic Alexa yelled at Samuel. "Honey, get into the house."

Belinda's hands on Samuel's shoulders squired him into the kitchen. Alexa collapsed onto the swing. Belinda allowed the screen door to bang behind her. "Samuel's in the parlor with his Legos." She gazed directly at Alexa. "You okay?"

"Don't know." The emotional inflection strange to Alexa's ears.

"Brad," Belinda asked, "Isn't there something you can do?"

"Let me talk to the Sheriff." He cleared the porch steps in one bound.

"Why's this happening?" Alexa's wail circled the tree tops. She fought to steady herself. "This is my worst nightmare. Mother's not a saint, but she's no devil either."

Belinda sat on the swing with her right arm around Alexa's shoulders. "Deep breaths. We'll get through this. Maybe Brad can help."

"He hasn't so far."

Belinda brushed two strands of Alexa's hair from her cheeks. "It's all a mistake. We don't need F. Lee Bailey or Johnnie Cochran. Brad can straighten it out."

Alexa buried her face in her hands.

"Consider this a case our stupid, SOB of a supervisor has given us, or you. Against all odds we'll . . . you'll prevail. Savor a little glimmer of we won one for the gipper."

Alexa splayed her hands as if she played peek-a-boo with Samuel. "What?"

"Okay. So we're not football fans or Ronald Reagan movie fans. You get the picture, right? You're Superman, Batman, David Hasselhoff, whoever battles to win against daunting odds."

Alexa laughed.

"That a girl. That's the spirit. When Brad returns you square those shoulders and light a fire under him. He'll be Perry Mason."

If only Belinda could forever soothe her fears. "What would I ever do without you?"

"Take Samuel and me to dinner."

Alexa tied a bow on her promise never to be beholden to any one person. "Why?"

"Overcooked the spaghetti into mush and burnt the bread."

Alexa wiped dried tears from her cheeks. With a pinch of impatience, she clutched Belinda's right hand as she asked Brad what he'd learned.

"Sheriff wouldn't divulge all, but the critical evidence is the state crime lab detected your Mother's fingerprints on the coffee can matchbook."

"But . . . but that wasn't the one in the mobile home."

"I know. I know." He appeared wounded. "It's all circumstantial."

The emotional hurt exhausted her. Her cheeks stung from the constant wipe of her fingers. *Why did she have to be so vulnerable?* "Can you help? I can't write you a check, not now."

His cheeks quivered. "That's your mother's decision. She has to hire her own attorney."

"I need to see her."

Chapter Fourteen

Alexa had visited clients housed in crummy jails. Lakeview County Jail ranked with the worse. She expected the peeling battleship-gray paint and recycled steel furniture. The wall graffiti unforeseen. Paint gouges dabbed with mismatched paint heightened Alexa's depression and added to her worry about Mother's continued sanity.

Alexa recognized Caroline, the officer from yesterday and Mother's arrest. "Ms. Hovey, I need to pat you for contraband."

Without argument, Alexa complied and sat at a green metal table across from Mother in a stark room with a three-foot wide mirror. First sight of Mother's haggard facial lines caused Alexa to shudder. Mother's squint failed to hide her rebellious eyes. While Caroline had excused herself, Alexa imagined the one-way glass offered an ideal vantage point.

"They treating you decent?" Alexa asked Mother.

"How should I know?" Mother whined, "Did nothing except come to this God forsaken state in response to the Sheriff's threats. God knows I don't deserve this."

"You have an attorney?"

"Asked for one. The sheriff said the public defender would talk to me this afternoon." Mother lowered her gaze to the tabletop. "I'm terrified, past scared."

"What if I asked Brad to represent you?"

With her fingertips on her cheeks, Mother whispered between her fingers. "Would he be better than a public defender?"

"Can't answer. Don't know Iowa." Alexa lowered her voice. "Chicago public defenders not always the most skillful. DNA evidence reversals prove that. If I ask Brad, would you consider?"

154

Mother nodded. "I think he likes you."

"Good. At least that's settled."

Alexa departed the jail and headed to Brad's office. A sign on the vacant receptionist desk said to have a seat. She leafed through the men's magazines fearful her jail scent would scare others. The secretary to Brad's partner appeared after Alexa paced for what seemed to her an entire afternoon. "Mr. Haberkorn will be here shortly."

When the familiar blue blazer crossed the front door threshold thirty minutes later, Alexa rose. "I need your help for Mother."

Brad didn't break his stride. "Let's go to my office."

Alexa didn't recall if she'd ever been in Brad's private office. Books stacked so high they resembled visitors in the two chairs they filled. He deposited an armful of books onto the floor, waved her to the cleared chair, and continued to stand.

"Criminal law isn't my forte. Will do misdemeanors if my partner's overwhelmed."

"Let me help," Alexa offered. "I'm not an attorney, but I'm experienced with youths charged with crimes, serious violent crimes." She readjusted her cheeks that sat on the unforgiving pain-in-the-butt cushion. "It's Mother. I'd never live with myself if I didn't do the most I can."

"But the reality is the prosecutor, elected five times, wouldn't file charges without a strong case. The sheriff respects his expertise. So do I. Then there's what I said at the farm."

"Mother can't rely on a public defender. I'll promise money from the farm."

"Guess no one told you."

Nerves combined with the chair's cushion required Alexa to stand. "What?"

"My partner, Stanislaw Baker, is the public defender."

"Must be Polish? You hear Stanislaw in Chicago all the time."

155

Donan Berg

"He definitely prefers Stan." A smile edged his lips. "Only disgruntled clients use Stanislaw." Brad took one step to his desk chair and then stopped. "You should meet him. If there's something about him that irritates you, we'll discuss your possible next step."

"Is he in?"

"Still in court. If his trial ends early, I'll drive him out to the farm."

* * *

Alexa shut the driver's door of Belinda's SUV. She had entrusted Samuel to Belinda's watchful eye for a drive into Lakeview. It would ease her tension to stretch her legs. Other than Rosie's parking lot and the street between the jail and Brad's office, she'd never strolled Lakeview's streets. The town squeezed its business district into six blocks with Main Street addresses. After that Friday night Alexa and Joe went to the movie, Belinda hadn't mentioned a single unique store. The moveable band shell unhitched and abandoned on the first side street Alexa passed.

When she came upon the jail, she reversed direction to where she'd entered Lakeview. Two blocks ahead and across the street hung a Waspi Bar sign. The hardware store next door should have the Pine-Sol she sought.

She spied a tandem-wheel parked on the street near the bar. The Ram's metallic gray finish dulled by a heavy road-dust layer. Alexa glanced to determine if anyone watched before she bent low to inspect its rear wheels. The tire treads on the first dual set similar to the machine shed impressions, except no notch or nick. Alexa's right forefinger traced a suspicious tread notch on the driver-side outside wheel.

"It ain't for sale."

The female voice startled Alexa. She wobbled erect to face Margaret. "I'm sorry. If you remember, I'm Alexa from Chicago."

156

"Sorta." She carried a plastic bag from Lakeview Hardware.

Alexa's brain cells whirled to craft the right words. "My pickup's old. I've never seen one with extra tires this big up close."

"Too big, if you ask me." Margaret patted her baby bump.

Alexa assumed Margaret meant the truck.

"My husband usually drives it."

Alexa heard a door bang. A stocky man, Alexa estimated to be forty, marched towards her carrying a beer twelve pack. This man probably the Carl she'd heard of.

"Margie, we gotta git on home."

"This here's Alexa. Her grandmother owned a farm next to the Erickson's."

Alexa, her arms at her sides, tried to smile.

"Serves that jerk right. He gittin' burned and all. Good riddance, I say."

Margaret's downcast gaze misdirected her words. "If you'll excuse us."

"Nice seeing you." Alexa stepped onto the sidewalk. "Good luck with the baby." She couldn't make out the muttered words of Margaret's husband as he deposited his beer under the pickup's lifted bed cover.

After her Pine Sol purchase, Alexa cut short her discovery walk. To the rolling clouds she offered a prayer for Margaret and her baby. While Alexa agreed first impressions often wrong, she preferred no husband to an abusive one.

She'd seen in vulnerable street girls the cowering reflex that radiated from Margaret's eyes. If she learned where Margaret lived, Alexa calculated the delivery of a baby gift could be her access for a conversation, if her husband wasn't there.

On Alexa's drive to the farm, she grappled to make sense of Margaret's husband's truck as creator of the machine shed tracks. Hatred between Joe and the husband added a plausible motive. Alcohol could've fanned the flames of discord.

While she stumbled to create the why, the how also nagged Alexa. Joe's meticulous and artfully planned fire not the inevitable result of a sudden rage. She visualized Margaret's husband more likely to toss a Molotov cocktail.

After she parked Belinda's SUV near the porch, she entered the kitchen to bounce her sleuthing off Belinda. "Where's Samuel?"

Belinda pointed. "He's in the bathroom. I said he'd have to do it all by himself."

A door squeaked and Samuel, squealing and waving his arms, toddled toward Alexa. She dropped to her knees to give her son a huge hug.

Samuel extended his right hand. "Sucker."

"No, not today." Alexa remembered the sucker jar near Rosie's cash register, next to a box of matchbooks. The revelation forged an easy answer to Mother's matchbook possession. The entire community and strangers enjoyed free access to Rosie's matchbooks. How would the arsonist know he or she pocketed a matchbook with Mother's fingerprint? Mother could've shared. That's it. With whom? She'd have to wait until her next jail visit.

"Tried your spaghetti again." Belinda's words deadpan. "Better results. Like to try?"

"While we eat, can I tell you about what I discovered?"

"Your mother doing okay?"

"As well as can be expected. C'mon Samuel. Let's tie on your bib for Aunt Belinda."

With one eye glued to Samuel, Alexa's explanation lingered on her tire tread discovery linked to Carl and Margaret Skelton's truck.

Belinda skipped truck questions to ask if Brad would represent her mother. Alexa detailed how that remained up in the air with Brad's partner being the public defender.

"Well, without Pine Sol, I guess we're done," Belinda said, glee in her voice. Her quirky smile expressed escalated delight.

Alexa's tightened facial muscles couldn't disguise a smirk Belinda must've seen.

Belinda frowned. "Guess you bought another bottle, didn't you?"

Alexa, without a word, returned from Belinda's SUV with her newest Pine-Sol bottle.

"Sorry," Belinda quipped. "No time." She crossed her raised heels on a nearby chair. "I'm babysitting."

Alexa chuckled for the first time since Brad left the porch. No need to kill Belinda's friendship. If flexible enough to pat herself on the back, she'd say they'd done a respectable farmhouse clean job. Belinda's labor and her camper counted as a multiple blessing.

Chapter Fifteen

"**Y**oo-hoo, anybody home?"

Hesitant to answer with tattered news clippings and recipes from Grandma's binder in her lap, Alexa gazed out the parlor window. She stacked the loose content inside the binder's front cover and closed it before she shouted through the window screen. "Go to the rear porch."

The heavy-set woman unsteady as she waved and struggled across the grass in low heels.

Lydia Skelton's unannounced farm appearance intrigued, but didn't upset Alexa. She hid the recipes in a kitchen drawer. On a Lakeview bond referendum article Grandma retained, her scribble said, "Lydia's too pushy."

Alexa lacked enough information to judge.

Lydia's right hand rested on the porch-step railing. Her huffs and puffs exhibited determination if nothing else. "Truck conked out. Just my blasted luck on a day when I needed to deliver a dining set for tomorrow's open house. Do you mind if I smoke?"

"If we stay on the porch." Alexa observed Lydia's nicotine-stained fingers.

Lydia closed a Lakeview Motel matchbook cover and struck a match. Her quick puffs reddened the filtered slim cigarette's end.

"Where's the, whaddya say, truck?"

"Up the road a piece. Thought I'd have to walk to the Erickson place until I saw the SUV."

Alexa's right foot pushed her swing; Lydia leaned her ample backside against the porch railing. Belinda poked her head out the kitchen door.

"Thought I heard voices. Samuel's napping. I'll be reading my *A Body To Bones* mystery."

Small smoke rings rose above Lydia's head. Her raised left arm jacket sleeve blocked a choked-off hacking cough. "Don't see a for sale sign. I could do you a bang-up job."

Alexa kept her voice casual. "Waited for the Sheriff's investigation. Couldn't have buyers gawking at or tramping near a destroyed trailer."

"Right, right. Saying says the 'Good die young.' Don't believe it, but not Christian to speak ill of the dead." Lydia stepped to and sat on one of the basement dining chairs Alexa had carried to the porch to save her shifting kitchen chairs on and off the porch. Lydia's kinder tone carried the same hostile implication as son Carl's uttered words about Joe when Alexa encountered him, Margaret, and his truck. As much as Alexa desired to defend Joe, fighting the entire Skelton family earned no reward and she risked breeding Realtor antagonism.

Alexa noticed a leg wobble. "Is that chair okay?" She

160

hadn't thought the glue meant to secure the legs to the seat may have dried out.

"It's fine. I don't move too quick." Lydia's cough and laugh simultaneous.

"Would you like me to telephone a mechanic?" *Stupid question. She must have own cell.*

"If you give me a lift, it might start with the rest. We could finish your listing agreement for this farm. I've forms in my briefcase."

Alexa hesitated. "I've signed a listing. Doubt I could sign two."

"Nonsense. We Realtors understand if a client wants to change, especially in first sixty days. Did you?"

What had Susan done? "Believe so."

"Didn't see this farm listed in the multiple. Thus, the other Realtor hasn't committed to a listing fee. Makes it easier to switch."

Alexa fidgeted with her jeans buckle. "Need to think this through."

"What's the deal breaker?"

"Huh?" Alexa thankful Lydia paused to light a second cigarette.

"What's holding you back? Commission? I wouldn't mess with what we Realtors write into contracts." Lydia's eyes didn't blink. "I'm sure the new owners might not want your grandmother's old furniture. With my handshake I'll agree to buy it for, say, $20,000, drive it to auction, and, if the auctioneer does better, we'll split."

Alexa stopped swinging. "Like I said, need to think this through."

Lydia gazed at where Joe's mobile home stood. "Great they moved that piece of junk. The eyesore would've discouraged squeamish buyers."

Didn't I say that? "Excuse me, I'll get the SUV keys."

Lydia's tossed cigarette missed gravel and smoldered in the grass. Alexa slowed Belinda's SUV behind Lydia's tandem-wheeled Ram two hundred yards east of Grandma's farm. Straps secured a dining table and chairs into the truck's box. She trailed Lydia to her pickup.

Five yards from its tailgate Alexa dropped her SUV keys and crouched to pick them up. Her right hand swept aside four road-shoulder grass blades. The soft earth tire-tread impression identical to Grandma's machine shed tracks. This clinched it in Alexa's mind.

A heated tailpipe puff struck Alexa in the face. The engine missed a third time before it ran smooth. By then an erect Alexa strode to the driver door.

Through a rolled down window, Lydia said, "Must have been a vapor lock. I should be okay. I'll let it run and get my listing form."

Alexa crossed two right-hand fingers behind her back. "Let me think before I get confused."

"Don't wait too long. You'll lose money. Call me in the morning."

"I'll watch until you get out of sight before I leave in the SUV."

"Oh, by the way, you find your grandmother's recipes. Never too early to think about the fall county baking contests."

Alexa avoided eye contact. "I need to keep searching." Her answer half true as binder page gaps existed. With a quick backtrack to Belinda's SUV, she waved to foreclose explanation.

She met Belinda in the kitchen as she filled a water glass at the sink.

"What did that woman want?"

"Me to accept a bribe."

Belinda rounded the table. "Sit down. Tell me."

"I'll wake Samuel and meet you on the porch."

Alexa didn't have to wake him. He rubbed his eyes at the stairs' uppermost step. She led him to the bathroom, waited outside the door, and they joined Belinda on the porch.

Belinda sat on Alexa's favorite swing cushion. "Was the bribe worthwhile?"

"Twenty thousand dollars to list the farm."

"Whew! Cash or check?"

Alexa shook her head. She sat on a porch chair; her eyes followed Samuel. He peeked over his right shoulder as he halted before the steps. "Can't break my word to Susan. And Lydia asked again about Grandma's recipes."

"With the interest they've generated, maybe you should auction them off."

Alexa repositioned herself to straddle the chair. "No way."

"Why? Something about your analyzing each recipe?"

"Partly. Intuition tells me a missing page may relate to Grandpa's gold."

"You worry too much. Those jeans used to hug your thighs, fitted and snug, now there're loose and there's a hollowness creeping in under your eyes."

"Temporary." She called out to Samuel. "Don't you touch that cricket."

Samuel poked his right index finger along the porch railing base. The cricket jumped.

Belinda let out a loud laugh. "You show him who's boss, Samuel."

The cricket dived into a punched-out knot hole and disappeared. Alexa, ready to corral her son, continued to sit when crunched gravel announced a visitor. Alexa presumed Brad.

Belinda rose and sauntered to the porch railing. "It's a Buick. Guess who?"

Alexa's cheeks warmed.

Within a minute, Brad and a heavier man with horseshoe hair mounted the steps.

"Let's go in the kitchen," Alexa suggested. "More chairs." She sidestepped Brad to reach Samuel. "C'mon, honey. We'll get you water."

"Sucker."

"No, honey."

The four adults surrounded the kitchen table. Three said
no to Alexa's drink offer. Brad introduced law partner
Stanislaw Baker who clicked open a portfolio with a yellow
legal pad. Alexa explained her suspicions about the Skelton
truck and its tire notch that matched the machine shed
impression. She highlighted Carl's caustic anti-Joe
comments and Lydia Skelton's innuendos.

"The animosity between Joe Erickson and Carl Skelton
is common knowledge," Mr. Baker said. Stanislaw's
fluidity of speech impressed Alexa. His crow's feet about
his dark eyes hinted his age to be twice Brad's. She waited
for him to continue.

"Carl's first on the Sheriff's list of suspects. His alibi
supported by the Waspi bartender who told me Carl drank
heavy from six p.m. until close. While only his wife
supports his early morning whereabouts, hard to be
hungover and have the dexterity to rig the mobile home."

"What about the early evening hours when Alexa and I
were gone?" Belinda asked.

"Covered by the bartender."

Brad gazed at Alexa. "Your finding the tire to match
the impression impressive."

"And—"

Stanislaw interrupted Alexa. "Timing's all wrong. You
found the impressions, what, a day or two before the fire?"

"Guess."

"Then, they weren't made by the arsonist the night of
the fire."

"Oh." His logic caught Alexa off-guard.

Belinda tried to save her. "What about casing the
scene?"

Stanislaw scribbled a note Alexa couldn't read.
"Possible. You know any other reason a person would drive

that truck near the shed?"

Alexa shook her head. "Shed's empty."

Belinda surprised Alexa with a raised right hand. "Well now, but how about before."

"Hold it everyone." Stanislaw clicked his pen. "I need a couple answers."

Belinda contorted her lips. Alexa stared at Brad whose eyes slipped closed.

"Good. Now. Who here spoke with Ruth Hovey that Friday, and when."

"Belinda and I had lunch with Mother at Rosie's. Ended about one." Brad's eyes reopened as Alexa spoke. "Wouldn't you agree with that Belinda?"

"Yes. And Joe Erickson stopped in and then left."

Stanislaw scribbled a second note. "Okay. Alexa, was your mother smoking?"

"She smokes, trying to quit. Didn't smoke in the restaurant."

"What about a matchbook?"

"One lay on the table next to the salt and pepper. No one touched it." Alexa gazed at Belinda before Stanislaw's next question.

"Did either of you two ladies see Lydia Skelton speak with Mrs. Hovey?"

Alexa blurted out, "No." Sheepishly she modulated her volume. "I heard mention that Mother approached Lydia. But that had to have been before Friday. Don't think Mother had time. Her attorney could vouch for time after court. His car left Rosie's parking lot."

Belinda shook her head.

"Thanks." Stanislaw closed his portfolio before he stood.

"Brad, time to have a private word?" Alexa asked.

He gazed at his law partner and Alexa detected no secret sign. She'd learned dozens from street kids. "Let's walk to the barn. Stan, you said you wanted to survey the mobile home site. It's that tarp I pointed out when we drove in."

Stanislaw nodded.

"Go," Belinda urged. "I'll watch Samuel. He and I are becoming best buds."

Alexa pressed the barn handle to slide it and realized she'd locked it. No matter. No one could hear their conversation. "Heard little new from your partner. You think he cares?"

"Don't let his demeanor confuse you. He's on top of your mother's case. You must realize attorney-client privilege limits his candor."

"What's that mean? Samuel's writing a column for the National Enquirer?"

"It's okay to let it out." Brad clasped his hands at his waist. "No defense attorney would've received the state's discovery this early."

"But Mother's sitting in jail. All that happens is wait, wait, and wait. If the judge hasn't said who owns the farm, I can't even use it as bail bond collateral." She leaned against his left shoulder and then straightened faster than a stretched rubber band. He didn't move or flinch.

"I'll review your Mother's case with Stan. He won't leave a stone unturned."

"Thanks." She wiped three right-hand fingers across her dry left cheek. "Do you know where Margaret Skelton lives?"

Brad described the house on the northern edge of Lakeview although he couldn't remember the exact house address. His final comment—look for the green shutters. They joined Stanislaw at Joe's trailer site. Alexa observed him snap digital pictures from varied angles.

"Find little that helps," he volunteered.

"What about that St. Christopher medal?" Alexa asked.

"Dead end," Brad said. "Fireman said he lost one; the inscribed initials add credence."

Alexa strolled to the porch as the two men departed in Brad's Buick. An old-time rock 'n' roll blared from the radio inside the kitchen. Belinda sat with her feet on a second chair. Samuel's soles clomped onto the porch planks in a dance step unrecognizable to Alexa. She laughed until his antics deserved multiple claps.

Samuel again lifted her spirits that real-life events submerged, pulverized, and/or drained.

Chapter Sixteen

Alexa eased Belinda's SUV to the curb near the squat house with the green shutters. She'd driven past the Waspi Bar and spotted Skelton's tandem-wheeled Ram parked outside.

With a wrapped child's sippy cup and eating utensil set in her hands, she knocked on the doorframe. The porch light glowed although the sun hadn't yet set. Alexa assumed she was visible through the door's peephole. Slowly the door eased inward.

"Yes," Margaret Skelton said.

"I don't mean to bother you." Alexa extended her right hand with the baby gift.

"Please come in?" Margaret didn't wait for Alexa's refusal. "Please excuse the mess. I have a hard time bending."

"Very understandable." Alexa's living room survey found papers scattered everywhere. A tabby cat jumped from the coffee table and raced off without a peek. She assumed three popped beer cans clustered on a table next to a fabric recliner to be Carl's.

Margaret shoved the spread newspaper on the sofa into a pile atop its far cushion. "Please sit. You really didn't have to bring a gift."

"Just a little something." Alexa placed her gift on the coffee table. "I've used two or three."

Margaret reached for it, grunted softly as she brought her shoulders erect, and tore the wrapping. "This is wonderful. One blue, one pink, very considerate."

"So when's your due date?"

"Six weeks." Margaret's legs spread her skirt wide as she plopped rearward onto an armed chair. "Some mornings I think it'll be today. Then not."

"Bet your husband's excited?"

"I think so. However, he's been through this before." Margaret grasped both chair arms. "Before I forget, I must apologize for his street rudeness. He and Joe never saw eye-to-eye."

"I gathered that."

"Alexa, your name's Alexa, right?" Alexa nodded. "Sorry. I sometimes forget names. Did your husband drive out with you?"

"No." Alexa didn't wish to elaborate. "Just Samuel and me. Samuel's my son."

"Always great for a man to have a son."

"I've read that. Yet, Samuel gets along fine." Alexa bit her lip. She hadn't meant to say anything that stated or implied she didn't have a husband.

"In this town if you're a single parent, unless widowed, your friends drift away." Margaret shifted awkward in her chair. "Your child can't go to the playground without vicious taunts."

"Wouldn't believe a small town or any neighborhood could be that cruel."

"Perhaps not all, but Lakeview is. Worse than a caste system documented on public TV." Margaret's hands tightened on her chair arms and the wood creaked. "Word says you dated Joe."

"Wow, news travels fast." Alexa spied the tabby's peek around the kitchen doorjamb.

"Small town, nothing else to do."

"You know Joe well?"

"Could say that. Dated him briefly."

"Oh."

"Don't be surprised. Joe dated every eligible woman in this county. Started early. He traded crayons with girls in grade school and then escorted one or two to the high school prom and such. All knew he loved Chanel No. 5." Margaret chuckled. "Have a bottle I could've shared."

"Sounds like a forever ladies man."

Margaret averted her gaze from Alexa. "I'd like to thank you for the gift. Perhaps we can share coffee at Rosie's sometime."

Alexa understood she'd probed an unspeakable topic in Margaret's life. She wouldn't push, nor did she wish to be in Margaret's home if either Carl or Lydia walked in. She needed a female source, such as a trusted Margaret, to counterbalance Brad and Oscar. "I'd like that."

"Call me. If you have your Grandmother's apple cake recipe, maybe I could copy it?"

Disappointment crossed Margaret's eyes when Alexa failed to offer a quick yes. Alexa apologized. "Still looking. Must be something special about that recipe."

"Your grandmother baked several award winning recipes. Apple cake was the best."

Alexa attempted to learn more. "Did she add rum?"

"Don't remember. Carl's mother always tried to duplicate it and never could. Anyway, my number's in the book. If Carl answers, hang up; don't leave a message. He'll think it's a telemarketer. Best time is after supper."

"Thanks. My prayers you'll have a glorious delivery." Alexa departed.

On the street in front of the SUV, two youngsters on

bicycles pedaled with their backpacks to her. She lamented not finding her old fat tire bicycle in the machine shed. Grandpa might have given it to a needy kid. Where the bike might have gone filled her thoughts as she sped to the farm. An update on Margaret for Belinda would be mandatory.

She found Belinda with Samuel on the rear porch. Samuel's eyes the widest she'd ever seen as he crawled after a jumping toad.

"Where'd you get the frog?" Alexa asked.

"Not a frog, a toad." Belinda's words instructional, not condemning. "Samuel and I checked out the front yard. Haven't caught one of these critters in years."

"See, you could enjoy farm life."

Belinda laughed. "You kiss it. I don't need no Prince Charming."

"Samuel, not too close." At the sound of his name he glanced at Alexa. When she didn't approach, he resumed stalking the toad into the porch's far corner.

"What did you learn from Margaret? You try your sandpaper or bubbly friend approach?"

"Neither. Spoke calm, friendly."

"Learn anything?" Belinda squeezed a lotion dab on her right palm and rubbed her hands.

"Not confirmed." Alexa sunk into the swing cushion. "But I think her baby's father is Joe."

"Whoa!"

Alexa didn't slow to Belinda's command. "She as much said she dated Joe. Referenced his infatuation with Chanel No. 5."

"Big question is how does that unlock your mother's jail cell? Brad blew your theory about the tire tracks leading to the arsonist. The husband, what's his name? Oh yeah, Carl. He had an alibi. You mom's attorney seemed to think it tight."

Alexa's cell phone rang. She flipped it open, listened for several moments, spoke, "How did you do it? I mean

170

get him to offer that."

Belinda craned her neck. She strolled to the kitchen door to reach inside and turn on the porch lights. Alexa, with her left hand fingers, flashed Belinda an okay sign.

Alexa didn't mention aloud the name of the person to whom she talked. The news beyond belief. Things like this didn't happen in Chicago. "Thanks. That'll be great. We'll speak tomorrow."

"What'll be great?" Belinda asked. Her shoulders tense as she swung.

"I'll tell you everything. First, I should get Samuel upstairs to bed." Samuel lay sprawled on the porch deck, his head bowed. "Looks like he collapsed before the toad."

"I'll help. Then we can sip a glass of wine in the night's breeze."

Alexa nodded. Belinda held the door as Alexa lugged Samuel into the kitchen and up the stairs. While she figured a soaking bath best, she deferred to wash his hands and face, to wake him long enough to use the toilet, and then to slip on his pajamas. She kissed him good night and went to reclaim her porch swing seat.

"Forgot where I stashed this." Belinda finished her porch-step climb. "Remembered my car."

Belinda set two wine glasses on the porch railing and filled each half full. The first she handed to Alexa with the toast: "Cheers." "Now tell me about your new stud on the phone."

Alexa gulped. "That was Susan."

"Whatever works."

"Quit it. She's convinced a contractor to fix the foundation on credit. Seems with the slow economy he'd rather take a chance than sit on his butt while the summer work season passes."

"Sure she didn't offer other inducements? You could be the farmer's daughter."

"Drink your wine. That'll dull your overactive brain."

Alexa never doubted Belinda's genuineness no matter how often her friend's inquisitive manner pushed Alexa's self-imposed opposite sex boundaries.

"Why? My changing from maid to matron of honor isn't any big deal."

"You talk like Margaret."

"Come again."

"Well, remember us earlier talking about her quickie marriage?" Belinda nodded. "She said point blank that a pregnant woman in this town better have a husband, or be a widow."

"Could that have motivated Joe's death?"

"Yikes." The wheels in Alexa's mind whirled. That made little sense. Margaret married. She didn't need to be a widow. The baby, if alive with Joe's DNA, would face small-town taunts in a no-man's-land if Margaret divorced Carl. Which Alexa would do in a heartbeat. The entire scenario didn't jive. Joe had no visible assets. He'd provide better support if he lived. Perhaps he'd have a future Erickson land share, but Oscar's vitality didn't forecast his father's early demise.

Belinda shoved the swing. "Whatcha thinking?"

"Don't think Margaret drove the Skelton pickup to this farm."

"Who?"

"The mother-in-law, Lydia."

"And you come to this conclusion how?"

Alexa swallowed a wine sip. "Deduction. Although I believe her breakdown a ruse to confront me to switch my listing, she proved she can drive the truck. Brad said he overheard Lydia and Margaret fight about continuing the pregnancy." When Belinda lifted the wine bottle, Alexa put her left hand across her glass. "If Lydia is anything like my mother, there'd be no end to the pressure. I feel sympathy for Margaret."

"Presume you're right about Lydia. What motivated

her? I'd say Margaret was as much to blame as Joe's thrusting, assuming she wasn't drugged."

"Have heard nothing but that Joe was an old-fashioned lady's man. Didn't see drugs in his home's bathroom or experience his spiking my drink. Will agree Margaret's as accountable as Joe when one considers all the birth control available these days."

"There's another."

"Huh?"

"You. With Joe's truck known, the gossip underground spies you and him at the drive-in. Word gets passed to Lydia who you rejected. Gossipers speculate you'd sleep in his trailer."

"Omigawd." Alexa clasped both hands to her face. "Can't be. Timing wasn't super-fast."

"If Lydia scouted the farm for the listing, no reason she can't utilize that knowledge."

Alexa shook her head. "Na, too much unexplained."

"Don't you recall she lost the Oscar Erickson sale? That spurs revenge."

"Farfetched, if possible, but I doubt it's realistic."

"Didn't that other farm buyer have a mysterious unexplained car accident?"

"A feminine, plump Dr. No on retro movie night?" Alexa's throat stifled a sarcastic laugh. Why had Fate delivered blow after blow? It was as if Belinda had asked her if she heard water dripping and she didn't, but then that's all she heard. Alexa needed a solution that began with a for sale sign in the farm's front yard.

Headlights wavered and pebbles spit by tires rippled the mobile home tarp. A pickup jolted to a stop. A dust cloud obliterated it. Belinda dashed to the porch railing. Behind her, Alexa ducked when Belinda did.

A deep voice yelled, "My kid ain't going to use your stupid gift."

Alexa discerned pieces of the gift she'd given Margaret

173

scattered on the lawn. She crouched behind Belinda and whispered it might be Carl Skelton.

"If you're Mr. Skelton," Belinda shouted, "I'd suggest you leave and leave now."

A second headlight pair wheeled into the farmyard. Red and blue strobes pulsed. A Sheriff car spotlight circled a burly man.

"Everyone stay put," shouted a male voice from behind an open driver door. "Carl, put your hands behind your head. Kneel on the ground."

With slow steps, the uniformed officer approached a compliant Carl Skelton. One by one the officer cuffed Carl's hands behind his back and led him to a second arriving cruiser.

"You ladies all right?" Sheriff Edwards asked.

Alexa, next to Belinda, stiffened her spine, pivoted, and faced the Sheriff who had climbed to the top porch step. He laid a plastic dish and fork on the railing.

"We're fine," Alexa said. "You chasing him?"

"Not really. His pickup hit the shoulder once when leaving town. With his history, we thought it worth the effort to tag behind. Anyway, no need for you to worry. We'll tuck him in for a few hours."

"Don't recall if anyone told you that the strange tire marks I noticed near the machine shed match Carl's pickup. One tire has this distinctive notch or gouge."

"Show me."

Alexa returned from the kitchen with a flashlight. She gave the Sheriff a look at the machine-shed tire treads and then had him feel the notch on Carl's driver-side tandem-wheel tread. The Sheriff jotted a note.

"If it's okay, we'll lock and leave Carl's truck here."

"No problem," Alexa replied.

After the Sheriff bid good night, Alexa dug out an old kitchen phone book and tapped in the number for Carl and Margaret Skelton on her cell phone.

"Margaret, this is Alexa. The Sheriff arrested Carl."
Alexa heard soft sobs.

"I'm so sorry. You all right?"

"I'm fine." Alexa trusted Margaret wouldn't say she
called. She leaned against the sink.

Margaret's cough echoed through the line. "Carl . . .
erupted . . . no excuse."

Alexa didn't wish to explore what justification spawned
Carl's actions. "I thought it best you know the Sheriff will
have Carl at the jail in a few minutes. They've just left
here."

"That was a beautiful thing, bringing that gift. I
should've put it away."

"Don't fret. When you have that beautiful baby, I'll get
you another."

"Carl shouted so loud. I guess I should be glad the
sheriff was patrolling. When he stormed out after shouting
that nothing good comes from anyone living on Joe's farm,
I shoulda called."

"No harm, Margaret. Stay calm and I'm sure Carl will
be all right." Alexa pressed end call.

A third headlight set illuminated the kitchen window
with a more sedate arrival. Alexa recognized the Buick
under the yard light and stepped onto the back porch.

Belinda crisscrossed the lawn in search of kid utensils.
She waved to Brad as he passed.

"What brings you here?" Alexa asked.

"Police scanner. Big news when backup requested.
RFD identified this farm."

"Well, excitement's done."

"I can see that."

"We can offer wine," Belinda yelled. "Stem glasses no
longer available."

"No thanks," Brad replied.

"Mommy, read story." Samuel's face was a light
patchwork of bars created by the screen door. Alexa went

to lift him and the storybook his left hand squeezed.

"I can read," Brad offered. He plopped into a chair. "Set him on my knee."

Alexa did without objection by Samuel. She ensconced herself on the swing. Belinda split the remaining wine with Alexa. The picture of Samuel's shoulders nestled snug in Brad's right arm warmed her soul.

Brad turned the first picture page. "There once lived a small rabbit."

"Toad," Samuel said. He pointed to the porch corner.

"No, that's a bunny. See the ears."

"Brad, Samuel found a toad today. He might think every animal's a toad."

"Let me look closer." Brad peered into the book. His expression obscured from Alexa by the book's pages. "You're right. There's a toad, maybe a frog, in the picture's corner." He stretched his left arm to return the pages to Samuel's reading distance. "Good job, Samuel. Now this bunny wanted to be big."

Brad's sweet voice droned on in Alexa's mind. Samuel's face enchanted in the dim light. She knew the wine didn't influence her observations for her untouched glass rested at her feet.

When Brad turned the last picture page, Alexa arose to take Samuel to his bed.

"I can carry him," Brad said.

"That's okay. It's important I tuck him in." She turned her head. "I'll be but a moment."

Alexa and Brad's tentative steps led them to the backyard oak. Alexa's right hand fingertips traced a rope tied to an upper branch. Her subconscious filled with the conviction that Jeffrey the Monkey, from a high branch, showered them with attention.

"That you read to Samuel deserves more than a simple thank you."

"He grows on one. Makes you wonder how any person

176

can ever forget being that age, the wonderment of it all."

"It's hard to express." She gazed skyward at Jeffrey for strength. "But you shouldn't create a bond with Samuel."

"Why? You can't worry I'll abduct him."

The sliver of a descending moon failed to bolster the melancholy wattage of the distant yellow porch light. "He and I will be here only a short time. I can't bash his joy."

"Samuel lives in the present. I doubt he worries about the future or remembers yesterday."

"You quoting Dr. Spock?"

"Never read him. Did Clarence Darrow defend him?"

Alexa laughed despite her serious fundamental concern. Her date with Joe her experiment, not a billboard announcement. Samuel hadn't traveled with her. Metaphorically, her tiptoe into rural dating stubbed her toe. While she desired a father figure for Samuel, she remained a little selfish for herself. While Brad had past connections with Chicago, he'd made it clear in the lakefront park he wasn't uprooting himself. "Can't be silly with my son's future."

"My apology. I didn't intend to insult."

"Accepted." The mental guardians that protected her heart marched at the ready. "I told the Sheriff about the tire tracks and the pickup's identifying notch."

"Thought that was a dead end?"

"Three people drive that pickup. Two eliminated. That leaves Lydia." Alexa repeated the scenario she'd explored with Belinda. A glance past her right shoulder distinguished from the porch shadows a figure in the swing's full extension. She assumed the person was Belinda.

"I'll mention this to Stan."

"And the more I think the more it makes sense that Lydia duped Mother into giving her a Lakeview Motel matchbook. It could've been a simple request for a light since Lydia smokes."

Donan Berg

"But the lab found only your mother's prints."

"Maybe Lydia wore gloves, or touched only the edges, or remembered where she touched it and wiped it." Brad's face turned from the light and eliminated even a sideways profile. *Why is he disinterested?* "How stupid of me."

A curt breath propelled his facial engagement. "What?"

"Wasn't there a partial unusable print? That would bolster my ideas."

"Not if the print had been a diner patron who fiddled with the matchbooks or a server who stuffed scattered or new ones into the box before your mother reached in for one . . . or two."

Alexa didn't regret the subtle tease in her voice. "You're no fun."

"I'm a lawyer."

Alexa laughed a second time. "And so you are. I've a question."

"Don't know if I can answer." Brad's tone switched to serious.

"If I were to have work done on Grandma's foundation, there'd only be a lien against the property and not my weekly earnings, right?"

The porch light silhouetted his face. "Depends."

"Gee whiz." Alexa shook her head. "Forget I asked."

The porch light blinked.

"Good night you two," Belinda called out.

Alexa shouted, "I'll lock up."

"Guess it's time for me to go." Brad's right hand waved toward the porch. "I won't kid. No pun intended. I know you're serious about my interaction with Samuel. There's no way I wish to distress his pretty mother."

The warmth rose in Alexa's cheeks. He'd said the identical words in Chicago.

"You should know." He paused, swallowed. "As a student I met Chicago girls, no disrespect, complete flatbread crisps. Couldn't locate that elusive one to remind

178

me of apple pie. All I'll say is, you kinda do."

"What kind of riddle is that?"

"Something to mull over." He stepped away. "Oh, Stan told me he had hopes to get your mother released on bail, but it should take another week."

His reference to Mother distracted Alexa from trying to unravel Brad's obtuse symbolic references to food. She watched him walk to and enter his Buick. She folded her arms across her flat abs. No flatbread above her arms, at least in her translation. Apple pie, baseball, and Chevrolet an advertising jingle. Odds were, he, as a young Chicago male law student with one sheepskin on his wall, wasn't on the prowl for mothers. It all made little sense. When he gunned his Buick engine, Alexa returned to her happy Jeffrey thoughts.

In the morning she'd have to pack up Grandma's recipes. If a Skelton torched Joe's mobile home, wasn't her Grandma's unattended home without Lydia's listing an arson target? Had her tight lips not to tell others she found the recipes given the house a reprieve?

When Belinda greeted Alexa, Belinda sat at the kitchen table in a loose T-shirt and Capri pants two sizes too big. "Don't see any smudged lipstick."

"Not wearing any. It's Saturday in the country."

"Sly devil, you. Can you help me with the wine? I couldn't gulp the liter of wine you two left in the bottle." Belinda flipped pages of Grandma's recipes.

Alexa tolerated Belinda's friendly teasing. She hurled no jabs at Belinda for sticking with her yoga program. Alexa praised Belinda's hard work. "Find an interesting recipe?" Alexa slid out a table chair as she spoke.

"Tuna with horseradish. Never heard of that. Does have common things like celery, mayo, or sweet relish that Pat and Ron chat about during blowout Cubs games."

"You should email them this recipe. Grandma listened to the Iowa Cubs."

"Nah, producer would delete before it got to their booth." She stirred a powder into a glass of water. "You find that apple cake recipe everyone talks about."

Did Belinda, behind her back, join the gold fanatics? "Not yet." That Alexa was but an obbligato to Samuel, her greater disquiet. Wherever she traveled, there was no way she wouldn't all-out protect him.

Belinda stared. "Then tomorrow morning we tear the attic apart. Binder was there."

Brad's shower of affection threatened to entice Samuel from her. "If you say so."

"Knock it off. Your distracted mood tells me it didn't go well between you and Brad. Even I picked up the way Samuel adores him."

Alexa poured herself a glass of wine. "That's problem number one."

Belinda's spoon clinked her glass. "Huh?"

"You know I want what's best for Samuel and an adult male role model heads my list."

"But Brad doesn't pluck the heart strands of your harp."

If the complexity baffled Alexa, how could she explain? "Didn't say that; wouldn't say that. I asked him to back off Samuel."

Belinda appeared to peel her tongue from the roof of her mouth. "Why?"

"Don't want Samuel hurt. As soon as I sell the farm, we're Iowa history. Brad will always be here. He's hinted as much. While going to law school he learned to despise Chicago females. And a daughter of a Chicago cop is nothing but a purebred Chicago female."

"People change." Belinda's voice didn't hide her tint of cheerleader discomfort.

"Chicago will never be Iowa; Iowa will never be Chicago."

"Here's a soda bread recipe with golden raisins. The margin note says to use the same Leprechaun raisins as in

180

the apple cake."

"So." Belinda's misdirection eased Alexa's escalated tension. "Grandma often wrote notes to herself around recipe edges."

"Don't you see the connection?" Alexa shook her head at Belinda's enthusiasm. "Golden raisins in the apple cake recipe could be the missing clue and lead to the real thing. Leprechauns guard a hidden pot of gold. That's a possible reason why the apple cake recipe isn't in these pages and why everyone questions you for a copy of Grandma's apple cake recipe. These people may be Iowans, but they ain't stupid."

For the first time since Brad left, anticipation coursed Alexa's veins. "You think?"

"Yeah, I think. With a flashlight we should attack the attic now."

"No. We'll wake Samuel."

The shine of adventure dulled in Belinda's eyes. "Guess you're right. We'll do it first thing tomorrow after I drain the last milk drops and ladle out our breakfast pancakes."

Alexa excused herself to recheck Samuel. She picked up his kicked-off blanket and covered his pajama-clad body. His mouth clamped his right thumb tight. Alexa fought her great impulse to pry it free. Her legendary toad hunter probably dreamed of multiple conquests.

Alexa blew her great hunter a kiss and, with a sigh, retreated to Grandma's bedroom. She left the door cracked to hear Samuel if he cried.

Switched on, her table lamp warded off the dark shadows. Its light dwarfed the halogen glow of the yard light creeping through the curtain's perimeter gap. As Alexa unbuttoned her jeans, she envisioned a future gobbled by wide-mouthed alien creatures. Her psychic energy pooh-poohed her imagination. She counseled her cases to make a decision and stick with it. Why shouldn't she feel confident in her own advice? Brad had to

181

understand. Perhaps he was correct Samuel lived only in the present. Samuel would forget his Iowa book readings when hugged by and read to by her and his Chicago caregivers.

She'd forgotten Grandma's friends and numerous experiences. Yet, dandelion fluff floated and Jeffrey the Monkey lived. What guarantee did she have Samuel wouldn't resent her for denying him Brad's book readings and/or park visits?

Alexa had fervently prayed for her three-week-bank of memory cells to evaporate after Nina's deception, but they wouldn't. They re-emerged at terrible times to overpower her psyche with agony and fear. One therapist advised she create positive, newer experiences to squelch the past. Better memories eluded her.

Alexa sank into Grandma's claw-footed tub. The warm water subdued her physical aches, but that's as far as it went. Her toes broke the water's surface tension. Soapsuds floated. Water drops dripped off her shoulder blades and calves before her bath towel chased all from her skin.

She ambled to Grandma's bed in her tight-wrapped robe. She'd never freely slept nude and wouldn't tonight. Her nightshirt fluttered above her knees as she climbed into bed. Curled under the covers, Grandma's love helped Alexa drift into slumber.

* * *

Loud bangs frightened Alexa.

"Yo, Sleepyhead." The voice Belinda's.

"It ain't morning."

"Open your curtains."

Alexa's barefoot soles thumped against the hardwood floor. Her right hand separated the curtain's center to prove Belinda right. "I'll be dressed. Bring Samuel."

"He's already playing in the kitchen. You've earned the cold toast."

182

Alexa didn't mind. The extra sleep beneficial until her realization that Mother remained in jail while she'd planned a trip home to resume her everyday life. Her cell phone lay on Grandma's dresser where she'd put it the night before. She activated the menu option and speed-dialed Brad. His voice mail, not he, answered.

She'd try later, perhaps after she determined why her strong impulse to call him existed.

When she entered the kitchen, Samuel raced as fast as he could around the table. Belinda, on his heels, exhibited no effort to catch him. Alexa did and lifted him high into the air. "Winner," she cried out. Samuel giggled. Belinda sank into a kitchen chair.

"About time," Belinda said.

"I'm ready to find that cake recipe in the attic."

Alexa gathered the blocks to occupy Samuel's attention and deposited them along with her son on the upstairs landing. After she followed Belinda to the attic, she left the attic door ajar.

"Where do we start?" Belinda asked.

Alexa stepped to where she'd found Grandma's binder. "Well, I found the recipes we have under this plank. Doubt her one recipe would be hidden like the rest."

"Do we have to go through all these boxes?"

"I'd say, 'fraid so."

Without any prearranged plan, Belinda and Alexa delved into each box and crate within a full radius of the upended floor plank. After an hour, Belinda slumped onto an overturned crate. "It's not here," Belinda lamented. Her crestfallen expression echoed her voice.

"I'll agree," Alexa replied. She rubbed off the cobweb strand stuck to her jeans. "We'll have to think like Grandma."

Defeat edged Belinda's voice. "You knew her. I didn't."

Alexa thought of the unsent letter she'd found beneath

183

Grandma's dresser drawer. There'd been no recipes. An idea struck her. "Let's go to the kitchen."

"What's the kitchen got to offer?" Belinda asked.

"What've we got to lose?"

Samuel squawked when Alexa kicked the blocks he'd piled opposite the attic door. Alexa's "I'm sorry" didn't erase his frown. She lifted him to her right hip and proceeded to the kitchen. Belinda followed.

Alexa handed Samuel the piece of toast she hadn't eaten. "Let's pull every kitchen drawer."

Belinda's expression migrated from a stare to befuddlement.

"Please, I'll explain later."

Alexa's spirits soared when her third removed kitchen drawer revealed a folded piece of paper, yellowed around its edges.

"What's that?" Belinda asked.

Alexa raised the unfolded paper in triumph. "Grandma's apple cake recipe."

"Let me see."

Alexa's hands smoothed the paper's four-fold creases against the kitchen tabletop. The recipe typed on six by nine stationery had no smudges or margin notes common to binder recipes.

"Why the troubled look?" Belinda bounced a chair on the floor before she sat. Samuel grabbed a graham cracker she extended to him.

Alexa, bent forward, rested both her forearms on the table with the recipe between them. "This doesn't look right." The ingredients all seemed plausible except for the one-half cup cold coffee and three tablespoons salt. Coffee strange. Salt too much.

Stuck in Alexa's memory were times she helped Grandma bake. Grandma often said, "You do one and I'll do one." She loved exact measurements. "This ain't Grandma's recipe."

"Then why would it be in her kitchen?"

"Who knows? Someone gave Grandma this recipe. She stuck in it a drawer. It got jammed to the rear and pushed out. Who knows?" Alexa stared at the recipe. *Something's missing. Leprechaun raisins.* "This isn't the apple cake recipe. I'm certain."

"How? The original recipe could've been retyped."

"No. No. The leprechaun raisins are missing." Alexa's right hand began to push the recipe in Belinda's direction. "See for yourself."

"I believe you."

Alexa left the recipe on the table. Samuel, perched on a chair, reached for it.

"No, honey. I'll get you another graham cracker."

"What'll we do now?" Belinda asked.

Alexa challenged the disappointment that bubbled in her chest. "Scour the attic again." Alexa gazed at Samuel. Cracker crumbs ringed his mouth and half-a-dozen fell to the floor when he flashed his hungry grin. His mirth peppered Alexa's spirit.

A knock vibrated the kitchen door. Alexa called out, "Come in." When the knob didn't rotate, she rose to unlock and slide the security chain free.

"Mr. Erickson, come in."

Alexa stepped aside to allow his entrance. He greeted Belinda and his eyes widened.

"You've found the apple cake recipe?"

Before Alexa spoke, Oscar raised the recipe page to his eyes. She hadn't known him to need eyeglasses; yet, he twisted and turned the paper in three directions before his quick strides to the sink window to hold the recipe up to streaming sunlight.

Belinda shook her head in slo-mo.

"See anything special?" Alexa asked.

"Rumor has it the recipe contains a secret code. Don't see one. Perhaps you have a candle?"

Donan Berg

Belinda turned her shoulders toward him. "For what?"
Oscar rested his backside on the sink's edge. "Guess it won't do no harm to tell you. You've probably heard that years ago your Grandmother cashed in a twenty-dollar gold piece at the bank. Rumors swirled your Grandfather stashed dozens he wouldn't admit to."

Alexa sighed. She raised Samuel to her hip.

"But that's only rumor, right?" Belinda asked.

Oscar glanced at the recipe. "Don't mind telling you I've been a fool. Searched every last acre, the barn, and the shed from high to low. Mind you, never hurt anything."

Alexa swore Samuel gained weight as she lifted and set him on his feet. "And, you found no gold?"

"Not even fool's gold. Joe said I was crazy. He chased people armed with flashlights and shovels when they awoke him in the middle of the night."

"What's with the recipe's importance?"

"A treasure map you might say. That old 1930s junker is, I believe, the start point."

"You're confusing me more."

"I tried to convince your grandmother to let me tow the car behind the machine shed to the salvage yard. She always refused. Said it had sentimental value. Its only value to Joe existed when he decided to hide his spare mobile home key in its glove box.

"Unless there are dried vinegar clues, the proper sequence of recipe ingredient amounts in steps, yards, or rods set forth a trail from the car. I've run a metal detector around and under that car twice and there's not even a rusted nail in the ground."

Alexa reached into a drawer. "I've got this candle. Let's see what we find."

Belinda continued to shake her head until her eyes focused on the recipe a seated Oscar held parallel to the tabletop. Alexa restrained her breath as she slowly waved her yellowish candle flame under the recipe. No telltale

186

brown lettering surfaced.

"That's enough," Oscar exclaimed. "We've struck out."

Alexa bent her right elbow to place the candle in front of her lips. She blew hard. Its flame disappeared into a rising column of white wispy smoke. She wetted the wick under the sink's faucet and returned the candle to its drawer.

"Guess we're not lucky," Belinda said.

"Reckon so." Oscar rose. "Mind if I take this recipe home? Lydia Skelton quizzed Leah about it." He gazed at Alexa. "And, of course, Leah's itching to try it."

"Don't see why not," Alexa replied.

"I could find paper and we could copy it for you," Belinda suggested.

"No, that's okay," Alexa said. "Take the recipe. Leave it in the car's glove compartment if I'm not here. What else did Lydia ask about?"

"If I still maintained an interest to sell. She hinted she'd be your Realtor."

"Oh." Alexa's shoulders tensed. She didn't wish to fuel that conversation. Susan would be her Realtor and the foundation crew could be starting within the week.

"I'll make sure the Mrs. has a piece for you the next time you're here." Oscar twisted the kitchen door knob and let himself out. Alexa didn't hear Old Betsy's putt-putt, or any tire on gravel. Oscar must've either parked along the road or hiked from his farm.

Belinda, at the kitchen sink window, uttered, "That's strange."

"What?"

"Oscar's turned toward the machine shed."

"Did he forgot something? We're not always here, you know."

Belinda eased the kitchen door ajar to peer through the crack. "He's walking around the machine shed, not going into it. We need a closer look."

"Yes, Watson."

Belinda frowned. Alexa, uncertain as to what to do with Samuel, hoisted him onto her right hip. If she lagged behind and let Belinda do the sleuthing, there'd be less chance Samuel would cry out and expose them. Belinda rounded the machine shed's right side and left Alexa's line of sight. When Alexa arrived, she spied Belinda peer around the far end. The only things there were the old car and planted cornstalks.

Alexa separated Samuel from her right hip, ready to put his feet on the ground. She stopped.

Belinda, waving her arms wildly, ran toward Alexa.

Alexa hurried to the backyard and set Samuel on the grass near the oak tree. Belinda ran to the machine shed's left side.

Within a minute, Oscar re-appeared. His strides stretched toward the backyard oak. "Needed to check if Joe's mobile home key was still in the old car."

Alexa dismissed the explanation as a ruse. "Was it?"

"No. I'll be off now. Car's on the road." His fast-paced strides kicked up gravel dust.

Alexa waited for Belinda. Samuel crawled safe on the grass, intrigued by a grasshopper. As a little girl she hated yucky insects. Samuel's actions genuine proof that boys were different.

When Belinda neared, she slowed her steps to match her shallow pants. "He paced away from the car in several directions. First, he did a box. Then different angular directions."

Alexa grabbed Belinda's right hand that seemed to flutter every which way. "He did what?"

"Paced one step, say north, then one west, then two north, then west again. Repeated in different directions, different step counts. I've no idea what he was up to."

Alexa released her grip. "With no secret clue, he had to figure the measured amounts were the clue. Like the word

188

'egg' indicated east."

"Don't think so, Sherlock. 'South' could be sugar, but I don't remember any word beginning with an 'n' or 'w' to indicate north or west."

"Suppose you're right. We better think about our trip home. Tomorrow's a work day."

"You're no fun."

"Have a seat on the grass. If you'll watch Samuel, I should go into Lakeview and visit Mother at the jail. I'll stop for sandwiches."

"Sounds like a plan." Belinda reached into a pocket for keys. "If not, we could fry up a mess of grasshoppers." Belinda chuckled.

Alexa didn't see what Samuel cupped in his hands. An ant crept through his weaved fingers.

"Oueee, Samuel."

Belinda tossed her keys to Alexa. "You get going. I'll make sure he washes up."

Chapter Seventeen

Alexa never relished a jail visit. At least this Iowa jail didn't require a telephone receiver to converse with inmates seated behind a glass pane. The droopy eyelids, sallow skin color, and reddened eye sockets weren't becoming on Mother. She kept pleading for Alexa to get her out. Alexa didn't intentionally wish to hurt Mother, but the words there was nothing she could do were honest and her best realistic answer.

Alexa, despite the drag on her finances, promised to visit the upcoming weekend.

Donan Berg

After the jail matron announced her visiting time had expired, Alexa departed for the farm and Rosie's for sandwiches, plus a fill up for Belinda's SUV gas tank at the Stop & Go. She splurged with an impromptu chip purchase.

Belinda chased Samuel on the back lawn. Both stopped when Alexa approached, two plastic shopping bags in hand. "Let's eat in the kitchen and then we can pack for home."

* * *

Alexa had finally laid a fussy Samuel in bed Tuesday evening when her cell phone rang. Her eyes grew wide at Brad's number.

"Can't you initial the payment papers?" she asked. "This will only be more delay until I'm at the farm this weekend."

"Wish I could, but there would be a conflict."

"Yes, I know. You represent the estate, not me. Couldn't you ask the contractor to check his tool belt and then you sign my name?" She realized his silence meant no. "Okay, wasn't it worth a shot to ask?" Alexa heard a laugh. "Don't make fun of me, Brad."

"I'm not . . . . And, this phone isn't bugged."

"It's all that stupid judge's fault. The sooner I can reinforce the house's foundation, paint, and caulk the better. Also the quicker I can rid myself of Iowa."

"I, for one, would miss your visits."

Alexa stretched her torso along the straight contour of her living room sofa. She had to test what he meant. "What? Don't you have enough clients to challenge you?"

"Not pretty ones."

Alexa kneaded the side of her neck. A prior warmth returned. "Bet you say that to all your female clients."

"Not really."

Alexa heard Samuel cough. She didn't know why. "Excuse me a minute." She left her cell phone on the coffee table and tiptoed to Samuel's bedroom. He'd turned over.

190

She waited. No second cough. Had she activated her imagination? Alexa hurried to the living room. Picked up her cell phone. "Sorry."

"Was that my bud, Samuel?"

Alexa inhaled a deep breath. No man ever referred to her son as a buddy. "Samuel coughed; I thought he might be up, but he turned over."

"Good. He's a great kid."

"Agree. But then aren't I what you lawyers label a biased witness since he's my son."

"Not speaking legalese. Samuel's inquisitive, treats life with joy."

Alexa elated Brad recognized Samuel's traits. Trouble was; would he be so kind when he learned the truth of Samuel's coming into this world. She hadn't explained Samuel to any man. Nor was she willing to. "Thank you. I'll be in Lakeview this weekend. Do I need to set an appointment to have the foundation work started? Or do I need to contact Susan?" Alexa kicked off her slippers.

"Speak to Susan. That would be best. The less I'm involved the better."

"Right." Alexa hated lawyers. They wanted to know everything, yet deny what they know. "Quick question. Does Stanislaw have any news about Mother?"

"None. Arraignment went as expected. Judge said enough evidence existed to mandate a trial. Stan's still winnowing leads with a concentration on the Skelton family."

Alexa grabbed the television remote when she hung up. The ten o'clock news wouldn't be on for another ten minutes. She speed-dialed Belinda.

"That's great he likes Samuel," Belinda said. "You bringing your bikini this weekend?"

"Why would I do that? Weather's predicted to be cloudy. My hairdresser rents burkas."

"Sometimes you can be aggravatingly naive. If you

don't expose honey, they'll walk on by."
"Quit it."
"Okay then. Give him a chance to love the real you."
"If you say so."
"Remember, this is not about me. You still willing to double date with Richard and me Thursday? My mother's on board to watch Samuel."
"You know I am."

Chapter Eighteen

Brad telephoned again Wednesday night. Alexa didn't understand the urgency. The probate judge hadn't ruled. That had been her first question. Samuel was doing fine, she said in response to his inquiry. Yes, he could bring hot dogs to the farm Saturday evening for grilling; a double yes that Samuel would accompany her.

When she relayed Brad's call to Belinda Thursday at work, Belinda smiled.

"He likes you," she said. "He's thinking up any excuse to hear your voice."

"But he jabbers most about Samuel."

"A ploy. Doesn't Samuel's mother come with him?"

"Guess so."

"Now forget Brad. You bring Samuel to my mother's before six-thirty and I'll drive from there. We're going to have a great time. Richard says you'll like his friend."

Reunited at daycare, Samuel acted normal until Alexa arrived at Belinda's mom's house. He clutched at Alexa's ankle-length skirt unwilling to let her go. "You'll see mommy later. You like Belinda's mom." She pried

Samuel's fingers loose. At her nod, Belinda's mother grabbed him. Alexa didn't know what had gotten into Samuel. She steeled herself to Samuel's cries.

Brenda's shop talk didn't assuage Alexa's loneliness as she counted Eisenhower exits until the I-494 Hinsdale exit. Alexa recognized the huge neon-lighted chicken sign featured in culinary guides. A guidebook asterisk indicated membership required to enter.

Alexa gawked at the pillared entry. She tapped Belinda on her right shoulder. "This where your secret society meets?"

"Take a deep breath and you'll do fine. I've never been here either."

Alexa exhaled twice before she spotted Richard near the hostess stand next to a suited gentleman with golden-tousled locks, widely spaced eyes, and weathered tan skin. When Richard introduced him to Alexa as Ira, his placid face burst into a generous smile. His introductory hug caught Alexa off guard.

Richard apologized for the ten minute table wait. Belinda touched Alexa's right elbow. "Excuse us ladies. Come, Alexa, we'll find the rest room."

Belinda beamed as she washed her hands. "What do you think? Hunk?"

"Scandinavians usually aren't touchy-feely. Name Ira threw me."

"Adopted. That's what Richard says."

Alexa tossed a crumbled paper towel. "Richard's eyes brightened at your sight. Not sure you should have invited me."

"Samuel's fine. This will be a great evening."

The restaurant's interior reflected a refined classic taste. Rich mahogany woodwork, artwork by European masters, and pastoral green-painted walls. Alexa's menu listed no entrée prices. Ira leaned toward her and whispered to select whatever she desired. His musk cologne overpowered her senses.

"Ira, you've chosen a great place." Belinda's voice bubbled higher than a nearby fountain.

Alexa recalled her and Brad and Luigi. That decor less elegant, but Luigi's friendliness engaged her while the erect, stiff waiter who enunciated three specials and the wine didn't. When Ira requested a bottle and four glasses, his perfunctory glance not a request for her opinion.

Alexa ordered chicken to avoid what she believed to be expensive entrees. She understood that there'd be no dent in her wallet, but the dinner's quid pro quo apparent when Ira, under the table, placed his left hand on her knee. She brushed it off with her right hand. The expression of shock on his face caught Belinda off guard. Richard, his eyes riveted on Belinda, missed the silent feminine signal.

When they awaited dessert, Belinda excused herself. Alexa took the cue for a rest room rendezvous.

"You're not enjoying Ira?" Belinda asked.

"I've a fear that Ira thinks we shouldn't end with dinner."

"Ira drove Richard so Richard expects he'd ride home with me."

"I know you've tried to help me forget 2007, but a one-night stand only reinforces the pain. Still, I don't want to make a scene."

"Let's do it this way. I'll say I need to go to my mother's, forgot an allergy prescription or some such thing. Since Samuel's there, best you ride with me. The guys won't understand, but I'll explain to Richard tomorrow."

Alexa's mind overflowed with Brad memories. He'd been considerate, like Joe. But Alexa couldn't play what-if games. Samuel was uppermost. She shrugged. Belinda wasn't to be faulted. "Thanks. You're a great friend."

Belinda bowed, her right forearm pressed her waist.

Alexa laughed. What would she ever do without Belinda?

Chapter Nineteen

Belinda's nonstop chatter since Chicago interrupted when Alexa answered her cell phone to inform Brad when they'd be arriving at the farm.

"Richard's glad you threw a roadblock in Ira's after dinner plans."

"How so?"

"Explained to him, in general terms, what can happen in our job." Her gaze at Alexa cut short as she passed a van. "Didn't use names. If he surmised, he didn't say."

"You shouldn't have."

"He's going to marry me. He should understand the nitty-gritty."

"You'll scare him off. He's such a great guy."

The radiant glow on Belinda's face shifted into overdrive. "He works in an office with no idea of the kooks that exist."

"Doesn't he read about disgruntled employees killing co-workers? Seems to happen with alarming frequency."

"I'd say he does. Anyway, he didn't acknowledge Ira's aggression and I made a couple choice remarks. Richard apologized with abandon. He said he'd explain to Ira that you were a friend of mine and a little shy."

"Ah, c'mon. I wasn't tossed off the boat yesterday."

"Protest if you must. You don't trust men. You certainly can't deny that."

Alexa's throat clamped tight; her sharp retort

swallowed. "Won't."

"You've peeked, if not turned the corner, in Iowa."

"Quit it."

"Don't I speak true? Joe and the drive-in. A dinner with Brad. If you want my opinion, Samuel in the back seat has a better instinct for men than you."

"Then you should've invited him to dinner with Richard and Ira."

"Don't distract me. These country roads don't have signs."

"There's the church sign. We're okay."

"You know what I'm saying. Tell me to 'quit it' and I'll know I'm right."

Alexa realized Belinda had, by quoting Alexa's own words, turned the tables on her. Their now familiar drive ended with Belinda's SUV turn into Grandma's farmyard.

The construction truck with huge timbers surprised Alexa. A wave from a man wearing an orange vest directed Belinda to park near the barn. While Belinda unbuckled Samuel, Alexa strode toward the construction truck.

"Howdy," boomed a lanky man wearing a white hardhat. The seven others Alexa saw swarm Grandma's house wore blue hardhats. "You Alexa Hovey?"

"Yes. Who are you?"

"Conrad Young. We spoke on the telephone about your project here."

"Yes, but I thought you needed a written agreement or payment before you'd start."

"That was before I talked to Brad. He said you were like Mrs. Anderson. My father built the machine shed. Your grandparents were upstanding. I knew I couldn't go wrong."

"I didn't expect this."

"Truth is, this project fit in perfect. Two . . . three days at most. We finished a project in neighboring Rock County on Wednesday and weren't scheduled to begin the next until Monday in northern Lake. Can't afford downtime when the winter winds aren't blowing."

"But I don't have a guaranteed loan. Without it I can't pay you."

"Don't worry. Men can't collect unemployment for less than a week. Better they work than moan with hangovers. They trust me. Brad said you'd not stiff me."

Two men whistled when Belinda reached the gravel's edge. She smiled. The whistles grew to six until Conrad shouted at them to knock it off and get back to work.

"Nothing so beautiful as pecs glistening with sweat, be it on State Street or in Iowa," Belinda whispered to Alexa.

One important question troubled Alexa. Could they sleep in the house? They hadn't towed the camper. She tapped Conrad on the shoulder to ask. He assured her that in three hours, four at the most, the house would sit firm on its reconstructed foundation and be better than new.

Alexa released Samuel's hand and chased him to the barn. She telephoned Brad on her cell and left a voice message to bring hot dogs and fixings for twenty. Nothing fancy about the Saturday night celebration she planned to host.

She relinquished Samuel to Belinda and strode to Conrad.

"If your crew's willing, we'll have a hot dog roast here tomorrow night. If any wish to bring beer, that'll be all right with me."

"Much obliged. One guy may want to cuddle his wife at home. But the rest, me included, kindly accept your invitation. I'll pass the word."

The twinkle in his eye overwhelmed her. He had to be fifteen years her senior without a ring or white mark on any finger. Alexa found Belinda at the barn with her taut features etched with concern from her brow to her tightened lips.

"You're playing with fire. Bet my last dollar you are."

"What?" Alexa pursed her lips.

"That foreman's gaze ogled you head-to-toe as you pranced your butt to this barn. Bet his memory cells cataloged every hip sway and fantasized you in the sack."

"Quit it. He's only interested in cashing my check. He said they'd finish in a few hours. Let's go to Rosie's."

The cafe server pointed to an empty booth. Alexa carried Samuel while Belinda followed.

Before they ordered, Brad appeared. Belinda scooted across the vinyl to allow Brad to sit.

"Saw the SUV. What's this twenty hot dog message?"

Alexa covered her lips with her right hand. "Trying to soften the contractor's expected sting for having to await payment. You never said I could get a loan."

"Well, blame Susan. She convinced Conrad."

"So, you're bringing the dogs?"

"Susan will."

"What about a grill?" Belinda asked.

"I'll speak with Susan."

Chapter Twenty

Uncertain about what today's party would entail, Alexa woke Samuel early after both had slept in their Iowa beds. She padded after him to the refrigerator stocked with fresh milk and cola.

With Samuel fed, Alexa waited for Belinda. "I've been paging through Grandma's recipes. Found no apple cake recipe with leprechaun raisins. You ready to search?"

Belinda grabbed a piece of toast and joined Alexa and Samuel in the attic.

Alexa's Gold

Alexa fumbled with an open box. How did Grandma think? The recipe binder hid beneath a floor plank. Alexa discovered no other loose or disturbed plank. At the office Alexa had dismissed Belinda's idea to search the barn and machine shed on the rationale that Grandma's entire world and comfort zone encompassed the farmhouse.

"Can't find no recipe," Belinda whined. Her right foot accidentally kicked a wooden crate.

"Let's use our heads," Alexa replied. A sock monkey smiled at her. *Jeffrey?* Its wide red lips said not him. She picked it up by its left arm, and it dangled by her right thigh.

Samuel grabbed the monkey around its stomach. A crinkling sound surprised Alexa. The monkey's stuffing to her recollection had always been cotton or rags, not paper.

"Honey, let me see the monkey. I'll give it back."

Alexa inspected the sewn seams. Stitches on one side were red and not black-colored thread. Her right hand fingers pressed inward.

"That sounds like paper," Belinda interjected. "Weird."

Alexa bit a seam thread with her incisors. With her right forefinger nail, she unraveled a half dozen stitches. With the seam breached, she stretched the opening wide and shook. Several four-fold paper sheets fell to the floor at Alexa's feet.

Belinda rushed to her side. "You find it?"

Alexa squatted. "There's writing. Recipe ingredients. Yes, its apple cake."

"Yahoo," Belinda shouted.

"Let's go to the kitchen and sew him up. Samuel deserves this monkey." Alexa couldn't have been happier. Jeffrey's legend lived. When Samuel grew, Alexa would explain how Jeffrey the Monkey brought joy to her life. Grandma must have expected Alexa's memories to guide her to the apple recipe. *Smart Grandma.* Next question: Did the recipe lead to gold?

Chapter Twenty-one

Alexa and Belinda tried to count paces from the old car as Belinda had witnessed Oscar Erickson try. They decided three eggs in the recipe meant three unspecified units east. Their first attempts at paces, then yards, and then feet didn't locate one gold coin. After a brainstorming break, they decided the map measured distances in rods, a surveyor's tool. Three rods translated into forty-nine and a half feet. Two cups sugar interpreted to be two rods south. No west or north direction decipherable.

Belinda stuck a wood stake next to a cornstalk row. "Be right back with a shovel."

Alexa's sneaker toe dislodged dirt crumbs. Samuel's handfuls of black loam miniscule when compared to the healthy full shovels lifted by Belinda. With the dirt pile at twelve inches, Belinda's shovel blade struck either a rock or concrete.

Alexa reached for Belinda's shovel. "Let me give you a break." She scraped at the obstruction until she uncovered the edges of a square concrete block. The soft sides of the dirt hole thwarted her effort to pry the block loose.

"My turn," Belinda said. With straight stabs, Belinda cut a two-inch channel on four sides of the block. "Think we can lift it out?"

Alexa nodded and dropped to her knees. "Samuel, give mommy room."

Belinda chuckled and then lower her body to be opposite Alexa.

Alexa stretched her hands into the hole. "On count of three."

Belinda grunted as she and Alexa tossed the block aside.

"What's that," Belinda asked.

"A cylinder," Alexa replied. Her right hand raised a hard plastic cylindrical container four inches in diameter and twice as long. Both ends sealed with an unknown adhesive. "We may need to saw this open in the basement."
"Can you shake it?"
"Sure, but there's no rattle."

Chapter Twenty-two

Alexa tossed Grandpa's hacksaw onto the basement table. With one end open, she reached into the cylinder. "I hate this."
"Why?" Belinda asked.
"There's nothing but a crude hand-drawn map. There's no gold piece nor any metallic coin. No wonder Oscar's metal detector didn't buzz."
"That's it? Geraldo's lucky he didn't answer my email."
Emotional overload and exhaustion gnawed at Alexa. "You didn't?"
"Of course not, silly." Belinda's right hand searched the cylinder's interior. "While digging is yucky for me and disheartening for you. We need to keep our find quiet."
"Huh?" On second thought, Alexa saw no reward in arguing. Failure made laughingstocks.
"If people think there's gold. That'll boost your sale bids."
"I couldn't do that. That would be dishonest."
"Perhaps not. Why'd your grandfather hide this map? Had to be important. He figured people might run metal detectors to find buried gold, so he stashed it elsewhere.

Smart if you ask me."

"There are numbers on this map that might be surveyor stuff." She pointed to numbers along the bottom and up one side. "I'll put it back in the cylinder and hide it under the attic plank until I can think of a better place."

"Good girl. Time to powder my face for the party."

"Thought you told Richard it's boring in Iowa."

"Not trucking out here for me." Belinda winked. "Somebody's got to chaperone you."

Chapter Twenty-three

After Susan arrived, seven cars and a motorcycle filled the farmyard. With Alexa's concurrence, Brad lined up two grills, one charcoal and one propane, three feet from the front entrance portico. The foundation reconstruction steadied major roof supports without repair of all deficiencies. An extension cord strung across the front door threshold powered the vibrating boom-box speakers. Brad, decked out in a bar-b-que apron, supervised the grills.

Alexa sidled up to him. "Didn't expect you after you shunted the hot dog buy to Susan."

"Unless Samuel invited a two-year-old lass, wanted to keep him company."

"Sure, right?" She felt a coy smile stretch her lips. "Maybe you wanted to coax him into a poker game to swindle him out of his inheritance."

"You found the gold?"

"Didn't say that. You're supposed to be the one with good news from the judge."

"Soon, soon."

Alexa's Gold

"Hi, pretty boss lady," Conrad interjected. Chest muscles strained the blue cotton fabric of his short-sleeve shirt. Wafts of Stetson Cologne ringed his head. His designer jeans made him and Alexa matched bookends although her dark sneakers less pretentious than his polished calfskin cowboy boots.

"Call me Alexa."

"Okay, pretty Alexa."

She gazed at Brad for help. However, he'd slipped away to assist Belinda carry charcoal and packaged buns. Circumstances persuaded Alexa to be gracious. Conrad's repetition of the word "pretty" hadn't warmed her skin as Brad's utterances had.

"Do all men in Iowa like that word?"

One corner of Conrad's mouth tilted. "Don't rightly know, but I reckon you hear it often."

Alexa experience the delayed warmth of her blush.

"May I join you?" Susan asked.

"Of course," Alexa replied. Her sigh more audible than she would've liked.

"Great job, Conrad," Susan cooed. "House sits sturdy."

"It had great bones, but we're not here to talk shop are we?"

"Heavens no." Susan's volume elevated to battle a new boom box tune. "Tonight's a celebration. A welcome to Alexa. Have you met her son?"

"Neither he nor the dad."

A raspy whisper squirted past Alexa's lips. "There's no dad." This was truth, yet, its release as toxic to her as lead in Samuel's water.

For the first time in their short acquaintance, Conrad's macho facade cracked. "Sorry." Sincerity seeped from his eyes in contrast to the bushels of bluster his lips directed at friend or foe within earshot.

"No reason to be." She glanced around. Pickups blocked the early car arrivals. "Question: Do this many

203

people work for you? Didn't see the half dozen females in blue hardhats."

"Most don't. Word spread about a party."

A tall, redheaded hunk strolled behind Conrad toward the parked vehicles. Alexa ignored him, asked Conrad, "Was this farm known as party central?"

"Won't lie. We construction workers connected with Joe before his, you know . . . ."

The redhead returned with two uncapped beers. He tried to hand one to Conrad who shook his head. When the redhead extended one to Alexa. She waved it off. "Joe liked to party?"

"What can I say?" Conrad shrugged. "Anyone who works hard, likes to party."

The redhead persisted. Conrad gulped his first swig. "Take the beer. Let's toast Joe."

Alexa succumbed to Conrad's toast appeal to drink twice to his repeated "Here's to Joe." When curious eyes multiplied in her direction, Alexa beat a retreat. "Excuse me, need a hot dog."

Alexa skirted dancers who grooved next to the boom box and weaved through a dozen lawn chairs sprinkled across the lawn and past two guys who straddled cooler lids. She waved off three offered beers. While all the guys smiled and offered bits of conversation, not one tried to impede or woo her.

She strode to the rear porch to check on Samuel.

"It's about time." Belinda's singular intensity crackled in her criticism.

Alexa cupped her mouth so her words didn't travel to Samuel's ears. "Why you pissed?"

"Stuck here, hearing the music."

"You could've—"

"Yeah, right? I could've." Belinda stared into the cornfield, her shoulder blades to Alexa.

Alexa hugged her. "You're my best friend. I'll do

anything for you."

When Alexa's hands felt the tension ease in Belinda's shoulders, she let go. "Go grab a hot dog, guzzle a beer. Didn't see wine."

Belinda flashed a thumb's up. Alexa bent forward to pick up Samuel. The furry caterpillar he stalked scurried to safety. Soft footstep thuds sounded on the deck.

"So is this the little guy?" Conrad asked.

"Name's Samuel." Construction textbooks must refer to small boys as "little men or little guys" for that's what Alexa remembered as Joe's initial reference to Samuel.

"Right, Samuel." Conrad stared at Samuel. "How ya doing?" When Samuel didn't respond, he turned toward Alexa. "You oughta know we didn't find a time capsule in your foundation."

"That unusual?"

"In old buildings, I'd say so. History and keeping records were important to the pioneers. When they settled down, they sealed newspaper clippings, photographs, and family heirlooms for later generations in foundation boxes meant to survive fires and tornados."

"So, if you had found Grandpa's gold, you'd be long gone?"

His mouth slack-jawed, Conrad's eyebrows jerked toward his hairline.

"Your expression says a thousand words. You'll get paid, but I'll not be hiring you again."

Conrad glared at Alexa. His right foot stomped a step forward. Alexa didn't twitch. He pivoted on his heels and hurtled the porch steps.

"Bitch," she heard him utter. She clamped her jaw. Jerks didn't deserve a response.

A new song streamed in from the front yard. Samuel danced to Alexa's delight.

Brad, still wearing his bar-b-que apron, rushed up the porch steps. "What did you say to Conrad? He kicked a beer case. Uttered a string of profanities."

Alexa trusted her feeling she faced a barrage of unjustified accusations. For the briefest instance she perceived Brad's lips to be soundless flapping until she heard "He said he's never coming here to work for, and I quote, 'that bitch.' When I left, two employees pinned him and the guy he picked a fight with."

She chalked up another reason for Iowa not to be her destiny. "You can join him."

"Whatever you say, please lower your voice. Don't label me the same as Conrad."

Alexa inhaled a deep breath. "Why not? You've dragged out Grandma's will forever. You hope to find the gold before I have a legal right to stop you?"

"I'll neither condemn nor praise the legal system. I've often curled my toes on its tightrope, always with your best interests at heart."

"Doubt that. You've a goal no different from the men that raped me." She slapped her right palm against her mouth. She staggered to and collapsed into the swing.

"Mommy," Samuel cried. He grabbed her right leg.

Alexa kicked out.

"Samuel, she's okay. Stay here."

Chapter Twenty-four

Alexa brushed the cold compress from her forehead. She forced her words vertical to the ceiling. "Belinda, how'd I get upstairs to Grandma's bed?"

"Brad carried you."

"Didn't drink but two beer swallows, yet, made a

classic fool of myself. Still dizzy."

"Don't worry. No one except Brad saw what happened, and he's only said you seemed to faint from exhaustion. Susan asked everyone to please go home, and they did with quizzical looks, but no one pestered her with questions."

"Conrad?"

"He lost two shot contests and tomorrow he's unlikely to remember you or me. A henna-maned hunk drove his truck off the farm with Conrad slumped in the front seat."

"All they want is the gold. I've inherited a nightmare."

"I think you're wrong to lump Brad in with all."

"Why?" Alexa handed the compress to Belinda. "He's just like all the rest."

"You're wrong. You really shook him. Did you tell him he pissed you off as you did me?"

Alexa shook her head. "And, you know, I didn't mean it."

"You need to open your heart and soul to Brad or just let him screw you and toss him away like a rag doll. Anything else and he'll not understand."

Alexa closed her eyes.

Belinda's footfalls signaled her departure and return. "You still thinking?"

"Sort of, trying to find decent words to tell you you've now really pissed me off."

"Bull dung. Let your emotions out. You can talk dirty with the best of our clients, but that's not real emotion. You're playacting. When you told me earlier I'd pissed you off that was the first real raw emotion you've expressed in three years."

Contriteness lathered Alexa's voice. "I didn't mean to hurt you."

"Far from it. Never once in my training did I expect someone telling me I sprayed urine would sound gratifying or lift my spirits."

Alexa cocked her head, laughed. "I must be a self-

Donan Berg

centered jackass."

"You said it. I didn't." Belinda, her grin ear to ear, bent forward and hugged Alexa.

"Mommy, cracker all gone."

Alexa shoved Belinda away to attend to Samuel. At Belinda's urging, she dialed Brad only to leave a voice mail message. "Sorry. Please call me." She pressed end call.

Alexa tucked in Samuel with a kiss goodnight. Across the hall, she pulled the sheets on Grandma's bed up to her neck and dozed off.

* * *

Alexa woke to her cell phone's vibration hum on Grandma's dresser. Before she reached it, the ring tone announced an outside call. In a groggy, half asleep voice, she said, "Hello."

Static progressed to absolute silence. The Caller ID number meant nothing to her.

Alexa flopped onto the crumpled sheets. If she had heard Samuel, she'd have flipped and crabbed herself out of bed, but she didn't. She lay back and sealed her eyelids.

"Alexa, get up."

The pounding on Grandma's doorjamb too high to be Samuel. She deduced Belinda and shouted, "Come in."

Belinda, in a wrinkled nightshirt, announced, "There's a Buick outside. My guess is Brad knocks on the kitchen door."

"You answer. If not, he must wait until I can find my clothes."

Alexa zipped her jeans, ducked her head into a tie-dyed T-shirt and padded toward the kitchen door. "Who's there?"

"Brad. Wanted to know if you're all right."

Without opening the door, Alexa shouted, "I'm fine. You can go."

"You can hide, but I'll stand here until you open it."

208

Damn, thought Alexa. Belinda's words floated through her brain. She could spread her legs, fake pleasure, and discard him like a broken toy. But no man had ever entered her unless violating her. She shivered. Being a rag doll no better than what she had experienced in three weeks of captivity. Alexa undid the chain; pulled the inside door.

"Satisfied? You can leave now."

"Sorry I didn't return you call."

His words lingered. He didn't call. Who did then? "Sure you didn't pocket dial?"

He drew his cell phone from his pocket and swiped its screen. "Positive."

Alexa, pushed by a hand in the middle of her back, bumped into Brad and let the outside door bang. She pivoted in slow motion. Belinda's smile checkered by the metal screen.

"I'm making breakfast for me and Samuel. If you're still talking when we're done, I might scramble an egg or two for you." Belinda shut the kitchen door.

"What'd I do?" Alexa asked to no response. She smoothed her bunched T-shirt fabric three times. Her to-the-swing-footsteps reversed to lead her to a one-person chair.

Brad slumped onto the swing seat.

"I should thank you, I guess, for getting me into bed." Her cheeks warmed when she realized the double entendre that lurked behind her words.

Brad squirmed. "Nothing special. Lot of guys at the party would've done what I did."

Alexa switched the subject. "How's Mother?"

"Heard she's doing okay. Stan didn't tell me anything, but his facial gloom didn't show there'd been a positive breakthrough."

"You hear why I upset Conrad?"

"Just assumed he messed up or pressed for payment."

"Neither. He only took the job to find Grandma's gold."

"Stupid." He gazed toward the barn. "Okay there's a rumor. But anyone with common sense knows it's hype. Geraldo proved that."

"Grandpa Anderson had gold. Bought one hundred acres. You think maybe that's why the judge takes so long?"

"That's not apparent if he is." Brad stood, resettled. "You positive there's still gold?"

"A hidden canister tells me I'm on the right path."

"Oscar Erickson has said many a time his metal detector searches came up empty-handed."

"Canister wasn't metal."

"But the gold would be. And, if secreted in the old car's tires, the metal detector's beeps discounted because of its proximity to the car's wheels or axle. No one the wiser. That's always the trick. Make an object disappear or appear like something it isn't."

"True." Alexa hoped her spun cocoon of indifference hid her intrigued expression she prized Brad's tire reveal. She rose, prepared to head in for breakfast.

"Wait a minute. You said the canister wasn't metal. You find it?"

She cobbled her confidence. "A canister, yeah. Not the gold."

His tongue made a clicking sound. "You're smart or your grandmother clued you in."

"I'd say both." Alexa laughed.

The back door creaked.

"Oh, you're still here." Belinda shrugged.

Chapter Twenty-five

The Sheriff's dingy interview room absorbed what little radiance Mother's straggly hair retained after what Alexa assumed to be harsh shampoo. The matron stood guard outside the door.

"How've you been, Mother?"

Mother's acerbic reply swift. "How do you think?"

"You can't let this place sap your spirit."

"That's easy for you to say." Mother's hands trembled. "I'm dying in here."

"You get any word?"

"My Public Defender tries to call, but it's easier if I call him collect. You know that Lydia woman?"

"Lydia Skelton, the Realtor?"

"That's the one. She visited a couple days ago. Smuggled me a piece of what she claimed to be your grandmother's apple cake. It must have taken in this place's odors. It didn't taste like your grandmother's apple cake at all."

"Was the cake the only reason she visited?"

"Who knows?"

"What did she want to talk about?"

"The farm. She implied she could be instrumental in a quick contractor foundation fix for a faster sale. She dumped on young women. Presumed her rant included the Realtor you chose."

"Foundation fixed. Marbles don't roll as they once did."

"Good." Mother fingered a cigarette pack without digging her fingernails into the cellophane. "That Lydia woman is an odd duck. She visits, never takes off her cloth gloves."

"You know, Mother, this isn't the cleanest place on earth."

Donan Berg

"Maybe not, but she wore gloves the day she and I talked."

"What day was that?"

"Oh, I guess it won't hurt to blab now. Day before the fire, she wanted me to be her ally to get the farm's listing. She stood outside smoking. Wore gloves."

"Strange you remember now."

"She asked me if I'd a match without a glance into her purse. Now that was strange."

"You give her a match?"

"Whole book. One of those diner books. Stuck them in her purse. Stupid she asked if not going to use. Then, maybe she changed her mind. You shouldn't worry."

"Anything I could bring you next weekend."

"A cell key." She glanced at the room's mirror. "Just kidding. Could use toiletries, but they'd only get ripped off. Perhaps you could mail me cigarettes, better yet, have my lawyer deliver. I'm sure to get them that way."

Alexa waved for the matron. She paused at the door to wave good-bye to Mother.

* * *

From the farmyard's edge, Alexa shouted, "Samuel, Samuel." *Where is he?* He didn't appear. Alexa's footfall creaked the lowest rear porch step. She shouted, "Belinda, you there?" Silence ruled. No breeze teased the swing.

When Alexa scaled the top porch step, she saw the kitchen door half ajar. Her stomach churned and her chest muscles squeezed tight, released, and tightened.

"Belinda, Samuel." The drip, drip, drip of a kitchen faucet she knew she hadn't used ratcheted her dread sky-high. Her jail trip to visit Mother lasted but an hour.

Her right-foot heel stopped on its rear sole edge. What was she walking into? Assess, assess, her brain commanded. Overturned table and kitchen chairs littered the floor while the cabinets appeared untouched.

212

Adrenaline fueled her legs to flee; her brain braked her muscles.

Alexa retreated. She ran to the barn, locked. Machine shed, locked. No strange vehicle. She scampered to the cornfield's edge for a farmhouse side view. Nothing. Her cell phone messages stymied by voice mail. Nine-one-one required stronger facts.

A double time march to the rear porch let her yell a third time, "Belinda, Belinda."

A fading solitary echo of her own shout reverberated inside the house.

Courage surfaced as her sole weapon.

With stealth footfalls to the kitchen door, her every-which-way glances added nothing new until she gazed at the kitchen floor. Four dime-sized blood drops. Alexa crouched. The closest one sticky to her fingertip touch. Erect and on her heels, she backed rearward to the porch.

Her cell phone connected with nine-one-one. "Don't know if anyone's injured. There's small blood drops. Looks like a fight. My son, Samuel, and my friend, Belinda, don't answer. Only three steps into the kitchen. . . . I'll wait for the Sheriff."

Alexa ran to the old car behind the machine shed and expected slashed tires. They weren't. Alexa's breathing pulsed in spurts from chest tension, not her running. While Brad mentioned the tires as gold safes, she envisioned no reason he would steal from her.

Faint sirens in the distance hastened her jog to the farmyard. She stood on the gravel; her shoulders slouched when Sheriff Edwards exited the first of two Sheriff Department cruisers.

"Tell me what's happened."

"Came home minutes ago. Called out for my son Samuel and my friend Belinda. No answer. The kitchen door left open. Saw blood on the kitchen floor."

"Did you go in?"

"Called nine-one-one."

"Good. Stay on the far side of my cruiser?" Alexa nodded. The Sheriff gazed at the second officer. "Jones, watch the front door. I'm going in the back."

Agony dragged Alexa's seconds into minutes. Vivid images of bruised children flooded her mind. Light beams behind the parlor window curtains pinpointed the Sheriff's location until the light traveled from one upstairs window to the next.

A second siren blared into the farmyard. Bar lights pulsed. Alexa pointed to the front yard. The officer gone. The fire department ambulance angled wide left, stopped in the dust cloud it had created, and beep-beeped in reverse across the grass. Two EMTs left a gurney at the base of the porch steps to meet the Sheriff and Jones who supported a person between them.

Alexa shouted "Belinda, Belinda" as she ran to the gurney.

"Slow down, ma'am," the Sheriff cautioned. "She's shook. The EMTs will take care of her."

Belinda pressed a white handkerchief to her lips. Vertical rips frayed her blouse. Her left foot missed its shoe.

"Belinda, where's Samuel?"

Stammered words emerged from her swollen lips. "The-y . . . the-y took him. Tr-ied . . . tr-ied hard. Could . . . couldn't stop them."

A frantic Alexa shrieked, "Who, who?"

"Two . . . maybe three men. Don't know . . . Men surprised me."

"Ladies," Sheriff Edwards interrupted, "we'll sort this out, but first we need the EMTs to check for serious injury. Anyone have a picture of this Samuel?"

Alexa tried to sharpen the thoughts in her cloudy brain. "Yes, yes. In my purse." She dashed to Belinda's SUV. Her purse on the front seat contained her wallet and Samuel's

picture. Her rearward SUV exit bumped into Sheriff
Edwards. "Sorry, here it is. Taken four months ago. Can I
check the house?"

"He's not there. Jones will double check."

"Watched your flashlights. You didn't check the
basement."

Sheriff Edwards yelled, "Jones, Watch your step in the
kitchen. Check the basement."

Officer Jones disappeared into the house. A flashlight
beam crossed a basement window.

"Nice catch, Alexa." The Sheriff brushed his chin with
his right hand knuckle. "You upset anyone lately? Someone
hold a grudge?"

Alexa, on purpose, didn't mention Brad. "Conrad
Young. There was a party Friday to celebrate the
foundation repair. He drank too much. We had words, but I
doubt he'd do this."

"He threaten you harm?"

"No." Her word sounded fragile. Alexa gazed at an
EMT administering Belinda oxygen. "Can I speak to
Belinda?"

"Give me a couple minutes with her, then yes."

Alexa paced in front of the oak tree with her gaze fixed
on the Sheriff. As he bent forward at the gurney, he
obstructed her view of Belinda. After four minutes, he
strode toward Alexa.

"EMTs suspect cracked or broken left forearm bone.
They're taking her to the emergency room. I'll issue an
amber alert, check at the office, and meet you at the
hospital in, say, forty minutes. Expect I'll know more
then."

Alexa's facial pores chilled by the absence of blood.

The Sheriff studied her for a moment before the
ambulance door slammed. "You okay to drive? I'll have
Officer Jones give you a lift."

Alexa exhaled a shallow breath. "I'll take the ride."

Chapter Twenty-six

Alexa hated hospitals with a passion, even if her former therapist charted her fear as irrational. Nowhere else did Alexa find human carnage in abundance. As a probation officer her duties weren't supposed to entail victim statements. Her need to save children mandated hospital visits not job-description compulsory. Compassionate hard-scrabble reality trumped genteel rules.

Crime infested her cases. The tentacles of violence gripped probationers and never relented. Safe houses provided temporary shelter until a trial ended. Beds then released for new victims. Long-term new identity creation a wistful pipe dream.

Alexa wasn't mentally prepared for mayhem to strike Iowa. Had the perps crouched in cornfields until Belinda's SUV headed into Lakeview? Why Samuel? He hurt no one. She had to be the target. Belinda attacked by happenstance. A nurse wearing black-rimmed eyeglasses and clad in a crisp white uniform approached. "You Belinda's friend?"

"Yes. Yes." Alexa tossed aside the unread *Health* magazine she'd picked up.

"Aide's transferred her to Room 204. If you wait five minutes, I'll bring you to her."

When the nurse disappeared, Alexa climbed the stairs to the second floor and tiptoed into Room 204. "Belinda, you awake?"

"Just resting my eyelids. They were heavy from fluttering and calculating the biceps of that one EMT. Had to be a foot or more."

"Let's get your clothes. You're fine."

Their laugh sliced through Alexa's tenseness. "What happened?"

"Heard what sounded like fake owl hoots outside.

Samuel was playing with his blocks, you know, in the
kitchen. Took three steps onto the back porch. A hand
pressed a cloth into my face. Tried to scream and couldn't."
"I know, I know."
"Four hands and a knee forced me to the porch deck.
Two arms twisted mine behind me, rolled me, and rope
bound my hands and ankles. A voice asked, 'Where's the
gold?' I stayed mum. Voice again asked, 'Where's the
gold?' I replied don't know. A fist slugged my mouth."
Alexa caressed Belinda's left hand, careful to avoid the
inserted port. "Did Samuel hide?"
"Heard Samuel cry Mommy. Then nothing."
Alexa gulped, her dry throat unable to produce saliva.
"Two grasped my shoulders and feet, carried me face
down until tossed onto a couch. No stairs said living room.
Ripped cloth noises startled me. Didn't see until later what
had happened to my blouse."
"Didn't you hear me shout?"
"Couldn't with cotton balls stuffed in my ears. You
ever hear of that?"
"Once. Learned later the abductors expected a long
siege. But forget that. They touch you?"
"Had my driver's license in my back pocket and felt a
hand. Then nothing until the cops."
"I'm sorry. Your license told them they had wrong
person. Instead they abducted Samuel rather than wait for
me."
"Don't be sorry. I shoulda put up a better fight. Kneed
one jerk."
"Don't talk that way. You coulda gotten killed."
"Like you said before, let's get outa here. Samuel needs
you."
A figure appeared at Belinda's hospital room door.
"Neither of you are going anywhere. That's orders from
Sheriff Edwards."
Alexa recognized the bearish physique of Officer Jones.

Belinda stretched her neck forward. "Who are you?"

"Corporal Wilson Jones. Sheriff detailed me to chaperone the both of you." His tight lips more a grimace than a smile. "Consider it house arrest with room service."

"I've got to find Samuel," Alexa pleaded.

"We've mobilized search and rescue. I'd rather suspect you don't know this county as we do. I understand you're both big city probation officers. Then you know the first hours critical. The Sheriff can't waste his time worrying about your whereabouts. You're both going to be right here. Isn't that so ladies?"

Alexa gazed at Belinda and Belinda shook her head. Then it dawned on Alexa. She'd ridden to the hospital with Corporal Jones. Belinda transported by ambulance. Their escape vehicle, Belinda's SUV, stranded miles away at the farm.

"You play gin?" Alexa asked. The ache in her heart for Samuel grew.

"Not on duty." The officer's shoulder blades wedged square between the room's doorjamb.

Alexa calculated his posture had to change sooner or later. What could she do? Her gaze wandered while Officer Jones never twitched. The vivid pastels of a framed watercolor faded as the sterile fluorescent bleakness replaced sunrays that had filtered through Belinda's window.

Alexa broke the latest silence. "Don't see a cast on your arm."

"Forearm's broken. It'll be casted after the swelling goes down. The ER doctor wrapped it tight in a pressure bandage." Belinda frowned. "He's married."

While Alexa tried to appear nonchalant by stuffing her fingers in her front jeans pockets, her biggest fear wouldn't go away. "Do you think they hurt Samuel?"

"Don't even go there."

Alexa paced in slow motion from the head to the foot of

218

Belinda's bed.

"Mind if I use your chair?" Corporal Jones asked.

"It's yours," Alexa replied. Now might be her chance if she got the officer's keys.

With his eyes fixed on Alexa, he stepped forward, grabbed the chair's curved handhold and screeched its feet across the linoleum floor until it rested parallel to the door. Corporal Jones sat. He blocked Alexa's exit with his boot sole at the doorjamb base.

Alexa searched for a distraction diversion to give her an opportunity to hurdle his right knee. With the officer's keys not visible, her snatch and hallway jump thwarted.

He pulled his size twelve black boot from the doorjamb to allow a nurse with a tray and a filled iced water pitcher to enter. She offered to roundup a second chair and Alexa agreed.

When audible dispatcher broadcasts blared on Corporal Jones' walkie-talkie, he dialed the volume to vibration. Alexa heard mention of the Waspi Bar.

With the nurse departed and a chair added, Alexa positioned herself alongside the bed at Belinda's head. Her left knee struck the lowered bedrail.

"Sorry," she whispered. Her back faced the corporal. "Could one have been Carl Skelton? Did you hear a large pickup?"

Belinda's head wobbled left to right before her eyelids closed. Alexa assumed sedation.

Alexa rose and ambled to Corporal Jones. "Sheriff should find the whereabouts of Carl Skelton. His pickup's been at the farm before."

"You sure?"

"Positive." Alexa pleaded, "What harm can come of it?"

Corporal Jones radioed Alexa's suggestion to the dispatcher with instructions to pass on to the Sheriff. "Roger" the only response.

"You know this Carl?" Corporal Jones asked.

"Brief acquaintance." She explained the tandem-tread gouge discovered at the farm.

"Interesting. He parks the pickup four to five nights a week at the Waspi Bar. Also seen it loaded with furniture and driven by his mother."

"You mean Lydia?"

"Had a cousin who tried to sell real estate for her office. Said Lydia's a real piece of work."

Chapter Twenty-seven

Alexa's battle with boredom dragged into the wee morning hours. The times Corporal Jones needed to use the restroom, he posted a nurse sentry. Each time static crackled his walkie-talkie, Alexa jumped. Belinda's light snores didn't spur a response from Alexa except a smile to Corporal Jones. When the clock-face hands reached two a.m., Corporal Jones rose. Alexa raised her left eyelid and didn't stir from her chair until he left the room. She tiptoed to his chair. Peeked into the corridor. He jogged toward her.

Alexa awoke at three a.m. to the left shoulder touch of a haggard Sheriff Edwards. "Your boy's in the ER."

Wild thoughts galloped through Alexa's mind. "Is he all right?" She rubbed sleep from her eyes. Her right knee crashed against the chair Corporal Jones had sat in.

The Sheriff caught Alexa by her shoulders. "Hold on. I'll escort you to him." His firm grip on her right elbow kept her pace equal to his. She wiped away tears as the mechanical whir of her one-floor elevator descent vibrated her soles. Alexa poked the "open door" button twice.

A nurse departed the interior Emergency Room with a tray piled high with bloody bandages. Alexa gasped.

Sheriff Edwards halted his steps. "You all right?"

Alexa inhaled deep and exhaled. "I want to hold Samuel."

Bright ER lights, eye moisture, and hummingbird-wing blinking blurred Alexa's vision. A man in scrubs pinned a child to a stainless steel table. A small stick protruded from the child's mouth.

Alexa rushed forward to hug her son. "Samuel, Samuel."

A male nurse restrained her. "Hold on. He'll swallow his lollipop."

Samuel rotated his head. He spit out the sucker. "Mommy, Mommy."

The doctor with a stethoscope draped around his neck and two hands on Samuel's torso, gazed toward Alexa. "He's fine. No broken bones, no lacerations. Bet he's hungry."

She hugged Samuel, squeezed him tight, and closed her eyes to the external world. Her entire world encased within her arms. She couldn't blame Belinda. She felt a tap on her left shoulder.

"Wife made sandwiches," Sheriff Edwards said. "I'll share. There's likely milk in the canteen vending machine." The doctor nodded his head.

The canteen location required they walk the hospital's entire first floor length. Sheriff Edwards switched on an overhead fluorescent light. Four tables ringed by seven vending machines left little room for private conversation. Alexa's concern moot unless others arrived. Sheriff Edwards plopped a child's lunch bag on the first table and plugged quarters into a milk machine. A carton clunked into its bottom-dispensing bucket.

"Thank you, Sheriff." With Samuel on her lap, she

ripped open the milk carton and inserted the straw the
Sheriff handed her. She touched the straw to Samuel's lips.
He bit into it.

"No, Samuel, suck, don't bite."

A sheepish smile lightened Sheriff Edwards' face as he
sat and unwrapped a sandwich. "Guess tuna on whole
wheat. Wife says this is better than liverwurst and onions."
He chuckled.

Alexa unwrapped a speckled sandwich from its clear
plastic. Samuel sucked on the straw. He refused to let it fall
from his mouth when Alexa waved half a sandwich.

"Do me a favor," the Sheriff said.

"Sure."

"Don't ask Samuel questions about his adventure until I
can talk with him. It's important."

She understood, and she didn't. "Okay."

"His memories can be helpful, although he can't yet
express them. If you ask him if this or that happened, he
might incorporate your words."

"Can I take him home?" Alexa waited until the Sheriff
finished chewing. "Can you tell me where you found him?"

"Wrapped in a blanket in a pickup. I shouldn't say
more."

Carl Skelton's name danced on Alexa's tongue. Her
lips didn't allow its escape.

"I presume you were the citizen to alert Corporal
Jones." Alexa bobbed her head twice. "Carl's got an alibi.
Passed out in a booth at the Waspi. His truck wasn't outside
the bar when we first checked. We thought he mighta
walked so we checked his home."

"And."

"Truck there on the street. Flashlights showed it to be
empty."

Samuel squirmed on her lap. She kissed the top of his
head. "Honey, eat your sandwich."

He tried one bite, then a second, and gazed at his

mother. "Sucker."

"Tomorrow, honey."

"I sent Jones home. I'll give you a ride to the farm."

Alexa handed Samuel to the Sheriff to visit Belinda. A groggy Belinda asked to see Samuel, and the Sheriff stepped into Room 204. Samuel pressed his face to the Sheriff's left shoulder.

"Sorry," Alexa said. "He's tired. Give me a ring on my cell and we'll drive in to pick you up. I've left a voice mail with our office supervisor."

Samuel's eyes widened, fascinated with the shining colored dashboard lights inside Sheriff Edwards' cruiser that often blinked. Samuel's fingers twined around the wire mesh that separated him and his mother from the Sheriff seated behind the steering wheel. Alexa pried Samuel's looped fingers free to fasten his seatbelt.

Alexa rambled that her suspicious office supervisor unlikely to buy Belinda's injury after Joe's fire caused their earlier delay.

"You suggest he call me. I'll vouch for both of you."

"Thanks." The Iowa countryside without a moon filled Alexa with an eerie sensation.

"You've got company," the Sheriff said. His voice edgy.

"Blue Buick should be Brad Haberkorn. SUV belongs to Belinda."

"You want me to ask him to leave?"

"Let's wait and see."

After the cruiser stopped, Alexa handed Samuel to the Sheriff. A lone figure approached and the Sheriff shoved Samuel into Alexa's arms. "Who goes there?"

"Alexa, it's Brad. You all right."

Alexa was so damn exhausted she didn't question Brad's presence. "Fine."

"Official scanner broadcasts translated into a county search and this farm."

"You sure?" the Sheriff asked. "We weren't public."

"You don't have to be. When there's periodic calls from four of your department cars notifying of locations and pit stops and the fire chief's mobile, it's a search. Anderson farm can only mean this one. You care to dispute?"

"Not now. It's been a long day."

In silence Alexa agreed a second dawn without sleep frayed her nerve endings. She lacked the energy to worry if a haggard Brad was alert enough to drive himself home. "Sheriff, I'll be okay. If you'll stay until you see the upstairs light, I'd appreciate it."

"Good night." The Sheriff walked to his cruiser, shut its rear door, and stood next to his driver's door.

Alexa fumbled in her pocket for the house key and couldn't find it.

"Here, let me." Brad mounted the rear porch steps and inserted a key into the kitchen door. Alexa hesitated at the door. Brad switched on a light. The upset table and chairs remained. She sidestepped the floor blood and carried Samuel upstairs to his bed, where she changed him into pajamas, kissed him twice, and tucked him in.

On the stair treads, she heard the Sheriff's cruiser depart. Brad leaned on the counter next to the sink. "I can sleep on the living room sofa. You look beat."

Alexa forced her lips into a smile. She noticed her purse on the counter.

"You take the house key from my purse?"

"No. Remember I've had a spare set."

She noticed no crime scene tape nor markers. "Help me lift this table."

They restored the table and chairs to usable positions. Alexa excused herself and climbed the stairs to the second floor. She peeked. Samuel slept. From her bedroom she lifted a blanket and pillow and returned to the kitchen to lay both on the table.

"Guess that means I can stay?"

Alexa considered she had no choice. Two cars in the farmyard could deter a second intruder invasion. At least no apartment neighbors lurked to wag their tongues. "I'll get a couple hours sleep and make breakfast."

"Sleep in. Stan'll backstop our office."

"Good night then." Alexa used the handrail to help her again climb the stairs to Grandma's bedroom. She let her T-shirt ring her neck until she unhooked and removed her bra. After slipping her arms into its sleeves, she kicked off her shoes, and stretched out on the bed. Sleep gushed into her body, and once ensconced, dulled her every sensation.

* * *

Bacon aromas filled her nostrils. A sizzling sound hip-hopped into her exposed left ear. Alexa rolled from her right side onto her back. Memories of honey-cured, hickory bacon enlivened her taste buds. Anxiety of no sound from Samuel sprung her legs to life.

Across the hall, Samuel's empty bed alarmed her for a second until she heard his downstairs request for a sucker. Brad's voice spurred her to splash water on her face, find clean underwear, and change into fresh jeans and a blue-striped tee.

"Mommy."

Brad, at the sink, twisted his torso toward her. Samuel slid from his chair and toddled to her. Alexa's one swift pendulum arc swung him side to side. When her arms tired, she hugged him tight. "No sucker." Samuel stared at her. She continued to shake her head no.

"Gee whiz, give him a break," Brad said. "He's been good."

"Some dad you'll be." Alexa's impromptu comment struck her silent. She feared further explanation would be a step, if not a jump, into quicksand.

"I try." Brad gazed out the sink window before he

225

shuffled his feet to face Alexa. "I spied the waffle package. Hope that's okay. There's only two eggs, and I didn't want to use your last."

"Belinda bought them. If blueberry, I'll take two." She wondered if Brad saw anything in the yard. His fork lifted six bacon strips from a stove pan. After two kisses and a hug, she let Samuel slide from her arms onto the floor, far from the blood stains.

Brad popped two waffles into the toaster. He poured a glass of orange juice without asking and set it on the table. Alexa sat and sipped. He served the waffles on a plate with a knife and added two bacon strips plus maple syrup. "Eat," he commanded.

Alexa drizzled syrup and cut the waffles and bacon into bite-sized pieces. Brad sunk his hands into the sink suds. His dishtowel under the drying rack exhibited training. His and Samuel's plates rinsed and stacked upright.

"You sleep well?" Brad asked.

"Like a rock. You?"

"Flashlights on the front lawn woke me, but disappeared when I found the front porch light."

A numbness settled within Alexa's body, unreplenished by adrenaline. "You hear a vehicle?"

He wiped his hands on a dishtowel. "That was the strange thing. I didn't."

"Any person in the yard?"

"Later, saw Oscar Erickson. He drove his old tractor, but I doubt he'd been in the fields."

"What makes you so sure?"

"Corn's too high. His tractor still had its row cultivator attached."

"You talk to him?"

"Nothing earth shattering. His boots had dirt on them, but not surprising for a farmer."

"He's been very nice. Don't doubt he comes by because of Joe."

"Thought he dug that hole in your cornfield."
Alexa finished her last waffle bite. "What hole?"
"In the field, east and a ways from that old car."
"Oh. I dug that hole. Oscar didn't."
"The canister?"
"You remember. Yeah, guess I'd better push dirt back."
Alexa's cell phone rang. She ran upstairs to Grandma's
bedroom and lifted it from the dresser. "Hello. Belinda."
She listened. "I'll be there at two-thirty." After her pivot,
Brad's presence in the bedroom doorway required Alexa to
corral her wits. "Belinda's being released from the hospital.
I'm to pick her up after lunch."

Embarrassed by her clothes strewn haphazard on the
floor, she announced in a strong voice, "Let's go
downstairs. I'll finish the dishes."

Alexa brushed Brad's left shoulder as she hurried from
the bedroom. Alexa stepped past Samuel playing with his
blocks and gazed out the window above the sink. She felt
Brad's breath on her neck. "I peeked in on you after the
lights awoke me."

She stiffened. "You needn't have."

"Didn't know if it were you outside on a search."

"For what?"

"Gold comes to mind."

Her shoulder bumped his chest in her pivot. "Is that all
anyone in this county thinks of? Gold? If I could toss this
gold into the air like a bride's bridal bouquet, I would.
Then maybe no one would terrorize Samuel and Belinda."

Brad's hands on her waist prevented her exhaustion
collapse. "Let it out, all of it. You're wound tighter than an
old wind-up wristwatch."

Alexa sobbed. She couldn't speak. Without his coaxing
her head rested on Brad's right shoulder. His left hand
rubbed her left shoulder blade. She closed her eyes. Iowa
without Grandma wasn't her world. Samuel was her world.

The brush of his lips to her hair condensed the space

between them. Her vulnerability frightened her. His compassionate non-threatening arms still rang the alarm. She jerked her head from his shoulder. "I've messed up your shirt."

"Trust me, we have wash machines in Iowa."

They both laughed. Alexa's sobs and laughter encapsulated potent medicine. The spell, if she could call it that, broken by Samuel's tug on her left leg.

"He craves attention," Brad said. "You sit. I'll chase him around the backyard."

Alexa sat, content to let her emotions simmer until Samuel's laugh exploded. She hustled to the porch to experience Samuel's joy. Samuel's absence, if less than one day, had horrified her.

She swung on the swing. Jeffrey the Monkey waved from an oak tree branch. Samuel rolled on top of Brad. When tickled, Samuel erupted in gleeful giggles. She remembered her dad's tickles, but he'd not romped with her in such a physical fashion. She guessed little girls were princesses in their father's eyes. Her dad had said she was.

"Mommy, help me."

Alexa gazed at her son and Brad lying in the grass. "You're doing great, Samuel."

"Tickle him, mommy."

Alexa exited the porch and reached her right hand to Brad's side. Before she realized it, she laid flat on the grass. Brad's thighs were at her sides and Samuel clung to Brad's neck. Suddenly his thighs pinched her no more.

"Speak, Alexa. Speak to me."

She opened her eyes to see Brad standing. She wouldn't explain the nightmares.

"You okay." He'd twisted Samuel around to his stomach and set him on the grass. Brad reached both of his hands toward her. He helped her to her feet.

"Guess I'm not cut out for men games."

"You terrified me. That expression on your face, I

couldn't describe it. When Samuel called you, I thought it was a game you'd played with him and, perhaps, his father."

Alexa trembled.

"Let me assist you to the porch; you're white as a ghost. If it was something I said, I'm sorry." He prodded Alexa by her shoulders. Samuel, distracted by a brownish moth, followed. "Here, sit in the swing. Can I get you a glass of water?"

Alexa grabbed Samuel's left hand. "Yes."

When Brad returned with three glasses, he handed one each to Alexa and Samuel and kept the third for himself. Samuel spilled his and Brad collected the empty glass and offered Samuel a drink of his. Brad's dramatic pause suggested he was thinking about possible constraints more substantial than Samuel's thirst. "I'm glad your color's returned."

"If you're a lawyer, and I tell you something, everything's in confidence, right?"

"If it's about the will, no. There's no lawyer/client privilege between us. I represent the estate . . . and you're the major beneficiary." His slow enunciation scared her. "You can't quote me . . . that'll disrupt in detrimental ways."

"You're thinking about the gold, aren't you?"

His gaze landed on her direct. "My thoughts are about you."

"And, the money I'd bank if I owned the farm."

He rotated the water glass within his hands. "I'm not rich, but my law practice elevates me above the income of most except . . . maybe a successful farmer."

Alexa regretted her attack on his motives. "I shouldn't have asked." The cases she handled resembled a costume ball. Attendees with small minds masqueraded in grand rented splendor with schemes to whisk away treasure.

"If I'd desired income, I'd have accepted the offered

Chicago associate position. I'm convinced I could've
earned partner and retired comfortable. Mind you, I don't
regret I chose Iowa." His voice grew stronger. "There's
positives here, if not always dollar signs."

"Guess Grandma recognized that when she wrote about
you."

"What?"

"Want to see the actual letter that Grandma never
mailed." Alexa wiped her brow.

Brad paced the porch railing; his left hand slapped the
wood.

Samuel squealed. Alexa swallowed hard, then relaxed.
A grasshopper leaped free of Samuel's right hand. He
crawled after it.

"My Grandma, bless her soul, always tried to be my
matchmaker. She praised Joe, rest his soul, and you." Alexa
failed to catch a hint of Brad's reaction or a late glint in his
eyes. "I'm not near desperate. I've made my way in this
world and that won't change because of Samuel."

"If I seem confused, it's because we don't know each
other."

"You've set your sights on women I haven't met?"

"Didn't say that, or, at least, didn't mean to."

"You closed your face, looked away."

"That's because I'm confused. You don't expose your
inner feelings, except where Samuel's concerned. Suspect
you've blamed me for the multiple delays with the probate
court."

"Who else should I blame?" The shrill in her voice
surprised her.

"Maybe the judge. He's making all the decisions."

"In Chicago, lawyers control judges. Operation
Graylord proved that."

Brad's eyes flashed. "Well, not in Iowa. Judges rule and
they, pardon my repetition, rule regardless of lawyers and
the latter's wishes for speed or justice ideals."

Alexa leaned her backside against the swing's support.

"Truce." Brad tucked his elbows to his sides and displayed his palms.

"Truce with one question. Did you tell anyone about that hole dug in the field?"

"No one. Cross my heart. Although Oscar mentioned it."

"When?"

"Told you I met him in the yard."

Alexa's right hand grabbed the swing's support. "He mention anything else?"

"No words of consequence. Chitchat, that's all. Why?"

"Maybe nothing. He seemed to know Grandma's apple cake recipe held the clue to finding the gold. Although he never said such, he always exhibited an insistent desire to get that recipe." Alexa's right hand covered her mouth.

"You're hiding something. What devilish trick did you play?"

She glanced at her wristwatch. "Give me a minute." Alexa picked up Samuel and carried him into the parlor. She adjusted the TV rabbit ears for the available cartoon channel. "There's your favorite talking cars." She left Samuel sprawled on the floor to return to Brad in the kitchen.

She sat in the chair Belinda favored. "Grandma had two apple cake recipes. I gave Oscar the one intuition told me Grandma didn't bake."

"How could you be certain?"

"Grandma had a margin-writing habit. Wait here."

Alexa bounded two stairs at a time to Grandma's bedroom. Grandma's recipes had become her traveling keepsake and occupied an inner suitcase pocket. Careful not to let a page fall, she carried the recipes to the kitchen and set them before Brad.

She lifted the first twenty pages. "See, this one, the next, and so on. I recognize Grandma's swirls and dots."

Brad elevated his eyes from recipes to Alexa. "And the one given Oscar?"

"Typed. No writing."

"Interesting. But you've no way to know he wanted the recipe for the gold."

"Think so. He paced the field near the old car once his hands secured the recipe."

"So? Everyone in the county has ideas about the gold."

"Like your stuffed tires?"

"We could check to see if I'm right."

Alexa shook her head. "Don't think so."

"With the hole . . . the canister . . . you know where the gold is, don't you?"

She tried to disguise her stiff voice. "Sorta." To lie wasn't her forte.

"Can't believe anything that vague. Your strained expression says you do."

"It's not important. Gold can't guarantee Mother's freedom or revive Joe. Besides, Grandpa's money was his and he could've bought a hundred acres or farm livestock."

Her cell phone rang. "Yes. Don't know exact time Belinda will be released from the hospital. We both hope it's soon. I'll update no later than tomorrow if that's okay?" She ended her call and gazed at Brad. "Chicago boss. One of his better days."

"I can help. Two heads often better than one."

"Let me think. I should check Samuel. He's too quiet."

Her chair footpad squeaked on the linoleum. In the parlor she found her mischief suspicion unfounded. Samuel's feet noiseless on the carpet. He danced along with the animated hands and feet of the cartoon stop sign.

When he finished, she clapped, and he toddled to her with a big grin.

"Bathroom?" Alexa led Samuel by the hand, closed the door, and left him inside.

"Flush?" she asked.

He reversed his steps and complied.

Brad waited in the kitchen.

Alexa's cell phone rang. "Great news. Samuel and I'll be there." She flipped her phone closed. "Belinda. She's being released in an hour."

Crunching gravel in the farmyard diverted Alexa's attention from Samuel. She released his right hand to stride to the sink window.

"Sheriff Edwards." Alexa dashed to the table. "Give me those recipes."

"But I'm not through trying to find what your Grandma said about me."

She squared her stack; her right hand bumped Brad's hand. Her day-one tingling nerve sensation reborn. Without time to race upstairs, she concealed the recipes in an upper cabinet.

She stared at Brad. "Not one word."

Alexa opened the kitchen door. "Come in, Sheriff."

"Thanks. Came to speak to Samuel. You can listen." He glanced at Brad. "No one else."

Brad rose. "I'll roam outside." He closed the kitchen door.

The Sheriff reached into his pocket. When his right hand emerged, he offered a shiny silver badge to Samuel. "Please raise your right hand for the oath as an official youth deputy."

Alexa coaxed Samuel from his hug of her left leg and raised his right hand.

"You swear to tell me about the bad guys, help your mom, and speak the truth."

"Mommy."

"That's a 'yes,' Sheriff. Let's sit in the parlor." She pulled Samuel's right hand without waiting for the Sheriff to agree. She propped Samuel on the center sofa cushion and plopped beside him. The Sheriff perched his body on an armchair's front cushion half. He slid his hat onto a nearby lamp table.

"Samuel, you remember yesterday with Miss Belinda?"

Samuel gazed at Alexa. His hands clutched his silver badge.

"Tell him, honey."

Samuel switched his gaze to the Sheriff. "Me like Bla . . . linda."

"Good boy. Samuel, how many men did you see?"

"Not like lady."

"What lady?" The Sheriff gazed at Alexa. His eyes registered confusion. "Miss Belinda?"

Samuel shook his head no.

"Was this lady you didn't like with a man?"

Samuel rubbed his left forearm. "Lady hurt me."

"Where? Can you show me?"

"Arm." Samuel raised and continued to rub his left forearm.

Alexa saw no scab or other evident wound.

"Any other place, honey? Maybe your leg or head?" She pointed to the spots she mentioned.

Samuel gazed at Alexa. He again shook his head.

"Did you see a man, Samuel?" the Sheriff asked.

Samuel nodded.

"How many men? Can you show me with your fingers?"

Samuel's right hand displayed two fingers.

"Good, Samuel. Did they take you anywhere?"

Alexa witnessed a veil of confusion lower itself across Samuel's face.

"Honey, did you ride in a car?"

Samuel shook his head no.

"A truck, a pickup like mommy has?"

"Big truck. No talking car."

Alexa strangled a chuckle at the Sheriff's arrested expression. Samuel's vital memory wasn't to be distracted. "He watched talking-car cartoons before you arrived."

234

"Thank you." The Sheriff relaxed and focused his gaze on Samuel. "Samuel, can you tell me the color of this big truck you rode in?"

Samuel shook his head three times.

"Did the lady hold you?"

"Not like lady."

The Sheriff's eyeballs rotated to Alexa without a head movement. "I'll take that as a yes. Was a man there with the lady?"

Samuel nodded twice.

"Did the bad people wear jeans like your mother?"

Samuel continued his nods.

"What color shirt? You remember the lady."

Samuel gazed at Alexa. He tried to roll off the sofa, and she caught him by his shoulders.

"That's okay, Samuel," the Sheriff said. "You've been a great deputy."

Samuel extended the badge to the Sheriff.

"You keep it. That's yours. You're my deputy, Samuel. Remember, I'm counting on you."

"Thanks." Alexa rose. "Don't know he helped."

Samuel hid behind Alexa's legs. His eyes peeked once and then disappeared.

"He did great," Sheriff Edwards said. "Confirmed the pickup we found him in more than likely at the farm earlier. The thing I can't figure out is why there was no ransom demand. Reading between the lines, his abductor didn't exhibit pedophile tendencies. Was food stolen?"

"None I can determine."

"Supports persons not strangers." The Sheriff stood to join Alexa.

"What about the lady Samuel spoke of?"

"With the truck I thought of the Skelton's, but Lydia's not the type to wear jeans."

"I thought of her, too."

Samuel still hadn't released his grip when Alexa waved

good-bye to the Sheriff from the rear porch. Brad leaned against the oak. Alexa's stride sluggish with an attached Samuel.

"Samuel help?" Brad asked.

"Big time. He's a full-fledged deputy." Alexa lifted Samuel's right hand with his badge.

"Wow. All I ever had was a decoder ring." Brad reached for the badge and Samuel swung his hand behind his back. "I'll see it later. He naps, right?"

Alexa laughed. Samuel toddled away as fast as his legs could motor. He held his badge high, stopped, and plopped onto the grass. To avoid Samuel's hands, a white-winged moth fluttered above his head.

"See, you lost your chance. He's rejoined his insect world." Her belly laugh bubbled past her lips. Alexa couldn't remember a time she'd laughed as much. She heard her cell phone ring.

She ran to the kitchen. After a gasp for breath, she avoided the phone's voice mail activation. She listened. "I'm sorry. Right away."

Alexa tossed her phone into her purse. She didn't remember it open. No worry. From the porch she shouted to Samuel. "Honey, do you need to go to the bathroom?"

"Brad, you must excuse us. I've lost track of time. Belinda's waiting at the hospital."

"Ride with me."

"You've done enough already. I shouldn't impose. Besides, I should get Samuel lunch."

"No imposition. The four of us can stop at Rosie's. My treat."

Chapter Twenty-eight

The lunch rush no longer evident when Brad, Belinda, Alexa, and Samuel entered Rosie's. Alexa switched Samuel to her right hip to hide the counter suckers. At least, he wouldn't nag her until after he'd eaten nutritious food.

The server led them to a large booth still wet.

"You talk to the Sheriff?" Alexa asked Belinda.

"This morning."

"Near lunch for me. He visited the farm and Samuel earned a deputy's badge."

Belinda frowned. "I'd rather eat lunch than talk about it."

"Why? Didn't the hospital serve you lunch?"

"Sure they did." Belinda's voice gruff. She glared. "Did I eat it is a separate question?"

Alexa cringed. She hadn't experienced Belinda in such a foul mood since the aftermath of a broken relationship two years ago. Alexa skipped Richard's name and a mention of the dazzling engagement ring on Belinda's finger. "Let's order. Samuel will have the chicken nuggets. Me, whatever the special is."

Brad and Belinda succumbed to Alexa's forceful conduct. They ate their served meals without further allusion to the prior day's traumatic events.

Brad dropped the two women and Samuel at the farm. He held Alexa's right hand and whispered for her to telephone him if he could help. Her half-hearted promise left the when unresolved. She wasn't ready to go any farther.

The television blared from the parlor as Alexa entered the kitchen. A peek confirmed the recipe's cabinet presence. She strolled into the parlor. Samuel played with blocks on the carpet. Belinda sat slumped in the chair warmed by the Sheriff.

"Belinda, stretch out on the sofa. I'll sit in the chair."

Belinda ignored Alexa's request and her tears escalated into out-of-control sobs. Alexa's right arm embraced Belinda's shoulders.

Belinda gazed at Samuel, then tilted her eyes to Alexa. "Let's go into the kitchen. Samuel can watch TV."

Alexa aided Belinda to her feet and guided her trembling friend. She pushed two kitchen chairs together to allow them to clasp their hands. Alexa permitted Belinda to start slow.

"One man forced me onto the sofa, face up, knee to my stomach, hand on my throat. Heard a zipper and didn't think it was my jeans, no tug. One whispered he'd not hurt me if I'd be nice. Ran fingers against my jeans. Threatened to have me."

"Belinda, I'm so sorry."

"Rubbed my diamond finger. Taunted me that my fiancé could enjoy seconds."

"Did he?" Alexa couldn't mouth additional words.

Belinda shook her head twice. "He said he'd save himself for you."

Alexa trembled. The blood drained from every vein in her brain. Violent flashbacks caused her to shudder. She told no one in Iowa about Nina and her boyfriend's attack. No one she'd met in Iowa crossed paths with her in Chicago. A renewed shudder immobilized her. *Except Brad.* But she couldn't recall meeting him until after she'd required an attorney for Grandma's will. The will delays. Had he created them? How would she know?

Had Grandpa's gold been a smokescreen, a ruse? Anyone could've buried the canister. The crude map included no verifiable tidbit to prove Grandpa buried it.

Finally, Alexa mumbled, "Belinda, you tell the Sheriff?"

"What for? Can't DNA sample air, no semen traces."

"You forget your ripped blouse?"

"No big deal. Refused to unbutton it myself. Figured any delay I could impose would be to my benefit."

"The attacker ripped your blouse?"

"And more."

"Oh, Belinda." Alexa repressed her own memories.

"Don't sweat it." Belinda chuckled. "I've had firmer bra rubs and random skin pokes by the Amazon at Macy's who claimed to possess a professional Maidenform fit certificate."

Alexa once walked out on the lady. "Guess you didn't explain this to the Sheriff either?"

"Hell no. Don't want an Internet psychopath three months from now to wave a police report and extort Richard for the detailed story of his violated wife. You won't blab will you?"

"Of course not."

"Knew I could trust you." The relief on Belinda's face helped calm Alexa.

"Samuel said one attacker was a woman. You see or hear a woman?"

"Saw little blindfolded. Never heard a woman's voice. Cotton balls stuffed into my ears. Every time a breath warmed my exposed skin it preceded a groping hand."

"You smell any food?"

"Sherlock, you're good. But, no. I tried to focus. I'll swear one man; the one that spoke and poked me wore Stetson Cologne. Smelled it this morning in a hospital magazine."

"That's great. Remember anything else?"

"Tried. No spaghetti and meatballs or bar-b-que sauce. Does manure count?"

"You smelled manure?"

"No. Just kidding. There's no manure smell on your grandmother's farm. Well, only when that old tractor guy from down the road visits. But it wasn't him. I'm sure."

"What about the woman? Smell perfume?"

"No."

Alexa scrambled to put the chaotic puzzle together. "Hear heels click?"

Despite her words, no visceral comfort filled Belinda's eyes. "No, no, no."

Flooded instinct swerved Alexa in a different direction. "You hear Samuel scream?"

Belinda's answer quick. "Once."

Alexa trembled. Samuel said the lady hurt him. "Where was Samuel?"

"Don't know. Kitchen maybe. Like I said, blindfolded, carried into the front room, and kept there the whole time. The TV volume blasted after Samuel's scream and then the cotton balls stuffed into my ears. Saw Samuel at the diner; he wasn't hurt was he?"

"No cuts or bruises. However, I worry about his psyche."

Guilt ebbed. Belinda's mandible sagged. "I should've protected him."

"Chill. You did everything one could expect. Me included."

"Thank you. What about our boss? I never answered the hospital phone."

"Covered. Said you're hospitalized. We should ask the Sheriff to say he needs to have us stay the week. He hinted he'd vouch for us. You anxious to go to work?"

"Not unless it subdues my nightmares."

"Trust me, it won't." Alexa didn't explain; Belinda knew of what she spoke.

"Glass of chilled chardonnay would be comforting."

"We don't have wine."

Belinda squirmed in her chair. "Cold beer?"

"Sit still. Iced tea coming up."

Chapter Twenty-nine

Alexa sat at the kitchen table. Belinda's signature snores descended the stairs and floated to the ceiling. When first laid down, Samuel resisted a nap, but now lay curled on the parlor sofa.

With all that had transpired, Alexa likewise favored a nap, however, her active brainwaves refused to be tamed. She'd been the target in Chicago because she'd tried to help Nina, one of her cases. Nina's boyfriend objected and lashed out to protect his harem, well, more than that, to humiliate Alexa. She'd not tried to harm anyone in Iowa.

Was her periodic presence enough to inflame hatred? Had Grandma's reluctance to share her recipes maddened a tight-knit community against her extended family? Why didn't folks let her inherit and then sell? That struck Alexa as the most logical. Alexa feared she'd never understand. What sign had she missed? Who had she underestimated or misunderstood?

Belinda's flip-flops clattered as she descended the stairs. "You look serious. The boss call?"

"No. What if we and others have everything wrong?"

Belinda rubbed her eyes. "You're losing me. What wrong?"

"The gold. If Grandpa bought land, he couldn't admit where he got the money. Grandma helped him by spending one gold piece and then no more to squelch tales of untold riches. That did two things: 1) disguised the gold as spent, and 2) quashed rumors of Grandpa as a thief."

"Sherlock, you've gone crazy mad!"

"Remember that canister and the map to Wisconsin? Checked an atlas. There isn't town nor dam named 'Mahot' in Wisconsin. No Indian name close."

"Didn't two map lines unite into one?" Alexa nodded.

241

"Your grandparents weren't dumb. Two interstates merge in Wisconsin near Tomah. 'Mahot' is close if spelled backwards."

Alexa craved convincing. "You think?"

Belinda stared blindly at the kitchen door, her jaw set. "Now's not the time to doubt me."

"Still, even if true, there's no logical sense." Alexa slowed her mind to one step at a time.

"Does anyone know how much gold your grandpa stole from Al Capone?"

Alexa doubted the information's usefulness. "Best I know is two bags."

"Full?"

"Heavens." Had Belinda lost her grip on the pragmatic? "How should anyone alive know?"

"If your grandmother counted salt teaspoons, she surely stacked gold coins."

Alexa shrugged. "If I grant you that, what says she told me?"

"Don't know, but I'm tired of being left out. Now who's that?"

The long absent, familiar putt-putt wafted through the raised kitchen sink window sash. Alexa rose to gaze into the farmyard. "Later. Must see what Oscar wants."

Old Betsy's brakes creaked in the farmyard. Oscar waved as Alexa descended the porch steps. On other days Oscar drove around the machine shed into the field. Alexa strode his way.

"Sorry to bother you." His quizzical bloom wilted. "Guessed you'd be gone."

Alexa shifted her weight to her right foot. "My friend was in the hospital."

"Sorry to hear that." His voice sincere. "Heard the Sheriff searched for your son."

Alexa reacted to blunt gossip without a full reveal. "He's safe."

Oscar's right hand lifted his wide-brim straw hat from his head. "Thank God."

She tested him. "Sheriff Edwards said the neighbors pitched in to help."

"Tried to do what we could." Alexa equated his earlier deflection to the Sheriff with protective ego. "That's why I'm here now." Alexa sought to understand without her interruption. "We don't like bad things happening. We're a peaceful folk, law abiding. Take pride in that. Help our neighbors when we can."

How could she argue? "Appreciate that."

"Came to tell you the menfolk from neighboring farms met at the church this morning at sunup. That was after the Sheriff put a temporary hold on his search." He donned his straw hat. "We voted unanimous to put a guard on this farmhouse when you returned."

"Your gesture is very kind." Alexa struggled to say no, then couldn't. "Is it necessary?"

"No offense, but with Joe gone, there's no man here. We've already divvied up shifts. I'll be here at sunset. We'll stay near the road, not trouble you."

Alexa elevated patrolling guards to the antithesis of freedom. "You sure?"

Oscar nodded. "We'd be proud to do it. If an intruder slips past one of us, you flip the parlor lights. The guard will contact the Sheriff. We all got womenfolk and a desire to keep criminals from our community. None of us shy away from his duty to protect his family or farm."

Alexa shied away from reading between the lines of Oscar's words that the entire county surmised what befell Belinda. Several Chicago police officers knew what had happened to Alexa. Their fleeting glances and hushed voices had made Alexa skittish around police officers, even those who were Dad's friends.

"Thanks, Oscar. We'll be here tonight. Don't know about tomorrow."

"It's the least we could do." He paused as he adjusted his hat. "Have a personal question."

Unexpectedly, numbness seeped from her heart. "Yes."

"You might not have seen it, but Joe had a small gun-shaped cigarette lighter. Authorities said they didn't find one. I tried to look. Wasn't successful. Maybe he gave it to your son?"

"Samuel doesn't have it. Sorry."

"You can understand I had to ask. My father gave it to me; I gave it to Joe." His right hand wiped across his eyes. "Well, guess no big deal," he muttered. "Can't pass it along, anyway."

Alexa gazed at the ground.

"That's all. Remember, flick the front room lights."

"Will do."

Chapter Thirty

Alexa parked in front of Carl Skelton's house and left Belinda and Samuel in Belinda's SUV. She rotated her eyes from the street to the neighboring houses for any clue Carl hadn't left. Mid-afternoon shadows failed to deter Alexa. A pregnant Margaret should be home. She knocked.

When the front door opened, Alexa blinked. Her eyes met Susan from Red Top Realty.

"What a surprise. I've been meaning to call you. Radio news said the search for your son found him safe."

"We're fine." Alexa deflected Susan to her main goal. "Margaret home?"

"Tell her to come in," a feminine voice behind Susan said.

After a step inside, Alexa glimpsed Margaret lying on the sofa. "Sorry. Is this is bad time?"

"No," Margaret replied. "Doctor's orders. Yet, I can't stand to lie in my bed all day."

"One question. You musta heard they found Samuel in a pickup similar to Carl's."

Margaret's eyelids drooped. Susan excused herself to the kitchen.

Alexa steeled herself. "Need to know if Carl wears Stetson Cologne."

Margaret scrunched her lips together, the upper one slightly twisted. "He doesn't even use aftershave." Her distended stomach rumbled. "Why you interested in Stetson?"

"Samuel's allergic to it," she lied. "Exposure means I have to have him checked."

Susan interjected, "Stetson's common in these parts."

Alexa frustrated Susan's doorway presence distracted from Margaret's unaided reaction. Susan's right hand grasped a glass of water, her left a brown pill bottle.

"Susan's right," Margaret said. "If you believe TV ads, most men favor Axe, not Stetson."

A whiff of Margaret's Chanel No. 5 perfume triggered Alexa's recall of their prior conversation. "Thanks. I'll see myself out." Alexa's right hand didn't allow the door to bang.

Before she hopped into the SUV front passenger seat, Alexa waved to Samuel in his car seat. She expected Belinda's huge interest. "Margaret said Carl doesn't use Stetson or aftershave."

"That wasn't Margaret at the door, or did she have her baby?"

"Susan from Red Top Realty. Jolted me, too."

Belinda's arms straightened, her palms on the steering wheel. "The Skelton's selling?"

"Didn't ask and wouldn't think so. Couldn't fathom

245

Lydia not getting a family listing."

Mirth faded from Belinda's eyes. "Stupid question."

"Then again, perhaps Margaret wants nothing to do with her husband and not listing with her mother-in-law her best choice at revenge."

Belinda twisted the ignition. "You don't see anything simple, do you?"

"Only trying to talk out the alternatives. Margaret's not a disrupter. That's my take."

"Then we'll go with that . . . that is until independent evidence is contrary."

"You saying we need a stakeout?"

* * *

Alexa tried to stretch her right arm. Its numbness proof she cradled Samuel too long. The tingling that pricked her fingers was a small price to pay to confirm her arm hadn't dropped off her shoulder.

Alexa yawned, "You see anything?"

Belinda lowered her binoculars. "Nothing. No lights in the house since Carl came home."

"Samuel can't sleep like this all night. This stakeout was a stupid idea."

"Shush. There's no light, but there's an engine noise."

Alexa didn't approve of being parked a block from the Skelton house. If she'd been able to do this stakeout alone, her scenario would've been different. Her logic hadn't persuaded Belinda at nine p.m., nor did it now when time slipped into a new day.

Both ducked as vehicle headlights crossed the intersection in front of them.

"Let's follow," Belinda whispered. "That's Carl's pickup."

"Maybe it's a hospital run?"

Belinda eased her SUV forward and into a right turn. "Doubt it. All the house lights would've been on."

246

Samuel rubbed his eyes. "It's okay, honey. Mommy's still holding you."

The tandem-wheeled pickup signaled a second right into the parking lot alongside the Waspi Bar. Alexa groaned when Belinda drove past the bar to park a block south.

Belinda scrambled from the driver's seat. "Stay here." She latched her door.

Unable to voice an objection, Alexa had no choice but to wait. Belinda's silhouette blended into the all-consuming darkness. If this had been a residential street, she would've expected a flicked on porch light. The sole change a pulled window shade in an apartment above a store. Samuel's closed eyes blocked his imagination from being excited by the unrelenting circles of a half dozen moths as they dive-bombed a glowing pole-mounted street lamp.

The driver's door handle clicked.

Alexa's shoulders stiffened before her head jerked left. She exhaled at Belinda's sight.

"Strange. Carl parked his truck behind the bar, didn't go in, and walked toward his house."

Alexa expressed her one concern. "He see you?"

"Nah. He didn't waste time gawking. Don't understand why he left home at all."

"No other vehicle lights disturbed us. He lock it?"

"Don't think so. Didn't see taillights flash. Be interested if someone goes near his truck."

"So would I. However, it's late and a sentry at the farm could set off a countywide manhunt if we don't sleep at Grandma's tonight."

* * *

Trying not to crush the two cigarette packs in her right hand, Alexa rock-stepped to an imaginary beat in the dingy Lake County Jail interview room. Mother would not expect her on a Monday. Mother's dropped jaw served as proof.

The metal door clanged shut behind the matron whose right arm pushed Mother into the room.

"Have a seat Mother." The door deadbolt screeched. Alexa unsure if oil in the penal budget.

"What's up? You're here, not at work." Mother smoothed a heavily starched blouse. "But grapevine buzzed with young Chicago woman kidnapped. Expected the worst."

"Guess good news needs time to travel through the walls. Sheriff found Samuel safe and sound. Belinda manhandled, but she'll be fine." Alexa held the smokes to her chest.

"Thank goodness." Mother eyed the cigarettes and gazed at the matron's face pressed against the door's small window. "If those are for me, leave them on the table between us when the matron stops staring. What she sees, she confiscates. Pull hand away slow. We can't touch."

Alexa's sideward glance saw no face in the window. She slid the cigarettes forward.

"How's your case progress?" Alexa asked.

"Can't get bail." Her Mother's left hand removed one pack, and it disappeared into her blouse. "Lawyer says not to say a word. Appear before a judge next week."

"Don't understand. Isn't your trial next? You've had an arraignment. Did your lawyer file motion for speedy trial?"

"Don't know. You're the one who needs to get me outa this rat hole."

Alexa ducked the devil's fire in Mother's accusation. She glanced to the ceiling, counted to ten, lest Mother's penetrating stare scorched her retina. Alexa imagined hatred oozed from Mother's heart like a rotten potato's grayish-white mush.

"Lawyer said one thing." Mother placed her left hand to her mouth, her index and second finger separated by the width of a dime. "Partial finger print not mine. Lydia Skelton."

Alexa skeptical. Mother once said Lydia wore gloves when they had their one conversation. If Mother took the matchbook, as she said, from the diner, when would Lydia's print adhere? Was Mother mistaken? Alexa, under the circumstances, initially doubted Mother schemed. Another matchbook? The wider her thought arced, the greater Alexa's confusion.

"How many conversations did you and Lydia Skelton have?"

The matron's nose again pressed to the window. She displayed two fingers and left.

"One," Mother said. Hard vocal edges matched her etched face. "I told you that."

"So what's the public defender doing about it?"

Mother slipped second cigarette pack into her blouse. "Wants to locate witnesses."

Alexa bowed her head and whispered. "How can he locate witnesses? The trailer was at Grandma's farm. Only Belinda and I were there that night."

"You sure Belinda's truly your friend?"

Alexa jerked her eyes wide. "Mother!"

"Sorry. My lawyer says Belinda's the jealous hot-headed type. She threatened a woman with a gun who approached her boyfriend in a bar. Charges withdrawn. Lawyer said she must've known influential legal system persons."

"She's like me, a probation officer. We're in contact with authorities all the time."

"Well . . . then."

"Well, what?" Alexa gazed at the room's door. The matron returned, held up one finger.

"Pull strings. I'm your mother for God's sake." Mother's voice rose two octaves. "You must be owed favors. Get me outa here."

"My job's in Chicago, not Iowa. There's no transfer."

"I'm gonna die in here." Mother trembled. She

squeezed her shaky right hand into a fist.

Alexa landed the mythical kite that represented her emotions to reassure herself and Mother. "You'll be fine, Mother. I know you didn't do it."

Mother pointed her right forefinger to the large glass mirror. "Tell that to them jerks."

A conflicted Alexa would've liked to give Mother a hug. Apart from the jail's no contact rules, she feared it would've been a cold experience. Outside, she inhaled a full breath to exhale the stale jail air. Belinda leaned against her SUV. Samuel squirmed in her arms. Circumstances dictated no separate trips.

"We need to stop by Brad's law office."

"Why?" Belinda asked. "You going through withdrawal since he hasn't stopped out at the farm in what . . . a day?"

"It's not like that. I've a question for Brad about Mother."

"You're confusing." Belinda stood tall. "Make little sense. He's not your mother's attorney."

Alexa grabbed Samuel. "Trust me."

Alexa, after buckling in for the two block drive to Brad's office, calculated she could've saved Belinda's gas and walked there faster, even toting Samuel.

The gray-haired lady seated at the Baker, Haberkorn Law Office receptionist desk smiled at Alexa. Her enlivened expression lingered longer on Samuel. She led Alexa and Samuel to the conference room where Alexa selected the chair she recalled from her first visit. She pulled it from the table to allow Samuel to sit on her lap.

The room's door opened. Samuel's eyes widened at Brad's familiar face.

"This is a pleasant surprise."

Alexa refused to let her voice waver. "Business, nothing else."

"Good. My schedule is jammed this morning."

"Mother says she sees a judge next week. Her public

defender says the print on the motel matchbook was Lydia Skelton. Why haven't they released Mother?"

"Wait a minute. It's not my case. As I told you before, Stan doesn't tell me everything."

"Well then you should tell him that Belinda isn't involved."

"Whoa. Only met her a time or two with you at the farm."

"Mother says Stanislaw suspects Belinda because of some jealousy incident in Chicago."

"Hold on. Take a breath. For the second time, let me repeat I don't know anything."

"You should." Alexa adjusted her grip on Samuel.

"No one's all seeing. Don't know why a man with a rifle stopped me last night just after sunset when I slowed near the entrance to your grandmother's farm."

"Why were you there?"

"To see you." He edged toward the door. "What else?"

"There was no reason for us to talk."

His right hand fingers rubbed his shirt button. A decision lurked behind his grim expression. "Don't understand big city girls." His gaze vacillated between Alexa and Samuel. "Never have. Guess I never will."

"What kind of put down was that?"

Brad's right hand dropped to encircle the doorknob. "An honest one."

"Samuel and I should leave. And, quicker the better. You've abandoned Mother and written off big city women, or should I be quaint and say girls."

"Before you leave please be advised the judge will issue a will ruling in three days."

"Whoa. You've told me lawyers can't know when judges will do things."

"I did, but the judge let it slip . . . . Who knows why? I think it was purposeful. I didn't ask. Anyway, you now know what I know." He slipped out of the room.

Alexa sat still. Three days. A lifetime. But should she confide in Belinda? She mumbled to Samuel that attorneys were no better than used car salesmen. When reunited with Belinda she put off Belinda's questions. They did agree not to stop at Rosie's. No sentry guarded the farm's entrance. Then she recalled no rifleman would materialize until darkness.

"Mommy, me hungry."

"Yes, honey. We'll be in the kitchen soon."

Alexa gazed at the oak tree. Jeffrey waved. Alexa tugged at Samuel's hand. The oak sported a fuzzy growth. Grandma had said not to worry because nature could heal its imperfections.

Alexa unwrapped two graham crackers from the upper kitchen cabinet to keep Samuel quiet until she prepared lunch. She gazed at Belinda. "I know you love Richard, but has he ever done anything that really upset you?"

"Don't think so. Was your visit with Brad so far off kilter you lost your voice until now?"

"What about another guy? Maybe threaten you with a gun?"

"What's going on?" The spoon from her glass clattered on the table.

"He added fuel to the fire Mother started."

She sipped as her gaze never wavered. "What?"

Alexa paced left. "Don't know how to say this."

Belinda steadied her cadence. "Say it simple."

"Mother's attorney is developing a defense she didn't do it because a jealous person close to me did it after I went on a date with Joe."

Belinda's eyes flashed. "Bull. There's only one person to accuse . . . me, right?"

"Yeah. But I don't believe you killed Joe, even if you threatened another woman with a gun."

"Bull." Belinda's fist pound flipped her spoon. "That bogus old story rears its ugly head."

Alexa regretted being caught in the middle. "It's true you threatened a woman with a gun?"

"Well, not threatened. A friend tossed me a gun when a loud woman held a broken beer bottle. I couldn't let it hit the floor, discharge, and hurt someone. That's the true story. The woman told police she overreacted. That's why the prosecutor filed no charges."

"You didn't pull strings?"

"Me? You with a police dad has pull, not me. Give your mother's attorney applause for digging. But I ain't doing time for a crime I didn't commit, even if it springs your mother."

"Didn't for a minute think you'd done it."

"Yet, after everything said so far, you and Brad didn't steal a kiss outside Samuel's view?"

"Why should we? He's Grandma's will attorney."

"Sure." A coy smile graced Belinda's lips. "So . . . Samuel likes him. Mommy doesn't?"

Alexa tried to keep her eyes cool. "I could like him."

Belinda stuck her spoon into her glass. "That's a step in the right direction."

"He doesn't cotton to big city girls, and in his mind that includes me."

"Let's skip that I caught your sense of longing. Why doesn't he like big city girls?"

Alexa had to rely on conjecture. "Bad experience is my guess. He lived in Chicago."

"But you'll agree all big city girls, or did he say women?"

Rather than unjumble Belinda's full question, Alexa relied on fact. "He said girls."

"Two demerits. Moving on." Belinda's voice exposed an undertone of challenge. "You're not typical. More sensitive than most. You don't go in for all those fashion dictates. Not to say, mind you, you don't dress nice."

"Knock it off. You can't make a silk purse out of a

sow's ear."

"Wow. What big city woman talks like that? Your not-so-big-city persona busts through. Has Brad seen this rural version of you?"

"Quit it. I'm me, not different people. And, I don't want to be different people."

"Didn't infer you have multiple personalities. Underneath you might not be the big city girl, sorry, woman the urban magazines highlight."

"Don't know where you're going. But if it's back to your prior statement, I should spread my legs to Brad and toss him away like a rag doll, I'm not going there. You can use any analogy you like. I'm not a Chicago girl ready to channel a bulging river upstream nor will I be an innocent virgin farm girl with a fertile field that awaits the plow."

"Wow, you've been reading best-selling fiction." Belinda's voice slowed. "Trust your own feelings when it gets to the nitty-gritty. Tell me, you've feelings for Brad."

Alexa stirred her boiling saucepan. "I'd say confused feelings."

"Don't explain. Been there. Don't need your explanation to befuddle me."

"Guess that's why we're best friends."

Belinda flashed a thumbs up. "Forever and ever."

"Mommy, cracker."

Samuel's request halted Alexa's theorizing. The give-and-take convinced her Belinda innocent of Joe's death. No matter how any lawyer tried to manipulate history, Belinda retained store receipts from that night. And, she was positive Mother hadn't ignited the fatal blaze.

Why did the criminal theories expand to tarnish the people closest to her? Why? Was this small town prejudice? Suspect only outsiders. Protect yourself and your neighbor by tossing blame outside the county? No subterranean connections to Iowa invaded her inner circle.

Alexa's resolve broke and she handed Samuel a graham

cracker half.

At the sound of vehicle on gravel, she moved to the kitchen window. A Buick entered.

"Brad's here. For what I don't know."

"Delay lunch," Belinda said. "I need a nap upstairs."

Alexa dialed a stove burner to off, hoisted Samuel onto her hip, and left the kitchen door ajar to meet Brad on the porch. She thought it unusual he carried a black attaché case. He set it on the railing. Alexa gazed into his eyes without speaking.

"You should be aware Sheriff Edwards said in a court hallway this morning he plans to question you again."

"What for?" Alexa sat Samuel on the porch deck. She handed him his second graham cracker half. She plopped onto the swing.

Brad straddled a chair. "From what I gathered, the hospital report states your injuries the night of Joe's fire were self-inflicted."

"What's that got to do with anything?" She flailed her hands, a useless gesture, like the spits of rain that threatened to dampen porch planks from a cloudless sky. "I wanted to save Joe."

Brad shoved his right hand through his hair. "Sheriff's fire question likely a smoke screen to disguise his inquiry into why a citizen last night spotted Belinda's SUV roaming Lakeview."

Alexa hardened her reluctance to cooperate. "That's personal."

A cold sharpness invaded his voice. "If you say that to me, I can't do anything about it. However, Sheriff Edwards can."

Alexa steadied the swing with her feet. Brad's threat didn't drive her into her protective shell. She stood and squared her feet shoulder-width apart. "We broke no law."

"Someone did." Brad's voice free of accusation. "A brick or steel pipe smashed the driver window on Carl

Skelton's pickup."

Alexa gasped. "Not us. Anyone who abandons a vehicle next to a bar tempts the possibility."

"You just confirmed that at some point last night odds are you were at Carl's truck."

Alexa swallowed. Even the wind seemed to hold its breath. "Didn't say that."

"Susan said you were at Margaret's yesterday asking questions."

The words jumped from her lips. "She on your payroll, too?"

Brad clasped and unclasped his hands. "Don't be snarky. I'm on your side, you know."

"Asked if Carl used a certain cologne." Alexa pursed her lips. "That's all."

An immeasurable challenge filled Brad's matter-of-fact eyes. "So?"

Alexa weighed the consequences of total honesty and left unsaid the cologne's brand. "Belinda smelled it on one of her attackers."

His jaw muscles relaxed. "She tell the sheriff?"

Truth gave her an out. "Only she knows. I wasn't present the entire time."

Hesitation bracketed his question. "You think Carl Skelton's after the gold?"

"Why not? Isn't the whole county?"

His lips regained their straight line. "Not me."

"Suppose Grandma confided in you that Grandpa spent it."

"That's confidential."

A thin catch in his voice struck Alexa as an abyss. Her left eyelid touched a fallen lock of hair, which she ignored. Her stomach released its twisted knot. "You're here to torment me and I'll bet it's for no good reason."

Brad rose, completed a stride, and unclasped his black attaché case. He half-turned toward her. His right hand fingers closed on a large white envelope. "Here." He handed it to Alexa and stepped aside to crouch in front of Samuel. "Dead cricket doesn't taste good with graham cracker." Brad flung the insect by its hind legs into the yard.

Grandma's handwriting she recognized. The envelope light enough to be angel food cake.

Brad gazed upward at her. "Open it."

Alexa's fingers trembled. "I shouldn't."

"I shouldn't tell you I promised not to deliver the envelope until the court approved the will. Since I didn't think you'd be here when the judge rules, I'm a couple days early."

"You didn't read what Grandma wrote?"

"Figured it wouldn't do me any good since I don't bake." He chuckled. "However, I'll be first in line to eat the apple cake. That's my guess. Your grandmother's prized recipe."

Alexa didn't think so. No reason for Grandma to hide it twice. Her index finger traced the envelope's sealed flap, then again. Samuel hugged her left knee.

Brad cocked his head to one side. "You going to open it?"

"Thinking." No tease grafted onto her words. "How long have you had this?"

"What difference does that make? I'll swear on the Bible it's your grandmother's."

The putt-putt of Old Betsy rode in with the fresh breeze. Alexa and Brad waited in silence until Oscar Erickson stomped the brake pedal. From the lawn's edge he called out, "Howdy."

Alexa dropped the unopened envelope into Brad's attaché. Brad closed it. She expected Oscar hadn't recognized what had been in her right hand. She proceeded in Oscar's direction.

"Sorry to interrupt. Wanted to tell you I'll be watching

the farm tonight. And ask if it'll be okay for me to borrow two plastic buckets from the milk house."

"Take what you need," Alexa replied. "Don't remember any being there."

"Were last week." She gazed at Brad who dallied near the backyard oak. "Again, sorry for the interruption. I'll be out of your hair now."

"Don't you need a key?" Alexa asked.

"Nope. Got one."

Alexa pivoted to Brad. "You track how many keys exist to the buildings on this farm?"

"Mrs. Anderson said two sets. I never questioned the accuracy."

"Or, she loaned keys to Joe and the hardware store made duplicates."

"Possible."

Alexa kept a suspicious eye on Oscar. He, like Brad, always seemed to hover. Belinda swore Brad eyed Alexa. That couldn't be Oscar's reason. His constant reference to Grandma's apple cake recipe didn't explain his visits after Alexa gave him the first apple cake recipe.

Then the thought struck. Oscar's wife tried the recipe and her refined taste buds detected God's truth: the recipe fake.

Alexa scurried to the porch. Samuel chased a second cricket, this one live. Alexa chuckled. Samuel's odds to catch a live cricket no better than a frisky grasshopper. Her sandals propelled her seated body to the highest swing possible. Brad dilly-dallied until Old Betsy's putt-putt faded and the dust settled.

"Here." Brad handed Alexa Grandma's white envelope.

"Don't want to open it."

"Suit yourself. I'm overdue at the office."

The sealed envelope rested on Alexa's lap as Brad, in his Buick, departed. She closed her eyes and twice activated a renewed swing with the ball of her right foot.

The screen door banged.

Belinda rubbed her eyes. "Heard the tractor. You and Brad makeup?"

"We didn't talk about us. He delivered this envelope."

Belinda stared at the envelope. "You ready to tell me what's in it?" Belinda squashed the cushion next to Alexa and bent her head and shoulders forward.

"You concentrating your Superwoman powers to read the words inside?"

Belinda shook her head. "Can't. Handwriting strikes me as your grandmother's."

"Right on. That's why the more I stare at it, the scarier it becomes to open."

Belinda's resistance stilled the swing. "You believe your grandmother would harm you."

"Never." The word crawled from Alexa's throat. She coughed.

"Then open it. There's little doubt your grandmother meant the best for you. Why else the will? Start at the corner."

Alexa raised the envelope to the newly arrived sun. An outline of folded paper inside darkened the envelope's center. With her right-hand thumb and forefinger, Alexa ripped an eighth inch wide fragment from the envelope's end. She compressed its top and bottom to extract lined white bond paper.

"You're killing me," Belinda said.

"Hold on. I'm doing it aren't I." Alexa unfolded the paper. Descriptive words and a crude map appeared on the page beneath two words: "Summer home."

Belinda pushed against Alexa for a closer look. "That's cool. You inherit a farm and a summer home."

Alexa's heart thumped against her sternum. "Remember that canister. This fits."

Belinda stood. "What fits?"

"The address, county road MM, Rock Lake, Wisconsin.

A post office box. A map can tell us if that's close to
Tomah, Wisconsin. That canister was like a diversion."
    "You think the gold's buried in Wisconsin?"
    "Don't think there's any gold." Alexa reached into her
jeans pocket for her cell phone. Punched in numbers.
    "Brad, please. Sorry. Could you do me a favor? Check
land records for owners of summer homes on Rock Lake in
Wisconsin, think near Tomah. Look for Anderson, my
grandparents." She closed her phone.
    "We should go there." Belinda sat. "I'll drive."
    Alexa hesitated. She ignored Belinda's soft plea to head
out. Since Oscar advertised he enjoyed keyed access to
locked buildings, she didn't wish to leave if Oscar prowled
the farm. Grandma hadn't trashed her attic. An unknown
person (Alexa reasoned Oscar) had rummaged it.
    Had Joe, with knowledge of his father's search, seen
someone else? The Skelton tread tracks existed in mud near
the machine shed. The timing fit.
    Alexa gazed at Belinda's expectant eyes. "We'll go
tomorrow with full daylight hours. Besides, you need a
restful night's sleep."

Chapter Thirty-one

Alexa, unable to sleep, wandered into the parlor and
toggled the lights. Frantic raps against the kitchen door
drew her nightgown-clad body off the sofa. A huffing and
puffing Oscar peered through the door's glass. Through a
door crack, she apologized profusely for her mistake.
    At six a.m. she woke Samuel. Belinda's kitchen
presence evident from a toaster pop and the stove pan

rattle. Alexa carried her overnight bag as she followed Samuel downstairs. The trio finished toast and scrambled eggs before Alexa buckled Samuel, who clutched a plush dog, into Belinda's SUV's rear seat.

"We still going through Dubuque as planned last night?" Belinda asked. Alexa nodded. "The gold or not the gold. That is the question."

Alexa groaned at Belinda's awkward Hamlet paraphrase. Three miles past Dubuque, the Mississippi River, and into Wisconsin, Alexa's cell phone rang. Caller ID said Brad.

"There's an Anderson who owns a Rock Lake cabin, but I doubt you'd be interested."

She pressed speaker. "Belinda's here. You have an address?"

"Before I read it to you, you should know there's an Alexa Hovey Real Estate Trust."

Alexa gasped. Belinda tapped her SUV brakes. She weaved right into a rest area and stopped in front of an open-sided pavilion.

Alexa pressed her phone to her right ear. "Say that again. My name on a trust?"

"Created three years ago. Trustee listed as Attorney Jonathan Hughes, Oak Grove, WI. His office on Main Street. You should find it easy. Don't have a phone number."

"Thank you." Alexa closed her cell phone and switched her gaze to Belinda. "I'll meet you outside after I take Samuel to the rest room."

Alexa, with Samuel in tow, grabbed a Wisconsin highway map from a pavilion information rack and met Belinda at a picnic table. "I need to spread this map."

"Why?" Belinda's face peppered with quizzical remnants. "We get revised directions?"

With Samuel content to sit at the picnic table and scribble on a flyer, Alexa shook her head. Her right index finger circled towns on the map until she located Oak Grove. The town's road dead-ended into Rock Lake. The map's black dot indicated it wasn't a huge town.

Alexa reloaded Samuel into his car seat and adjusted the map to be ready to answer Belinda's directional questions. On Oak Grove's Main Street the golden letters on the plate glass window said "Jonathan Hughes, Attorney at Law." A receptionist escorted the trio to a small room with three walls lined with law books. The centered round oak table seated four if each person occupied a ladder-back chair.

A stooped, bald-headed man who wore a white shirt with a dark-string tie and black slacks stepped through the door. His droopy eyelids shielded inquisitive dusky eyes. He carried a file. "Alexa Hovey, it's nice to meet you." His direct gaze preceded his offered his right hand.

"How'd you know me?"

"There's a photo in my file. Couldn't mistake your grandmother's eyes." He pulled out the last empty chair. "Your grandfather and I, those were the days, you know. Emma Sjodgren was the most beautiful lass. A skinny Irish lad like myself enjoyed little chance."

"You knew both of them?"

"Most glorious memory is when Emma kissed me the day she and Henri left for the Iowa cornfields." A loud sigh collapsed his chest. "Well, to business." He flipped his file to its first page. "Your trust owns 'Golden Coin Ranch,' a pretty site on Rock Lake."

"Wow!" Belinda exclaimed. "A ranch."

The attorney gazed at Alexa. "Don't let your friend get too excited. Your grandfather had a wry sense of humor. While he bought three lots, Henri sold two without shore footage."

"Why choose this name?" Alexa realized her question wandered close to the unanswered gold question that vibrated her vocal cords, eager to bust forth.

"Your grandfather carried a gold coin in his pocket the day he bought the lakefront land he desired. Cheap western paperbacks were all he read."

Alexa recalled an attic box full of Louis L'Amour. That now fit. "Are there horses?"

"They galloped only in your grandfather's mind."

Alexa rubbed away her forearm goosebumps. "I want to see it."

"You can, but you can't stay there. It's rented. Convinced Emma, after Henri's funeral, not to sell. I enjoyed her visits, coffee together at the cafe." He gazed to the ceiling as if a projector beamed a scene onto its white plaster. With the abruptness of a finger snap, he returned from his mind's diversion. "Was never to be, even though we were again single."

"Did Grandma visit often?"

"Last time when she signed the papers to rename the trust and add your name as co-owner of the First National bank account."

"Wouldn't the Patriot Act have required Alexa to present herself?" Belinda asked. She extended her right arm to distract Samuel with her wristwatch.

"Bank president said nothing. The trust named me trustee, and Emma was there. We're a small town. There'll be no hassle."

Chapter Thirty-two

Belinda drove her SUV underneath the parallel steel rods between two wooden totem poles that elevated the "Golden Coin Ranch" letters. A faded, posted sign on the right post announced "Unwelcome Visitors Shot Without Notice."

"We better be welcome," Belinda quipped.

"You heard Attorney Hughes call. He said the couple have rented for a year now."

The dirt road, slick from rain, led to a cabin with a six-foot-deep front porch. A woman in her thirties, green cotton dress, sandals, and a bandana waved to them.

Alexa unbuckled Samuel and carried him to the porch. Belinda followed. The introductions inside were informal. "Walk around as long as you like," the woman said. "Was told you're the family that owns this house."

Alexa and Samuel preceded Belinda to the home's rear exit. The lake's sandy beach shoreline but fifty yards ahead. Winterized cabins flanked both sides. Two fishing boats with one person each floated without direction on a ripple of shimmering blue.

"Wonder how many Chicagoans live here?" Belinda spoke aloud to no one in particular.

"That's not important," Alexa replied. "Lots of opportunity to bury . . . ah, things." Alexa's glance caught a window curtain flutter. Samuel squirmed to crawl. "No, Samuel. You have enough bugs at the farm." She waved at Belinda who paced the shoreline. "Let's go."

Alexa knocked on the rear door. "We thank you for letting us visit on short notice."

"You're welcome." The woman waved farewell.

* * *

The trip to the farm whizzed by. Samuel less fussy after a rest area stop and Alexa's switch from the front passenger seat to sit beside her son.

"Long day," Belinda said. Her stocking-clad feet propped on a kitchen chair. "No gold, but we now know you're landed gentry. The entire office will bow to Baroness Alexa."

"Quit it. The office gossips enough without injecting

264

the cabin."

"You think your grandmother and this Old Sod attorney had a fling?"

"She never mentioned him."

"Adds all the more intrigue. You search for gold and meet an Irishman. Maybe he's a leprechaun hiding Grandma's pot o' gold. I'd call his eyes mischievous. Isn't that what leprechaun's are, mischievous."

"It's myth, pure myth. Besides, Grandma always referred to Grandpa as her life's true love."

"Sad for the attorney. I'd say he pined for your grandmother. One-sided love, not returned is a tragic state of affairs. Sorta like you and Brad."

"Whoa!"

"Well it's true. The world can see it if you can't. And you put Samuel to bed so he can't save you from this conversation."

Alexa latched the refrigerator door. Experience told her Belinda wouldn't quit until she finished unburdening her overstuffed mind. "Sorry, did you want a pop?"

"No thanks. But Samuel could benefit from a real live one."

Alexa groaned and slumped into a chair opposite Belinda. Her tired right arm let the can clink against the table. She wasn't disappointed she hadn't unearthed a buried treasure box. Grandpa hid his gold in plain sight. He invested in land.

Attorney Hughes had shown her the trust's bank account. A respectable three thousand dollar balance since the current tenant stayed the winter. In prior years the summer-only rentals paid for cabin repairs, road assessments, taxes, and the trustee stipend with little profit. If Alexa weathered the current economic downturn, the attorney predicted a lakefront demand up-tick to represent the trust's greatest value.

Alexa heard a distant car honk. A fearful pang rippled

through her body until she realized it had to be someone's acknowledgment of the unknown entrance guard. The honk didn't repeat.

"Samuel's fine," Alexa replied. "I'm more anxious about Mother." Alexa's cell phone rang.

A sleepy-eyed and lethargic Belinda raised hands to her ears. "If it's Brad, I'll not listen."

"Don't. It's him." Alexa listened. "I won't lie." Alexa closed her cell.

Belinda let her feet flop onto the floor. "Well?"

"Brad said he needed my help. Sheriff Edwards accused him of thwarting his investigation by tipping me off to let you skip out before his questioning."

"So why would Brad ask you to lie?"

"He didn't. Suggested I might not recall, if the Sheriff asks, what he said."

"Splitting hairs. So, will you protect him? Samuel's happiness is at stake."

"Quit it."

"You do what you have to do. I can fend for myself."

Chapter Thirty-three

Alexa watched through the kitchen window as Sheriff Edwards' cruiser entered the farmyard, a half hour after his call to Alexa's cell. "Hello, Sheriff," Alexa said through the ajar kitchen door.

"Belinda here?"

"If you wait on the porch, I'll call her."

Belinda crossed the kitchen en route to the porch. Alexa hid her hands in a dishtowel to disguise her anxiety. She would've liked to eavesdrop, but she had confidence in Belinda.

When, through the kitchen window, Alexa spotted the departing Sheriff's dust plume, she scurried to the porch.

Belinda, a facial smirk evident, sat on the swing. "Bush league."

Alexa mashed herself next to Belinda. "What?"

"That Sheriff. Tried to intimidate me into admitting I tossed a brick through that pickup outside the bar. What's its name?"

"Waspi."

"Yeah. I challenged him. Said where'd I get the brick?"

"And?"

"He admitted it came from the Andersen Cement Factory in the next county."

"Anderson? That's Grandma's name."

"Close. Andersen with an 'e' not an 'o' and the Sheriff lacks proof either of us has been near the place. Then he asked a lot of dumb questions about our trips from Chicago."

"He should know about the will, the court delays."

"Suspect he thinks we transport drugs like cocaine. You know. Chicago. Drugs. Gangs. Secret trunk compartments. He hinted he knew about your attack."

Alexa's right-hand palm smacked her forehead. "That doesn't say we're drug runners."

"He thinks your attack is a cover story to keep your job to run drugs or you're an FBI mole or confidential informant."

"You're spinning a yarn."

"Well . . . he stacked multiple implications. Us in the criminal justice system, big city, your grandfather's Capone connection. His cake's icing is the fire evidence against your mother."

Alexa's head exploded with Belinda's rapid fire insinuations. "He's conspiracy central?"

267

"Righto."

"Who's he think heads this conspiracy amongst the cornstalks?"

Belinda pointed. "You."

"Me?" Alexa inhaled a deep breath. What Belinda said exceeded Alexa's comprehension. Her a drug kingpin? Not only had the Sheriff most likely smoked corn silk, he'd inhaled funny cigarettes. "What about Carl Skelton?"

"Sheriff didn't name him. But the impression he gave was that the person who ratted me out was a snitch hired to spy on Skelton. Guess they watch his truck as a drug delivery drop-off."

"If I give you that, why was Samuel found in the truck?"

"You want me to speculate like the Sheriff?"

Alexa shrugged. "Hell, why not?"

"Only after Samuel's abduction did the criminals realize that he was your son, the kingpin's heir. They mistook my farm presence as a nanny, or who knows. They couldn't face possible execution at your hands so they dumped Samuel and slipped into the night with the hope you garnered no knowledge of their identities. You know, deniability."

"Logical, except I'm no drug kingpin."

Belinda slowed the swing with her right foot drag. "You could be."

"Quit it. So I suppose this Sheriff connects me to Joe's death?"

"He didn't say and I couldn't read between the lines."

Alexa's left foot shoved the swing. "Fantastic, utterly fantastic."

"Agree. What do we do now?"

"What can I do? If I skip out and abandon Grandma's will, I look guilty. If I stay, bimbos etch the word 'guilty' in big letters across my forehead. You know how gossip travels."

"You can't leave; that's your worst possible option. Sheriff said couple nonsensical things."

Alexa listened out of respect. "Like what?"

"He referred to cocaine as 'corn.' Said it twice. And, he said 'gold' meant pure."

"Could see that. Gold represents a champion, numero uno."

"It's logical. No one in Iowa blinks twice at the mention of the word 'corn' and its first two letters are the same as cocaine. There's even an 'n' in both words."

"Drug dealers could fly below the radar. Any eavesdropping communications satellite wouldn't highlight the word 'corn' in Iowa-based transmissions. So where does that leave us?"

"Safe, I think, until you inherit the farm."

"Why? That's two days from now if you believe Brad."

"Once you inherit the farm, drug competitors will think you've set up a base, know where the stash is, establish networks, and be a distribution threat."

Alexa exhaled. "This boggles one's mind."

"Mine, too. But admit it, it's all plausible."

"Yeah. Nina's betrayal convinced me weird things happen, and I suffered until rescued."

"We must figure out who we can trust."

"We don't know many people here." Alexa processed that as a fact. She had to express the names. "Sheriff, Brad, Stanislaw, Oscar, Leah, Susan, Lydia, Margaret. Who else?"

Belinda winked. "Forgot Carl."

"Don't trust him." Stetson Cologne seemed to eliminate Carl from Belinda's assault, not Samuel's abduction. Alexa didn't dismiss idea Carl splashed cologne on his jowls as a disguise.

"Okay. Who else?"

Alexa's brain cramped. "Can't finger nor name drug dealers."

"What's your intuition say? Who's the one you trust most?"
"Guess you mean Brad."

Chapter Thirty-four

An hour later, Alexa's cell phone rang. She said hello to Brad.

Static laced his words. "Saw the Sheriff in town, you didn't tell him did you?"

"He never talked to me. Why you so nervous?"

"Agree to meet me for dinner at Luigi's tonight."

"People gossip." Alexa kept the proof to herself. "Come by the farm at supper."

"If that's my only choice, see you after six."

* * *

Alexa billowed a tulip-flowered tablecloth she'd found plastic-wrapped in the attic across the kitchen table. Her fourth attic search uncovered nothing else. To honor Brad's Luigi's offer, she boiled spaghetti and added a meat sauce from Grandma's recipes. Belinda's afternoon grocery store run had purchased the required sauce ingredients, toasted garlic bread, peas, and corn.

Samuel's fingers strained for an hour to shell peapods. When successful, Alexa let him crunch the peas in his mouth as she'd done as a young girl. Fortunately, Belinda's efforts filled a cereal bowl with enough peas to save the adult dinner.

Brad arrived at six-thirty. Alexa spooned soggy spaghetti, but no one complained.

Belinda rose. "You two go. Me and Samuel will do the dishes. Take a glass of wine."

Alexa gazed at Belinda. "We don't have wine."

"Added it to your list." Belinda filled two counter glasses. "Now git. Samuel and I have work to do." She slid a chair to the sink. "Partner, the bowl with suds is yours."

The kitchen screen banged, but didn't latch. Brad set his untouched glass on the porch railing. Alexa clung to hers as the swing swung.

Alexa blurted into the uncomfortable silence. "Who started the rumor I'm dealing drugs?"

Brad whirled. His right elbow knocked his wine glass onto the grass. "Who told you that?"

"Then it's true; there's a rumor."

"When you're paired with Carl Skelton, there's always loose talk."

Alexa snapped, "Ain't mixed up with him."

"People see you go to his house and then there's your friend near his truck in the middle of the night outside a bar notorious for unsavory connections to this and that."

"Drugs, right?"

Brad reached into his front pants pocket and pulled out a used envelope. From his shirt pocket he extracted a pen he clicked. He wrote: "Joe's home bugged. House?"

Alexa let her mind gallop. Questions swirled. Who? Why? How long? What about Joe's truck? Could that be the reason the Sheriff whisked it away the night of the fire? Alexa arose, held her glass high, and shouted, "Don't sell drugs. Never have. Stupid rumors all hogwash, every cotton-pickin' one."

Redness bloomed across Brad's cheeks. He shook his head and pointed to the porch steps. After his descent, he double-timed across the graveled farmyard to the spruce windbreak.

When Alexa caught him, he twirled, his face tense. She shortened her last step to give him personal space. "Bet you

271

thought my shouts too dramatic."

He swallowed hard. "Stupid." His right hand smothered the word. "No, foolish is better."

She disregarded the tone of her voice. "You wired?"

He tugged his dress and T-shirt from his trousers, lifted them to his armpits, and spun around. His exposed lower abs rippled. Alexa saw no tape, wire, or microphone. "Why warn you?"

"Make me think I was safe and execute a sting."

Brad shook his head. "That's TV cop shows and movies. Can I lower my shirt or maybe you'd like to pat me down?"

"Meant what I said. Don't mess with drugs, no way, no kind."

His shirt fabric dropped. "You must be the Chicago exception."

Alexa reached for a ground pebble and tossed it at him, careful to aim below his neck and above his belt. It missed and bounced harmlessly behind him.

Brad exposed his palms in a gesture of surrender. "Truce."

Alexa pitched aside the second stone in her right hand. "Tell me about the Sheriff."

"Tempest seems to have blown over. Belinda must have calmed his nerves. But he's not spending much time on Joe's fire."

"But Lydia Skelton's print was found on a matchbook."

Hair fell into his eyes with his strong head shake. "How'd you find that out?"

"Got my own wires." Alexa tried hard to suppress her chuckle, but couldn't.

"Touché." His brow glistened, and he wiped it with his white handkerchief.

Alexa didn't think the evening temperature that high.

"Rosie's matchbook box had several books with Lydia's prints. She's never denied she often takes matchbooks. Gives them to clients. Lydia earned a commission years ago when Rosie bought a house. Lydia likes to say she encourages visitors to eat at Rosie's."

"You think flimflam?"

"Plausible. Stan could mold it to create reasonable doubt."

Alexa gazed at the house. The kitchen light remained on. The shadowy figure likely Belinda. Her friend's image rekindled why Alexa visited Carl's house. "I went to Margaret only to ask if Carl wore Stetson Cologne. You can verify with her or Susan."

"Susan?" He again wiped his forehead. "What she doing there?"

"Don't have the foggiest. Assume they're friends chatting about the baby."

"Wouldn't have thought so. While at work, Margaret never had a kind word for Susan. But then, when Susan and Joe split, Susan spread ugly rumors about Joe and Margaret's hookup."

"Feuds die; misunderstandings get patched."

"Didn't register on my radar. But then I don't always understand women."

When Alexa perceived no tease, she asked, "What's that supposed to mean?"

"Truth. Saying I'm not perfect."

"You're quick." Clouds gathered above the spruce trees. "We should go back."

Brad glanced behind his left shoulder and then grabbed her right hand without tugging.

Surprised, Alexa didn't fight. Her stretched stride avoided a reluctant child impersonation.

Within three steps of the porch, Brad stopped. Without dropping her hand, he gazed into her eyes. "Why do we always speak of others? It's not like I'm unaware you've been with a man."

"It wasn't a happy time. Not that I don't love Samuel,

you understand."

"Your grandmother mentioned you. Said something about Samuel's father dying in the war. She was never very specific, and I didn't question her for details."

Alexa compressed her lips. She refused to step verbally into any sinkhole.

He continued, "You're different, totally different, than women I met in Chicago."

"I'll consider that a compliment." Alexa blocked her attempt to foresee her future.

His eyes glistened with challenge and his clenched jaw line bristled with tension. "It is, believe me, it is."

"I'm not trying to be difficult." Alexa struggled not to admit her life's blueprint didn't exist. "Things, even in Iowa, must reach a conclusion regardless if I fail to perceive how."

"Guess your grandmother's death, the will, the farm, the gold, Samuel and your friend's abduction, and the disruption to your job have all ganged up on you."

Alexa shuddered at the word "gang." She wouldn't explain. She hoped her inner fear had evaporated through her scalp and not coursed through her hand into Brad's. "I wouldn't put it that way, but yes I've felt overwhelmed."

"You can let me help. Not as a lawyer . . . a friend."

The north wind crashed in. The backyard oak swayed. Alexa didn't see Jeffrey.

After Brad stooped to retrieve his wine glass, they ascended to the porch. Alexa shared her full glass with Brad. His feet propelled the swing for both of them. The melancholy porch light cast faint shadows as it toiled to illuminate them. The kitchen dark behind the closed door. Alexa assumed Belinda shepherded Samuel upstairs. Misty air joined the wind to threatened rain.

Creases and shadows outlined Brad's facial features. Alexa tested Brad's motivation. "You should know there's no what we can't talk about in Wisconsin."

He sat as if locked in fierce introspection. "Only the cabin?"

"You unsealed Grandma's envelope." Her outrage real. "That's reprehensible."

"Hold on. When a Boy Scout years ago, our troop camped out there one spring weekend. Great swimming, little chilly. Neighbor stabled a mule. Gave us rides. We planned to go the next year but our scoutmaster said people rented it. Wisconsin mention triggered my memories." His features lightened. "And, to be honest, I guessed."

"Then why all this hubbub about buried you know what?" If the farm not wired, and she wasn't about to search the barn, her speaking in riddles amused her.

"People like to think they can dream. Thrilling barbershop tales filled with when, how, and where your grandfather traveled. No one believed he accumulated riches by farming, even with a dairy herd. The stories filtered through the years and in time, after inevitable exaggeration, became a truth staple."

"But Grandma?"

"Homebody. Arthritis in her knees. Loved baking."

Truth struck. Alexa admitted, "She complained at times about her right knee. Doctor told her surgery unwise."

"Real trooper. She never limped nor grimaced in pain in my presence."

"So I guess you're not convinced I'm a leprechaun hiding whatever."

Laughter erupted in both. Their shoulders touched, and neither recoiled. Alexa's right hand drifted to Brad's left knee. She hadn't planned it, nor did she know why she didn't lift it.

Brad leaned sideways and tilted her chin his way. His fingers cupped her jawline as if a fragile rose. His tender kiss followed by one that molded their lips together. Desire began to grow with Alexa. Breathless, she eased toward him.

Donan Berg

Alexa's eyes flitted into the shadows. The porch's openness subjected them to surveillance or interruption at any moment. She subjugated her fear to the moment's enjoyable warmth.

As quick as his first impulse, Brad slumped into his swing cushion. "I shouldn't have done that." He gazed away from her.

"Don't apologize." Her words candid and sincere. No way did she want to see him on his knees. Her inner voice kicked in. *"On a knee" could mean more than an apology.* Alexa's cheeks blazed, stoked by her heart's intensity.

"Did I kiss funny?" Brad's expression unreadable.

"Don't be self-conscious. I'll give it back." Alexa admonished herself for the employment of a teenager's trick. When her lips brushed Brad's, they lingered. Alexa's body temperature spiked as her heart tumbled like a wildfire whipped by out-of-control winds. Strands of her conscience gripped an imaginary fireman's hose.

Her chest heaved when Brad's fingers inched into her hair behind her right ear. Embers of her desire smoldered as he kissed her forehead from one eyebrow to the next.

"I was hoping we had a future," Brad said. He gasped for air. "A long future, not ships passing in the night."

While Alexa's pent up emotions demanded release, her inner voice chimed in with a reminder to think of Samuel. She knew where that voice originated. She'd had cases where multiple boyfriends paraded before a woman's small children. The children's development stunted, if not filled with terror. She'd opted for the opposite extreme where no visible or invisible male invaded Samuel's home.

Belinda had nagged her it wasn't natural and would warp Samuel's natural development.

Alexa whispered, "You've been kind. There's more to consider than myself."

"I can understand." Brad's arms released their grip.

Alexa believed her shoulders should've slumped, but

276

they didn't.

"Your neck vein," Brad said, "bulged like you're angry with my advances."

Alexa's left hand brushed her thigh. "There's much I need explain. Now's not the time." She'd pooh-poohed her therapist who had warned her that self-preservation instincts would involuntarily shutdown her ability to feel emotion and that her body's internal safety calibrator would be incapable of distinguishing physical harm threats from fear of the unknown.

"Why not?"

She couldn't elaborate. If she didn't rehearse what to say, any slip would categorize her as damaged goods. Alexa, proud of her resilient strength, couldn't be deceptive.

The gravel crunch catapulted Alexa to the porch railing. A sedan stopped alongside Brad's.

"Who's there?" Brad called out.

Alexa's right forefinger rubbed her upper lip. "Think it's Susan."

"You expecting her?"

"Maybe she has news on my listing."

From the railing, Alexa waved a welcome. Susan carried a portfolio and the two women met at the top of the porch steps.

Susan gazed at Brad. "You guarding the house? Guy at the road flagged me to a stop."

"Nope." He flashed a sheepish smile. "Just visiting."

"Alexa, can we talk in the kitchen?"

Brad interjected, "I won't bother you. Was ready to leave." He pocketed the envelope that littered the porch and handed his wine glass to Alexa.

"It won't take but a minute." Susan strolled past Brad.

Alexa's free hand reached across the kitchen threshold to flip on the interior light. Susan clopped after her. Alexa, seated at the kitchen table, watched Susan pull out a sheet from her portfolio. "Bank delivered this letter they wouldn't offer farmhouse mortgage money—"

"Hold on. Why?"

"This letter claims the foundation is substandard."

"That's ridiculous. Conrad repaired it. A buyer has other choices, right?"

"Only one in this county, but the bank's reluctance applies solely to the farmhouse. If there's an underlying logic, they'll finance a land sale."

Alexa's right palm rubbed the enlarged neck vein Brad had spotted. She'd indebted herself for the foundation repair. The bank's letter more troublesome than financing because Susan delivered it with Brad present. Alexa convinced his presence to add fuel to the gossip engine.

"Let's put the listing on hold." Alexa's impetuous statement shocked even her.

Susan corralled her shock to plead, "That's not wise."

How was Alexa to control her listing if no one listened? "I really don't care."

"I've tried to do everything possible for your benefit. Brad giving you contrary advice?"

Alexa's face burned hot. "Leave Brad out of this."

"Sorry. It's just he's always around. And, you're still in court."

"What you insinuating?"

Susan reached for the paper on the table. "You want this bank letter?"

"No. Let's forget about the listing."

"It's not that easy. You've got an unexpired, signed listing contract."

Alexa stared. "Let's not speak about it anymore."

"I'll call tomorrow." Susan let the screen slam. Her car's tires spit gravel.

Belinda called out, "What was that all about?" from the top of the stairs. "You there, Alexa?"

"Everything's fine. Need to check if Brad's still here."

Alexa stepped onto the porch. No Brad. A halogen yard-light glow reflected off his Buick. The upper oak leaves rustled. Brad hadn't climbed the tree, had he?

With her eyes focused on the oak, Alexa strode to it. She couldn't determine if Brad lurked on a high branch and she had no wish to tramp the homestead and adjoining fields with an available flashlight and arouse the road guard.

Alexa returned to the porch to find Belinda sipping wine while her feet steadied the swing.

"Is that Brad with the flashlight?" Belinda asked. "See his car."

A flashlight beam crossed left to right as if its owner had lost a valuable near the barn.

"Brad," Alexa yelled. "Whatcha searching for?"

"Is Susan gone? Somebody should tell her to add the hay in the barn to your listing."

"She's gone. As to the barn, that's Oscar's realm."

"I'll be heading upstairs," Belinda said. "Either a lot of barn hay is important stuff or you're trying to bore me so I leave." She winked at Alexa.

"I'll be upstairs shortly," Alexa replied.

Belinda grabbed the kitchen doorknob and pulled it after her. Brad clomped onto the porch. He teased Alexa by crisscrossing a beam across her sneakers.

"Why you searching the barn?"

"No reason. A barn on a cash-crop farm doesn't need to store hay. It should've been sold."

Their evening had turned into an enigma. "Since when are you a hay bale expert?"

"Not an expert. Courtesy says I listen to farmers at Rosie's."

"So . . . ." Alexa bit her lower lip. "What found?"

"Nothing. One can't navigate the hayloft with all those stacked bales."

"Could have told you that." Alexa's facial muscles

tightened, and she failed to stifle a yawn. Wasn't any reason for Brad to sneak inside the barn? "Can't worry about no hay. Susan said the bank won't approve a farmhouse mortgage."

"Craziest thing I ever heard. You sure that's what she said?"

"Positive. She had a letter."

Brad extended his right hand. "Show it to me."

"Didn't keep it."

Brad shook his head. "Who signed it?"

"Don't remember if I ever read that far."

"Stupid," Brad said under his breath. "I'll try to see James Halverson at the bank tomorrow. With 260 top-grade tillable acres, they're crazy to get sidetracked by an old house. Bank's been handing out loans for decades. Any buyer will adjust his or her offer on what they see and one who wants to live here can drag in a trailer."

Alexa gasped. Vivid flame memories caught her off guard.

"Sorry. Didn't think. Anyway, I'll straighten this out."

Brad spread his arms and embraced her. Her hands caressed his shoulder blades. He twisted his nose from their nose bump and kissed her. For a second he pressed his lips to hers and then slid them to her right. He gazed lovingly into her eyes. "I'll straighten out the bank tomorrow."

The words broke Alexa's spell. Bank. Business. Loans. Hay bales. They didn't exist in her blissful state. Stars twinkled in an overhead sky as rain clouds rode atop a westward wind.

The first drops dampened their foreheads.

"Duck inside; I'll telephone tomorrow." Brad stole a kiss and dashed for his Buick.

Alexa paused. What about . . .? She leaned across the railing; a rain spray hit her face. Brad's Buick taillights turned right. Too late . . . .

Chapter Thirty-five

"Guess we're not going to Chicago today." A wry smile contorted Belinda's lips. "Your cell phone on counter tells tales." Alexa ignored her to search an upper cabinet for Samuel's oat bits.

Belinda laid a spoon next to Samuel's table setting. She and Samuel faced empty cereal bowls. Belinda rattled her spoon. Alexa glanced at the table. Belinda continued. "Making out on the porch isn't very private."

"You were spying?"

"Went to close a hallway window when the wind howled. Was that why you grabbed on?"

Alexa closed the cabinet. "Samuel doesn't wish to hear this."

Samuel gazed at his mother at the mention of his name. "Cereal. Me Hungry."

"All gone, Tiger." Alexa added four cracked eggs one by one to the mixing bowl with the milk and cheese.

"Mommy scramble eggs."

Belinda tapped his spoon to divert Samuel's attention. "You two last night could've used the barn. I've heard straw can be soft."

"Quit it. Remind me later. I've forgotten to check if Brad locked the barn."

"Sooooo." Belinda re-activated her smile. "At least one of you had that idea."

"Brad said he searched the barn for something." She stirred her skillet's egg mixture. "He never said what he missed."

"Probably you." Belinda winked.

"You're one-track-minded this morning. More important is how you're feeling?"

"Ready to head home. Need but five minutes to fill and

zip my bag."

"Tomorrow early. That'll empty the refrigerator, if we eat dinner at Rosie's."

Samuel banged his spoon on the table. Alexa slid scrambled eggs into his bowl. When the toaster popped, she handed Belinda two slices and clicked in two ends.

By nine-thirty with breakfast cleaned up, Alexa watched Samuel crawl around the kitchen. She refused to allow him to play on wet grass or planks in his last pair of clean jeans.

Her cell phone rang. Hang-up. Restricted Number.

When she heard the gravel crunch, her hopes rose Brad had driven to the farm. Her kitchen window view confirmed: no Brad. A van with "Young's Construction" painted in red on a rear white panel swerved. Its wide U-turn halted when its rear wheels dug a trench in the gravel. Conrad ran out of her sight. His robust scowl more ominous than the muscles exposed or hidden by his sleeveless red T-shirt.

Belinda screamed.

Alexa grabbed Samuel's right arm and whispered, "Bad man, Samuel. Hide in the parlor."

She prayed her son might go undiscovered if he stayed quiet. She stuck his lawman's badge into her rear jeans pocket. Conrad marched Belinda into the kitchen. His right hand covered her mouth; his left pinched her waist.

Alexa bristled, her feet square. "You know I don't have your money."

"We think you do."

Alexa sidled to the sink window. No accomplice visible. She gambled Conrad's boast fake. "Think it best you leave. One scream and the Sheriff will be here."

Conrad's jaw line tightened. "Don't think you'll do that."

Alexa's right hand fingers traced her cell phone outline in her jeans pocket. Odds strong she couldn't extract her cell phone and use it before grabbed or kicked. "Why not?" Alexa needed to keep her wits. How could she distract Conrad to give Belinda a chance to break free and run?

"Your son's too precious not to have a mommy."

"That's right." Alexa recognized the female's voice before she cleared Conrad's shadow.

Alexa's first glimpse a blue ski mask, exposed cleavage pushed up beneath a wide V-neck tee, tight blue jeans, low heels, and a handgun's barrel pointed at her. "Susan?"

"Keep guessing," Conrad hissed.

Alexa didn't dare switch her entire gaze from Conrad. The odds against her and Belinda had doubled. If she angled her body right, not enough to let Conrad fade from her attention, perhaps greater information would give her an opportunity to disarm a woman whose unsteady right arm waved the .22 pistol.

"Stand back," Conrad ordered. He shoved Belinda into a chair. While he alternated glares between Belinda and Alexa, his left hand reached behind his back and reappeared with clothesline cord. He bound Belinda's hands behind her back.

Conrad waved his right arm at Alexa. "Lay on the floor, face down." She complied in slow motion. He ordered his accomplice to watch both.

When footsteps threatened to trample her, Alexa lifted her eyes without head movement to see Samuel's shoes. She swallowed hard.

Farmyard gravel crunched. Louder and louder putt-putts elevated Alexa's spirits.

Conrad hoisted Alexa by her right arm. Through the screen door mesh, the masked woman threatened, "No tricks. Two lives, if not three, depend on you shooing this farmer away." The woman and her handgun disappeared from sight after she said, "Conrad, you help."

Alexa expected Oscar, and that's who it was. Why he came, she didn't know. Even he had said it was way past

283

cultivating time.

Conrad whispered, "Don't you leave this porch."

Alexa cleared her throat. Her first greeting try resulted in an inaudible hoarse whisper. Conrad grimaced. Alexa tensed when his jabs to the small of her back prodded her to the railing. She coughed and bit her lip.

Oscar jumped off Old Betsy. He and his rain-stained boots stopped on the lawn halfway to the porch. His familiar straw hat dangled from his right hand. "Needed to check how long you'd be staying."

"Tomorrow." Her word barely audible. She cleared her throat. "Tomorrow. We leave tomorrow. Expect early."

"There'll be a man on guard tonight then. That's all I needed." He pivoted toward Old Betsy.

Alexa's mind frantically searched for a word to clue in Oscar she needed help. The parlor light wouldn't help if she couldn't reach the switch, besides daylight camouflaged its glow. "You thank the Sheriff for his help in finding Samuel?"

Oscar didn't respond. Alexa sighed. Too obvious and dangerous to try again. Old Betsy's putt-putt faded to silence within her ear canals.

Conrad's exhale warmed her neck's nape. With the wind calm, her nostrils detected Stetson Cologne. Belinda's attacker *de ja vue*? She didn't recall if he'd splashed it on for the construction wing ding.

The kitchen door hinges creaked. Conrad jabbed Alexa a second time and pointed his right forefinger at the door. Alexa heeded his direction with deliberate steps.

"Too bad your try to alert the hick farmer failed," the woman said. "I could gloat, but there's things more important." The woman pushed the screen door wide and pointed a right forefinger at Alexa. "One can suffer slow no matter how many others die fast."

A chill ping-ponged the vertebra of Alexa's spine. The woman's threat clear.

"Mommy." Samuel yanked into the doorway. "The lady's hurting me."

Alexa straightened her elbows with her hands face up. "Please give me Samuel."

"Why not?" the woman sneered. "Ankle biter deserves a final hug before mother departs."

Alexa embraced Samuel to her breasts. "Mommy will always love you." The woman's words puzzled Alexa. If Grandpa's gold buried at the farm, why travel? And the woman mentioned only her. Mounting dread of Samuel again being a hostage paralyzed her arms in place.

"Touching." Sarcasm dripped from the woman's utterance.

She gazed at Conrad. "Where's your buddy?"

"He'll be here."

Conrad herded Alexa and Samuel into the kitchen where Belinda's chin touched her chest. Belinda perked up with the commotion. Her raised eyelids exposed darkened pupils. Alexa hustled to occupy the chair next to Belinda. Alexa shifted Samuel to her opposite thigh and pinched Belinda's left forearm.

"You stay here." Conrad said to the masked woman. "Shoot all three if they try anything." The commands distorted Alexa's impression the woman had been in charge. She foresaw a difficult task to overpower Conrad. *Forget Conrad. Get the gun.*

"Where you going?" The woman asked Conrad.

"Oscar Erickson saw my truck. I'll scoot past him on the county road and do a circle double back via the township road. That way it's unlikely he'll think anything other than I left a tool."

Samuel squirmed on Alexa's lap. Belinda's head slumped.

"Now, Alexa, where'd you put whatever it was you dug up in the field next to the old car." The woman trained her gun on Alexa's forehead. "There's several holes out there."

This last statement puzzled Alexa. She'd dug one hole. Well, maybe two, but the second she'd filed in with dirt.

"Don't sit there silent. Conrad said he found no metal box or canister in the foundation."

A light dawned in Alexa's brain. This explained why a sober Conrad assured her no immediate was payment necessary. His work an orchestrated ruse to search for a cornerstone or similar metal receptacle cemented in to safeguard heirloom papers.

"Don't know what you're talking about."

The woman strode out of Alexa's vision. She dared Alexa not to move. Footsteps stopped behind Alexa and a cold metal object tickled her neck's nape. "Have you thought harder?"

Alexa whispered, "Can't tell you what I don't know."

"Don't be difficult." From the corner of her right eye, Alexa watched the woman stretch her right arm and square the .22's barrel end against Belinda's left temple. Belinda closed her eyes. "A cat may have nine lives. How many does a Belinda have?" The woman angled her body while she kept the barrel on Belinda's temple. "Blood splatter can be so messy."

Alexa couldn't risk Belinda's execution. Whether the woman bluffed or not, Russian roulette scared Alexa. Belinda's fingers in prayer position.

"Oscar has the apple cake recipe."

"Ain't falling for no three-dollar bill. His wife brought an apple cake to Rosie's for a big to do. All agreed it wasn't your grandmother's recipe. Think harder. I can count: three . . . two—"

"Wait. Don't shoot. There was a buried canister."

The wildness in the woman's sunken eyes simmered. "Now we're talking. Where is it?"

Chills challenged Alexa's cowardice. "Basement, far corner."

"Now we'll all wait."

286

Wrestle-the-gun scenarios filled Alexa's brain. Time expired when Alexa heard gravel crunch. Conrad's silhouette darkened the kitchen doorjamb outline.

"Bimbo here says a canister's in the basement, far corner. Get it."

Alexa hugged Samuel. Why hadn't Brad telephoned? He said he would. If she didn't answer, she expected him to drive to the farm.

Conrad's heavy footsteps bounced the kitchen floor. He disappeared from Alexa's sight and returned with the canister in his right hand's grasp. He extracted the crude Wisconsin cabin map.

"Don't tell them," Belinda whispered. She clamped her lips when the .22 touched her skin.

"Tell us what?" the woman demanded.

A defiant Belinda replied, "Nothing."

The woman paced the kitchen, waved the gun aimlessly, and flicked Belinda's ear with its barrel. Her splayed right hand cupped Belinda's scalp. "Don't believe mothers are as contrary as you. Perhaps Conrad can soften her up."

Nerves knotted Alexa's abdominal muscles while the woman's vague threat set off fear aftershocks. Her memory cells spooled her captivity for vivid replay.

"You can let us go," Alexa said. "Whatever you hope to gain isn't buried outside. House reconstruction proves it wasn't hidden in the foundation."

"Shut up. Give me that paper, Conrad."

The woman studied the paper. "This here is Wisconsin. No way we'll spin our wheels with Alexa guiding us. Day-old rumors had you on I-90. One doesn't need to be a big rig trucker or buy GPS to figure out I-90 traverses Wisconsin. Even a dummy can rule."

"Speak for yourself," Belinda blurted out.

The woman's left-handed slap reddened Belinda's cheek. "Uppity. You'll get yours."

Donan Berg

If only I were as fearless as Belinda. Alexa's hopes rose when gravel crunched. Oscar may have returned. Perhaps Brad. The Sheriff?

The woman hustled to and stared out the kitchen window. "Blindfolds."

Conrad snatched Samuel from Alexa's lap. With a second cord, he bound Samuel to a chair. The woman tossed Conrad bleached flour-sack material cut into four-inch wide vertical strips. Conrad folded and fitted one across Belinda's eyes and then Samuel's. He draped the third blindfold on Alexa's right shoulder. His left hand caressed her left breast. She shivered and flinched as if punched in the stomach.

"Sorry, hand slipped." He tightened the strip across her eyes and knotted it behind her head.

"Your buddy's here," the woman said. "Let's load the truck."

Alexa called out, "Samuel. I'll take Samuel."

"Don't fear, Mommy." Conrad's voice a hard snicker. "You be cooperative and he'll be alive to kiss you when we return."

Two strong hands from behind slipped under Alexa's armpits and hoisted her to her feet. One under her right shoulder released its grip and knuckles jammed into the small of her back. She stumbled forward. Two hands fumbled for a breast handhold. Fingers uplifted her. Thumbs compressed each breast into a vise grip to keep her upright.

"Nice," Conrad said. "I also specialize in denim zippers." He laughed.

When her soles supported her shoulders, Conrad's baritone voice whispered into her right ear. "I'd pay to learn what thrills tingle and excite you right now."

Alexa slumped, her legs wobbly. Alexa willed herself to be strong. She calculated any rearward kick she tried likely to miss a direct hit on his groin, a pain he deserved.

288

What did survival classes preach? She tried hard to remember.

"Mommy, I can't see."

Conrad tongued Alexa's right ear. He whispered. "Quiet if you want him to see you again."

Alexa silently counted from one to ten and repeated the numbers in reverse order. She inhaled as the seat belt clicked. From her required step up and the smells of dust-ladened air and stale beer convinced her the vehicle to be Conrad's van.

"Be nice," the woman said, her voice behind Alexa. "Conrad hates soiled upholstery so you tell me if you need a pit stop. Let's enjoy our little trip to America's Dairyland."

Light seeped under the bottom folds of Alexa's blindfold, but it didn't allow her to decipher landmarks she passed. The rough road jostle convinced Alexa they drove cross-country. The brightness of the filtered light narrowed her direction choice to either north or west. She couldn't believe they'd head west. A smoother stretch with occasional light thumps suggested a numbered highway or possible interstate. Two swings to the right suggested they traveled east.

Alexa kept her ears alerted for conversation to identify the woman. Nothing helped. At a rest stop, Conrad escorted her to a stall. She didn't dare loosen her blindfold to be embarrassed and grossed out if she confirmed he watched.

He pushed her to climb into her passenger seat. She sat still and heard neither Conrad nor the woman enter. Had they abandoned her? She slunk low, stretched, and reached past the bucket seat console for the ignition. No key.

After what Alexa judged to be an hour, two doors opened, and a breeze gusted into her cheeks. Both front-seat springs creaked.

"Miss me?" Conrad teased. "We ate lunch. Put out your hand. Saved a sandwich."

Alexa let the item rest in her right palm. It smelled like tuna. She nibbled two bites and gobbled a third to placate her hunger pangs.

"Tilt your head back," Conrad ordered. "Open your mouth."

Water chilled Alexa's gums and the back of her mouth. Drops dribbled onto her chest.

"Sorry," Conrad said. "I'll aim better next time."

"Quit your playing. Let's go," the woman commanded. Her tone the harshest ever.

After several turns and an occasional stop, Alexa lost her geographical bearings. The uncomfortable hours couple with stiffened her muscles.

"We're here," the woman announced.

Alexa sighed. She had no inkling where "here" was.

"Go knock on the door."

Conrad's open door sent a whiff of pine to Alexa's nostrils. She tasted no saltiness to suggest water. A Jet Ski roar switched her conclusion to a fresh-water lake.

"Sit still," the woman ordered. Her harsh directive constituted the rare snippet spoken by the woman since the last rest stop. Alexa didn't budge from her seat.

"No one's home," Conrad said.

Alexa's right elbow fell from the door's armrest. Her seatbelt buckle clicked and the harness strap tension eased. Fingertips on her left shoulder and a thumb on her right dug in.

"Can get myself down," Alexa said. She didn't believe the woman angry with Conrad for his touchy-feely actions or threatened that Alexa would break their partnership. Alexa dismissed Conrad's indignity from her mind to conjure an escape plan.

"Stand still," Conrad said. He removed Alexa's blindfold.

A home nestled among the shoreline pines displayed a "Golden Coin Ranch" welcome sign. *Grandpa's.* Alexa remembered the town-to-Rock-Lake road. It offered no escape if she were chased by a vehicle. A couple hundred yards to her left was a mobile home park that abutted a state wilderness area. Alexa calculated her odds above fifty percent to be able to run that far without being caught. She expected wilderness area staff at a ranger station.

She throttled her breath. Her first thought was to chide Conrad and the woman for a wild goose chase. Grandpa had buried no gold here. What her abductors lacked in knowledge, she could use against them. She'd have to be believable.

"What we doing here?" Alexa asked.

Conrad tightened his grip on Alexa's right wrist. "Play Dumb. It won't work."

"Right," echoed the woman.

"Can I stretch my legs?" Alexa asked. "They ache." She counted on bursts of adrenaline to soothe or mask her pain. Baby steps to clear the van's side without suspicion her goal.

"Don't try any monkey business," Conrad warned.

Heel-to-toe and a reversal amused Alexa, if not Conrad. The glimpse of the crossed-log fence across the road to enclose the mobile home park sufficient for Alexa. The woman had to be uncomfortable under her mask. Perspiration streaked across soft skin to her blouse's neckline. Alexa noticed no identifying chain, necklace or piercing.

"What way?" Alexa asked. She didn't care which direction. She needed time and an obstacle course. A straight dash and Conrad would catch her in fifty yards with no telling what his grubby hands would fondle.

"You tell us. We know the gold's buried on the property. The map tells us that."

Their conclusion better than what Alexa hoped for. "You bring the recipe?"

The woman's quizzical glance heartened Alexa. Her

vocal irritation escalated exponentially. "Conrad, did you bring a recipe?" He shook his head. She stared at Alexa. "What recipe?"

"Grandma's apple cake recipe. The ingredients tell the steps required."

"That's a frigging lie," the woman bellowed.

"No it isn't," Alexa replied. "That's how I found the canister."

The woman's eyes flashed at Conrad. "You idiot. I told you there was more." The woman grabbed Alexa's left hand and with Conrad's superior strength positioned Alexa's shoulder blades flush to a tree. "Stay put. I'm watching."

The woman motioned Conrad away from Alexa. With alternating glances at Alexa, they stopped ten feet from Alexa and shielded their mouths with cupped hands. Alexa arched her back to stretch smarting muscles. Beyond her, clouds slow-marched from white to reddish pink. No rain threatened. She estimated a half hour before the sun radiated from below the horizon.

The woman waved a cell phone high. "You wish to say your last words to Belinda?"

Alexa's exasperation mounted that she hadn't pulled the trigger on her escape. "What?"

The woman stomped two steps toward Alexa. "You're not cooperating."

Alexa shook her head.

"If that's the way you want it." The woman pressed her cell phone to Alexa's left ear. The phone's speaker pulsed sharp gunshot reverberations against Alexa's eardrum to throb deep within her ear canal.

"No," Alexa screamed. She fell to her knees. Her hands clasped her face. Tears flowed. Her eye sockets ached. "You Bastards," she shouted.

"We're not into games. I told you at the farmhouse, one death, two deaths, no matter. You want to say good-bye to your son?"

"Not Samuel." Alexa scratched her fingernails across her cheeks. "Tell me what you want. I'll do anything." Her eyes gazed at the woman through glistening eyes. She cringed at the smirk on Conrad's face. "Tell you everything."

Conrad loomed above her. "And then—"

"Shut up, Conrad. Your pleasure's not what I'm here for."

"If your grandmother's recipe is the key, you should know it by heart." The woman ordered Conrad to get a shovel from the van. "Bring rope, too," she added.

The woman's evil bore into Alexa as she pushed herself erect with her right hand. "Backyard. Count from the back door's concrete pad."

The woman wrapped her right hand around Alexa's left wrist. "You lead, slow and easy."

Alexa neither rushed her stride nor crushed flowerbed border plants. No parked car discouraged Alexa's window scan for a woman anxious to learn why strangers traipsed her lawn. The absent Jet Ski denied Alexa an opportunity to encourage a driver's curiosity. Without a distraction to enhance her escape, Alexa diverted her attention to calculate which way to pace the surveyed terrain. A thread of Alexa's memory recalled Kelly's Island near Mother's home in Ohio.

She hoped Ohio's historical glacier had western ice sheets. If so, Rock Lake existed as a spring fed rock depression surrounded by a glacial deposit of dirt and rock. Her task was to find a backyard spot with enough soil to enable Conrad to jab his spade twice.

Conrad caught up to Alexa as she stepped onto the rear door's concrete pad. He tossed his coiled rope three feet from Alexa's left foot. His hands fidgeted with a spade.

Alexa asked the woman to move six steps right. "Grandma's apple cake uses three eggs." Alexa counted three strides forward. She deliberately deleted all outward expressions of direction. "Two cups of apples." Alexa stepped off two right-angle steps from the last egg step. "Three ounces golden raisins." After a second ninety-degree pivot, Alexa hesitated. The greener lawn blades to her left portended deeper roots. Alexa pondered whether to adjust her stride or add another ingredient.

"Hurry up," the woman barked. "We're not doing this in the dark."

Alexa paced three steps and twisted a quarter-turn right to face two miniature rose bushes. "One cup nuts." Rose thorns snagged her blue jeans as her right sneaker landed between the two bushes. Alexa exhaled. For her sake she hoped rose bush roots extended deeper than Kentucky bluegrass. A dandelion bloom an inch in front of her right toe buoyed her spirits.

"Here." Her right sneaker toe scratched a shallow mark in the dirt.

"Conrad, you dig. Alexa, step to me."

"We should bind her hands," Conrad said.

"Not now. Dig. The homeowners may surprise us. We'll deal with her after the gold."

The spot chosen by Alexa also existed within four feet of a large hickory. If she'd guessed right, the tree's roots had either traced or created a gap in the underlying rock. Conrad's rope lay behind her. She angled rearward by twice kneeling to tie a shoelace. The woman's rampant attention on Conrad galvanized Alexa.

Conrad tossed a half-dozen full shovels of dirt into a mound. He flung the spade into the hole like a javelin. It bounced. "I've hit something," he called out. He stomped the full force of his right foot onto the spade.

With her captor's eyes focused on the hole, Alexa charged her right shoulder into the woman's side. The woman screamed as her face grated against the ground's pine straw stubble. The woman's phone flew four feet from her hand. Alexa scrambled to snatch the cell phone.

Conrad's pant snag slowed his sideways leap away from the hole.

Alexa plucked the loose coil from the ground and flung the rope as hard as she could at Conrad's feet. Conrad crashed to the ground with the rope entwined between his ankles.

In her bolt toward the street, Alexa pumped her legs as fast as she could. An adrenalin rush coursed through her veins. In a perfect getaway she would've disabled the van. Not only did Alexa lack simple tools like pliers or a screwdriver, she didn't know where the woman's .22 was to blow out a tire.

Alexa jumped a hedge and sprinted toward the mobile home park. Even if Conrad drove his van, she could dodge and weave between homes faster than he could navigate the gravel and dirt paths that served as roads. Where a top rail didn't exist, she vaulted the log fence.

Alexa grasped for breath after she upset an outdoor grill. A chained dog barked.

"You won't get away," a strong male voice shouted. "Think of your son."

Alexa couldn't gauge the distance the voice traveled. She'd thought of Samuel. If Conrad and the woman found no gold, her life and Samuel's would have been disposable. By running, she at least heightened the illusion she knew where Grandpa hid his gold.

A deep-seated determination not to be brutalized a second time energized her. Three years ago she promised herself she'd never submit to being a hostage again. She darted behind a fourth mobile home, tripped, and fell against an AC condenser unit. Left forearm scratches bled. Alexa wiped the forearm's warm sticky ooze on her jeans. She pushed herself erect with her right arm and slowed her pace while she lengthened her strides.

A six-foot wire fence loomed in front of her, the woods

beyond. In her escape plans she had calculated her ability to scale at least one fence. She shimmied up a support pole with her toes in the wire ovals. *No razor wire.* After her hands clasped the top horizontal rail, she flipped sideways, and let go. Her flexed knees initiated a roll as soon as her soles hit the ground.

Alexa inhaled deep to run past the scrub trees and onto a pine-needle carpet beneath a red pine canopy. Behind her she heard Conrad shout unintelligible curses. Darkness surrounded her. Swaying branches became shadowy figures. She encountered a small dirt path. It had no markers. She ignored it to take her chances with the distant water she heard gushing.

She reached for her cell phone. Hers with national coverage would've sprung to life, if not taken from her at the farm. The unknown off-brand her fingers grasped displayed no service bars.

She couldn't rest. Her right forearm protected her forehead against high brush and low tree branches. How close had Samuel been to the gun discharge and Belinda? *When I get out of here, whole families will pay, and pay dearly.*

She sprinted to a break in the trees and burst into a clearing. Alexa skidded to a stop. The glen was a rudimentary road comprised of two parallel ruts with grass between. Headlights buoyed her. To be cautious, she retreated into the shadows.

She hugged a tree while her eyes spied a white van. Conrad. *Damn.* He'd foreseen her route.

Alexa inhaled and clamped her mouth shut.

The van inched past. A flashlight beam from the driver's door illuminated the brush and pine needles four feet in front of her. When the beam didn't reverse course, Alexa exhaled.

Unsure of her next move, Alexa discounted rest. If the van doubled back, her safety wasn't assured. With the

296

van's red taillights visible, she bent her shoulders forward and scampered across the road. Five feet into the darkness she paused when her sneakers crunched gravel.

Water crashing into rocks rumbled. She wiped her forehead dry only to be wetted by a fine spray. One step forward and she almost tumbled. She would have if a sapling had not provided a last second handhold. Experience filled in her knowledge gap with the idea that water foamed through rapids beneath the ledge she stood on. Alexa thanked God for the gravel path.

While the ledge offered no opportunity for a drink, she followed the trail until wooden-trail-sign-arrows pointed to a campground and a ranger station. Her choice simple— ranger station.

To bolster her determination, she counted her steps. When she reached one hundred, she started anew. She fantasized she rode a merry-go-round where youngsters stretched to grab the brass ring. In reality she missed the brass ring.

The clock inside the closed ranger station said ten o'clock. She had encountered no activity, except the white van. The park's metal entrance pole padlocked in the no entrance/exit position. Not locked was the water fountain. The sulfur-tinged water gagged Alexa. She forced two swallows and dreamed of her mouth's saliva shrinking a peppermint Lifesaver to nothing.

She assumed Conrad and his white van meandered the campground and the rutted roads inside the wilderness area. Tire tracks ten feet from the padlocked pole presented proof lovers entered the wilderness area despite being warned not to. She tightened both shoelaces, skirted the pole, and jogged toward Oak Grove.

She expected neither constable nor help in Oak Grove. When she reached the edge of town, her premonition proved a direct bull's-eye. The only light and jukebox noise in Oak Grove emanated from the "Last Chance Saloon."

Donan Berg

It was a chance, last or not, that Alexa wouldn't take. She reduced her jogging stride to a brisk walk along the asphalt road white line that led out of town. A sign said I-90 intersected five miles ahead.

Two hours later she dove into the ditch, face first, when headlights appeared behind her.

She held her breath. The car didn't slow. When Alexa raised her head, she saw rotating red and blue lights reflect off the asphalt ahead of her. An audible sigh escaped her lips. She hadn't seen the colored lights approach. When the lights disappeared, Alexa's desperation mounted. She flipped her mental glass to half full. While she may have lost an opportunity, Conrad's white van hadn't reappeared.

She checked her cell phone. No service. Convinced she should chuck it, she resisted her impulse. Into the surreal dark night, she counted, "One, two . . . ninety-nine, one hundred. One, two. . . ."

When she reached the I-90 junction, she stood on the shoulder of the two westbound lanes and held her right thumb high. She'd read one or two road journey books and the author always reached his or her destination. She chuckled to herself. If the author didn't, who'd write the book? Good thing she wasn't writing any book.

Cars, trucks, and vans whizzed by. One semi changed lanes in deference to her safety.

Disappointed, she lowered her thumb and walked. The interval between vehicles grew longer and longer as time passed. Trucks in greater number motored east, not her direction.

Her body cast a long shadow that didn't quickly disappear. An eighteen-wheeler had geared down behind her. After it passed, its brake lights brightened. An enlivened Alexa jogged to the big rig that idled on the shoulder.

A burly, bearded T-shirted gentleman with overflowing chest hairs and shorts that allowed his girth to hang and wiggle stood at the truck's tailgate. "It must be Christmas early."

Depleted lungs delayed her response. After three deep breaths, she flung her arms wide to push her shoulders erect. "I'm sorry. What did you say?"

"Never mind. Never met a truck stop Lolita on this stretch of road."

"Get on then," Alexa snapped. "I ain't any whore."

"Feisty. I like that."

Alexa reached into her rear pocket. Samuel's sheriff's badge might look official in the dark, and she carried a cell phone. The trucker edged toward her. The fingers of fear fisted in her stomach. "Stand still." She flashed Samuel's badge. "I've got my cell phone here somewhere." She yanked it from her front jeans pocket.

The trucker planted his feet. "Look. There's been some kind of misunderstanding. I didn't mean no harm. I was teasing. Believe me."

Alexa didn't have many options: two, at most. Keep walking was not an option she favored.

"I got a pretty niece about your age. What say we forget what I said? If you need a ride, you're safe with me." He reached into his back pocket. "Here's my driver's license. You keep it and give it back when you hop off." His new tone registered sincere.

Alexa calculated the license could be bogus. Whether it was didn't alter her predicament. Wariness filled his face after her show of authority. She guarded her exact destination. "If you're heading west, I'll ride along a ways."

"Hop in."

At the Winona, Minnesota, mileage sign, Alexa realized I-90 West would take her too far north. When he pulled into the Mississippi River rest stop, she handed Jeff his license. He'd spun enjoyable stories of characters he'd met. She counted him one merry soul. Her thank you ended with the suggestion he tell others I-90 had new patrols.

Alexa befriended a second trucker who delivered fresh baked bread to Iowa towns. He offered her a ride to Lakeview. A stroke of luck concluded her day, albeit night.

Alexa struggled to separate her eyelids when dropped off at the Lakeview Sheriff's Office. By her overheard conversation, the dispatcher woke up Sheriff Edwards at home. Alexa catnapped in a lobby chair until the voice of the Sheriff awoke her.

"Who kidnapped who? Not your son again?"

"'Fraid so."

Alexa couldn't control her tears when trying to explain about Belinda.

"How many?" Sheriff Edwards asked.

"Conrad Young and a masked woman drove me to Wisconsin. The third drove up to the farm while I was blindfolded."

Sheriff Edwards without siren or lights slowed as he approached Grandma's farm entrance road. He stopped on the shoulder. "We need to wait for a deputy. You said neighbors posted a sentry. Don't see one."

"Thought it would be Oscar. He stopped by to confirm if we'd still be there."

"You mean Oscar Erickson?" Alexa nodded. "Stay here. No one will detect me if I circle."

Alexa observed the Sheriff disappear into a windbreak. The dispatcher's voice interrupted the Sheriff's car radio static. Alexa kept her hands in her lap. She interpreted the Sheriff's stay put order as her instruction not to move a muscle. A face appearing outside her passenger window startled her. Since she hadn't heard the deputy arrive, she assumed she nodded off.

Alexa lowered the car's window.

"Sorry. I'm Wilbur. Sheriff nearby?"

"In the trees."

Wilbur gazed across the vehicle roof. "He's coming.

300

I've got to get my vest."

Sheriff Edwards walked around his cruiser's rear bumper to stand next to Alexa's open window. "Only one vehicle in the farmyard. A SUV. Isn't that your friend's?"

"What about a pickup? I recall a pickup comment."

"Didn't see one." The Sheriff pressed the microphone button on his portable radio. "Elsie, who's on call." He listened. "Notify them for the Anderson farm, RFD 137. Ring the fire chief and have him dispatch the ambulance, no sirens or lights."

Alexa's pulse raced. It grieved her she couldn't hug Samuel close. Belinda bleeding at best. All this waiting couldn't be good. The cell phone in her pocket vibrated. Her reaction not fast enough to answer. She checked its caller ID. "Baker, Haberkorn Law Firm." Alexa couldn't believe a fifty-fifty chance Brad was involved with the masked woman.

Behind her, three vehicles clogged the roadway. The Sheriff huddled with the manpower he'd summoned. Old Betsy's familiar putt-putt joined the early morning chorus.

Alexa stayed out of sight behind the Sheriff's cruiser. She couldn't hear his words, but the clinking of metal buckles on oxygen tanks and the firefighter boot shuffle gave her clue to peek.

Sheriff Edwards led the farmhouse encirclement. He dispatched the deputy to the front lawn while he dashed to brace his butt against the rear porch railing. An eerie quiet belied Alexa's internal turmoil. Everything in the yard light shadows swayed in slow motion. Even Old Betsy silent as Oscar, arms folded, stood on his tractor.

Alexa sprinted to the windbreak. She'd re-interpreted the Sheriff's admonishment to reference the farmhouse, not the fields. She skirted the break's eastern end and turned right. At the old car she angled for the machine shed's corner, the rutted road, and, with a dash across the last open space, flattened herself against the backyard oak's mossy

Donan Berg

side. Alexa winked at Jeffrey. Her Monkey friend visibly
confused by the morning's activity.

Alexa peeked. The Sheriff tiptoed across the porch to
the kitchen door. An auxiliary officer in riot gear covered
the Sheriff's advance with an automatic rifle. The Sheriff's
extended right hand showed two fingers above his head.
Two rifle-fired tear gas canisters shattered glass. Alexa
sensed choking gas filled the front parlor. The second
exploded inside the west kitchen window.

The Sheriff twisted the kitchen doorknob to be engulfed
in a white cloud. His breathing protected by a gas mask, he
entered. Alexa held her breath, not so much to avoid the
tear gas as the wind carried it away, but with fingers
crossed for Samuel's safety. She pressed forefingers against
her ears for the expected gunfire.

When Alexa reached thousand one hundred and twenty
five, the Sheriff emerged empty-handed. Other than a third
gas canister, no shells exploded.

The pulled-off gas mask exposed the Sheriff's
contorted facial scorn when Alexa ran to him at the porch
steps. "I told you to stay put. I meant it."

"Samuel. Where's Samuel?" Alexa shrieked.
"Belinda?"

Sheriff Edwards grabbed Alexa's shoulders. "Hold on."

Involuntary tears, reflected in the Sheriff's helmet
visor, glazed Alexa's cheeks. She imagined Jeffrey's leap
had landed him on her shoulder.

Wilbur, the deputy Alexa met, charged out the kitchen
door. He shunted his mask aside. "House is empty, upstairs
and basement."

Alexa collapsed onto the ground. She hugged her chest,
trying not to suffocate Jeffrey. Fear, terror, and fatigue
sapped every last ounce of her strength.

"EMT," Sheriff Edwards called out.

Below Alexa's jaw, fingers pressed against her neck.
"She'll be fine, Sheriff. Elevated pulse slowing. Breathing

302

not near hyperventilation."

"No hospital. Must find Samuel."

"Calm yourself, Alexa." Sheriff Edwards' words more command than request. "We don't know if anything's happened to your son. You told me you heard a gunshot on a cell phone. Your friend's not in the house. There's no fresh blood. No evidence of a struggle. You know of anywhere else they might've been taken?"

"No. No."

The Sheriff ordered his deputy to carry two kitchen chairs to the oak tree. He and Alexa each took a seat. "Tell me again, best you recall, your activity and whereabouts since your abduction."

Alexa's throat constricted with each mention of Samuel's name. She skipped all but the sketchiest outline of her wilderness escape and her hitchhiking experience. She rubbed the itch of abrasions and the scabbing cuts on her left forearm.

Sheriff Edwards interrupted, "Yes, deputy. What is it?"

"Machine shed and barn checked, at least the lower level. No sign of anyone."

"What about the barn loft?"

"Hay, straw bales stacked full. Don't appear to be disturbed."

"That's fine. Vehicle said to be here earlier is gone." He gazed at Alexa. "Can you describe the vehicle? . . . Believe you said pickup."

Alexa swiped tears from her eyes. "Didn't see any vehicle, except Conrad's van. Think I heard them mention pickup when second vehicle arrived." Her right forefinger touched the tip of her nose. "Oh, I don't know. I'm so tired."

"Can I help?"

Alexa hadn't noticed Oscar join them under the tree.

"Doesn't look like there's much to do," the Sheriff said. "Do have one question. Who had guard duty last night?"

"That'd be me. However, I wasn't feeling well and went home about two-thirty."

The Sheriff stood to be able to gaze into Oscar's eyes. "What vehicles did you see?"

"The SUV, of course. One pickup. Left about ten-thirty. I recall I'd listened to the radio news. Didn't come back."

Alexa bowed her head while she kept her ears alert.

Straps blocked the Sheriff's right hand from his uniform pocket. "Can you describe?"

"Dodge. Big like Ram, dual rear wheels. Left in a hurry. Damn idiot almost ran me over."

"How many in this truck?" Alexa lifted her head to see the Sheriff's eyes fixed on Oscar.

"Driver. Saw no one else before I jumped into the ditch."

"Can you identify the driver?"

"Like I said. I jumped." Oscar pulled a red bandana from his back pocket. Wiped his brow.

"Carl Skelton," Alexa murmured.

"What was that?" The Sheriff pivoted toward Alexa.

"Carl Skelton drives a dual-wheel Dodge."

"Know that," the Sheriff replied. "It was observed last night parked outside the Waspi Bar from about ten-forty-five until three-thirty."

"You want names of two others with dual-wheel pickups?" Oscar asked.

Sheriff shifted his stance toward Oscar. "Got them."

"Okay if I offer Alexa a bed at my place?"

The Sheriff cocked his head toward her. "That sounds to be a good idea. We might lose her any minute." His right hand reached to shake her shoulder.

"Heard you," Alexa grumbled.

"Oscar, I'll drop her at your place in a few minutes."

"Good. Old Betsy needs a head start." As he departed, Oscar flashed a right-hand wave to two other uniformed men on the lawn engaged in an arm-waving conversation.

Alexa rose and wobbled briefly before her left hand on the oak tree steadied her. With Oscar out of earshot, she asked the Sheriff, "You pulling surveillance on Carl?"

"Can't comment."

"What you said matches pretty close to what Belinda and I saw."

"You have to draw your own conclusions. Can you walk? My cruiser's still parked on the county road."

"Yes." Alexa's willpower augmented the muscle power her legs temporarily lacked.

"I'll be there shortly. There's details I have to square away with the deputy and the EMT."

If there existed an ongoing investigation into Carl, Alexa realized the Sheriff wouldn't likely discuss. Reading between the lines, she figured one existed. She didn't wish to sleep, but her body wasn't cooperating. Her stomach growled. Naps hadn't cleared her head.

The Sheriff, without explanation, directed Deputy Wilbur to chauffer Alexa to Oscar's.

When welcomed, Alexa recalled Leah Erickson's string-bean body. "We've converted Joe's room into a guest room. There's towels in the hallway bath. Anything else you need, please ask."

"Point me in the room's direction."

Apprehension to sleep in Joe's room evaporated after Alexa pushed the room's door. Beige walls and a yellow twin-sized comforter decorated many a sterile bed-and-breakfast pictured in travel magazines. Not in pictures was the birch-log candle scent

Alexa kicked off her sneakers and lifted the comforter to expose a pillow encased in flower-patterned cotton that matched the sheets. She emptied her pockets on a table with a frilly shaded lamp before she laid, fully clothed, on her right side.

She tossed and turned in the stillness. Anxiety fought with exhaustion and, after three hours, neither prevailed.

She forced her eyelids closed. Visions of Samuel chasing insects danced on her lids' inner skin.

Her cell phone ring bolted her upright. Disoriented, she slapped her jeans' pockets to locate the phone. The rings ceased. *Rats.* Her right hand fingers grasped the cell phone lying next to her turned-on lamp.

She punched the <send> button to hear "What's up, Susan?"

Alexa's lips remained stuck together.

"Don't play games. I don't have time for games."

Alexa's voice wavered. "What do . . . do . . . do you have time for, Brad?"

"Not this."

The phone line went dead.

Alexa laid her head into her shallow pillow indent. In her groggy, unplanned semi-fog she'd baited Brad. She hadn't expected his reaction. Behind his actual words, she hadn't fathomed he maintained a deeper relationship with Susan.

Alexa began to count the cracks in the ceiling. When she blinked, the cracks streaked every which way. Her mental sleuthing stirred a dizzy potpourri of Brad recollections. She shivered and chastised herself. Samuel and Belinda were missing, and she fantasized a soap opera.

She flung her heels off the bed and onto the floor. Her bedroom door ponged against the rubber-tipped spring screwed into the wall an inch above the white-painted baseboard.

"Where do you think you're going?" Oscar asked. His plaid bathrobe belt tied in a haphazard bow, a towel in his right hand meant either to dry his damp hair or his bare feet. He blocked her hallway escape.

"Ain't doing no good here."

"We've got men, women, even teens, out searching. Another pair of eyes that can't see straight aren't a powerful help."

"I must."

"No you mustn't. I'm not your father, but as a father I can offer fatherly advice. I searched high and low beyond the point of exhaustion for clues to solve the fire mystery that killed my son Joe. Only ended up with sore hands and a painful heartache."

"But you searched. That's what I've got to do." Through the slits of her eyes, Alexa couldn't react to the glistening in Oscar's eyes. "But what you didn't find seems to be important."

"Huh."

"The pistol lighter. You said Joe had one, and it didn't show up."

Oscar rubbed his blue bath towel against his scalp. "There's a million reasons, all legitimate, as to where that lighter might have gone."

"Regardless of logic, your instinct told you its being missing was important."

"But what good is that now? Joe's buried over yonder."

Alexa retreated and sat on Joe's bed. "Other than Grandma and Joe, you know my grandfather's farm better than anyone."

Oscar rotated his shoulders against the bedroom doorframe as if bothered by an itch. "So."

"You helped search for Belinda and Samuel?"

"Just at the farm." A heavy exhale punctuated his speech. "Didn't go into town."

"And what did you find?" Alexa began to stuff her items from the table into her pockets.

"Neither."

"That's not my question. Since both are still missing, I assumed you'd not found either."

Oscar stopped his shoulder rotation. "Sorry. One of us is confused."

"You've been in the house and the other buildings?"

"Well, maybe not the house unless invited, but the barn

307

and machine shed often."

Alexa's right hand pushed her erect. "Well, the machine shed is empty."

"Guess so." Oscar tossed his bath towel across his left shoulder.

"And, hasn't it been pretty much that way all the time?"

"Yeah."

"Then there's the barn." Alexa didn't believe she was getting anywhere since Oscar's answers became shorter and shorter. She expected him to leave any second. "You've never run milk cows there have you?" He shook his head. "What else has the barn been used for?"

"After your grandfather butchered his last Hereford, not much except perhaps a few Spotted Poland China sows."

"Pigs you say? I didn't see any pens."

"Years ago your grandfather bought two prize breed sows. Wanted to strike it rich by capitalizing on less fatty lean pork. Had four pens, six at most. Two still in machine shed."

"Never heard of that." In reality Alexa hadn't heard much when it came to farming.

"Was revolutionary. Your grandfather never envisioned the scale that modern hog farms require to eke out a profit. He had pens, not engineered buildings."

"What kind of pens?"

"Steel cages basically." Oscar wiped his towel across his scalp.

"Think I saw two cages fixed to the machine shed ceiling. Were those them?"

"Should've been more. Didn't I say six?"

"Would the cages have been sold?" Alexa didn't know why she cared. She had not the slightest interest in raising hogs . . . or any farm animal for that matter.

"Doubt it. Costs more to ship them and no farmer hereabouts wanted to experiment."

"We need to check the machine shed." The thought

ejected from her mind, out her mouth.

"Hold on. Sheriff's more than likely checked. It'd be a waste of time."

"If Joe asked, would you do it?" Alexa turned her head to the far window. She didn't need to quilt-trip Oscar. She returned her gaze ready to apologize.

Oscar spoke first. "Of course. But this is different."

"No it isn't. You didn't find the cigarette lighter. I saw one at Carl Skelton's." Alexa realized she may have stretched the truth, but she didn't wish to walk to Grandma's farm. "Their association might tie Joe into drug dealing." Alexa clasped her right hand across her mouth.

"Never. Joe never swallowed an illegal drug in his life."

Alexa refused to split hairs. Illegal drugs didn't have to be swallowed. "Humor me. Let's go check Grandma's. If a wild goose chase, I'll profusely apologize and buy lunch."

"You'll have to ride Old Betsy. Leah drove our car to town."

Positive she'd irritated Oscar and piggybacked her pain onto his, she nevertheless achieved her search goal. She trusted her instincts. "My pleasure."

Old Betsy's putt-putt droned into her ears. Alexa spread her knees, planted her soles on two metal portions of Old Betsy's wagon hitch, and grasped Oscar's overalls-clad waist from behind.

"You doing okay?" Oscar asked. "Not much farther."

A giant dust plume rose ahead of them. Alexa asked Oscar if it came from Grandma's farm and received no response. Alexa leaned right as Old Betsy turned left into Grandma's farm. Oscar steered straight across the deserted farmyard to the machine shed.

Alexa gasped. Smoke spiraled from the barn's cupola.

When Old Betsy's pistons ceased their clatter, she pointed her right forefinger skyward. She shouted at Oscar, "Didn't the searchers see that?"

"Too recent," Oscar exclaimed. He pulled a cell phone

from his top overalls pocket. "Barn fire, RFD 137. We'll be here."

Alexa jumped to the gravel. "Isn't stored hay green or wet?"

"Not all. Plus there's straw, combustible in its own right if the conditions—"

Alexa didn't want to hear. "Can't we do something?"

"Stay here." Oscar jumped off Old Betsy and ran to the barn's milk house door. Alexa watched Oscar grunt at a door that didn't budge. "I'll be back."

Alexa paced as Oscar disappeared around the barn's corner and then returned.

He panted. "All locked."

Alexa gazed upward. While she didn't see flame, the gray smoke mixed with black streaks increased in volume by half. "Can we kick in a door? I don't have keys."

"We could pull the loft door down. It's on a pulley. The rope's hanging there."

"How? It's above our heads."

"Old Betsy can help." Without another word Oscar hopped on Old Betsy, turned her ignition, and backed her up to beneath the loft door.

Alexa bit her lower lip. She heard no sirens. "What can I do?"

"Stand back." Oscar added body height by standing on Old Betsy's tractor seat to yank a rope loop. Its end dangled from the rooftop barn loft door pulley. Nothing moved.

Oscar stretched the rope taut, jumped to the ground, and with a farmer's loop knot cinched the rope to Old Betsy's wagon hitch. Oscar hopped onto the tractor's seat, motioned Alexa clear, and gunned Old Betsy. Her two front wheels lifted a foot off the ground before she crashed forward. A large squeaky groan overhead promised success. The pulley's moveable wheels spun until the rope slipped into its track.

Alexa stood amazed.

Alexa's Gold

Old Betsy reversed toward the barn. The rope and
pulley worked to allow the loft door weight to activate
gravity. Smoke billowed from the exposed loft.

When Old Betsy quieted, Alexa called out to Oscar.
"How do we get up there?"

Oscar pointed out the two loft door handholds built into
the door's interior facing. Alexa grabbed both and held
tight. Old Betsy roared to life. Guided and lifted by the
rope, the door swung into its raised and closed position.
Alexa fell backward into an opening between two hay
bales. Sunlight hit her face as Oscar shifted gears to allow
the door to drop open.

Alexa, never trained for barn fires, instinctively tossed
each bale she could grasp to the ground below. The
exertion winded her. While smoke swirled above her head,
the fire's heat wasn't at her hands. She tossed bale after
bale. Whatever dent she made, didn't seem significant.

As she bent forward and inward, a hand tapped her
right shoulder. Sunrays shadowed Oscar's face. "How'd
you get up here?"

"Hard way. Rope and feet against the door. Learned the
trick as a kid."

"This is all smoke, straw, and hay."

"There's a fire here. Trust me. Unless we douse or
stomp it, the barn will be a goner."

Alexa winced at the words "barn" and "goner." She
swung a bale, careful to miss Oscar as he joined her to
make it their effort. Alexa yanked one hay bale free and six
cascaded to her feet.

"Whoa," Oscar yelled.

"What?" Alexa wiggled a straw bale off her right foot.

Oscar's eyes widened. "Secret Chamber."

"You're a kid again?"

Oscar shuffled forward and selectively chose hay bales
to his right to toss behind him. Alexa tugged four to the loft
opening and kicked them out. She couldn't believe what

Oscar uncovered. A rectangular room appeared. Its ceiling supported by planks.

His cough disturbed Alexa. "Stand clear," he rasped.

"Why?" She drew in a hiss of breath, prepared to jump if a back draft whooshed. "Fire?"

"Damn. Cages."

Alexa thought Oscar's histrionics overblown. She'd stepped aside after his secret room discovery. What did cages have to do with fire . . . or anything? Alexa peered forward past Oscar's thigh. "Omigawd!"

"Calm down, Alexa."

She couldn't. She wanted to barrel past Oscar.

"Hold on," Oscar implored. "We've got to go slow. Three or four of these roof planks aren't all that long. If there's a cave-in, the fire tumbles upon us. We'd be trapped."

Thick smoke choked Alexa. She coughed. Smoke plumes that had initially rose above her head heated her forehead and reddened Oscar's face. Horizontal smoke streaked through the gaping hole Oscar had burrowed to expose the secret chamber. She closed her mouth, held her breath. The heat warmed Alexa's cheeks.

A stooped Oscar edged forward. He struggled to drag from the secret chamber what Alexa couldn't see. Metal jangled.

When he slid a metal cage closer to her, she saw inside it a person, prone, hands and feet tied behind his or her back. A gag's knot tied at the neck's nape.

That blouse. *Belinda!*

"Help me pull to the opening," Oscar directed. "Don't do anything else."

Oscar's orders chafed Alexa's professional pride. His disaster qualifications blank after the listed word "farmer." Her right hand grasped the cage.

"Eeee Ooww. Ouch!" Alexa yelled. Her jolted fingers tingled like she'd touched an exposed low-volt electrical

312

wire. Jarring sensations rippled her arm as if she'd struck her funny bone. Why hadn't Oscar warned her? She glared at him and noticed he wore leather gloves.

"What?" Oscar asked.

"Pinched a finger. I'll survive."

Alexa crouched near the cage without contacting metal. Electrical leads from the cage's wire mesh wrapped to the terminals of a duct-taped lantern battery. She yanked the battery loose and let it fly. It bounced toward the loft opening. With both hands free, she tugged at the cage. The person inside didn't twitch. A gray cloth bag partially covered his or her head.

"Come here." Oscar's husky voice pleaded. "Need your help."

Alexa couldn't activate a muscle. Belinda, if indeed Belinda, didn't appear alive. She shouldn't leave her friend. Sirens blared in the distance.

"Alexa." Oscar strained to shout. "This might be Samuel."

The word "Samuel" shattered Alexa's emotional trance.

"Samuel, Samuel, is he all right?" Tremors racked her body.

"Don't know. There's a second cage. It's caught on . . ." He coughed. "Caught on something."

How could that be? Alexa had slid the first cage and Belinda weighed more.

"Hurry, Alexa. We don't have much time?"

Alexa reached Oscar's side. A collapsed roof plank lay wedged against the cage.

Alexa's left hand forefinger tapped the cage. No jolt. Without explanation to Oscar, she tugged and jiggled. The cage didn't budge.

"First you, then me," Oscar said.

Alexa complied. The cage edged her way, barely an inch.

"Great," Oscar said. He slid his side an inch and a half.

Alexa repeated her effort. Oscar grunted. The cage moved. How far Alexa couldn't guess. Buoyed by Oscar's result, Alexa tried again. Her strained biceps barked with pain. Alexa prayed her leg strength bolstered her arms. She blew out a breath to swallow heated air. *Can't faint now.*

"That's it," Oscar said, full of praise. "Two more tries should do it."

A plank clattered against the loft floor. A seated Oscar pushed with his feet. Freed from its impediment, the cage slid.

With the cage bathed in sunlight, Alexa cried out, "It's Samuel. He's dead." Her hands, as if guided by an inept apprentice puppeteer, fluttered aimlessly above her scalp. Alexa shrieked, "Oh, God, no. Make it all go away."

Oscar pivoted on his butt, coughed, and fumbled with the cage's latch. It squeaked twice as he slid the bolt free. "The boy's bound with cloth. Let me rip it free."

Alexa's hands covered her ears. She inhaled. Black smoke inflamed her throat. She counted to ten. The cloth puckered, but she didn't know if what she witnessed was real, caused by Oscar, or plain blind hope.

A weak cough fixated her stare at Oscar. A flame flickered and flashed behind him.

"He or she's alive. I feel movement." Oscar tried to stand, and couldn't. "Help me drag this cage to the other one. We've little time."

The cage bumped Alexa's left foot, slid across her toes, and nearly toppled her backwards.

Together they maneuvered the cage to the loft opening. Oscar cradled the cloth bundle in his arms and unwrapped the edge farthest from Alexa.

Alexa screamed, "Mommy's here. Samuel, say something."

Samuel's closed eyelids and chalky white face immobilized Alexa.

"Who's up there?" shouted a baritone voice.

314

Dread transfixed Alexa. The sirens had been so far away.

"He's got a pulse," Oscar said. Loft door bangs against the barn's side echoed. Oscar forced two fingers into Samuel's mouth. He flipped the toddler. Samuel's body extended along Oscar's right arm, his face in Oscar's palm. Oscar's left hand sharply slapped Samuel's back three times. A weak cough gurgled out of Samuel's mouth.

"Up here. Up here," Oscar called out. "Alexa, show yourself."

Alexa fixed her eyes on Samuel. Oscar's voice arrived as a faint distinct echo. A beam crack and flames that zigzagged to the roof's crest jarred her into the present. "What? What do I do?"

"The door. Signal the firemen."

Alexa scrambled to the loft opening. One fireman dangled halfway up the loft door as he grasped the pulley rope. Two others braced a ladder as a third started up the rungs.

"We're up here," Alexa shouted. "Help us, please."

Chapter Thirty-six

A blurry face topped with dark bushy hair stared at Alexa. Tight straps restrained her. She couldn't move her extremities. She strained to free herself.

"Take it easy, young lady. Breathe. You're going to the hospital."

Tears cooled her cheeks. "Samuel, Samuel, I need to hold my son. Know he's safe. Belinda. I need to speak with Belinda."

Donan Berg

"You will, you will. Patience."

Alexa tried to answer, but no words escaped the oxygen mask clamped to her face. Her lungs greedily absorbed the oxygen molecules. Her anger grew at the images, like bothersome flies, she couldn't swat away. Hags in black habits with long pointy noses shook bony fingers at her. She cringed at their admonishments: Allowing those men to take pleasure from your body. Alexa's heated raw vocal chords cried out, "No. No." The unheard struggle tormented Alexa. Her mind sprouted beanstalk fears of losing Samuel and Belinda.

Bells chimed and her gurney creaked until a Lakeview Hospital emergency room doctor loosened her restraints and raised her head and shoulders.

"Samuel, my son. I need to see him?"

"Give us a few minutes." He gazed at a clipboard. "He's doing fine."

"My friend, Belinda?" Wiggles freed her left wrist.

"She should be fine in time."

Alexa gasped. "Oh no." Her left hand unlocked her right-hand belt clasp.

The doctor's eyes blinked. "Didn't mean to distress you."

"I know hospital-speak." Hands prepared to push, Alexa glanced for a landing spot next to her gurney. "You're hiding something."

"Sorry, can't elaborate. It won't do you any good to worry about things no one can control. I'm prescribing pain medication. Your lungs still hurt?"

"Can I go?"

"Sure. Oscar's waiting for you." The doctor chuckled.

Alexa landed on both feet. "What's so funny?"

"You can't repeat this, but I've known Oscar for years. Stubborn Swede. He'll attend the devil's funeral."

Alexa covered her cough. "I'm okay."

316

"Take this prescription. I'll get you an update on Samuel."

Alexa awkwardly shook the doctor's hand and followed the floor arrows to the hospital's waiting room. She pushed the windowless double door open. Oscar sat on a vinyl chair, his head buried in a sport magazine.

Alexa's sneakers didn't stir him. She whispered, "Thank you, Oscar."

Oscar's head jerked. "Alexa, thank God."

She didn't wish to ask why. "Have you seen Belinda, Samuel?"

"Neither." He shielded his mouth from the nurse behind the reception desk. "Nurse Ratchet there claims privacy laws say she can't tell me anything. It just ain't neighborly, I tell you. What's this world coming to?"

"Doc said he'd tell me about Samuel. Belinda he wouldn't."

"Have a seat."

The vinyl squeaked as Alexa slid into the chair next to Oscar. Mrs. Erickson burst through the outside doors.

"There you are." Mrs. Erickson planted her feet in front of her husband. "Chief Johansson said you were playing fireman again. Lost Joe. I'll die if I lose you."

"Leah, it's no big deal," Oscar said softly.

"Were you helping him?" Mrs. Erickson glared at Alexa.

The quiet demur woman first met at Joe's funeral reincarnated as one of the accusatory hags in her nightmares. Alexa sank into her seat. "He's a hero. Saved my son." Alexa started to sob.

"Now, here, here, young lady, this ain't no time to cry." Oscar handed Alexa a tissue from a nearby box. Alexa squished left to allow Mrs. Erickson room to stand by Oscar.

The hallway door clacked. Mrs. Erickson pivoted. "How's my little Freddie?" she asked.

The emergency room doctor blushed. "Fine, Mrs. Erickson. You're welcome to drive your husband home. If his skin's redness doesn't fade, have him see his regular doctor next week."

"Oh, I ain't worried about him. He's got a tough hide." Oscar's sheepish grin caused the receptionist to shake her head. "It's this young lady that worries me. She's skin and bones. Needs a bowl of my winning stew so you better be releasing her, too."

"We are. I came out to take her to see her son."

Mrs. Erickson completed a half rotation and patted an erect Alexa on the left shoulder. "How do they say it these days? You go, girl. We'll wait here."

Alexa squeezed Mrs. Erickson's right hand before she followed the doctor. Past the doors into the hallway she asked, "Do you go by Dr. Fred or Frederick? I'm sure it's not Freddie."

"How could you guess?" He smiled.

"That receptionist couldn't keep a straight face."

"Your son's in this next room." The doctor completed three long strides and entered a room to his left. Curtain rings clattered as he exposed Samuel's bed. Samuel lay curled as if a baby inside the womb.

Alexa rushed to him. "Samuel, mommy's here."

Samuel's eyes lit up and his brief smile displayed the gap between his lower teeth. "Mommy, my tummy hurts."

"He'll need several days' rest," the doctor said. "He was dehydrated. Understand he was wrapped in cloth. It tended to suffocate him, but probably prevented smoke inhalation. That's likely what caused him to black out."

"Can I hold him?"

"I'd suggest not. His veins aren't very strong to hold his IV."

Alexa patted and rubbed Samuel's right hand. She glanced at the doctor. "Belinda?"

"Really can't say."

318

"Please, doctor. She and I are Chicago Probation Officers. We depend on each other."

The doctor gazed out the window. He laid a clipboard chart on the portable tray at the end of Samuel's bed. "Excuse me, I must be going." He activated the door's pneumatic close.

"Doctor—" Alexa's eyes latched on to the clipboard. "Excuse me, Tiger."

Alexa, with her eyes on the room's door, sidestepped to the foot of Samuel's bed. The chart's top listed Belinda's name. Alexa scanned its information. "No, no way," she muttered under her breath. "Never happen." She heard a cough in the hall and hustled to Samuel's side.

"Excuse me," the doctor said. "Forgot my chart. You can stay as long as you like."

Alexa lifted a plastic chair next to the bed. "Mommy's here. Mommy loves you. You're my greatest joy. Will be always."

"Sucker?"

"We'll have to wait, honey. Tomorrow. I promise." Alexa said a silent prayer to God.

Oscar stepped inside the room's door. "Is he doing okay?"

"Doc says he needs to rest."

"I needed to ask if you'd want to go home with Leah and me."

"That's very generous, but Samuel and I need each other."

"Understand. Need to hurry or Leah will be in deep trouble with Nurse Ratchet. You see she distracted the nurse so I could sneak in here."

"Is Nurse Ratchet her real name?"

"Heavens no. Thelma Nicholson. She just likes to act high and mighty with rules and all. You be ready tomorrow for the best stew you've ever tasted."

Chapter Thirty-seven

Alexa heard feet shuffling in the hallway. "You can't be here," a high-pitched female voice scolded unidentified persons.

Samuel's closed eyes soothed Alexa. He appeared to breathe normally.

The room door burst open. A man braced his body against the wall.

"Brad," Alexa gasped.

He pressed his right forefinger to his lips, stepped into the bathroom, and closed the door.

A nurse in green scrubs cracked the door and peered in. "Everything all right in here?"

"Sure." Alexa didn't dare glance at the bathroom door. Counting to ten after the nurse departed, she knocked on the bathroom door before walking to the foot of Samuel's bed.

Brad strode out. "Thanks." Khaki pants and a green polo shirt replaced his lawyer's suit.

"What's going on?"

"Don't know. Two reporters from Des Moines acted boorish to Thelma. Saw my chance."

"Reporters? Don't want to talk to any reporter."

"And, a nurse stopped me. Claimed visiting hours were over."

Alexa raised her gaze to the room's clock, nine p.m. Brad spoke truth.

"Said I needed to speak with a client."

"You told me at the farm you're not my lawyer."

He raised his right forefinger. "Doesn't matter. You know about Belinda?"

"Doctor wouldn't let me see her."

"Rumors filled Rosie's today that one of the Chicago

women was murdered. And, I feared it was you."

Alexa erupted into sobs; rivulets of her tears flowed like lava from a volcano's summit crater. She grabbed the bed's end for support. Brad's hands pinched her waist and guided her into the room's solitary chair.

Alexa mumbled, "But there wasn't any blood."

"Don't know about that. Oscar was in the cafe this afternoon, but he wouldn't open his mouth, not even to Rosie. He sat in a booth, head bowed, his coffee cold, and muttered, inaudible to all except Rosie who later told me he said his farm's cursed. Not the Oscar I grew up with."

"And . . . and Belinda?"

"Couldn't ask or I'd never have gotten in."

"We gotta find her." Alexa's arms pushed her body erect, and then she slumped.

"Not so easy. Security patrols came on duty at nine."

"I'll find her."

"How? You might be able to check a few nearby rooms, but this hospital has three floors, security camera centrally monitored."

Alexa racked her brain. What numbers could she remember from that chart she saw? There'd been a twenty-four. "How many rooms on each floor?"

"Thirty, maybe thirty-six."

The Lakeview Hospital layout couldn't be radically different from those she'd often visited in Chicago. ICU and maternity would be isolated. The first floor with its ER, operating rooms, and offices narrowed Alexa's focus to the second and third floor.

"How are the rooms numbered?"

Brad shook his head. His eyes concurred with his eyebrows drawn together.

She'd find out easy enough by walking the corridor to the upper-floor stairs. With Samuel a patient, she'd been given a 24-hour visitor pass.

"You hatching plans?"

"Can't sit here."

"Word of advice, all stairwell doors have non-visiting-hour activated alarms. Don't ask how I discovered." A faint smile emerged before it evaporated beneath his stoic lawyer mask.

"Watch Samuel. If his IV pops, press the call button. Explain I needed to stretch my legs."

Brad stepped aside. Alexa, in the corridor, tugged the room door closed. Two out of every three ceiling lights were dark. She carried her purse high against her right side and estimated the elevator doors to be fifteen paces away. Of her two choices, Room 224 or Room 324, she decided on the first because it required the shortest elevator ride and, if Belinda remained hospitalized, the second floor represented the shortest operating room gurney trip.

Alexa shuddered at the thought. She dipped her head as an orderly carrying a cylindrical oxygen tank passed. Fortunate for Alexa, his eyes were focused on a chart.

She pressed the higher of two elevator buttons.

Waiting gnawed at her insides. When she heard the elevator door mechanism, she scanned the corridor, ready to hide her face. A muffled door slam caused her to jerk rearward. Silence. No security patrols. The elevator door presented an empty car.

Alexa resumed breathing. She scurried in and pressed the "2" button once, then twice.

The fear of exposure that had gripped her before the elevator door opened on the first floor returned when two chimes sounded. Then a clunk. She faced a murky corridor. Which way?

Samuel lay in Room 111. Her logical thought said to walk right. Stronger lights reflected on the corridor floor in that direction. She assumed a nurse's station and a duty nurse ready to notify security to abort her Belinda mission.

A tinkling chime, in double repetition, accompanied a light blink above a room two doors from her, kitty-corner across the corridor.

Alexa ducked into the elevator car. The door began to slide closed. Her right forefinger pressed the door open button while her left hand obstructed the door's path. She peeked. A green blur and white-soled shoes entered the room with the lit light.

Alexa executed an Olympian's walk step toward the nurse's station. Not until fully exposed did she contemplate more than one nurse per floor. She slowed and paused in partial hiding next to a fire extinguisher, its glass case jutted six inches into the corridor. One nurse toiled, for how long she didn't know, in a room she passed. The room number stenciled to her right—217.

Her new goal: third door on the left. She accelerated to a purposeful stride. Head up, eyes forward. Desperation forced a fake air of confidence. A second nurse at the nurse's station buried her attention in computer printouts.

Alexa didn't stop. Praised China for quiet sneakers.

Without knocking, she entered Room 224. The dim light outlined two beds. The one to her left empty, and the bed to her right exhibited uneven bumps beneath a cream-colored blanket. In the movies a Man-in-the-Moon beam would've illuminated the entire room. Her right hand squeezed the doorknob behind her to initiate a careful closing absent a loud latch click.

"Belinda," she whispered. Alexa tiptoed toward the lumps.

A huge monitor dwarfed its portable cart at the bed's head. No miniature blips traveled across its darkened screen. Unconnected wires dangled loose.

Alexa's chest tightened. They disconnected machines and pulled the plug when life ended.

Her heels contacted the floor. She had to think, think hard. Her mind perceived a blanket ripple. An overhead vent's cool air swish chilled her skin and minimized any blanket flutter.

"Belinda," she whispered a second time.

The vent's exhaust ceased. The blanket rose at the bed's head and collapsed at its foot.

"Belinda, it's Alexa." Her voice inched above a whisper. "Can you hear me?"

A muffled voice beneath the blanket muttered, "Huh?" Alexa couldn't recognize if it was male or female.

She dialed her voice a notch louder. "Belinda, it's Alexa."

An arm, unencumbered by the blanket, swung free. "Turn on the light. Switch by the door."

Alexa braced herself for gunshot and surgical scars. After the flick of a switch, Alexa saw Belinda sitting up in bed. No bandage encircled her head. Alexa rushed to hug her best friend.

"Rosie's Cafe had you dead. The doctor wouldn't tell me anything." Alexa wiped tears from her cheeks. Her happy tears commingled with Belinda's.

"I'm okay, except I'm beginning to understand now why people leave the farm."

Alexa's muscles relaxed when Belinda laughed. Belinda shifted her legs to allow Alexa room to sit on the bed.

"You say I'm dead?" Belinda asked.

"Obviously you're not." Alexa pushed a stray singed curl behind her right ear. "Brad told me tonight that's the big gossip at Rosie's. I saw firsthand that awful cage."

"That cage wasn't the hardest thing. The guy kept repeating you'd been killed in Wisconsin for not disclosing where the gold was. Said Samuel next if I didn't tell him where it was."

"Omigawd. You know there's no gold."

"That's what I kept saying. He punched me. Told me to quit lying." Belinda reached for a covered glass with a protruding straw and sipped.

"You recognize the guy?" Belinda shook her head.

"Well, has to be cohort or friend of Conrad. I'm ninety-eight percent positive the woman who abducted me was Susan. It was Conrad's contractor truck and the woman called Conrad by name. How'd you get into the loft?"

"Blindfolded and prodded by the cold of a gun, climbed what seemed to be boards nailed to a wall. My shoulder guided by a hand. Stumbled over bales."

"Samuel?"

"He had to have gone first. I lay on the front room floor repeating to myself 'Alexa had strength. I can free myself. I can protect Samuel.'"

"Could the stay behind thug have been an athletic woman?"

Belinda shook her head. "You sure this Conrad wasn't an imposter?"

"Positive. When I said the canister was in a basement spot, he went directly there. Conrad's repair gave him full basement layout knowledge."

"Reasonable." Belinda scooted against the headboard. "And, the woman was Susan?"

"Revealed herself in Wisconsin. What confuses me is, if she dated Joe to gain access to the farm to search for gold, why do that when she could've easily snooped when Joe wasn't there. Everyone knew Grandma's absent for church or community baking contests."

"You're not being analytical. Susan got dumped and the father of Margaret's baby is more likely Joe than Carl."

"Whoa, sister." Alexa jumped off the bed. "If that's so, Susan's a prime candidate for Joe's murder with revenge her motivation. However, why wouldn't Susan go after Margaret?"

"Haven't figured that out. With all these county interconnections, who knows?"

"More important, when's the doctor discharging you? You look good."

"Could leave tomorrow, but I'm not."

"If the farm's out, I'll ask Oscar to let you use his spare room."

"That's okay. I'm being switched to a third floor private room tomorrow. Then the Sheriff announces there's a $10,000 reward for information leading to the arrest and conviction of my killer."

Alexa's insight lost in the translation. "Come again."

"If you'd not been so rambunctious and searched for me, the Sheriff's plan was to let you in on our scam in the morning. Made him promise he'd do that before I agreed. No way did I want you to become an unknowing target with weirdos loose."

Alexa performed a slight bow. "Why thank you."

"Don't you think that ER doctor is cute?"

Alexa sighed. "You mean Freddie?"

"Huh? It's no fun always having you a step ahead."

"This plan with the Sheriff puts you ahead. I've a need to get to Samuel's room. Brad's there."

"You can't tell him. Sheriff wouldn't tell me who he suspects."

"Okay. If it'll make you better faster."

Chapter Thirty-eight

Alexa kissed Samuel and promised she'd return with a sucker. She slid into Brad's Buick, which idled outside the hospital's main entrance.

"What's at the farm?" Brad asked. He accelerated before Alexa's answer.

Alexa's disquieted intuition demanded her peace of mind be found at the farm. How? She didn't know. That

Brad acted on faith convinced Alexa of his goodness.

Brad parked where he always did, under the farmyard security light. He exited after Alexa and joined her at the backyard oak.

Alexa gazed skyward. Jeffrey the Monkey clapped after his jump to a middle branch. To her right the barn's huge shadow darkened Oscar's wavy green cornstalks in Grandpa's field.

Brad broke their silence. "Firemen did a great job to save the barn."

"Let's start in the machine shed." Alexa braved Brad's skeptic look and set off. After Brad unlocked the padlock, he assisted her with the door. She gazed to the ceiling. Her hunch correct.

One of two metal cages no longer hung from the ceiling.

"It's deserted." Brad waved his right arm in a circle. "What's so important?"

"The cages that imprisoned Belinda and Samuel were Grandpa's sow containment pens. That they were used is only vital if they identify the criminal. Fingerprints, snagged cloth, all unlikely. Bottom line is we must search."

"Sheriff's office collected duct tape, a battery, burnt fabrics, and swept your kitchen for clues. Authorities in four states unleashed the bloodhounds to track Conrad, Susan, and the third conspirator when he or she's identified. Why not wait for the Sheriff?"

"Can't. Belinda's in jeopardy. Maybe Samuel. They've suffered more than I can ask. Based on what you said, I'll skip the hayloft. What Belinda told me leads to the rusted stanchions."

"Whatever. I'm with you. If you were all blindfolded before the third perp arrived, how can Belinda have identified the person? Was it a voice? Words spoken?"

"Don't expect to find hidden tapes, but there was a pickup. And there's the connection to Conrad."

Alexa's right forefinger rubbed her nose itch. "Truth is I can't add evidence that Susan conspired to swindle one of your real estate clients with Conrad's inflated home repairs."

"It's a fed problem. They'll do it right."

"Nevertheless, your calls to Susan identified the masked woman since I grabbed her phone." Alexa started to close the machine shed door. Brad pitched in.

Alexa left Brad and double-timed it to the barn only to wait for Brad and his key set. She entered first. Smoke-filled air required her to find a door block. Drag marks in the caked dust indicated a removed metal cage. Alexa bypassed how it was hoisted to the hayloft.

"What's the logic that drove you here?" Brad asked.

"Intuition. I need to poke around."

"Go at it. Don't see anything but dirt and rusted metal."

Alexa stalked the rusted stanchions. Brad's conclusion gained credence. While the wire cage couldn't have passed through the hayloft opening at the top of the nailed two-by-fours crafted into a barn-wall ladder. Disassembled cages could be. She hustled to the one against the far wall. Metal clips fastened the sides. Pliers or a screwdriver could unsnap them. *Another dead-end.* Alexa wrung her hands. She rattled the cage with a kick.

Brad leaned against the makeshift hayloft ladder. "We can leave at any time. Did you throw all this hay from the loft?" Brad kicked a broken bale.

"Tossed mine out the big door." Alexa glanced at the hay at Brad's feet. None of it blackened. Frustrated, she kicked a bale slab. It split apart without offering calm.

"Is this a new game?" Brad kicked hay in a manner that reminded Alexa of Samuel.

Alexa chuckled when Brad's right foot became tangled in a loose sisal fragment. Then she saw it. A streak of black. She crouched to flick hay stalks aside. A black ski mask.

Brad chewed on a six-inch straw piece. "Was that Conrad's or Susan's?"

"Doubt either. Susan wore blue. Never saw Conrad wear one. You gotta pen?"

Brad handed her one.

Alexa split the head opening. "There's two red hairs."

"That's a lot of people, men and/or women."

A discovery thrill crackled through her when she paired red hairs and Conrad. Not him for his hair was brown, but the red-haired worker who had handed her a construction party beer. She recalled her refusal and Conrad's insistence she toast with him.

"While I couldn't explain my sudden light-headedness then, Conrad must have stirred his worker's frustration into his own twisted scheme to ditch home repair scams with one master gold strike." She doubted the legal system would second her strong conjecture. "Let's go."

Chapter Thirty-nine

Brad had been contrary, but Alexa convinced him a white lie to protect her, Belinda, and Samuel violated no law. Alexa sat in the Lakeview hospital waiting room fully confident Nurse Ratchet offered all the physical protection she required. Alexa's triangular walking course between three parking lot security lights settled her nerves.

Brad's call confirmed he'd spread during Rosie's busy breakfast hour the rumor that Belinda had not died, but was in a coma. The Sheriff confidentially briefed Alexa the feds and his deputy checked out leads on Conrad and Susan sightings. They both lingered outside a hospital room while

Belinda's slept. Alexa desired further clues to confirm her identity of the red-haired man who had caged Belinda.

Alexa was satisfied the Sheriff's plan had potential. The Sheriff had carried Samuel to Belinda's third floor room and posted a twenty-four-hour guard. A life-sized toddler doll "slept" in Samuel's room numbered 111. Brad had transported to the hospital a dressmaker dummy with a wire skirt that Alexa found in Grandma's attic. With the dummy underneath, she puffed up the bed's blanket in Belinda's former room number 224.

A uniformed security guard winked at Nurse Ratchet before he left for outdoor rounds.

Alexa's waiting room page flips through sports and farm magazines didn't tranquilize her nerves. Each clock minute-hand click like an intensified gusty wind to sway her anxiety like a mountainous rope bridge. Her effort to zoom in on each noise met with unintelligible static. Alexa fretted when she overheard Nurse Ratchet gleefully mention she hoped the last thirty minutes of her three-to-eleven p.m. shift would gallop by. Alexa's grand idea to lure Conrad leisurely impaled on the pitchfork of unreliable gossip.

Oscar interrupted her reverie. "There's a hospital guard tied up in the bushes."

Alexa gulped. Why Oscar showed unimportant. "You call the Sheriff?"

"Nine-one-one. Pity the poor guy because his assailant stole his clothes?"

Alexa rushed to Nurse Ratchet. "How many security?"

"Normally two, but John called in sick. What's the problem?"

Alexa kept her silence. If she confided in anyone, it would be Oscar. "Can Mr. Erickson join me to check on my son?"

"Highly irregular this late. Rules don't allow. He can visit tomorrow."

Alexa whispered to Oscar to distract Nurse Ratchet and then wait outside. Oscar approached Nurse Ratchet from the side. "You're not neighborly the way you disrespect mothers."

Alexa didn't hear Nurse Ratchet's response as she slipped into the first floor corridor. To disguise her true intentions, she stayed on the first floor, peeked into room 111 for two seconds, and then headed for the elevator. The second floor quiet calmed her. The nurse who manned the floor's station said she hadn't bumped into a red-haired male under fifty years since last week.

Regretful her plan subjected her ridicule, Alexa dragged her right hand fingers across the top of the fire extinguisher glass en route to room 224. That she hadn't heard sirens didn't dissuade her the Sheriff cordoned off the hospital's parking lot. Odds high the guard's attacker, a thief, long gone. She'd return the useless dressmaker dummy to Grandma's attic.

Alexa slammed the palm of her right hand against the room 224 door. It resisted for a second and then conceded to her hand's force. She reached for the light switch.

An arm grabbed her about the shoulders and spun her against the wall. Light bathed the room. A mouth, its right corner upturned, said, "Welcome. Been waiting since I saw you prance across the parking lot." A nine-millimeter pistol barrel glistened when he twisted his right wrist.

Alexa recognized the male's red hair. "You're Conrad's friend. Gold's not here."

The side of his mouth crooked into a brief smile. He snickered. "If you don't tell Conrad, I won't. Split fifty-fifty with me, keep your mouth shut, and you'll keep half. Oppose me and, well . . . ."

Alexa tried to assess her bargaining power. Buried gold that promised a better life had invited new evil into her and Samuel's life. Nevertheless, without the gold or its myth, her cards were singletons of multiple suits. "Who's saying I know where it is?"

"If you don't, there'll be one less person who can finger me."

Clammy chills invaded Alexa's hands. "You'll never succeed."

He raised his left hand to brush strands of hair from her forehead. His fingers brushed her cheek. They ignited no longing in her. She locked her knees lest her legs collapse.

"Too bad I left my special beer outside." Wicked glee danced in his eyes. "I could enjoy a party this time."

Alexa exhaled between clenched teeth when he retreated. She desired a sharp object against her suspicion the hospital purposely cleared each room of objects harmful to patients. No terra cotta flower pot rested on the window sill. Alexa desired a weapon more than air to breathe.

He lifted the blanket off the dressmaker dummy. "This black wig will help. In two minutes a new hospital shift will make our exit less noticeable. You'll like my new wheels."

Alexa shook her head. She didn't care if she annoyed him or not. With his attention focused on her, Samuel and Belinda were safe and she was going to do nothing to change that. Then the image of Conrad and the masked woman filled her brain. She had no idea if the Sheriff stayed nor the strength or vigilance of the posted guard.

"Stand by the bed and don't move. I've got to see if our exit is blocked."

He edged the door two inches from its jamb.

The crash against the door surprised Alexa. She'd heard of misdirected gurneys. This violence magnified. The red-headed male rocked on his construction boot heels. A second crash knocked him on his backside. Alexa scurried into the bathroom and leaned her right shoulder against the door. She trusted the metal door to deflect a bullet.

Seconds passed into a minute. Alexa peeked through the slimmest crack. A nine-millimeter pistol lay across the room. A hand stretched for it. Alexa couldn't see the hand's connected arm. A construction boot kicked out without contact to a second surface.

"Alexa, Alexa?"

Why is Brad here? Thank God he is. Alexa closed the door. She had no chair to prop against it. What sounded like a chair struck the wall. After two breaths she cracked the door. "Brad?"

He wrestled with the red-haired male. Brad rolled the construction worker away from the gun. Their bodies blocked Alexa's path to it. She winced when a punch bloodied Brad's chin.

Brad's right-fist retaliation glanced off his attacker's skull. A fire extinguisher not seen earlier by Alexa kicked away by the red-haired guy. It clanked on its slide away from Alexa.

Brad seemed to gain the upper hand, but his blow blocked by a forearm. Brad's right arm grabbed and used as leverage to drag and pin him to the floor. The red-haired guy straddled Brad's waist. Alexa horrified when Brad's head twists failed to avoid rapid-fire fists.

She ran to the bed and grabbed the dressmaker dummy by the wire skirt. She coiled her shoulders and swung. The dummy's soft thud against the red-haired guy's right shoulder failed to knock him off Brad.

"You bitch," he yelled. "You're next."

If her job experience tested one hypothesis, it was that verbal threats empowered her. She swung the dummy a second time. Her forewarned target ducked his head. He reacted to grab its shaped shoulders before Alexa readied a third try. Brad lay on the room's floor.

The red-haired guy hurled her backward with the dummy as a lance. She groaned when her shoulder blades struck the bed's railing. Her assailant yanked the dummy from her hands.

"You're lucky I won't kill you. You're boyfriend's a

different story."

Alexa's right hand grabbed a fistful of sheet, useless as a weapon. "You can't kill him. Only he knows where the gold is." Alexa judged her assailant's slack jaw indicated her lie undetected.

He snarled at her. "You're lying."

Alexa swallowed hard. "He was Grandma's attorney. He couldn't tell me the gold's whereabouts until the farm was legally mine." She noticed Brad draw his right arm to his bruised chin. She tried to keep the red-haired guy's attention until Brad raised himself from the floor and it wasn't happening. "Didn't Susan tell you?"

Her attacker shook his head.

Alexa interpreted his action to answer her question, but she couldn't be positive. He fisted his right hand, squared his feet.

"Kick off your shoes and tear strips from that sheet."

Alexa feared the worst. Three-year-old memories tortured her. Her right toe against her left sneaker's heel slipped it off. She repeated the process with deliberate slowness. "Can't tear these sheets. Not strong enough."

"Use your teeth."

Brad's half-roll to his right advised Alexa he required a longer distraction. Samuel's badge, even if she carried it, wouldn't work this time.

Alexa's left hand undid her blouse button adjacent to her belt.

"You telling me I don't need to tie you down?"

Alexa's facial muscles too terrified to smile. She remembered Belinda's experience. Her forefinger traced the outline of her next higher button.

"Stop."

Alexa's spirit plummeted. He'd caught on to her attempt to delay until, if not Brad, then Oscar worried about her whereabouts. They represented her only salvation. No nurse scheduled to include this room on his or her rounds.

"We've time to satisfy your cravings later." He banished the dummy. "Tear that sheet. I need to tie your boyfriend's hands before we depart to load up the gold."

Alexa, dejected, stuffed the sheet's end into her mouth. Her last effort at defiance.

"Bitch."

Alexa tried not to gag on the sheet. She attempted to slow her breathing. Alexa choked off her impulse to cry 'watch out' at the uplifted fire extinguisher. She averted her gaze from Brad.

Blood spurted from the red-hair roots of the assailant. The red-haired guy staggered.

Fire extinguisher in hand, Brad towered above the supine red-haired male crumpled on the floor. Brad retreated to gather up and stuff the nine-millimeter into his waistband. Red welts seeped blood and bruises colored Brad's skin red and bluish.

Alexa spit out the sheet. "How . . . how did you know?"

"Luck. Oscar paced the waiting room and worried you'd been gone too long."

"God bless, Oscar. What about Conrad and Susan?"

"They're on the run. State police and FBI will do their jobs. What about Samuel? Belinda?"

"Well protected."

Alexa hugged Brad.

Epilogue

Two white linen-clad banquet tables on Grandma's rear porch displayed one special apple cake, cheddar and Swiss cheese, crackers, pickled herring, suckers, wine, beer, chips, iced tea, and colas.

Alexa didn't believe it had been six months plus since her pickup bounced on an Iowa country road to visit a farm where her fondest and greatest memory consisted of chasing dandelion fluff under Grandma's watchful eyes. She waited for Belinda to cross the gravel.

"Great to see you."

"Wouldn't miss it. The office expects I'll enthrall them with juicy new gossip." Belinda waved to Brad playing horsy with Samuel under the spreading oak branches. "And, I'll start with that sparkling diamond on your ring finger."

Alexa's cheeks warmed. After two months of no, she'd rewarded Brad's persistence at Luigi's last week with a marriage-proposal yes. "Never imagined I'd stay. I wavered and wavered until I convinced myself it would be best for Samuel. Of course, grasshoppers do for Samuel what airborne dandelion fluff did for me."

Belinda plopped a red cooler next to the swing. "Does your mother visit?"

"Wild horses couldn't drag her here."

"But they exonerated her for Joe's death."

Alexa tugged her T-shirt. "Even after I offered to pay her lawyer fees, she stormed off after I refused to surrender my will rights."

"So . . . the Fire Marshal was wrong? Joe died in an accidental fire?"

Alexa's discomfiture rose she hadn't kept Belinda updated. "Radio news said a search uncovered a miniature Colt .45 cigarette lighter in Lydia's garage. She claimed it couldn't have started the fire. I told the Sheriff Joe's lighter didn't work and Oscar failed to find it in the debris. Brad said Lydia confessed days after Margaret gave birth."

Belinda sighed. "Did Margaret have a boy or a girl?"

"Boy. Gossip, one Iowa attribute I hate, says Margaret won't say Joe's the father. Who knows? Sunday church

336

whispers claim the child's nose and mouth not Carl's."

Belinda's right hand shielded her upper lip before she whispered, "Have you spent the gold?"

Alexa rubbed her left hand ring finger. Next to the circular diamond was space for her special gold. She expected her and Brad would agree on a date within the year. She loved his patience. She appreciated the time it would grant her to be honest about her past and Samuel's father.

"There were few gold coins. After Oscar sold the hayloft bales, ten 1925 gold Liberty coins were found in an old coffee can. Grandpa devised a grand buried treasure scheme and then stashed the coins in the most common of places."

Belinda murmured, "You didn't tell me if you spent them."

"Put all in a safety deposit box for Samuel. Brad's the trustee until I agree to his adoption offer. Until then I can't wait to help you send your assailants to prison. Sheriff says state police nabbed Conrad and Susan in Clarinda. Russel, the red-haired guy, locked up in Lakeview's jail."

"Good riddance." Old Betsy's putt-putt filled the farmyard. Belinda smiled. "Now this party can begin."

Alexa's right arm raised her diet cola while her left hand waved at Brad. His offer to adopt Samuel stronger than words. Without question, she basked in the warmth of being Brad's last and only Chicago woman.

The End

If you've enjoyed *Alexa's Gold*, don't be bashful, write a review. A simple 'I liked it or like this author.' is sufficient. Author Berg's books are available at your favorite book retailer. In 2016, Author Donan Berg won the Gold 1st Place Award for Romance awarded by Feathered Quill. The novel is available today through major book retailers.

Ask your local librarian to reserve you a copy.

Here's a taste:

Excerpt of *One Paper Heart*

A seated Alicia kicked her left foot to elevate her dress hem. She stood and let the skirt drape her legs. She strode to reception's hallway door. "Thanks," Alicia said as she reached for the envelope offered by her editor.

"Engaging story. Call me if there's any question."

"I'll have to look at it tonight."

Alicia bade her editor good-bye and added her manuscript to the extra-large handbag she had carried to work for this very purpose.

Anxious to read her editor's suggestions, Alicia hurried to her apartment elevator after her seventy-year-old neighbor, stationed in the lobby, coaxed her to sign a protest petition. Upstairs, Alicia threw open her bedroom window. Pungent horse manure vapors, spiraled three stories from a foundation flowerbed, gagged her. Alicia slammed her window shut, comforted by the scent of fall mums. The bouquet was Vicky's gift to celebrate Alicia's novel completion.

As evening darkened into night, Alicia labored to accept and reject her editor's suggested revisions. Weary eyed, she put off the critical proofreading until the next evening.

Satisfied with her punctuation and story tweaks, she decided to mail her manuscript submission and have it appear like any other writer submission. She telephoned her adoptive parents to inform them she'd be using their suburban Minneapolis/St. Paul New Brighton, Minnesota, address. Alicia explained a publishing guidebook tip suggested the benefit of a residential street address to indicate the author's stability and maturity. Alicia also happy the address choice further disguised her authorship from Norma, Wanda, Carol, and Mr. Van Gilleran.

While Alicia didn't divulge her pen name, she explained to Mom and Dad that publishers often confuse and/or mangle author's names so if any letter or package arrived, no matter to whom addressed, they were to accept it and telephone her immediately. Alicia inhaled until her stomach pressed her spine. She crossed her fingers for luck that all her deception didn't confuse.

After she hung up, a steeped small fear grew into a dull headache. How would she easily identify her three-chapter submission from the other mailed envelopes received? Alicia dared not deviate from standard white or manila. A gaudy pastel would be a submission faux pas rewarded by immediate summary rejection.

She rummaged through a bedroom dresser drawer where she'd stockpiled classroom supplies should she ink a new teacher contract. A pad of leftover Valentine Day paper hearts hid under an eraser package. Alicia's fingers traced the round heart edges to their points.

The brilliant red color, shaded to imply depth, exuded cuteness, well, Alicia thought, cuteness for an eight-year-old.

Inspiration struck. Each heart's adhesive presented a definite plus.

One paper heart would be an inconspicuous corner addition to her envelope to identify her manuscript submission from the multitude.

2

One Paper Heart

With her rubber-banded story pages, a synopsis, and a SASE reply envelope tucked inside, she sealed her envelope after her umpteenth recheck. On the exterior, Alicia affixed a typed New Brighton return address and a completed mailing label. Onto the lower left front corner, her fingers pressed her one paper heart doubly hard.

With her submission mailed, she dared not leave her *New Romance Delights* reception desk even for a minute. When Aunt Agnes telephoned Tuesday morning with an offer to buy lunch, Alicia tried to put her off and failed. The best Alicia did was to get a persistent Aunt Agnes to agree to postpone lunch to Thursday.

Later than usual, the letter carrier dumped two huge envelope piles with an untypical groan. Alicia estimated three dozen. After a hand swipe into his leather pouch, he and Alicia traded good-bye waves. She quick-stepped letter-sized correspondence to the in-office mail center. Startled when a co-worker said hello from behind, a jumpy Alicia responded with a curt, "Hi, must get back to the phones."

When Alicia glimpsed her paper heart point peeking out from the left pile, third envelope from the bottom, she tried a normal breath. With both reception doors closed and no one waiting, Alicia leaned forward to separate her manuscript submission from the others. She considered it inane to be holding her breath. Her left hand lifted the envelopes above hers as her right hand tugged it free and laid it front and center on her desk. Her stuck fast red paper heart marred by a black streak.

Alicia maneuvered to tuck her knees and the desk chair's front casters beneath her desktop. Her red heart had admirably fulfilled its mission to easily identify her manuscript's arrival. Prepared to say good-bye, she reached her right hand index finger forward to slide its nail under the heart's right edge.

3

A male voice interrupted. "Let me take those slush pile novels."

Alicia froze, her right arm in midair six inches above her affixed paper heart.

The speaker, one Randall Van Gilleran, acquisitions editor for *New Romance Delights*, stood three feet from her arm, his manicured hands outstretched at the waist. The interior office door edged shut behind him.

Caught red-handed, Alicia's constricted throat blocked all larynx efforts to utter even a grunt.

"Oh, you saw it too." Van Gilleran chuckled. His intense and intelligent eyes bypassed her presence to scan reception's empty chairs.

Alicia's heart thumped to conquer her brain's suspended animation. "Saw what?"

"That paper heart." He advanced a step. "Some wannabe author is so foolish."

Alicia pressed her lips together to force her lungs to breathe slower. Why didn't her hand drop faster and hide her paper heart? No answer came to her. "Oh, that." The two words uttered whispery and hoarse. Yet, she wasn't ill, not yet anyway. Was she frightened by what Mr. Van Gilleran might do next, absolutely?

He lowered his hands to his sides. "He or she must think romance publishers are impressed by envelopes with cutesy red hearts." No compassion encircled his words.

Her paper heart became the electrical spark to race her chest's heart. Alicia prayed for a visitor or a telephone ring. No Luck. Her gaze darted to the ceiling and then to Mr. Van Gilleran.

"Don't you agree it's foolishness?" He charged on without giving Alicia a chance to respond. "It deserves to be tossed without reading."

Alicia's hands sunk faster than gravity's pull to squish the last remnants of trapped air out of her envelope. Her left shielded the return address from Mr. Van Gilleran's view;

her right obscured her red paper heart. "What . . . what," she stuttered. She forced her voice to increase its volume. "What if . . . what if there's a postcard or reply envelope inside."

Her left hand slid off the New Brighton return address. She twisted her face to Mr. Van Gilleran. The animated facial gayety of his first chuckle absent. His pressed together eyebrows and pursed lips forged horizontal parallel lines.

He snatched the heart manuscript from her desk.

Not until he'd completed his swiping action did she realize her right hand rested on his left forearm's white shirt sleeve. Alicia pleaded. "We request submitters to send us a way to tell them we received their submission." She glanced at her manuscript clamped in her boss's hand. "Shouldn't we honor that? Our website promises authors that courtesy."

Alicia retracted her hand from his arm. She couldn't bear to gaze at his face.

Mr. Van Gilleran walked to the front of her desk. With her white envelope still gripped by his left hand, his right pawed through both desk submission stacks.

In a moment of panic desperation, Alicia envisioned a dash around her desk, a grab of her manuscript, and a hallway run to catch the lobby elevator. If she were lucky, an Orange No. 34 bus awaited. If not, Plan B was a jog to disappear into one of the Nicollet Mall shops.

She dismissed the asinine Rambo exploit as foolish and impractical. To have her manuscript published remained her cherished goal. If she didn't expose herself as Lady Victoria Dash, Alicia foresaw her flash drive backup copy reprinted and mailed under a second pen name.

That is, if an angered Mr. Van Gilleran didn't mount a crusade to unearth Lady Dash's identity. Alicia breathed easier. She'd built a firewall to hide her connection to Lady Dash. There existed no listed telephone, Facebook page or

Google search listing. Alicia's bliss dissipated in three seconds. Her *New Romance Delights* personnel file contained her parents' New Brighton telephone number and address for emergency contact. He could easily check. Connect the dots. She needed to divert his attention.

In her three-week tenure, Alicia garnered one Mr. Van Gilleran habitual tidbit. He always planned his every move. He wouldn't lower himself to walk into reception to collect and carry unprocessed manuscript submissions to his office. She crossed her two right hand fingers behind her back. *Be consistent, please, please, please.*

"Was there something else you came out here for?"

"Right." He glanced at her desktop.

Alicia's eyes followed his. His unwillingness to lift his head or speak provoked an impatience in her brain incapable of release.

"Wanda said she gave you a statistical report." He tucked Alicia's manuscript under his right arm. "You were to double-check her calculations. Have you completed that?"

"Yes." The nerve-racking suspense that coursed her veins excised, for now.

Alicia reached to her left for a manila folder, transferred it between hands, and balanced the folder atop a manuscript pile. Wanda Swanson, Mr. Van Gilleran's personal secretary, had been the first office person introduced to Alicia. An office friendship blossomed.

To support the opened calculations folder, Mr. Van Gilleran slid her manuscript envelope beneath it. While he read, Alicia's hands in her lap fidgeted.

When he closed the folder. Alicia's slightly relaxed body tensed. She gasped. *He's taking the manuscript with him.* Her right hand stifled the sound of a second gasp.

Mr. Van Gilleran stopped two steps from reception's interior employee-only exit door.

"Perhaps you're right." His right hand tossed her paper

6

heart manuscript onto her desk corner. "Guess I'll have to at least skim it. Process it along with all the others."

Alicia quietly sighed. "I'll do that."

She gazed at the black-streak scarred red paper heart.

"Expect it'll be below our acceptance standards, although we're more liberal than the industry giants in New York City."

A light blinked on Alicia's phone. Intercom. She ignored it. *Please hurry, leave now.*

"Another thing, has a Mr. Jackson Grant stopped by?"

Alicia didn't recognize the name. Her fingers tapped her manuscript, but she didn't have the courage to slide it further from Mr. Van Gilleran. "Only morning visitor was the mailman."

"Jackson's a good friend, collaborated on a documentary that won an Oscar." Mr. Van Gilleran's facial features softened, especially his sharp, taut forehead lines.

"Impressive. I'll ring Wanda if he shows." Alicia rotated her chair a quarter turn.

"Thanks. I'm trying to enlist his help."

Alicia stretched her left arm to grab three envelopes to stack atop the paper heart. "What kind of drama does he write?" After the words emerged, she realized her question delayed his exit.

"Doesn't really. He's more involved in screenplay promotion."

Alicia sat quiet, hands folded in her lap. The connection between screenplays and novels seemed simple enough. A dozen seconds, each silently counted by Alicia, elapsed as Mr. Van Gilleran leafed a second time through the manila folder he carried.

"Later."

End of *One Paper Heart* excerpt.

About the Author

Author Donan Berg won the 2016 Feathered Quill First Place Gold Award for Romance for his novel *One Paper Heart*. An excerpt is included above. Author Berg previously landed four times in the romance winner's circle of the 2014 Ninth Annual Dixie Kane Memorial Contest. In 2013 he garnered three awards in the Eighth Annual Dixie Kane Memorial Contest.

His vibrant writing talents, honed as a journalist, corporate executive, and lawyer, are displayed in his three Skeleton Series Mystery novels entitled *A Body To Bones, The Bones Dance Foxtrot,* and *Baby Bones. Adolph's Gold,* a police procedural mystery, has many attributes of his Skeleton Series Mystery novels while *Abbey Burning Love is* a fast-paced, novel-length, small city murder mystery/romance e-book.

A native of Ireland transplanted to the United States Heartland, he's also authored a collection of short stories entitled, *Bubbling Conflict and Other Stories*, where the lead story highlights the never-ending sectarian violence in Northern Ireland.

His novels have earned the praise of entertaining mystery, heartwarming romance. He blogs at www.abodytobones.blogspot.com.